A Fête Worse Than Death

A FÊTE
WORSE THAN DEATH

Dolores Gordon-Smith

Constable • London

Constable & Robinson Ltd
3 The Lanchesters
162 Fulham Palace Road
London W6 9ER
www.constablerobinson.com

First published in the UK by Constable,
an imprint of Constable & Robinson Ltd 2007

A copy of the British Library Cataloguing in Publication
Data is available from the British Library.

ISBN: 978-1-84529-595-0

Printed and bound in the EU

To my husband, Peter, because of all the Saturday night steak dinners followed by the requests to 'Read another chapter,' and to the Gordon-Smiths (junior editions), Jessica, Helen, Elspeth, Lucy and Jenny, without whom life would be twice as peaceful and half as much fun.

Chapter One

With a feeling of relief, Jack Haldean walked into the dim green interior of the beer tent. My word, it was like an oven out there. A noisy oven, where the laboured thump of the Breedenbrook band mixed with the shrieks of excited children on the helter-skelter, hoarse shouts from the hoop-la and coconut shies, sharp cracks from the rifle range and the hollow, oddly mournful music of the steam organ on the roundabouts, all grilling under a blazing sun.

He took off his straw hat and fanned himself. It was easily as hot as Spain, the difference being that no Spaniard, and certainly none of his relations, ever expected him to do anything in the middle of the day but sleep. They certainly wouldn't lug him out to a village fête.

Haldean found a space on a bench and wriggled his backbone into a comfortable position against a sturdy tent pole. His cousin, Gregory Rivers, was standing at the trestle-table bar, waiting patiently to be served. Haldean relaxed, soaking up the low rumble of conversation, savouring the contrast between the muffled din outside and the slow, placid voices within. The smell of hot canvas, the smell of hot grass, the pungent reek of tobacco and the sweet smell of beer . . .

'Cheers,' said Greg, handing him a pewter mug. He took a long drink. 'Good Lord, I needed that.' He looked at Haldean suspiciously. 'You seem jolly pleased with yourself.'

Haldean gave a contented smile. 'I'm just enjoying it all, I suppose. I mean, I know we've more or less got to come, with Aunt Alice helping to run the fête and all, but I'm glad we did. It's . . . it's peaceful.'

'You're having me on,' said Greg as a boom from the trap-shooting thundered across the park.

Haldean put down his mug. 'Not peaceful because there's no noise, but peaceful because – well, because all this sort of thing really makes me believe the war's over . . . *Damn!*'

'Whatever is it?' said Greg in surprise, his mug halfway to his mouth.

'Over there,' hissed Haldean. 'By the bar. Don't look now. Thin dark bloke with Oxford bags and a moustache. This is the last place on earth I'd have expected to see the rotten little creep.'

'What's he done?' asked Greg. 'It's not like you to go overboard like that.'

Haldean raised his eyebrows. 'Isn't it? You don't know him. His name's Jeremy Boscombe and he's a swine. He was in my squadron. He was a mutton-fisted pilot and a lousy shot with a huge chip on his shoulder. God knows how he survived, but he did. He only joined the Flying Corps because he expected it to be a soft touch after the infantry, and he held me personally responsible that it wasn't. He had the cheek to look me up a few months ago at the magazine offices to see if I could help him publish a book that he's writing, a cynical thing about what a ghastly time he had in the war.' He paused and added, with reluctant fairness, 'Well written, though. I recommended him to Drake and Sanderson.'

'It sounds putrid,' muttered Rivers. 'Uh-oh, he's seen you. Bad luck.'

With a weary sigh, Haldean got to his feet. Boscombe was threading his way through the crowd, a supercilious smirk on his face.

'Well, if it isn't Major Haldean.' Haldean caught the smell of drink and sighed. Boscombe always had a weakness for whisky. 'Whatever brings you here?'

8

Haldean decided to play it absolutely straight. 'My aunt, Lady Rivers, is on the committee.'

Boscombe's eyebrows crawled upwards. 'Is she, by Jove? I never suspected you of having such well-connected relations.' His smile grew. 'Damned if I thought you had any English relations at all.'

Haldean smiled back. 'I'm flattered to know you gave it any thought whatsoever.'

Boscombe searched for an answer, couldn't find one, and slumped on to the bench. 'Bloody awful affair, isn't it?' he said after a pause. 'I can't stand these yokels and their high jinks.'

'A fête worse than death?' asked Haldean smoothly. There was a snort of suppressed laughter by his side.

Boscombe stared at him blankly, then caught the grin on Greg Rivers' face. 'Don't tell me you're enjoying it?'

Greg's grin vanished as he took in Boscombe's slurred speech and flushed face. 'Yes,' he said bluntly.

'Yes? Well, there's no accounting for taste, is there? I don't think we've met, by the way. I'm Boscombe, Jeremy Boscombe, and you are . . .?'

'Rivers. Gregory Rivers.'

They looked at each other with mutual distaste. Boscombe shrugged and turned to Haldean again. 'I read one of your stories in the train, old man. Why on earth don't you write something other than those mindless detective things?' He leaned forward. 'I don't say it was bad – it had a lot of promise – but the *subject*! Murder. I ask you. Absolute rubbish.'

'Thanks for the advice,' said Haldean, with every appearance of sincerity. Boscombe preened himself. Haldean took out a cigarette and lit it, without offering one to Boscombe. 'Damn good of you to take an interest. Er . . . How's your first book coming along?' There was a very slight emphasis on the word 'first'.

'My book?' Boscombe crossed his arms and leaned back, narrowly avoiding falling off the bench. 'Rather well, actually. Who did you recommend? Drake and Sanderson?

9

Hopeless, old man, hopeless. I mean, they wanted it all right but the sales they predicted would make a cat laugh. No. I've got other fish to fry.'

'Oh really? What?'

'Private publication.' Boscombe tapped the side of his nose and laughed to himself. 'Private publication. I can reach a truly appreciative audience . . .' His glance flicked up. Haldean followed his gaze, but could see nothing to draw his attention. A tall, fair-haired man came into the beer tent and stood in the crowd at the open flap, looking around. Without another word, Boscombe levered himself up and walked over to him. They heard his voice above the buzz of conversation. 'Colonel Whitfield? I thought it was you . . .'

Greg Rivers let his breath out in a heartfelt sigh. 'Of all the obnoxious little toads . . . *Murder. Absolute rubbish.* Supercilious little runt. I wouldn't be surprised if you murdered him yourself, talking like that. I *like* murders.'

'Between hard covers, so do I. Bump off Boscombe. That's a thought. *Outraged author kills critic.*' He sighed regretfully. 'That'd never do for a motive. I wonder what really happened with Drake and Sanderson? He's barking up the wrong tree if he thinks publishing it privately will do him any good. *Tout au contraire*, as the Frenchman said on the Channel steamer when asked if he had dined. Who's he cottoned on to now? That tall bloke in riding kit who looks too handsome to be true? He seems vaguely familiar.'

Rivers glanced across the tent. 'That's Colonel Whitfield. You know, Jack, the Augier Ridge VC. We met him at the Meddingholme point-to-point. He owns a livery stable on the outskirts of the village.'

Haldean nodded. 'Of course it is. I couldn't place him right away. The Augier VC, you say? That explains why Boscombe's glued to him. He was mixed up in that Augier Ridge business too. It's all in his wretched book.' Another memory clicked into place. 'I say, Greg, is he the bloke Marguerite Vayle's keen on?'

10

'Yes, that's the one.'

Haldean looked at the Colonel. 'I hope everything works out for her. I've got a soft spot for Maggie Vayle. I think she had a rotten break, losing her parents. She's only a kid, after all.'

Rivers pulled a face. 'Kid or not, she's nineteen and old enough to get married. You know my parents are responsible for her? She's giving them a real headache. My mother's very iffy about her marrying the Colonel because he's so much older. I know he's not *old* old, if you see what I mean, but he must be nearly forty.' He tapped Haldean's arm. 'Come on. We can get away from your pal Boscombe if we slope off now.'

They walked out of the tent into the brilliant sunshine. All Haldean's content had evaporated. That Boscombe – *Boscombe!* – of all people should be at the fête beggared belief. Well, the beer he'd been so looking forward to had been ruined, but he was damned if he was letting the little rat ruin the rest of the afternoon. With Greg following, he plunged into the crowd as far away from the beer tent as possible, fetched up at the coconut shy and then on to the darts and hoop-la.

Quarter of an hour later, having proved his skill and won two coconuts, a celluloid doll in a carry-cot and a large and violently coloured packet of sweets, Haldean, his temper restored, strolled between the stalls towards a tent advertising *Zelda, Seer of the Future*.

'What on earth are you going to do with that lot?' asked Greg, looking at his friend's winnings.

'Oh, I don't know.' Haldean looked around for inspiration. A small girl, wearing a green velveteen frock which was too hot and too tight, materialized beside them. Her eyes fixed longingly on the carry-cot and the sweets. 'Here – d'you want any of these things?' The little girl nodded enthusiastically but timidly. 'Come and get them then,' said Haldean, stooping down and holding them out. 'It's all right, really. Don't be shy.'

11

The little girl took one step forward and two back. 'My mummy says I'm not to take sweets from strange men.'

'Hmm.' Haldean dropped down on one knee so he was at eye-level with this cautious child and pondered the problem. 'I'm not really a strange man, you know. Shut up, Greg. Have you seen Lady Rivers? She's my aunty and Sir Philip Rivers is my uncle. And Greg here is their son and my cousin, so you know quite a lot about me really.'

The little girl put her thumb in her mouth and regarded him gravely, reassured by this burst of genealogy. 'You've got a face like a gypsy's,' she said eventually.

'No, I haven't,' said Haldean indignantly, ignoring the crack of laughter from Rivers. 'Not a bit of it. Look, old thing, I'm blowed if I'm carrying this stuff round any longer. Sweets give me tummy-ache and I never played with dolls. Here you are.' He put his unwanted prizes on the grass and the little girl, with glowing eyes, picked up the carry-cot with the coconuts and sweets and scurried off.

'Talk about suspicious,' said Haldean with a laugh. 'At her age I'd have killed for a bag of sweets as polychromatic as those.' He looked round the stalls. 'What else is there? Let's have a go on the rifle range. Unless, that is, you feel tempted by Zelda, Seer of the Future.'

Rivers laughed. 'Not me. You know who Zelda is?' he asked, picking his way towards the rifle range through the guy ropes which stretched out over the grass. 'Mrs Griffin, who used to be the cook at Hesperus.'

Haldean stopped. 'What? I must call in and see her. She used to be very generous in the matter of biscuits when I was a kid, to say nothing of letting me lick the bowl out after she'd made a cake.'

'It's cakes which are the bone of contention, so to speak.' Rivers raised his voice to carry over the band, which, after a brief period of silence, had plunged into *The Pirates of Penzance*. 'Apparently Mrs Griffin has won the home-made jam section every year but she's never got more than an Honourable Mention for her cakes. Isabelle tells me that Mrs Griffin thinks it's because Mrs Verrity's cook always has an entry and Mrs Verrity, the big bug to end all big bugs, is on the judges' panel. Mrs Griffin took the hump a bit, and my mother and my sister had to put in some heavy charm to persuade her to come and read the fortunes.'

'Prejudice, eh?' Haldean put down sixpence on the counter of the rifle range. 'Well, she may be right.' He squinted down the barrel of the air rifle. 'Let's see if the old skill still lingers . . .' He pointed the gun at a battered tin lion's head which formed part of the Big Game Jungle Safari for the marksmen of Breedenbrook.

'My mummy says I've got to say thank you,' said a voice from just above his knee-cap. Haldean jumped and the pellet thudded into the wooden boards at the back of the stall. He sighed and looked down at the little girl in the green velveteen frock.

'I'm going to call her Daisy and I'm going to dress her and take her to bed and take her for walks and make her a teatime with mud pies and she's going to eat it all up like a good girl, even all the nasty bits *and* her greens and at bedtime I'm going to get her undressed and she's going to stay in bed all night and . . .'

'Good for you,' said Haldean kindly, loading up and sighting the gun on the lion once more.

'So there you are,' said a voice from behind them. 'I was wondering where you'd got to.' Haldean flinched and once more the pellet thudded into the wooden boards. It was Isabelle, Greg's sister. 'I expected to find you in the beer tent.'

'As if,' said Greg with a grin. 'We did look in, actually, but we didn't like the company. There was a complete outsider who used to know Jack.'

'And she's going to be my very own dolly and stay with me for ever 'n' ever . . .'

'I think I saw the man you mean. I didn't like the look of him at all. He was shovelling down whisky or something from a hip flask and arguing with Colonel Whitfield.'

Isabelle glanced down and smiled at the little girl. 'What a beautiful dolly, sweetheart. What's her name?'

'She's called Daisy and that kind gypsy man gave her to me.'

Isabelle gave a gurgle of laughter. 'What, this gypsy here?'

Haldean put down his air rifle with a sigh. 'Look, girls and boys. I used to have a reputation as a crack shot. This is now in tatters. I still have tuppence worth of enjoyment to get out of this gun and I'm going to pot that lion.' He looked down at the little girl. 'Why don't you go and have a ride on the chair swings or something? They look awfully good fun.'

'I've spended all my money.'

'Here's sixpence. You ought to be able to do something with that.'

'My mummy says I'm not to take money from strangers.'

'Oh, good Lord!'

'I'll take you, darling,' said Isabelle bending down to her. 'I'm not a stranger, am I?'

'No. You've got a pretty dress.'

'Why, thank you, sweetheart. I'll have that sixpence, Jack. It belongs to your little friend here.' Hand in hand they walked off to where the chair swings were whirling madly amid shrieks of pleasure. Haldean shot his lion and turned to find Rivers looking out over the crowd.

'There's that blighter Boscombe again. He's still got Colonel Whitfield in tow, I see.'

Haldean's eye's lit up. 'That means the beer tent's free once more. Shandy?'

'Shandy it is.'

They made a leisurely progress back to the beer tent, slipping round the back of the hoop-la stall to avoid Boscombe. Boscombe saw them and looked as if he was about to follow, when he was stopped by a very elegant woman who had come over to speak to Colonel Whitfield.

'Have we shaken him off?' asked Haldean, pausing at the entrance to the tent.

'If you're quick. Damn! Here he comes again.'

Boscombe, weaving slightly, walked across to them and linked arms affectionately with Haldean. 'Thought I'd missed you, Jack old man. You don't mind me calling you old man do you, Jack, old bean? I used to have to call him sir,' he confided to Rivers. 'He wanted me to chase Huns all the time. It was *bloody* dangerous.'

Haldean unlinked his arm. 'You're drunk.'

'Just a little. Seen anyone you know? I've seen someone. Bloody surprising that was, all things considered. Bloody funny too, if you think about it. Give a man enough rope and he'll hang himself.' He started to laugh and Haldean and Rivers looked at him wearily.

'Look, Boscombe, why don't you go somewhere and sleep it off?' asked Haldean with diminishing patience.

Boscombe stopped laughing. 'Don't tell me what to do. I don't need you any more, *Major* Haldean. You see that woman with Whitfield? She needs me.' Boscombe gave a knowing wink. *'Nice* woman. We go way back.'

'Glad to hear it,' said Haldean with false cheerfulness. 'Don't let us keep you.'

He shook off Boscombe's groping hand and went into the tent, Rivers following. Boscombe was left swaying gently outside. 'Little tick,' said Haldean briefly and applied himself to a pint of shandy. 'Who was the woman, by the way? The one Boscombe was being revoltingly suggestive about, I mean.'

'That's Mrs Verrity. I can't see what she'd have to do with the likes of him.'

'Me neither.' There was a long and liquid pause. 'Has he gone yet?' asked Haldean, finishing his drink.

'Yes,' said Rivers, glancing outside. 'All clear.'

'Thank God. I want to see Mrs Griffin to talk about old times and I don't want him around while I'm doing it. Let's go and see if she's free.'

Mrs Griffin wasn't busy; in fact she was standing outside

15

the fortune teller's booth, looking extremely hot in a long and artistically tattered skirt, brilliant red blouse and heavily beaded shawl. She greeted Haldean with delight. 'Do excuse what I'm wearing, Master Jack, but I've got to look the part. I mean, everyone knows it's me and when I'm just doing the tea-leaves at home I don't bother dressing up, of course, but it's different here. People like you to make an effort.'

'Do you really tell fortunes then, Mrs Griffin? I mean, it's not just something you make up?'

Mrs Griffin looked shocked. 'Oh no, Master Jack. T'wouldn't be right, that. I could read your hand now easy as wink. Of course in the general way I don't charge for it – I don't want no trouble with the police – but I have a stall at the Stanmore Parry fête to oblige her Ladyship and she asked me ever so kindly if I'd do Breedenbrook as well, as the usual lady they had was laid up and Mrs Verrity couldn't get no one. Well, I don't mind. It's not very far, not really, and I did wonder if I did Mrs Verrity a favour it might count for something when it came to the home-made cakes. Twelve years I've been doing cakes for this fair now, and nothing more than an Honourable Mention to show for it. Still, it's not what you know, as I always say, it's who you know that counts. Speaking of who you know, I think this gentleman's looking for you.'

With a feeling of ghastly inevitability Haldean turned and saw Boscombe walking towards them with Colonel Whitfield behind. 'Oh, God damn it, not again!'

Mrs Griffin sized up the situation and stepped forward. 'Do you want me, my dear? Have your fortune told?'

Boscombe gave a short laugh. 'Why not? Although I know it already, why not, eh, Whitfield?'

Colonel Whitfield shrugged. 'Just as you like.'

A small boy came hurrying through the crowd. 'Mrs Griffin? You've got to come. They're announcing the winners for the cakes and I've been told to come and fetch you.'

She clicked her tongue. 'Just as I was going to see this

gentleman, too.' She turned to Boscombe. 'Why don't you go and sit down inside my tent, my dear? I won't be very long and you look as if a little rest might do you some good.' Boscombe blinked at her. 'You'll be more comfortable in the shade,' added Mrs Griffin, tactfully. 'I think you might have a touch of the sun and no wonder in this heat and with all the noise there is too.' She opened the flap of the tent. 'In you go. Settle yourself down while I go and see about my cake.'

'Cake?' repeated Boscombe uncomprehendingly, but went in all the same.

Mrs Griffin peered in after him. 'There. He's resting nicely now. Might even have a little nap, I dare say.' She adjusted her headscarf and took the small boy by the hand. 'Come on, Michael. I don't want to miss this.' Hitching up her inconveniently flowing robe, she set off across the field.

Haldean looked at Colonel Whitfield. So this was the man Marguerite Vayle had fallen for. It was obvious why. He looked as if he should be on the front cover of a film magazine. Whitfield had melancholy sky-blue eyes, a sensitive mouth, broad shoulders and crisply curling blond hair. 'I saw you in the horse trials this morning,' said Haldean conversationally.

Whitfield brightened. 'Did you? Nice mare, that. She's inclined to shy a bit so I thought I'd bring her out locally before trying any of the major events. I thought she was going to get a clear round but the noise from the trapshooting startled her. I'm sorry,' added Whitfield, 'I know we've met before, but I can't recall your name.'

'Jack Haldean. You know Captain Rivers, of course.'

'Indeed I do. Haldean . . . You're Sir Philip's nephew, aren't you? And don't you write or something? It sounds damn clever,' he added dubiously. Obviously being clever was not an unalloyed compliment in Whitfield's eyes.

'It pays the bills,' said Haldean, easily. 'D'you know Boscombe well, Colonel?'

'Not frightfully. I've had a couple of letters from him.

Apparently he's writing a book about the war for some reason and he was one of the men to come out of that Augier Ridge affair I was involved with. I hardly know him. Do you?'

'Yes . . .' The way Haldean said it made Whitfield smile. The smile made his whole face lighten. Haldean grinned. 'He's a bit much, isn't he? He transferred to the Flying Corps and was in my squadron for a while.'

'You poor beggar. I never had the dubious pleasure of serving with him.'

'Lucky you.'

Whitfield laughed. 'He's a bit hard to take, isn't he? Goodness knows what . . .' He stopped as the vicar, Mr Steadman, approached.

'Ah, Colonel, there you are. Excuse me butting in, gentlemen, but I have to leave soon and I was looking forward to a word with the Colonel. It's about this pony I'm interested in for my son, Whitfield. I believe you have it here with you. Thomas is waiting by the loose-boxes at the moment and it seemed an ideal opportunity to let him try it out.'

A shade of annoyance crossed Whitfield's face. 'Can't it wait, Mr Steadman?'

Mr Steadman looked annoyed in turn. 'I'd rather see to it now. Thomas is off on a visit to a school friend's on Monday and I'd like to get everything arranged before then.'

Whitfield's lips tightened, then he shrugged in resignation. 'Very well. Now's as good a time as any, I suppose.' He turned to Haldean and Rivers. 'Nice to have met you again.' He tipped his hat and walked off between the tents, the vicar by his side.

'He is a bit old,' said Haldean thoughtfully, accepting the cigarette that his friend was offering. 'For Marguerite, I mean.'

'Oh, he's all right,' said Rivers, striking a match. 'Isabelle's funny about him. She thinks he's deadly dull, but that's because he talks about horses and not about her.

18

She's so used to having blokes dance attendance that she can't credit anyone simply doesn't notice she's around.'

Haldean grinned. 'Don't tell me she's jealous of Marguerite.'

'Good grief, no. I mean really no. But Marguerite's terribly intense about him and Isabelle finds it all a bit wearing.'

They finished their cigarettes. The band, wearied of Gilbert and Sullivan, started on Jerome Kern. '*And if I tell them . . .*' hummed Rivers. A series of renewed shrieks bit through the air. 'Your little pal on the chair swings is kicking up a rumpus, isn't she?'

'I'll say,' agreed Haldean with a lazy smile. 'Mind you, I don't suppose she's making that din all by herself.' He glanced at the tent behind them. 'If Boscombe manages a nap in this racket he's doing well. Is he asleep in there?'

Rivers lifted the tent flap and peered inside. 'Dead to the world,' he announced briefly. 'Hello, here's Isabelle.'

'Have you got your trumpets and drums handy?' she asked. 'Do give me a cigarette, Greg. I haven't had one all afternoon. Thanks. Mrs Griffin won the cake competition and she's making a sort of royal progress across the fair. Virtue rewarded and all of that.' She sucked in the smoke gratefully. 'Thank goodness, that's better. I hoped to be able to slope off after the cake judging but Mother was there and although she wouldn't actually say anything, she'd look, you know. She's still got the idea that smoking is a thing that a lady does in private, so I went round the side of the cake tent and that was no better because Mrs Verrity and Colonel Whitfield were there and three was definitely a crowd.'

'I say!' said her brother. 'They weren't . . . were they?'

'No, Greg, they weren't. Although I wouldn't be surprised if there was something going on. She's still awfully good-looking in that preserved kind of way, even if she's old enough to be his mother.'

'No, she isn't,' countered her brother.

'Well, she's getting on a bit at any rate. And I wouldn't

19

put it past him,' she added darkly. 'No, they seemed to be having an argument. They stopped when they saw me, of course, but Mrs Verrity wasn't happy. Unlike Mrs Griffin who's on cloud nine. Jack? What is it?' For her cousin had stopped listening to her and stepped forward. There was a small green blur and the little girl in the velveteen frock flung herself out of the crowd and into his arms, sobbing.

Kneeling down, he patted her back and looked helplessly at Isabelle.

'What is it, sweetheart? Tell us,' she said.

The arms tightened round Haldean's neck. 'It's Daisy,' she said between sobs. 'My dolly. She's broken. I put her cot down all safely to go and play and when I got back someone had thrown Daisy out of her cot and stood on her.'

'Oh dear,' said Haldean soothingly.

'And her cot's all dirty and her pillow's gone and it had roses on it. It did.'

'Look,' said Haldean, attempting to disentangle himself, 'what if I win you another one? Would that make it better?' The little girl stopped sobbing and nodded. 'We'll go and do that now, shall we? And perhaps a glass of lemonade would help too.' He looked up as the flushed and happy Mrs Griffin came towards the tent with Mrs Verrity in approving attendance.

'Master Jack? I won. I won the cakes. And Mrs Verrity here says I did it fair and square.'

'You certainly did, Mrs Griffin,' said Mrs Verrity. 'I thought your entry was outstanding and said as much.'

Haldean, still on his knees, glanced up in pleased surprise. Mrs Verrity was a remarkably good-looking woman with beautiful eyes, but it was her voice which captured his attention. It was low and clear with a zest of an accent. Italian? French? French, he decided, and lovely to hear.

Mrs Griffin was beaming. 'Why, thank you, mum.' She looked at the little girl in Haldean's arms. 'Sally Mills? Whatever's the matter with you?'

'It's my dolly. She got broked but this nice gypsy man's going to get me another one.'

'Don't you call Major Haldean a gypsy, Sally. It's not polite. I think that's very nice of the Major and you should say so.' Haldean rose gratefully to his feet as Sally haltingly thanked him. Mrs Griffin beamed once more. 'That's better,' she continued. 'Now wipe your face. Here's a hanky. You've got sweety-stuff all over it.' Mrs Griffin spat into a corner of her handkerchief and rubbed Sally's face vigorously. 'There. No harm done. Is my gentleman still waiting for me inside the tent, Master Jack?'

'He certainly is, but . . .'

'Then I'd better see to him right away.' She disappeared inside, only to reappear seconds later, giggling. 'I think you'd better come and have a look at this. Has he had a drink or two? Yes, I thought I could smell it. Talk about the Sleeping Beauty! We'll have to wake him up. I can't have him there if I'm going to do the fortunes.'

Mrs Verrity raised a perfectly plucked eyebrow. 'Is Mr Boscombe the gentleman in question? He'll have to move. Really, Mrs Griffin, this is too bad for you, after you were good enough to step in for us at the last moment.' She looked at Haldean and Rivers. 'Perhaps you would come in with me?' She opened the tent and stepped inside, Rivers and Mrs Griffin close behind. Haldean was stopped by a small hot hand thrust into his.

'I won't be a minute,' he said reassuringly, looking down at the tear-stained face. 'You be a good girl, Sally, and wait with Miss Rivers. Belle, d'you think you could . . . Thanks, old thing.' He walked into the tent to find Mrs Verrity bending over Boscombe, hand on his shoulder.

'Mr Boscombe. Mr Boscombe . . .' Mrs Verrity suddenly paused and stared, gazing down at the man sprawled out in the chair. She straightened up and looked at the little group by the door. Her eyes fixed on Haldean. 'I think,' she said, in a very controlled voice, 'you'd better take Mrs Griffin out of here. And get that child away from the entrance.'

21

Haldean started forward. 'What . . .?' he began but was stopped by a gesture.

'Please do as I say. And afterwards I think you'd better get some help. Please.' Her plea for understanding was compelling.

Haldean dropped his eyes to the body and slowly nodded. 'I see. Mrs Griffin, would you mind coming outside? It's all for the best. That's the ticket. Come on.'

'But why, Master Jack?' asked Mrs Griffin out in the open air once more. 'What's wrong? Has the gentleman had an accident?'

Haldean steered her away from Sally Mills who was still clutching Isabelle's hand. 'I think you'll find,' he said as gently as possible, 'that he's dead.'

Chapter Two

Superintendent Edward Ashley closed his notebook. 'I think those are all the questions I have for you now, sir. I may have to get back to you, of course.'

Jack Haldean smiled. 'Any time, Superintendent. Can we offer you a cup of coffee or do you have to make any further calls this evening?'

Ashley considered the matter. He'd had a busy afternoon which had turned into an even busier evening, and he supposed he should get back to the station to start putting the information he'd gathered into an official report, but he was tired and Hesperus was the last place he had to visit.

Through the open library window drifted the smells and sounds of a summer evening; the sleepy coo of wood pigeons, the rich perfume of stocks and roses and, from far away across the park, the faint lowing of a cow as it settled down for the night. It was peaceful here; a sight more peaceful than his last important case which had led him into the docks at Newhaven. There were two other considerations as well. The first was simple curiosity. He had heard of Hesperus, the 'big house' of Stanmore Parry, of course. He had occasionally been a guest at the same public dinners as Sir Philip Rivers and he had met Lady Rivers, who took a keen interest in local affairs, at the police charity ball in Lewes over a year ago. However, that was very different from being a guest, however fleeting, in Hesperus itself, and he had a hankering to see how the other half really did live. The second consideration he hardly expressed to himself, but it was nothing more than a desire to get to know this Major Haldean better. He didn't know why, but he kept on feeling as if he should know something about him. Odd, that, and he was obviously friendly enough, so . . .

'Thank you very much, sir. That'd be very welcome.'

Haldean smiled – a slightly shy smile – and led the way into the drawing room.

Lady Rivers was in the act of pouring coffee from an agreeably large pot.

'I've asked Superintendent Ashley to join us, Aunt Alice,' announced Haldean, walking over to the mantelpiece and propping himself against it.

Ashley's spirits drooped. The last time he'd been in a room like this was on holiday when he and his wife, Elsie, had taken a charabanc trip to a Stately Home on Visitors' Day and paid half a crown to get in. It was one thing interviewing witnesses in the library; he was Superintendent Ashley with the authority to ask any questions he pleased. It was a familiar situation and the library, with its mellow oak, leather-spined books, well-used chairs and cigar-scented comfort was not an intimidating room. The drawing room was, and Ashley envied Major Haldean's complete ease. Why, the room must be nearly forty feet long and at least half as wide. His own neat semi-detached, the source of such pride to his wife, could fit between these four walls. The garden would make it a bit of a squash, he thought defiantly. No, you couldn't fit his garden in here. Mind you, talk about gardens! Hesperus didn't have a garden, it had *grounds*. Grounds that went with a house that had this sort of room, with its huge stone fireplace, ornamental pillars, rich Turkish rugs and a decoration – a frieze, was that the right word? – of Greek girls in floaty dresses waving tambourines and suchlike that ran right round the high ceiling.

With a feeling of prickly defiance, Ashley became aware that Lady Rivers was speaking to him. Wondering what he was doing here, no doubt . . . And then he saw her smile.

24

It was a totally unselfconscious, welcoming smile. She wanted him to feel at home and, by George, he was going to feel at home. He'd been invited, hadn't he? Well then.

'Would you like some coffee, Superintendent?' she said. 'Milk, cream or black? I believe we've met before, haven't we?' She frowned slightly. 'Now where was it?'

'It was the police ball in Lewes, your Ladyship,' said Ashley. She remembered him. Lady Rivers, a real lady who owned this house and these grounds, not only was perfectly happy to have him sitting in her drawing room but actually remembered him. That'd be something to tell Elsie. 'Milk, please.'

She handed him a cup. 'That's right. It was an awful crush, but it was a good cause, wasn't it?'

The coffee was excellent and so was the cigar which Sir Philip offered him. Ashley sat back in the brocaded armchair taking stock of the people in the room. Sir Philip Rivers he knew, a short, stocky man with a military moustache and, as if to soften his appearance, laughter lines round his eyes. Lady Rivers, still a very handsome woman with a kindly expression and that lovely smile. Sharp, too, if he knew anything about it. Captain Rivers, their son Gregory, who was now leaning with one elbow on the mantelpiece talking to Major Haldean, he had, of course, interviewed earlier. He had his father's stockiness and sandy hair but was a taller man with a frank, open face. Trustworthy, said Ashley to himself. Then there was their daughter, Isabelle.

Ashley quietly drew his breath in. He had heard she was a beauty and, by jingo, she was. Chestnut hair with a gleam of red where it was touched by the evening sun and vivid green eyes. I bet she plays merry hell up in London, thought Ashley. It's not just her looks, or her dress, a modern, square-necked, flat-chested thing, which would have made some women look as if they'd dressed in a sack, but which Miss Rivers carried off perfectly. It wasn't any of those things, it was that air she had about her. Why, you'd hardly notice any other girl . . . With a shock he realized he *had* hardly noticed the other girl in the room.

Marguerite Vayle, she'd been introduced as. Goodness knows where she fitted in and by the look on her face she didn't want to fit in. A poor little dab of a thing with mousy hair who looked as if she'd dressed any old how. A schoolgirl? No, too old for that, but not by much. Sulky or worried? With a faint question mark in his mind, Ashley flicked his gaze to the man at the fireplace.

Major Haldean. Surrounded, as he was, by the unmistakably English faces around him, he stood out like an orange in a basket of apples. And yet his speech and his name were English enough, belied by his foreign darkness of hair and eyes. Those eyes suggested humour and friendliness but the chief impression he gave was of a nervous intelligence. And Ashley couldn't rid himself of the idea he should know something about him. What, for heaven's sake? Major Haldean; despite the title he was a young man – Ashley had long since ceased to be surprised by the youth of commissioned officers who had served in the war – and Ashley also knew from his statement that he'd been a pilot in the RFC. He walked with a slight limp. An air accident? An air ace? No, that wasn't right. And why did the feeling chime in with the tugging memory of the last cup of tea before bedtime, a good book and the pleasant drowsy feeling that sleep was on its way? Why . . .? Got it!

Ashley looked at Major Haldean with triumph. *Jack Haldean*, that's who it was. The author, of course, and damn clever stories they were, too. Interesting, as well, as if the murders and what-have-you were happening to real people and not just people in a detective story. And that wasn't all. Hadn't he heard that some detective story writer had been involved behind the scenes with a real case up in London? It wasn't generally known or the newspapers would have made a meal of it, but Ashley had heard as much at a police dinner. He was sure the name was Haldean.

'Major Haldean,' he asked. 'I don't suppose you write books, do you?'

Haldean gave a smile in which shyness was once again uppermost. 'Books and short stories, yes. It's mainly short stories, but some of those have been collected into books. Er . . . Have you come across them?'

'I have indeed,' said Ashley enthusiastically. 'I thoroughly enjoyed them. I'll tell you something else, too, sir. You managed to get the police more or less right, which is a thing that most detective stories never seem to bother about.'

Haldean laughed. 'That's my pal Rackham for you. Inspector Rackham of Scotland Yard. He tells me where I'm going wrong. The trouble is, you can't get it completely right, otherwise it doesn't work as a story.' He paused, and Ashley heard the unspoken question. 'The thing about stories is that the police are happy to welcome an amateur. I don't know if they always would in real life.'

Ashley stroked his chin. 'I suppose it depends who the amateur is.' He was probing now. 'Didn't you get involved with a case yourself?'

Gregory Rivers grinned. 'Your secret's out, Jack.' He looked at Ashley. 'If you know about that, Superintendent, I wish you'd tell us. We can't get a thing out of this human oyster apart from the fact it happened.'

'It was confidential,' muttered Haldean.

'So you tell us,' retorted Rivers. He shot a sideways glance at Haldean. 'However, I don't think I'm breaking any confidences when I tell you old Jack's just dying to have a crack at working out what went on this afternoon.'

The ball was firmly at Ashley's feet. 'I've got your statement, of course, Major,' he began cautiously, then caught the eager, rather anxious expression on Haldean's face. He gave the ball a careful nudge. 'What do you think about the murder, then? After all, you were an eyewitness.'

Haldean raised an eyebrow. 'So it was murder. I wondered if it was.'

'*Murder?*' echoed Lady Rivers. 'But how can it have been? Are you sure?'

Ashley nodded his head, taking in the reactions of the people in the room. Interest – curiosity – and then he realized that Marguerite Vayle was looking at him intensely. Fear? Maybe. However, she was only a bit of a kid . . .

Sir Philip stared at him. 'Murder? Damn me.' He glanced at his son. 'You said nothing about the feller being murdered. How can he have been murdered?'

'I'm afraid there's no doubt about it,' said Ashley. 'He was shot through the head, you see, and we can't find the gun anywhere. Believe me, we looked for it. I'd like to see the gun, I must say. It can only be a tiny thing. The bullet hole was very small and there obviously wasn't much wallop behind it. There was no exit wound.'

Haldean nodded knowledgeably. 'That'll be a .22. They can be very nasty weapons. The bullet lacks the force to get out of the other side of the head and ricochets around inside the skull. It does an awful lot of damage.'

'Jack!' said his aunt with a warning glance at Marguerite. 'Please don't. You'll give us all nightmares.'

'No he won't,' said Isabelle cheerfully, taking Marguerite's hand. 'We're all as tough as old boots nowadays and, after all, it's not as if we knew him, is it? You're all right, aren't you, Maggie?'

'I . . . I . . .' began Marguerite Vayle, then stopped. 'Yes, of course it's all right. Aunt Alice, if you'll excuse me, I think I'll go to my room now.'

'Just as you like, dear,' agreed Lady Rivers.

The door shut behind her and Isabelle looked at her mother in exasperation. 'Honestly, she's so *wet*! The slightest thing brings on the heebie-jeebies.'

'I think it shows very proper feeling,' said Sir Philip.

'Oh, Dad, it doesn't. If Mr Lawrence isn't clucking over her like a mother hen when the slightest bit of a thing goes wrong, she goes running up to her room. I can't think why you have her to stay.'

'I think you're being too harsh, Isabelle,' said her mother. 'You know perfectly well why poor Marguerite's here and it's only natural that a girl of her age shouldn't want to listen to a catalogue of horrors. We're talking about murder, which isn't the slightest bit of a thing, as you put it. Jack, you should be more careful. Bullets and skulls are all very well in your stories, but I don't see why we have to talk about them.'

'I don't mind talking about them,' muttered Isabelle rebelliously, 'and I don't see why Maggie should. She's only a couple of years younger than I am.'

'But you really are like an old boot,' said her brother.

She gave him a charming smile. 'Thank you, Greg. How beautifully put.'

'Actually,' said Haldean, 'I was surprised how upset you were about Boscombe popping off this afternoon, though, Isabelle. After all, as you said, you didn't know him.'

'I'm not so hard-bitten that I can't whack up a bit of sympathy for the poor soul. It was bad enough when I thought he'd just died, what with having Mrs Griffin to cope with, but murder . . .' She stopped and shuddered. 'It's awful to think that while we were all enjoying ourselves and thinking of ordinary, everyday things, someone was planning *that*. They'd be all smiling on top and underneath . . .' She shook herself. 'And what makes it worse is that you were there. Right outside the tent, I mean.'

Greg nodded. 'It's rotten, isn't it?' He glanced at Ashley. 'But that's the point, Superintendent. We were there all the time. It can't have been murder. Jack and I and Mrs Griffin saw Boscombe go into the fortune teller's tent and not another soul went in after him.' He sighed uneasily. 'We were talking – joking, I suppose – about him being bumped off. It sounds dreadful now, but he was pretty drunk and very offensive. I can't believe he was murdered. Are you quite sure it wasn't suicide?'

Ashley knocked the ash off his cigar and sat forward. 'Perfectly sure, Captain Rivers. Not only could we not find the gun, but there were no powder or burn marks on

Boscombe's skin either, which you usually get with a suicide –'

'If the gun's an automatic then there might not be anyway,' interrupted Haldean. 'They've got smokeless powder in them so you often don't get the burning you do with a revolver. I got it wrong in a story I did last year and received a very learned telling-off from a bloke at the Home Office.'

'Trust you to know that,' said Greg with a grin. 'I'm sorry, Mr Ashley, what were you saying?'

Ashley coughed. 'I wouldn't take anyone's opinion about firearms marks as gospel. It always seems to depend on whom you ask.' He put down his coffee cup thoughtfully. 'As for you not seeing anyone go into the tent, Captain Rivers, there's no great mystery about that. After all a tent isn't like a house or even a hut. The canvas walls are laced together and what I think must have happened is that someone pulled apart the lacing and shot him through the hole.'

Haldean frowned, visualizing the scene that afternoon. 'You could get under the wall of the tent quite easily, you know. Especially if you pulled out a tent peg or loosened a guy rope. Anyone who's reasonably active could wriggle underneath.'

'They could,' agreed Ashley. 'They'd have to be quick, though, and there's the risk they'd be spotted. I think someone saw Mr Boscombe go in and took a shot through the tent walls. They can't have done it from the back of the booth because of the angle of the bullet.'

'Isn't that awfully chancy?' asked Haldean, filling his pipe. 'I mean, with Greg and me standing round the corner?'

Ashley shrugged. 'A murderer's got to take some chances, otherwise they couldn't do it at all. And really, what would you see? A man peering into a tent. The gun would be concealed by his body and the odds are you wouldn't remember it especially. What I can't understand is why you didn't hear anything.'

Haldean laughed. 'Hear anything? In that racket? You don't know what you're asking. The place was like Bedlam. There were children shrieking on the swings, the rifle range cracking away, people shouting through megaphones, a band thumping out selections from Jerome Kern and what sounded like a heavy artillery barrage from the trap-shooting. If someone had decided to take a machine gun to Boscombe then a faint susurration of sound might have reached us, but a .22? Absolutely not.'

'Nevertheless,' persisted Ashley, 'I think the murderer was taking a pretty big risk. Are you sure you didn't hear the crack of a shot while you were standing outside?'

'Not a thing. Greg? How about you?'

Rivers shook his head regretfully. 'I only wish I had,' he said. 'To think of us standing there chatting while the man was murdered . . . I mean, it makes you feel a bit feeble, doesn't it? I actually looked in the tent and saw Boscombe.'

'You said he looked "dead to the world", as I remember. And I, God help me, felt pleased about it because it meant he was out of our hair for the time being. As I mentioned in my statement, Mr Ashley, Boscombe had been an unmitigated pest that afternoon and I'd tried to avoid him. But . . .' He paused. He wanted to phrase this correctly. Greg was quite right. He was itching to be involved with the case, and although the Superintendent seemed friendly enough, he might freeze up if he thought he was being pumped. 'You said you didn't find the gun. Did you – er – find anything significant?' Ashley frowned slightly and Haldean hurried on. 'The trouble was that I, detective story writer or not' (it wouldn't hurt to remind him of this admittedly thin reason for being taken into his confidence) 'was, considered as an eyewitness, about as much use as a chocolate fire-screen.' That made him laugh. Haldean had hoped it would. 'I did manage to keep everyone out of the tent.'

'And believe me, Major Haldean, I appreciated that.'

Haldean gave him a quick smile. 'Thanks. Mrs Verrity

was a great help where that was concerned. But I had my hands full with Mrs Griffin and a little girl who had taken a shine to me.' He nodded to Isabelle. 'Belle helped of course, and so did Greg, but it did mean I couldn't have a dekko on my own account.'

Ashley returned the smile. 'The little girl – is that Sally Mills of 17, Landsdown Cottages?' Haldean nodded. 'The thing she was chiefly concerned about was that she'd got a new doll to replace the one she'd lost. I gather you provided that for her.'

'Absolutely, I did. It was the only way to keep her quiet. After the doctor and the police arrived I took little Sally off to get a doll and my cousins took Mrs Griffin to the tea tent.' Was the Superintendent going to count him in?

'She told us that she'd had an awful foreboding all day that something was going to go wrong,' said Isabelle. 'She was unnecessarily graphic about it. "I had a feeling in my water," was how she put it. Poor Greg had to look the other way.'

'Well, honestly, Isabelle,' put in Rivers. 'It was a bit rich, wasn't it?'

'She calmed down after a gallon or so of tea. She had shrieking hysterics when it turned out he'd shot himself, as we thought. Thank goodness Mrs Verrity kept her head. I wouldn't be surprised if she broke down later on because she was marvellously controlled at the time.'

'She gave her statement very clearly,' said Ashley. 'You asked about physical evidence, Major.' Haldean gave a silent breath of relief and tried not to look too pleased with himself. 'There wasn't much. The ground was baked hard so there weren't any footprints. What we found was a collection of negatives. No gun, nothing disturbed, nothing dropped at the scene, and as to the outside of the tent it was the same story. As far as I could tell, no one had taken out a tent peg or fiddled about with the guy ropes or, if they did, they replaced them very carefully. It wouldn't take much, though, to loosen the fastenings of the tent walls. I tried it on the other side of the tent and it would have been easy enough to poke a gun barrel through and make it look untouched afterwards, but that rough canvas is useless for fingerprints, so there's not help there.' He finished the last of his coffee and looked at Haldean with the beginnings of a wry smile. 'It seems a simple murder but as I remember reading in one of your stories, they're the most difficult to solve. It'll be a case of . . .' He broke off as the door opened.

Haldean swore under his breath. It was one thing having got the Superintendent to spill the beans to them. It was quite another now a stranger had entered the room. He liked Mr Lawrence but he could wish the man had timed his entrance better.

'Rivers?' began Mr Lawrence, then broke off as he saw Ashley. 'I'm sorry,' he continued as Ashley got to his feet. 'I didn't realize you had a visitor.'

'Not at all, my dear fellow,' said Sir Philip quickly. 'Come on in. Superintendent Ashley, this is Mr Hugh Lawrence from Canada. He's staying with us for a few days. This is Mr Ashley of the Sussex police, Lawrence. He's looking into this affair at the Breedenbrook fête this afternoon.'

'A most unpleasant occurrence, Superintendent,' said Lawrence gravely. He was a squarely built man about the same age as Sir Philip, with an attractive, mobile face that showed, at the moment, nothing but deep concern. 'I regret to say I knew nothing of it until I went to the car for the homeward journey and then the chauffeur told me what had happened. I was glad I was able to break the news to Miss Vayle. She's a sensitive girl and was upset at the thought of a man dying and even more so when the chauffeur told us he had shot himself.'

'He didn't,' said Isabelle quickly. 'It was murder.'

Lawrence raised his eyebrows and looked around the room. 'Where's Miss Vayle now? Does she know?'

'She went to her room when we started talking about it. She didn't want to hear the gory details.'

'That shows very proper feeling,' said Mr Lawrence

approvingly. He sat down in an armchair as if settling himself for the evening.

Haldean decided to take the initiative. 'Er . . . would you care for a pipe on the terrace, Superintendent? As I said, I was Boscombe's CO during the war. I might be able to fill you in with a few more details about him.' Would that fetch him?

Ashley got to his feet. 'That might be very helpful, sir. Thank you.'

It had worked.

The terrace looked out on to the sweep of the park. Haldean propped his elbows against the stone balustrade and gazed at the dusky landscape. There was still just enough light to see the line of trees edging the river but the stars were beginning to come out and a faint gleam over the eastern horizon showed where the moon was rising. It was a *rich* night and Haldean felt a sudden stab of sympathy that Boscombe, much as he disliked him, had been so forcibly prevented from enjoying it. He drew a deep breath and turned to the man beside him. 'So Boscombe was murdered, Mr Ashley? To be honest, I can't say I'm surprised, you know. Granted that one shouldn't speak ill of the dead and so on, he was a little brute when I knew him and I don't think he'd improved. But as to who murdered him and how – well, that's another matter, isn't it?'

There was a stone bench with a lion's head at the end of the terrace. Ashley sat down and snuggled himself into the angle between the back of the seat and the carved lion's body which served as the arm. 'Those are the questions, aren't they?' he said, taking out his pipe and tobacco pouch. 'The who and the why. Talking of "who", who's Mr Lawrence?'

Haldean smiled. 'Do you always answer one question with another?'

'I just wondered about Mr Lawrence. Apart from Miss

Vayle and Mr Lawrence I can see where everyone else fits in. I mean, you're all members of the same family. Are they relations as well?'

Haldean shook his head. 'No, they're not. Mr Lawrence is a Canadian copper-mine owner. Nice bloke. He and Uncle Philip are Marguerite Vayle's trustees. Her parents died some time ago and Marguerite stays here from time to time. She's taken a shine to Colonel Whitfield – you've met Colonel Whitfield, of course? – and Mr Lawrence came over to do a bit of polite inspection. From what I can gather, he's quite a big bug in Canada. He endows libraries and so on and was a sort of war profiteer in reverse. He let the government have copper at knock-down prices during the war which earned him everybody's grateful thanks.'

'Good for him,' said Ashley, filling his pipe and inspecting the bowl. 'You come across so many stories of fortunes made by those who were out for what they could get, it's nice to hear about someone who wasn't in it for themselves.' He put a match to his pipe. 'What did you have against Boscombe?'

Haldean shrugged. 'As I said, I had the misfortune to be his CO. He'd only joined the RFC to escape from the infantry – not that I blame him for that – but he had a genius for fermenting trouble. And the worst of it was, you could never pin it on him. The Flying Corps wasn't like the army. It was fairly free and easy and everyone did their bit without making a great deal of fuss about whose responsibility it was, but he was a real barrack-room lawyer.'

'I know the type,' said Ashley with feeling.

Haldean nodded.'It wasn't just that he always insisted on his rights, he was clever, too. He had a flair for hunting out someone's weak spot and leaning on it. He had a bad name with women, too. He was in my squadron for about three months and caused me more trouble than a whole *Jagdstaffel* of Germans. I must say I was fairly relieved when he managed to smash up his plane and get invalided home. That was a few months before the end of the war. The details'll be on his record. Granted all that,

35

I'd still like to know how he came to be murdered at Breedenbrook fête.'

'Well, we do know the "how",' said Ashley with a half smile. 'That's something, anyway. The "who" is another matter.' He pulled at his pipe reflectively. 'We know when the murder took place, which is always a help. You saw him go into Mrs Griffin's tent at about twenty past three. It was approximately four o'clock when Mrs Griffin returned so that means anyone who wasn't in sight for the whole of that period is theoretically suspect. Now although I don't suppose I should be telling you this, there are some people we've more or less excluded right away. You and Captain Rivers should be the chief suspects of course, but . . .' He shrugged. 'I just can't see it somehow.'

'Is it my honest face?'

Ashley grinned. 'Partly that, but I don't suppose you'd be so keen to tell me how much you disliked him if you were the murderer.'

'If I was writing this, that would automatically make me very suspicious indeed.'

'Maybe, but Captain Rivers would have to be in it with you, and that I can't believe for one minute. All the local lads said what a decent bloke he is and that's how he struck me.'

'I'm glad you see it that way,' said Haldean thoughtfully. 'It'd upset Greg to know he was suspected of murder. Really upset him, I mean. If you suspected Isabelle she'd laugh herself stupid, but Greg's not like that. Who else is out of it?'

'Mrs Griffin, of course, Mrs Verrity and the rest of the judges' panel for the cake competition – which .includes Lady Rivers, but it doesn't rule out Miss Rivers, Colonel Whitfield or Sir Philip.'

Haldean raised his eyebrows. 'I say,' he began in a different voice. 'You don't actually suspect Isabelle or my uncle, do you? I know I said Belle would laugh herself silly, but it's a nasty business to be mixed up in and as for my uncle . . .'

'Don't concern yourself, Major. There are plenty of other people who could have done it without dragging in either Miss Rivers or Sir Philip. The point I was making was that they *could* have done it, which is a very different thing from saying they did do it. I've got the local men started on the business of taking statements from the villagers but it's a long-winded affair and there's nothing to say that they're going to be completely accurate. Fortunately the cake competition fixes a time in people's minds otherwise we wouldn't have a chance. After all, when you're out for the afternoon at a village fête you're not checking your watch, even if you have one, every five minutes.' He blew out a wreath of smoke. 'All of which makes me think that "why" might be a more fruitful question to ask. Any ideas?'

Haldean hitched himself on to the balustrade, resting his feet on the arms of the bench. 'Why? He wasn't a nice man, but you don't get murdered because of your lack of charm. Why does someone get murdered?' Haldean meditatively scratched his chin with the stem of his pipe. 'I suppose there are several reasons,' he said eventually, 'but the ones I can think of off the top of my head really boil down to gain or fear. There's revenge, of course, and simple insanity, but gain or fear strike me as the most common. Who would Boscombe's death benefit? Did he have any money?'

Ashley shrugged. 'We know precious little about him. He was staying at the Talbot Arms and he gave his address as London. So far that's all I really know. I've asked Scotland Yard to try and find out where he lived. They should be able to trace him through the odds and ends in his pockets. Amongst all the usual things he had a lady's wristwatch, so there might be a woman in the case, but he also had a bill from his club which ought to tell them something.'

'Will you be going up to London?' asked Haldean.

'When I get the all-clear from Scotland Yard, yes. But locally speaking, you're one of the few people here who seem to have known him. What was he doing at the fête in the first place?'

'He wouldn't say. He obviously knew Colonel Whitfield though, if not very well. I asked the Colonel about it. Boscombe was involved in the Augier Ridge affair where the Colonel won his VC and Boscombe had corresponded with him about a book which he – Boscombe, I mean – was writing. I gather that was the extent of their acquaintance. Come to think of it, that's probably why he was down here. From what he said, he knew Mrs Verrity, too.'

'Yes, she told me that when I talked to her earlier. She didn't know him at all well, though. She had a private hospital in France during the war and he'd been one of her patients.'

Haldean gave a short laugh. 'Is that what it was? I might've known it was utterly tame. He said they went "way back", and gave a revolting leer. That was typical of him. He was not a nice man, Mr Ashley.'

'He doesn't sound it. Had you run across him since the war? Before this afternoon, I mean?'

'Only once. It was some time ago. Last August or September, I think. I can check the date if it's important. As I said, he'd written a book about the war, an auto-biographical thing telling us all how foul it was and his own part in it as a Doomed Youth. I know he lived to tell the tale, but that's neither here nor there. He breezed into the offices of *On the Town*, the magazine where I work, and presented me with a chunk of manuscript which he wanted my unbiased opinion on.' Haldean laughed. 'I don't suppose he wanted anything of the kind, but I read it anyway and it was all right, if you like that sort of thing. I recommended him to Drake and Sanderson and they offered to take it, but when I saw Boscombe this afternoon he said that the sales they'd predicted were hopeless and he was going to publish it privately. Goodness knows why.

It costs a bomb to bring out a book yourself, so he might have had some money to play about with. I suppose the truth of the matter is that he'd fallen out with the publishers. He quarrelled with just about everyone else.'

'Can you remember anything about it? His book, I mean.'

Haldean frowned. 'I read the first four chapters or so. There's a lot about the Somme and a long passage about the tunnels under the Augier Ridge. As far as I can recall, Boscombe says he was wounded and rescued by Colonel Whitfield and his party. Boscombe was frightened to death down in the tunnels. That bit's really well done. Damn! I wish I could remember it more clearly.'

Ashley shook his head. 'Don't worry. I can't think that it's going to be so important, but I'd like to see what he wrote. It might give me some insight as to who he was.' He knocked his pipe out and stood up. 'I'd better be getting along. I'll probably find out more in London about him than I can locally.'

Haldean paused. 'Look, Superintendent. Don't take this the wrong way, but I'd really like to help if I possibly could. If you contact Inspector Rackham of Scotland Yard I'm sure he'd speak for me and all that. At the very least I can give you a lift to London. I've got my car down here.'

Ashley hesitated. 'That's very good of you. Inspector Rackham, you say? I'll have to contact the Yard in any case if I'm going up to Town. By the way . . .' He paused. 'What was the case you were mixed up with in London? The real one, I mean?'

'It was the affair at Torrington Place. A nasty business altogether.'

Ashley's eye's widened. '*That's* the one.' He looked at Haldean with increased respect and thrust out his hand. 'About that lift, Major. I'd be delighted to accept and it's been a pleasure meeting you.'

Haldean shook the outstretched hand, a smile illuminating his dark eyes. 'Believe me, Superintendent, the pleasure is mine.'

In the billiard room the conversation, which had also ranged round the fête and sudden death, with diversions into the weather and the comparative merits of celluloid and ivory billiard balls, had settled on Richard Whitfield. 'If you want my opinion, Rivers, he's too old for Miss Vayle,' said Lawrence, sighting his cue.

Sir Philip wrinkled his forehead. 'Old? Damned if I'd think of him as old. He's what? Mid-thirties? My word, that was a thin cut. Well done.'

'I'd say he was nearer forty. She's nineteen.' Lawrence chalked his cue again and lined up for his next shot. 'I guess I may be being overly protective,' he added in his soft Canadian drawl, 'but there's a good deal of money at stake and I'd like to see her happily settled. As one of her trustees, it's my responsibility.'

'And mine too,' said Sir Philip. 'Oh, bad luck. Just whispered past. I know that as trustees we've got to be careful of fortune hunters,' he said, frowning at the white ball, 'but I don't think Whitfield's one. I'm not saying he hasn't been feeling the pinch a bit lately – who hasn't? – but there's no reason to believe he's only or even mostly interested in Marguerite's money.' He stood back and stroked his chin, watching the white ball kiss the red into the end pocket.

'Well, from what I hear, it sounds as if his stables need some money spending on them. I gather they're not what they were.'

'That's not his fault.,' objected Sir Philip. 'Old Mr Whitfield tried his hand at a bit of speculative investment during the war. He tied a lot of capital up in foreign securities in the hope of a big return and, of course, it all went wrong. Whitfield was telling me about it the other day. He's done very well to keep the place going since his father died. He manages, but a lot of men in his position

40

would have sold up long ago.' He bent over the table, sighting the angle of the cue ball. 'But that's academic in a way. It's Marguerite herself who worries me. It's a damn difficult situation, Lawrence. Once he knows the truth he might cry off altogether. There's no point pulling a face, man,' he added as he walked round the table. 'We have to look at facts.'

'You're saying he might . . . er . . . throw her over?'

'Not exactly,' said Sir Philip, lining up his shot. 'They're not engaged yet. But he wouldn't be human if it didn't count for something.' He sighed. 'I feel horribly responsible, you know. She first met him when she was staying here for Christmas and the affair or interest or whatever you want to call it had got well under way before I knew anything about it. It was Alice who warned me about the possible pitfalls. I did hope it might peter out, but it didn't. Hmm. Difficult angle, that one. But I do think,' he said, walking round to the score board, 'that we'll have to tell Whitfield.'

'I really think,' said Lawrence mildly, 'that we should tell Miss Vayle first.'

Sir Philip gloomily regarded this prospect. 'You're right, of course.' He brightened slightly. 'Perhaps Alice'll do it. I can always rely on her for this sort of thing.'

Haldean strolled back into the house after having seen Ashley to the door. Going to the sideboard he poured himself a whisky and soda and curled up in a corner of the sofa.

'You're looking very pensive, Jack,' said his aunt. 'Did Mr Ashley want you to help him?'

Haldean half smiled. 'You saw what I was aiming at? I *think* I've done it. With any luck he's going to ring Bill Rackham and sound me out. I rather liked him – Ashley, I mean.'

'So did I,' said Lady Rivers, putting down the book she had been reading. 'He reminded me of a terrier we used to have. You remember Tucker, don't you, Isabelle? He was very solid and totally dependable. He got very slow in later life, and was very nearly blind, but once he'd got on the scent of a rat nothing could shake him off. He was devoted to you, Isabelle. He was such a loyal little dog.'

Isabelle rested her chin on her hand. 'Poor old Tucker. He was loyal, but I've never known such a dog for digging. He would keep on bringing dead rats into the house as well, and I hated finding them in my bedroom. If you wanted to dig something up, Jack, so to speak, I wish you would find my emerald pendant. You know, the one you gave me when I was twenty-one. I haven't seen it for ages and I wanted to wear it for the Red Cross ball.'

'Not again,' groaned her brother. 'If you'd look for it instead of grumbling all the time we'd all be a lot happier. You wouldn't have lost it in the first place if you weren't so scatty.'

'I'm not scatty!' said Isabelle indignantly. 'Not with things which really matter. And I wanted my pendant because everyone else'll be wearing pearls. Everyone does now and . . .'

'You want to be different,' finished Haldean with a grin.

'Well, I do. It's the ball next week and if I can't find my pendant then I can't wear my green georgette and I know Ethel Tibberton will be wearing blue, so that's ruled out, which only leaves the cream with burgundy trim and I've *got* to wear pearls with the cream because nothing else goes and Diana Hesketh's got a long string of pearls, about twice as long as anyone else's, and she's dying to crow about them.'

'Gosh,' said Haldean. 'Putting on a white tie seems easy by comparison.'

'You don't know the half of it.'

Gregory Rivers stretched out luxuriously. 'And all in the name of fun.'

'Well, it's in the name of charity, actually, dear,' said his mother. 'I'm extremely grateful to Mrs Verrity for hosting it. She goes to a great deal of trouble and expense and last year we raised a considerable sum of money, which, of course, is the main object. However, there isn't any reason why we shouldn't entertain ourselves at the same time.'

'Jack doesn't need to be entertained. He's got a murder to keep him happy. It's your idea of fun, isn't it, old man?'

'No it isn't,' said Haldean. 'You make me sound positively morbid. I'm motivated by nothing more than feelings of civic duty.'

'Come off it!'

'No, really,' said Haldean with a lazy grin. 'It's fascinating, but I don't know that I'd call it fun.' He met Rivers' raised eyebrow. 'All right, guv, I'll come clean. There is an element of that about it but . . .' He locked his fingers together and stared at them. 'I wish I'd liked Boscombe. I'm blowed if I can't feel a certain sympathy with the murderer. Is anyone the worse for Boscombe being ex of this life? Is there a grieving relict and a row of orphaned children? I doubt it. I know he's dead and I sincerely hope he does rest in peace and all of that, but he was an unpleasant little runt all the same.'

'Jack!' said Lady Rivers, shocked. 'You can't condone murder simply because you don't care for the victim. Why, if people were murdered for being unpleasant, half the County would be dead tomorrow.'

Haldean caught Isabelle's eye and laughed. 'That's an appalling slur upon your neighbours.'

'You know exactly what I mean,' said his aunt severely. 'And you have to get on with people in the country otherwise life is simply impossible.'

'Even if Diana Whosit has better pearls than yours, Belle,' murmured Haldean. 'Unforgivable. Talking about neighbours, what d'you think of Colonel Whitfield? I'd not really met him properly before today and . . .'

'Whitfield?' said Sir Philip, coming into the room with Lawrence behind him. 'We were just talking about him, weren't we, Lawrence? Can I get you a drink, by the way?'

'I know Marguerite's interested in the Colonel,' said

43

Lady Rivers, 'which is why I wrote to you, of course, Mr Lawrence, but until he met Marguerite I would have said that it was Mrs Verrity who had caught his eye.'

'He's done precious little about it if she has,' said Sir Philip, pouring a glass of whisky for Lawrence. 'Say when. Help yourself to soda. Mind you,' he added warmly, 'I wouldn't blame him if he *was* keen on Mrs Verrity, even if she is a few years older than him. She must be the most attractive woman in the district. She's got the most marvellous auburn hair. I can't think how she does it at her age.'

'You might care to notice, Philip,' said Lady Rivers acidly, 'that Anne-Marie Verrity is only slightly younger than me and that even I haven't succeeded in becoming completely grey.'

'Oh . . . er, no, of course not, my dear,' said Sir Philip, regarding the pit which he had dug. 'Completely grey, indeed! What an idea! Besides, it suits you. Very . . . becoming. Not that it would matter if you were, of course. Grey, that is. All over.'

'Who is Mrs Verrity, anyway?' asked Haldean, throwing his uncle a lifeline. 'I've heard her mentioned, of course, but I only met her this afternoon. She seemed a very capable sort of person. Is she English? I thought I heard the trace of an accent.'

'She's French,' said his uncle gratefully, 'but she's lived in England for years.' He added soda water to his whisky and rocked the glass thoughtfully. 'She married Michael Verrity, whose family owned Thackenhurst. You remember him, Alice? He was in the diplomatic corps and we ran into them in Cairo before the war. They got posted to Vienna for a time and I gather she made quite a stir in society there. Verrity was well on the way to making a name for himself when he fell ill and got sent home. He must have died about 1914 or was it '15? Anyway, Mrs Verrity developed a taste for nursing and after his death set up a hospital near Auchonvillers. Ran it jolly well, too. As you say, she's a capable woman.'

'You still find her slightly exotic though, don't you, Mother?' asked Isabelle.

'Well, I do, dear. I suppose a lot of it has to do with the way she dresses. She wears country clothes, admittedly, and nothing out of place, but such *style*! She looks more like someone from a magazine rather than a real person. The house is like that, too. Thackenhurst was always very pleasant but in a lived-in sort of way, but after the war I believe Mrs Verrity had someone down from London to design the rooms for her and it shows. It's hard to realize it's actually someone's home. Of course she often has visitors and I suppose as she is French and lived in Vienna when it really *was* Vienna, she feels she has to make a show.' She stood up and yawned delicately. 'Oh dear. I think if you'll excuse me I really must go upstairs. It's been a long day. The fête was enough and then with this tragedy on top of it . . . I feel so sorry for Mrs Griffin. I must call in on her tomorrow. She only stepped in at the last minute because I asked her to and I can't help but feel slightly responsible. Goodnight, everyone.' She left the room.

Haldean looked at Rivers. 'Fancy a last pipe on the terrace?'

'Don't mind if I do.'

Together they went outside and strolled the length of the house, smoking in companionable silence. The moon had risen and was riding low in the sky, drenching the lawns in silver light. A breeze ruffled the top of the grass, sending little dancing shadows flickering across the lawns. Moonlight was odd, Haldean thought. It was as if the shadows were real and the things they were shadows of were themselves unsubstantial tricks of the light. A bit like Boscombe. The real man, the living man with a body, organs, a brain and, he presumed, a soul, was gone, an unsubstantial memory. But his death – an event of minute importance compared to his life – was the part that cast the shadow. And as for him? He had to chase that shadow,

45

seeing whom it would darken. Better than chasing rainbows, he thought, with a touch of humour, and put
another match to his pipe.

'I've been thinking,' said Rivers eventually. 'About
Boscombe, I mean. Damn funny business altogether. What
was he doing at the fair in the first place, Jack? And why
did he go in that tent to be killed?'

Haldean turned the question over. 'He must have come
to the fair to meet someone,' he said eventually. 'I'm
assuming that was Colonel Whitfield.'

'You could be right, Jack, but I think he saw someone
else as well. Someone he knew, I mean. Don't you remember? He was rattling on about his book in the beer tent,
and I was wishing he was very much elsewhere, when he
looked up and sort of jumped. We were sitting by the tent
flap, if you remember, and I thought he'd seen someone in
the crowd. Then Colonel Whitfield came in and Boscombe
latched on to him.'

'And that somebody else might be the murderer? You
could have something there. In which case it's a chance
meeting . . .' Haldean shook himself. 'What else did you
ask? Why did he go in the tent to be killed? That's a good
question, Greg, and pretty rum, when you come to think
of it. I mean, once he's in the tent he's out of sight. No
one could know he was in there apart from those of us
who saw him go in. And that's you, me, Mrs Griffin and
Colonel Whitfield.'

'And anyone else who happened to be watching.'

'Was anyone else watching?'

Rivers shrugged. 'Blessed if I know. We weren't keeping
it a secret, were we? And although it all seemed innocent
enough at the time, if someone wanted to murder the chap,
then it doesn't seem very far-fetched to say that same
someone would be keeping a fairly close eye on where he
had got to.'

Haldean sucked his pipe regretfully. 'No, damn it, you're
right. I'll tell you something that's occurred to me, though.
It can't have been a planned murder. Someone just saw

their chance and took it on the spur of the moment. Hang on a mo. They'd have to have a gun on them, and that's odd, too. You don't go armed to a village fête unless you're expecting trouble.'

'And that knocks your idea of it being an impulsive murder on the head.'

Haldean half-laughed. 'If I go on worrying at it I'll end up thinking he wasn't murdered at all. I'm going to forget it until tomorrow.' He stretched his arms out lazily. 'I love staying here. I always sleep like a top.' He glanced at his cousin. 'Is something bothering you, Greg?'

Rivers leaned over the balustrade. 'Yes, it is. Murder, you know? I know I pulled your leg earlier about it being fun, but it's not fun, is it? There's someone out there who thinks it's up to them if another person lives or dies. I've got to go back to Town soon and I don't like the thought of leaving you all. You didn't like Boscombe. Lord knows, neither did I, but that's where it stops. But someone else . . . They've killed once and if you start stirring things up they might try again. It's a dangerous game, Jack. I'm not happy about you being mixed up in it.'

Haldean paused. Greg was right. Murder wasn't fun. It was a warm night, but he looked once more at the shadows on the lawn and shivered.

The next morning, lured by brilliant sunshine and what sounded like every sparrow in Sussex cheeping outside his window, Haldean got up at the indecently early hour of seven o'clock and, leaving the house swathed in Sabbath silence, climbed into his car and went to hear early Mass in Lewes, where the words of the offertory went home with unusual force: *Illumina oculos meos, ne unquam obdormiam in morte: nequando dicat inimicus meus: Praevalui adversus eum. Enlighten my eyes, that I may never sleep in death; lest at any time my enemy say: I have prevailed against him.* Enlighten my eyes: there were worse prayers for an

47

investigator and Boscombe had certainly had an enemy who had prevailed.

At the same time Superintendent Edward Ashley, who was also thinking of Boscombe but on a more earthly plane, was carrying a cup of tea up the stairs to his wife. Giving her a peck on the cheek, he explained that no, he really couldn't say when he'd be home, and he'd have his dinner heated up when he got back.

By the time Haldean had spiritually fortified himself, Ashley was sitting on a dilatory bus wheezing its way to the Talbot Arms, Breedenbrook, where Boscombe's room had been kept locked until he could look at it in far greater leisure than he could spare on the previous day.

Arriving back at the house, Haldean shed his suit and, arrayed in elderly, unfashionable but comfortable flannels and an open-necked shirt, spent an agreeable half-hour in, variously, ejecting the kitchen cat from his bed, relieving the housemaid of a cup of tea and leaning over his windowsill, cigarette in hand, whilst the perfect title and rudiments of plot for his next story formed themselves in his mind.

Descending to the morning room, he armed himself with a plate of scrambled eggs and bacon from the sideboard just as Ashley, in the company of Mrs Dorothy Plaxy, landlady, was ascending the old, oak and lethally polished staircase of the Talbot Arms. She was assuring him at great length that everything had been left just as he had told them to, and re-emphasizing that they'd never had any trouble in their house. No, not even after-hours drinking, which could be checked with Constable Hawley. As she panted on to the landing she was giving forcible and frequent expression to the view that it didn't seem right to her, not anyhow, that any guest of theirs should go and get himself murdered.

As Mrs Plaxy opened the door, Haldean was raising his coffee cup to his lips, but what Ashley saw in that room was not only the cause of Mrs Plaxy's violent hysterics but also the reason why the telephone bell rang in the hall of Hesperus Manor.

Haldean's breakfast (which he was looking forward to) remained half-finished on its plate.

Chapter Three

Albert Plaxy, a big, awkward man, still wearing the old clothes in which he cleaned out the beer pipes every Sunday morning, took the cup of tea and put it with clumsy sympathy into his wife's hands. 'Here you are, Mother. Drink this and you'll feel better.' He turned to Superintendent Ashley. 'I don't know what to say. We've never had nothing like this happen before. It's always been such a quiet house.' He glanced at the little maid who had brought the tea. She, round-eyed with excitement, was still standing beside him. 'What do you want, Betty?'

Betty swallowed and bobbed in a nervous essay at a curtsy. 'Please, Mr Plaxy, it's Mrs Jones and Mr Holroyd. They'm saying they won't stop here a moment longer if this sort of thing goes on.'

There was a renewed outbreak of sniffing from Mrs Plaxy. Albert Plaxy shuffled, unable to find words to express his irritation with this fresh nuisance.

'You tell the staff,' said Ashley, his voice hard with impatience, 'that . . .' He stopped, seeing the fright in the girl's eyes. She was only as old as his own daughter and he softened his voice. 'You tell Mrs Jones and Mr Holroyd that they're very valuable and important witnesses and I'm looking forward to seeing them again. They've already been very helpful and I'm sure they'll want to go on helping the police. You can do that for me, can't you, Betty? And I know that Mrs Plaxy can rely on you and them to keep everything running smoothly until she's feeling up to things again. And if the doctor, a Major

Haldean or any more policemen arrive, you'll send them to me, won't you?' He gave her a warm smile. 'I know I can depend on you.'

She pinked with pleasure. 'I'll tell them, sir.'

They turned to the door as a knock sounded and Haldean's long, dark face peered round into the sitting room.

'Hello. I couldn't see anyone at the front of the house so I came to where I could hear voices.' He took in Mrs Plaxy's tear-stained face. 'I say, I can see you've had a nasty shock.' He pulled up a footstool and sat beside her. 'Superintendent Ashley only told me that something was the matter. I don't know what's happened yet.'

That was true. Ashley had been urgent but uninformative and Haldean, knowing that every word he said would be heard with goggle-eyed enthusiasm by Mrs Sweetiman and her daughter, Gladys, who took it in turns to operate the local telephone exchange in the back room of Stanmore Parry Post Office, hadn't pressed him. And that, he thought as he looked at Mrs Plaxy, had been the right decision. Mrs Plaxy would usually emanate an air of kindly, well-fed, unruffled calm, but now her face had an unhealthy greyish tinge, she was breathing in little rapid bursts and the hand that held her handkerchief continually scrunched open and closed.

Albert Plaxy scuffed his feet noisily, wanting, at a guess, to find physical relief in vigorous movement, but that, in this comfortable, cluttered sitting room with its sagging chairs, lace antimacassars, dotted tables, silver-framed photographs and presents from Eastbourne, was impossible. Haldean felt real sympathy for Albert Plaxy, so anxious to do the right thing and so obviously incapable of doing it.

'I didn't want to say too much on the phone,' said Ashley, but Haldean ignored him, concentrating on Mrs Plaxy.

'Can you tell me what happened?' he asked quietly.

The concern in his voice was unmistakable and the

sympathy in the way he hunched forward, looking anxiously at her, was like soothing ointment to her wounded nerves. Her breathing slowed, her hands relaxed and she straightened up and managed a watery smile. 'It's silly of me to take on so, sir, but it gave me such a turn.' She took a deep, shuddering breath. 'I don't know what you must think of me, sitting here, but . . . but . . .' She caught sight of young Betty who was watching with undisguised interest and frowned. 'Betty, go and make a cup of tea for the gentlemen. Or would you like something else, sir?'

'No, tea'll be fine. Thank you very much. It's Mrs Plaxy, isn't it? Are you up to telling me about it?'

'Yes, I . . .' She stopped, looking at him doubtfully. 'Excuse me, sir, but are you a policeman?'

Haldean shook his head. 'No, but Mr Ashley asked me to come because I'd known Mr Boscombe during the war. I've driven over from Hesperus. You know, in Stanmore Parry. I'm Major Haldean, Sir Philip Rivers' nephew.' As he had hoped, she brightened at the mention of Sir Philip. Anything to do with Hesperus was known, familiar and respectable and gave her the comfort of being able fit him into local life.

She looked at him with gathering confidence. 'Well, sir, I was showing the Superintendent here to Mr Boscombe's room. Off you go, Betty,' she added in a near normal voice. 'Don't stand there gawking.' She smoothed the corner of her apron. 'The Superintendent came last night and told us what had happened to Mr Boscombe and we had a look at his room and there was nothing wrong, was there, Bert?' Her husband grunted an affirmative. 'And the Superintendent told us he didn't have time to look at it properly then but we was to keep it all locked up and he'd come along today, first thing. And we did that, sir,' she said, turning to Ashley, her voice rising. 'You were there when I locked it and not another soul went into that room, I can swear it.'

'I saw you do it, Mrs Plaxy,' said Ashley, reassuringly.

'Well then,' she continued, her fingers fluttering on her

apron. 'I took the Superintendent up there this morning and we opened the door and there was a man laid across the bed. I didn't see him at first, because the bed's in the corner, and when I did, I just screamed because – because –' her hand clutched, showing the knuckles white – 'because his face had blood all down it. He was a mask of blood, sir,' she gulped, falling back on the cliché. 'A mask of blood.' Haldean took her hand in his, feeling it tighten. 'I've read of such things – Bert always has the *News of the World* – but to see it with my own eyes in our own house . . . Well, I don't know what I did next, sir, and that's a fact. It was bad enough to hear of Mr Boscombe being shot but to have someone killed here and to see them weltering in their own blood . . . I'd give a hundred pounds not to have had it happen here.'

Haldean stood up. 'It must have been awful for you. Now, if I were you, I'd drink your tea. Have you got plenty of sugar in it? Good. It's the best thing for a shock. And perhaps Mr Plaxy could put a drop of brandy in it? Good man. You look as if you could do with one yourself, Mr Plaxy.'

'I'll be ruined when folks get to know what's gone on,' said Mr Plaxy with a groan. 'Ruined.'

'No you won't,' said Haldean briskly. 'Why, when this gets out it'll be standing room only in the bar for months on end. You'll be turning custom away if I know anything about it. People will come from miles around and Mrs Plaxy'll be the talk of the town if she describes what happened. They'll be queuing up to hear the real story behind what'll be in the newspapers. You just wait.'

'Do you really think so, sir?' asked Mrs Plaxy. 'That folks'll want to hear all about it?' Haldean nodded vigorously. 'Why, that's dreadful, wanting to dwell on such things,' but her voice showed a certain pleasure in the prospect.

'Mr Plaxy, can you stay with your wife? Superintendent Ashley and I are going to have a look at the room. You know the way, don't you, Mr Ashley? Good-oh. Then we won't disturb you any further for the time being.'

'You did that beautifully,' said Ashley with deep approval as they mounted the oak staircase. 'Calmed her down, I mean.'

'Thanks.' He frowned at Ashley. 'There's another body? It seems incredible.'

'I know. He was shot too, plumb in the middle of the forehead. Once again, there's no sign of the gun, so we can rule out suicide. He's about the same age as Boscombe and gave his name as Morton. He booked in late yesterday afternoon. He signed the book, but the only address he gave was "London". I did wonder, as you knew Boscombe, if you might know this chap as well. If you do, then it'll save a lot of work.'

Haldean shook his head. 'I've never come across a Morton as far as I know. I'm glad you were with that poor woman when she found him.' They came to the top of the staircase and Haldean glanced round. 'Nice old oak here, isn't it? If you were arranging a murder this would be a wonderful place to stage it with this high polish and these twists and turns. You could break your neck quite happily and who's to say that you weren't pushed?' He looked along the landing. 'Three doors, opening on to this corridor. Are they all guest rooms?'

'They are. The one at the end here is Boscombe's and the one at the far end belongs to our new body. If you don't know him we'll have to get Scotland Yard to try and find out who he is. Take a look anyway. The doctor and some of my men should be arriving shortly but I think we've got ten minutes or so before they show up.'

Haldean's first impression of the room was that of incredible untidiness. The chest of drawers stood open, the wardrobe gaped wide and a suitcase was upended on the floor, its contents thrown down beside it. All this he took in with a glance, then his eyes moved to the bed and stayed there. It was an old-fashioned, four-poster bed complete with steps and curtains. The pillows and the great bolster underneath had been flung on the floor. One of the curtains was disarranged, pulled away from its rail. The man lying on the bed had his hand entangled in the material, dragging it on to him so it half-covered his body. He lay with one leg dangling over the steps, the rest of his body flung back on the counterpane. Haldean's first thought was that his face appeared to be in odd shadow. Almost instantly he worked out that the shadow was dried blood. Instinct made him walk softly. Stooping down beside the man on the bed, he peered into the distorted face before turning to Ashley with a shrug. 'I've never seen him before, poor devil. His name's Morton, you say?'

'According to the register, yes. Reginald Morton. You can see why neither Mrs Plaxy nor I saw him right away, up in that dark corner. She was exclaiming at the mess in the room, which certainly wasn't in this state when I saw it yesterday, and she looked up and said words to the tune of "Oh dear, the curtain's been pulled off." Then she started screaming. My word, she didn't half yell! Mind you, it gave me a bit of a turn, seeing him like that. Mrs Jones, the chambermaid, who's an older woman in her fifties, came along and *she* started having a fit, which brought the barman up. He joined in the general hubbub and then Mr Plaxy heard the din and came upstairs with that little maid at his heels. I don't think she got to see anything, there were so many people in the way, thank God, and Mr Plaxy just stood there rubbing his hands through his hair, looking as if he'd been struck dumb. I got everyone out of the room at last and Mr Plaxy, once he'd taken a closer look, identified the body as this man Morton who booked in about five o'clock yesterday afternoon. We know a little bit about what Morton did after he got here. He put his things in the room at the end, then went down to the bar for a drink. He didn't say why he had come here and, although he only booked for one night, told Mr Plaxy he might be staying for longer. He ordered an early dinner which was served in the dining room at about ten past six. He was served by the barmaid, who only comes in in the evenings, because Mrs Plaxy, who usually waits on the guests, was showing me up here. Needless to say, the room was all right then.'

'Would Mrs Plaxy or anyone else have told Morton what had happened at the fête? After all, Boscombe's death must have been a pretty hot piece of gossip.'

Ashley shook his head. 'I asked her that, Major. She says not and I believe her. I rather gather they wanted to keep the whole thing as quiet as possible. It was talked about in the bar in the evening, of course, but after his meal Morton went out in the garden with his coffee and a brandy. No one saw him come in again, but the empty cup and glass were found by the table under the tree out there. The barman remembered the cup because, strictly speaking, the crockery isn't allowed out of the dining room and it was the only cup and saucer in use all evening. But what I can't get over is the fact that we've had two deaths on the same day. Morton's death has to be connected with Boscombe's murder, it just has to be.'

'Oh, undoubtedly,' agreed Haldean. 'You can't have two murders of blokes from London on the same day in a one-horse place like this without there being a common link. It stands to reason. Besides that, this is Boscombe's room, and that alone tells us there's some connection between the two men. Which means, of course, a common murderer and probably a common cause as well. Was anyone unusual seen coming into the pub? Anyone who wouldn't normally be here, I mean?'

'I asked that. There were just the usual faces. A few more, perhaps, than average, wanting to talk about the fête and what happened to Boscombe, but they were all regulars.'

'Of course,' said Haldean, walking to the deep window-sill, 'there's nothing to say that the murderer came in through the door at all. Was this window open all night?'

'It would have been, I imagine. It certainly wasn't shut

when I left the room yesterday. It was a sweltering day, after all.'

Haldean crouched down and peered at the windowsill. 'No marks that I can see. No dust either, unfortunately, disturbed or in its virgin state.' He looked out of the window. 'It'd be an easy climb, though. There's an old apple tree plonk outside the window. It wouldn't take much to shin up that and get across. This must smell lovely when it's in blossom.'

Ashley disregarded the apple tree's probable scent and joined Haldean at the window. 'I see what you mean. It's a bit of a stretch at one point, but nothing a man of reasonable size couldn't tackle. But there are at least three doors downstairs. Why should anyone climb through the window?'

'Because that way they wouldn't need a key. And talking of keys, how did Morton get in here?'

'I don't know,' said Ashley slowly. 'Boscombe's key was on his body, but there are spare keys for all the rooms on a board downstairs in the little office off the hall.'

'And come to think of it, I bet Morton's key would fit this lock with a bit of jiggling.'

'Well, that's something I can check easily enough,' said Ashley. 'I'll go and get the other key to Morton's room and see if it will open the door.'

Left alone in the room, Haldean walked back to the body again, seeing once more how the desperate clutch of the hand had brought down the curtain. Not an attractive-looking character, he thought, even discounting the ghastly evidence of death. A thin, sharp face, made sharper by the dark wisp of moustache. The clothes were new, smart and expensive. Very carefully he turned back the jacket, revealing the label of Sweet and Co. He'd been right about the expense. He crouched down beside the bed. What about the shoes? They showed a high polish under a thin layer of white dust. Unsuitable shoes for the country. Thin soles and a shape that belonged on a London pavement rather than a country road. An odd type to find in a rural inn. He looked as if his natural habitat was Piccadilly and that warren of nightclubs and bars which spawns out from the heart of London. So why had he come to Breedenbrook? If he had merely wanted to see Boscombe he could have done that easily enough in London. So that implied there was some business that the pair of them were engaged on down here. But Boscombe had arrived on Friday. Had Morton caught wind of it and followed Boscombe down? Haldean clicked his tongue impatiently, aware he was running on ahead of facts.

Ashley's entrance made him stand up. 'I've got the key to Morton's room,' said Ashley, inserting it in the lock. 'I think you might be right about this . . . done it! Morton's key fits.'

Haldean leaned back against the wall. 'In that case, let's indulge in a little speculation. Morton knows Boscombe. We'll take that as read. And as he was found in Boscombe's room, it's reasonable to suppose that Morton wanted to see him. Now when you arrived he was having his dinner – yes? So, unless someone told him, he wouldn't know about the murder. So he comes into Boscombe's room and waits for him.'

'D'you think that's all he did?' asked Ashley. 'I mean, he could have been the one who pulled the place apart.'

Haldean frowned. 'He *could* have been, I suppose. In which case our murderer comes into the room, finds Morton in mid-plunder, and shoots him. I must admit I'd thought of it the other way round. That our murderer comes in, finds Morton, shoots him and then starts to search for something. In fact doesn't it have to be like that? Otherwise there'd be nothing stopping Morton coming and giving Boscombe's room the once-over as soon as he arrived.'

'Not if he was expecting the man back,' argued Ashley. 'But say he *did* find out in the course of the evening that Boscombe was dead, there'd be nothing to stop him coming in here and searching for something.'

'True.' Haldean stroked his chin. 'But in any case we're

both agreed that someone, who is either Morton or the murderer, took the place to bits looking for something. What it is, I don't think we can begin to guess at yet, although . . .'

Ashley looked uncomfortable. 'I'd rather not start guessing anything just yet.'

'Right you are. So Morton is either sitting here placidly twiddling his thumbs or, on your hypothesis, looting the joint, when in comes the murderer and bang! End of Morton. Now, you locked the room up when? Half-past six? At which time our chap was quietly eating his dinner. Give him half an hour or so to finish it and drink his coffee and brandy and that gets us to seven o'clock or thereabouts.'

'By which time,' said Ashley in disgust, 'everyone was busy downstairs. In a place as solid as this it's not surprising no one heard anything. Unless . . .' He eyed the open window. 'Unless someone was sitting in the garden. They'd have heard a shot, wouldn't they? I'd better get on to that. Now, we're assuming –' He broke off as footsteps sounded on the stairs and Betty, the maid, ushered the doctor into the room.

'Morning,' said Dr Wilcott briefly. 'This sort of meeting is getting to be a habit, Superintendent.' He put down his case and jerked his thumb behind him. 'Your men are downstairs. I asked them to stay out of the way until I'd finished.' He gave Haldean a curious glance. 'You were at the fête yesterday afternoon, weren't you? I didn't realize you were in the police.'

Haldean hesitated and Ashley stepped in. 'This is Major Haldean, Dr Wilcott. He's helping us with this investigation.'

Dr Wilcott nodded. 'Pleased to meet you, Major.' He opened his case and took out his thermometer. 'Better get down to business, I suppose.' Haldean and Ashley stood to one side while Dr Wilcott examined the body. Haldean noticed Wilcott's abstracted eyes, so oddly at variance with the deft professional movements of his hands, and felt reassured. Whatever Wilcott said, he felt they could trust.

After a few minutes the doctor withdrew the thermometer and held it up to the light, lips moving silently while he worked out his calculations. 'He's been dead about fifteen hours – maybe fifteen and a half. What's the time now? Just on ten past ten. I'd say he was shot about seven o'clock last night. I can't give you the time to the minute, so there's no point asking. That's as accurate as I or anyone else could be. The cause of death is definitely this gunshot wound to the forehead. There are some powder burns round the wound which indicate the shot was fired from very close range. At a guess rigor set in straight away, as it often does with head injuries.' He stood back from the bed and seemed to look at Morton as something other than a subject for the first time. 'Poor young devil. I don't recognize him. He's not local, is he?'

'He's from London,' said Ashley.

'London, eh? Like the other one. By the way, Superintendent, I've done the post-mortem on Mr Boscombe. I'll let you have my written report, of course, but the only thing of much interest was the fact he must have been fairly drunk. The stomach contained a good deal of alcohol.'

'That's borne out by our reports from witnesses and the empty hip flask in his pocket.'

'There wasn't anything else that could have caused his apparent drunkenness, was there, Doctor?' asked Haldean. 'He couldn't have been fed a drug of some sort, could he?'

Wilcott shook his head. 'I wouldn't have thought so. There was nothing to indicate it and, after all, when you find a man who has been seen drinking, who appears drunk and has a fair load of whisky on board, then it's a fair supposition that he actually was drunk. Or wouldn't you say so?'

Haldean nodded. 'Oh yes. I was just checking, that's all.'

The doctor wiped the thermometer and replaced it in its

case, but hesitated for a moment before putting it in his bag. 'That's not a bad question, though. Appearances can be very misleading, Major, as I'm sure you're aware, but you can take it that it was drink, not dope, that Mr Boscombe was influenced by. I'll let you have my report as soon as possible, Superintendent.' He gave another glance at the twisted body on the bed. 'And let's hope you catch the man soon. Anyone as ruthless as that needs to be out of the way as soon as possible.' He snapped his case shut and picked up his hat. 'Shall I ask your men to come up?'

'Please do. And what,' said Ashley as Dr Wilcott left the room, 'were you getting at with that question about drugs?'

Haldean shrugged. 'It's just something that occurred to me last night when I was threshing it out with Greg. At first sight Boscombe's murder seemed impulsive. Only someone who saw him go into the tent could have known he was there, which points to the murderer apprehending a sudden danger. But the gun's a problem. After all, a .22 isn't something you take to a fair, and that implies premeditation. Boscombe's condition must have made life a lot easier for the murderer and I did just wonder if it was all his own doing. If he'd been drugged as well, that would have meant the murderer had really thought things out in advance.' He grinned. 'However, I'm wrong. Now a Sherlock Holmes would take one glance at the body and tell you the murderer was a left-handed manufacturer of artificial knee-caps from Peckham who smoked Trichinopoly cigars and walked with a limp.' He put his head to one side as the tread of official feet sounded on the staircase. 'I'll be off, Ashley. There's nothing more I can do here and I don't want to be in the way. Er . . . is there any chance you can let me know what happens?'

'I imagine I'll have to go up to London,' said Ashley thoughtfully. 'Is your offer of a lift still on?'

Haldean grinned. 'Just give me the word. By the way, if you do talk to Scotland Yard, Inspector Rackham will be able to reassure you I'm not a complete idiot. Not all of the time, anyway.'

Inspector William Rackham had been very reassuring. In answer to Ashley's telephone call he not only offered the Sussex police any help which he could provide, but testified to Haldean's abilities so warmly that any lingering doubts Ashley had were swept away. The warmth carried over to the next morning when Ashley, having decided to accept a lift up to London, was met at Breedenbrook police station by Haldean at the wheel of a blue and silver and extremely powerful-looking Spyker.

'I've spoken to Inspector Rackham,' shouted Ashley over the thrum of the engine. 'My word,' he added, as Sussex slid past, 'this is some car you've got.'

'Lovely, isn't she?' agreed Haldean. 'I won her in a bet. Are we going to meet Rackham at the Yard?'

'No. We're going to where both Boscombe and Morton used to live. They shared a flat together, so we were right about them being connected. Inspector Rackham'll meet us there.'

'That's pretty quick work,' said Haldean admiringly. 'Finding their address, I mean.'

Ashley shook his head. 'There was nothing to it. Morton had a criminal record. He's been nailed twice for illicit gambling and petty fraud, so he wasn't hard to find. The flat's in a block somewhere in Kensington. Vesey Mansions.'

'Vesey Mansions! My God, that's going it a bit.' Haldean caught Ashley's expression out of the corner of his eye and grinned. 'If you were a bit more au fait with London life, you'd know that was a very good address as the house agents say. Those flats must cost six guineas a week at least.'

'Six guineas!' Ashley was temporarily speechless. 'I'd want Buckingham Palace for that. We might find money's at the bottom of this, after all. Slow down a bit, will you? We're not at Brooklands, you know.'

'Sorry,' apologized Haldean, watching the needle flicker back down to forty, which was still, as Ashley pointed out, twenty miles above the speed limit. 'I got carried away. Nice straight road, London on the horizon, not a soul in sight. Didn't anything come out of the post-mortems?'

'Nothing we couldn't have guessed. Both men were shot with a small calibre pistol – you're probably right about it being a .22 – and the lack of scorching on Boscombe's skin indicates he was shot from a distance, which we didn't doubt anyway. Morton was shot from very close quarters, of course. There were fingerprints all over that room but God knows which ones belong to the murderer, if any. Babes in arms know enough to wear gloves these days.'

'Did you get anything from the statements?' asked Haldean, gearing down as they approached a village. 'For instance, did anyone hear the shot that killed Morton?'

Ashley grinned. 'There was an old buffer of about a hundred and three who was grumbling about "they pikey cars". Apparently he was in the garden of the Talbot Arms – the Gents is out there – and a car backfired at about quarter past seven. Now, although I didn't contradict him, he couldn't possibly have heard a backfire in the garden so I think it must have been the shot he heard. That was agreed to by a couple of other witnesses. It's funny how people's minds work. I asked did they hear a shot and they said no. Ask if they heard a backfire and they say yes. That's because "a shot" to them means a shotgun, which is a very distinctive sound.'

Haldean nodded appreciatively. 'You should have been a psychologist.'

'God forbid. Being a bobby's good enough for me, even if I can't afford a house with a fancy price. Anyway, it looks as if Morton was shot at about quarter past seven, which ties in with the medical evidence. No one at the pub saw anything out of the way and, of the people drinking there, I can't seriously suspect any of them. They're all so ordinary, and local, too.'

'Which doesn't number them amongst the elect, but I know what you mean. I tried a little experiment last night. I drove to the Talbot Arms, went in the side door, waited around a bit, pinched the key from the office and got to Boscombe's room without anyone seeing me. Being innately honest, I managed to replace the key without being copped. Then, seeing the night was still young, I went outside and shinned up that apple tree to Boscombe's window. It was as easy as falling off a log, if you'll excuse the rather apposite simile. I had to do a pretty decent impersonation of a branch a couple of times as divers rustics crunched past underneath, but no one saw me either going up or coming down. After that I felt I'd had enough amusement for one evening, so I went and had a well-earned pint of bitter. So you see, old thing, anyone could have got into and out of the Talbot Arms without Mine Host being any the wiser.'

'Or anyone else by the sound of it. Thanks. That's worth knowing. I spent some time going through the statements from the fête. I'm glad to say that your uncle's got a perfect alibi, as have Colonel Whitfield and the vicar, Mr Steadman.'

'So no murdering ministers, as it says in *Macbeth*?'

'Er . . . yes. The Colonel and Mr Steadman were watch- ing young Thomas Steadman put a pony through its paces, when they were joined by your uncle. Mrs Verrity arrived and took the Colonel off for a few minutes. He'd promised to lend her some men to clear up the fête and she wanted to get the details sorted out.'

'Isabelle saw them,' put in Haldean. 'They were by the side of the cake tent. She said they seemed to be arguing about something.'

Ashley shrugged. 'I don't know what they could have been arguing about, but if they were by the side of the cake tent they couldn't have murdered Boscombe. It's physically impossible. Your uncle and Mr Steadman say

64

Whitfield and Mrs Verrity were only gone for five minutes, if that. Then Mrs Verrity went to give her casting vote on the cakes and the Colonel continued his conversation with Sir Philip and the vicar about which horse would be suitable for young Steadman. They carried on chatting until the news came that Boscombe had been found dead. And,' he added, 'I don't mind telling you it's a relief that none of them can be involved. You know how it is with people in that position. If they're guilty there's no saving them, but I'd have to be pretty damn certain of my facts. So who the devil *can* it be? We know he was at the fair. We know he's murdered twice. He'll need strong nerves, a good bit of cunning, the willingness to take risks, a large slice of luck and the ability to brazen things out.'

'Yes . . .' Haldean sucked his cheeks in thoughtfully. The blue sky was fleeced with brilliant heaped clouds and the hawthorn bushes that ran down to the grass verges were thick with a summer snowstorm of white flowers. The heavy scent of the bushes caught him by surprise and he smiled at the unexpected pleasure.

'Go on,' prompted Ashley.

Haldean half-smiled. 'It's this. Granted the sorts of murders they were, I think we can guess something about the murderer. You mentioned money. I can't see why, if the murders had been carried out for gain, both Boscombe and Morton couldn't have been killed in the comfort of their own home, as it were. I think they were a danger to someone. There's a couple of other things I could guess, but I'd like to see what we turn up in London first. However . . .' He paused. 'Two murders. I think someone is very, very frightened.'

Haldean drew the car to a halt outside the white edifice of Vesey Mansions. Inspector Rackham was waiting to meet them. Haldean pipped the horn cheerfully and he and Ashley climbed out. Rackham had a companion with him. She was a small, dark woman with a brisk, buttoned-up

65

air. Not a person, thought Haldean, to stand any nonsense. 'This is Miss Edith Sheldon,' said Rackham, introducing them. 'She read about Mr Morton's death in the news-papers this morning and very kindly came round to the Yard to offer her help.'

'I hope I know what's the right thing to do,' said Miss Sheldon virtuously. 'My mum was dead against it. She said, "That Reggie Morton's been trouble ever since you clapped eyes on him, my girl, and I don't want you getting mixed up with no police." Never did like him, my mum, but she always means for the best, and she's right, in a way. She always did say he'd come to a bad end, and I suppose he has, in a manner of speaking. She said it was nothing to do with me if he's gone getting himself killed, but I said as how it was my duty to say what I know and I'm sure,' she added, pausing for breath and unleashing a quick smile on Rackham, 'that no one could have been nicer than this gentleman.'

'It was a pleasure,' said Rackham cheerfully. 'I just wish the circumstances had been different for you, miss.'

'You've been very kind,' said Edith Sheldon with con-scious bravery, laying her hand upon his arm. 'A real gent who knows how to treat a lady, and I'm sure,' she added meaningfully, 'it makes a nice change.'

Haldean smothered a grin. There was something about the big, friendly Rackham, with his untidy red hair, freckles and appealing greeny-blue eyes, that made most girls want to look after him and it was obvious Edith Sheldon was no exception.

Ashley interrupted them with a cough. 'It's very good of you to take the trouble, Miss Sheldon. Did you know Mr Morton well?'

'We were supposed to be engaged, not that I had any-thing to show for it. No ring or nothing. I didn't mind at first, because I knew he was hard up. That's how I met him. I'm a waitress, you know, a nippy as they call us, at the Lyons in Piccadilly, and Reggie'd come in and . . . Well, he was all sweetness and light, and . . . and good fun, too.'

She swallowed and blinked rapidly. 'I don't suppose you want to know all that, but . . . but . . . you could have a laugh with Reggie. He liked the Lyons, all bright and cheerful and with an orchestra and all. He said it was as good as a dance hall, any day. He was a good dancer, he was. I said he'd get me sacked, trying to get me to do the tango in uniform, but Reggie just laughed and said it was worth the risk. Funny, that was. He liked the food, too. I used to slip him a bit extra on his plate when no one was looking. Appreciated that, he did, and no harm done. I thought Reggie might as well have it as it go in the pig swill. But later, when he come into his money and there's still no ring and no good times neither . . .' Her mouth set in firm line. 'I'd had enough, I tell you.'

'Shall we go into the flat?' suggested Ashley. 'I can see your evidence is going to be very valuable, miss, but we might as well talk indoors.'

Rackham had spoken to the manager of Vesey Mansions on the telephone that morning, and the porter was waiting to show them into the flat. Once in the sitting room, Edith Sheldon looked round. She gave a shiver.

'Are you all right?' asked Haldean.

She shivered again and squared her shoulders. 'Yeah. Silly really, but I was only here on Friday and I was that angry with him. I was just feeling sorry, now he's not here any more, that I couldn't have said something nicer to him, but I couldn't have known what was going to happen, could I?' She gave him a deliberately bright smile. 'Thanks for asking. It's hard to think of him not being here.'

'Were you engaged for long?'

'Since last summer, only, as I say, it was informal like.' She heaved a sigh. 'It all changed when he moved in here, him and his high-and-mighty-friend, Jeremy Boscombe. I couldn't stand him at any price and he treated me like dirt, him and his wandering hands. I wasn't having any of that and I told him, straight. Oh yes, he didn't try that twice, no fear. Still, it's a nice flat, innit?' She looked round, again, wistfully this time. 'I used to tell Mum what it was like, but she thought I was making it up, all about the gold taps in the bathroom and a special lift to bring the meals up, all cooked and ready, and no fires to make, just these radiators, a char to clean up after them – kept it nice, she did – and carpets everywhere and a toilet inside and a telephone, too. Yeah, it's nice.'

It wasn't exactly nice, thought Haldean, but it was striking. The sitting-room window looked out on to Hyde Park and only the sound of traffic below told them they were not in the country but in the heart of London. The room was fashionably furnished in primrose and black, with a large black sofa and two armchairs. A vast mahogany gramophone, its soundbox faced with mother-of-pearl, stood against one wall. It was painfully ostentatious, but it looked expensive and, that, presumably, was the desired effect. The walls were hung with modern pictures in which planes and cubes jostled uncomfortably together, and across the room from the gramophone stood a sideboard with chromium fittings, two bookcases and a black lacquered roll-top desk.

'Yes, Reggie's ship came in all right,' said Edith Sheldon. 'One moment he was sucking up to me for free tea and toast, the next he had money to burn. He used to have lodgings in Bloomsbury and wasn't above asking for help with the rent. Then he moved in here and I wasn't good enough any more.'

'That's rotten,' said Haldean. 'I don't think Mr Morton knew when he was well off. I'm surprised you stuck it for so long.'

She smiled at him again. 'Thanks. But I wasn't going to be made a doormat of, oh no, and if Reggie had had a bit of good luck, it was only right that he should share some of it with me, after all I'd done for him. To tell the truth, Reggie was all right when he didn't have Jeremy Boscombe egging him on. Bad influence, he was. I couldn't see what Reggie saw in him. He was always sneering and had a real down on things. You know, a chip on his shoulder. He used to rave about America, how he'd be properly appreciated over there. I said to him, well, if America's that good, why don't you go then, hoping he'd push off altogether and leave us to get on with it, but he never shifted. He hardly ever went out of London. I think it was all talk, this carry-on about America and New York and so on, to make him look big. I think most of the time he was saying it to get Reggie worked up, knowing that Reggie wouldn't be allowed to go, not since he had his little bit of trouble, so to speak. Terrible strict they are, aren't they, about who they'll let in, I mean?'

'How did Mr Morton and Mr Boscombe come by their money?' asked Ashley.

'They had a big win on the horses. Always did like his betting, did Reggie, and this time he picked the right one and no mistake. I don't know how much, but it must've been a mint. Last October, it were. The pair of them moved in here and started acting as if money was water. Nothing was too good for them. Clothes – beautiful clothes they always had – dancing at all the posh places, the Ritz and what-have-you – and parties with enough champagne to sink a ship.' She laughed. 'Not that that made them popular. They're stuffy here and didn't like the noise, nor Jerry's arty friends.'

'Arty friends?' asked Haldean.

'Yes, all painters and writers and suchlike.' She indicated the pictures on the walls. 'Not that I call that *real* painting. You can't see what it's meant to be half the time, can you, and where you can it doesn't look much like.'

'Rupert Lister,' put in Rackham, reading the signature on the portrait of a lady who seemed to be composed solely of triangles.

'That's one of them, yes. Big bloke with a beard and holes in his jersey.'

'Boscombe had written a book, hadn't he?' asked Haldean.

She half-laughed. 'You'd have thought he was ruddy Shakespeare, the way he carried on. All about the war, it was, and not even made up. Well, anyone can say about what's happened to them. It's not proper writing, that. Were you a friend of his, then?'

'I knew him, if not very well,' said Haldean. 'I haven't disagreed with anything you've said so far.'

'Do you know what happened to his book?' asked Ashley.

She walked to the desk and opened the top drawer. 'I think it's in here. Yes, that's right.' She took out a cardboard folder and held it out to Haldean. 'This is his book. You're welcome to it. I've heard enough about it to last me a lifetime.' She turned back to the drawer. 'That's funny. The diary's gone. It was here on Friday, I know it was. Reggie was waving it about.'

'What –' began Haldean, but Ashley interrupted him.

'Why don't we sit down, Miss Sheldon, and you can tell us what happened. Now,' he said when they were settled, 'what brought you round here on Friday?'

She accepted the cigarette Haldean offered her and sat back in the chair. 'I'd got tired of it all,' she said. 'I knew Reggie wasn't playing straight and I'd had enough. Like I said, I'd stuck to him through thin times and it wasn't fair how I was being treated, so I decided to sort things out once and for all, tell him he wasn't the only fish in the sea. Anyway, when I got here – that was about eight o'clock – I was pleased at first because Jerry Boscombe wasn't around, so I thought that's all right, then, but it wasn't, not really. Reggie hadn't known Jerry was going away and he was furious. He said that Jerry Boscombe was a double-crossing . . . Well, I won't say what he said, but I had to remind him there was a lady present. Awful language he used and he was in a terrible state, proper worked up. Not that I minded that much, because it was Jerry Boscombe he was shirty with. All about what he'd do if he got his hands on him and so on.'

'Did he say how Mr Boscombe had double-crossed him?' asked Ashley, pen poised over his notebook.

She shrugged. 'It was something to do with that diary, but what I don't know. Funny about that diary, he was.

Always had been. Reggie got it from a friend of his who'd died. I don't know when that was, but it was ages ago. It was because of that diary he got to know Jeremy Boscombe, worse luck.' Haldean looked a question. 'Somehow or other – I don't know how – Jerry knew Reggie had the diary. You know his book that he was always going on about? Well, he said he'd been a friend of this man who'd died and he wanted to look at his diary so he could put it in his book or something. Anyway, he and Reggie got together.'

'When was that, Miss Sheldon?' asked Ashley.

She frowned, considering. 'It must've been August or September. Yes, that's right. End of August, it was. Reggie was meant to come to Margate with me and showed up with Jeremy Boscombe in tow. I didn't like him much, even then, but Reggie said he was all right and he was a bit curt with me, saying they had a bit of business together and I wasn't to mess things up. I don't believe in holding back, you see. I speak my mind, and Reggie was afraid I'd put Jerry Boscombe's back up.' She sniffed. 'I wouldn't have minded if I had, but Reggie was very particular about it. Anyway, Reggie thought he was wonderful at first. The sun shone out of him, according to Reggie. I bided my time, but then, as I say, they had this win on the horses and they moved in here and that was that. I wish he'd never cast eyes on the blessed diary, no, and Jeremy Boscombe neither.'

'And you say Mr Morton still had this diary on Friday night?' asked Ashley.

'Like I told you, yes. He was ever so precious about it. He kept it in that desk, all wrapped up. It was a big thing, more like a book, really, with a leather cover.' She smiled humourlessly. 'He found me reading it once. My word, you've never heard such a carry-on. I wasn't having that, so I threw it at him, said he could keep his old diary. I said a few other things, too.'

'I bet you did,' put in Haldean.

'Yeah. Ruddy cheek. Anyway, I had the best of it. He

picked it up and said something very offensive about pearls before swine, then he laughed and said I wouldn't understand a word of it. I didn't half tell him. He slung it back at me and said I could read the whole thing for all he was concerned. I tell you, if there'd have been a fire I'd have chucked it on, speaking to me like that.'

'Good for you,' said Haldean warmly. 'Who was the friend? The one who died, I mean?'

'Goodness knows. Funny name. Peter? No, that's not right. Petrie, that's it. The thing is, there was nothing in it to get worked up about. This Petrie had died, as I say, and left Reggie some money – not much – and his bits and pieces, including this diary. It was wartime stuff, all about the army and so on. Who wants to read all about that now? I said, I'm the one who's important, not some old book, but he wouldn't have it. Not Reggie.'

Haldean went to look in the desk. 'I'll just check it's not here. A leather-covered book, you say?'

'Yes. It looks like a map case.'

He opened the top drawer. 'Not in there.' He looked through the other drawers. 'It's not here,' he said eventually. 'Address books . . .'

'I'll have those,' said Ashley.

'And campaign medals and a photo album.' He opened it, holding it so Edith Sheldon could see. 'There are some pictures of you in here.'

She bit her lip. 'That's right. That top one. Him and me. That was on a boat last year. We'd gone up the river for the day and had a picnic. It was nice. I was fond of him in his way. Poor Reggie . . .' She sniffed and, taking a hanky from her bag, blew her nose. 'Can't you find the diary, then?' she asked after a pause. 'He must've taken it with him to . . . Where was it? Breedenbrook? I don't know why he should, but it had something to do with it. He got it out the desk and said, "I'll show him" – meaning Jerry Boscombe – "I'll show him. I've got this and he'd better not forget it. It's mine." Don't ask me what it's about because I don't know.'

Haldean slid back the roll-top part of the desk. 'I don't suppose it's in here. No, there's not enough room. Pens, stamps, pencils, bills – lots of bills – and a collar-stud box. Odd place to keep it. I suppose it's got paper-clips in.' He opened it idly and then stood, his body rigid, staring into the little box in his hand.

'Jack?' asked Inspector Rackham quickly. 'What is it?'

Edith Sheldon craned her head to see. She gave a startled gasp. 'It can't be real.'

Haldean looked up. His voice was quiet. 'It is.' He tipped the contents of the box on to his hand and showed them to Rackham.

'Jewels,' said Rackham in surprise.

'Not just jewels,' said Haldean grimly. 'This is my cousin Isabelle's emerald pendant. It was made for her and I'd recognize it anywhere. But for heaven's sake, Bill, what the dickens is it doing in Boscombe's desk?'

Chapter Four

Inspector Rackham leaned against the windscreen of Haldean's Spyker, watching Edith Sheldon's departing back. 'That woman,' he said with great feeling, 'ought to have a prize for talking. Good God, I thought she was never going to shut up.'

'I thought her tongue was running on wheels,' put in Ashley.

Haldean grinned and climbed into the car. 'Some people are never satisfied. After all, Ashley, it was only this morning you were yearning for someone to Tell All about our two blue-eyed boys. Why don't you hop in the car, by the way? Don't hang about on the pavement. And now the loquacious Miss Sheldon has answered your prayers, all you can do is grumble.' He reached in his pocket for his cigarette case. 'Smoke?'

'The thing is,' said Rackham, climbing into the back seat and taking a cigarette, 'how much can she be trusted? Not factually, I mean, but in her impressions of their characters. Jack? You knew Boscombe. How did her account add up?'

'Fairly well,' said Haldean, blowing out a mouthful of smoke.

'What I'd like to know,' said Ashley, speaking over the noise of the traffic, 'is how Boscombe got hold of Miss Rivers' necklace.'

'Yes . . .' Haldean pulled the collar-stud box out of his pocket and opened it. 'It's certainly Belle's, all right. It's a unique design.'

'You're sure of that?' asked Rackham.

Haldean smiled. 'I designed it.'

'Did you, by Jove?' Rackham leaned over and took the box. The pendant was a delicate twist of gold wire shaped like an elongated star with tiny emeralds for its points. 'You did a nice job, Jack. It's a lovely thing.' He passed the box back.

'Thanks. I've got a friend who's a jeweller. He made it for me. It's not terrifically valuable, but Isabelle will be glad to have it back.'

'Not only that, but I'd say it answers one question, at least,' said Rackham. 'There's no doubt about where those two got their money from. Horses, indeed! I don't care if Morton did have a name as a gambler, I'd say robbery was much more likely, wouldn't you, Superintendent?'

'It looks that way,' agreed Ashley.

'But . . .' began Haldean impatiently, then shook his head. 'You might be right. In fact, in one way you've more or less got to be right. He could have pinched this pendant at the Ritz, I suppose, or at the Savoy or any of the other places Isabelle can be found when she's in London. We know from Miss Sheldon that Boscombe liked the high life.'

'But you're not happy,' stated Ashley.

Haldean wriggled in irritation. 'Not completely. Never mind. Scrub it for now. Can I give Belle her pendant back, Ashley? She'd be very grateful. She wants to wear it at Mrs Verrity's Red Cross ball. I know it's evidence and all that, but I'll give you a receipt and promise that she'll produce it as and when necessary.'

'I can't see why not,' said Ashley after a moment's thought. 'It is Miss Rivers' property, after all, and it should be restored to its rightful owner. But this idea of Boscombe and Morton being thieves, Inspector. Have you got any more unsolved thefts on file at the Yard?'

'There are always a few hotel thefts we can't nail down,' said Rackham. 'I can't think of anything particularly out of the way, but it's a common enough occurrence. Having

75

said that, your cousin didn't realize the necklace was stolen, did she, Jack?'

'She thought she'd mislaid it.'

'I wonder if anyone else has mislaid anything? It's your case, Superintendent, but it'd be worth asking the people who knew them.'

'That's a very good suggestion,' agreed Ashley. He opened one of the address books he'd taken from the flat and flicked through it. 'This is Boscombe's. Quentin Manderton? He lives in Chelsea. That's not far from here. Shall we go and see what he has to say?'

'Quentin Manderton?' repeated Haldean with a groan. 'Yes, all right. If we must.' He started the engine and slipped in the clutch. 'I've run across him a couple of times. He's a great poet, according to his own estimation, and exactly the sort of person who would be friends with Boscombe. He talks more undiluted eyewash than anyone else in London.'

Undiluted eyewash, thought Ashley, sourly. Yes, that just about summed it up. Quentin Manderton had flung open the door to them. He was giving, he said, a poetry reading and ushered them into a room crowded almost to bursting point with people. Inspector Rackham told Quentin Manderton they were policemen. Manderton roared with laughter, pulled a supposedly funny face, sang '*A policeman's lot is not a happy one*,' and immediately started a conversation about unsubstantial realities with a young man in an orange waistcoat. No one asked their names. No one questioned their right to be there. Haldean, who seemed to know at least half the people in the room, was greeted enthusiastically by a young man in a brilliant purple tie who then completely ignored him. The only time everyone was quiet was when Quentin Manderton, announcing himself by banging on a tin tray, read his poems. And the best you could say about *them*, thought Ashley, was that they were short. Incomprehensible but short. The fumes from a gas ring over which an earnest young woman in khaki trousers was frying bacon and onions made his eyes sting. Everyone seemed to be talking at once and no one, as far as Ashley could see, was listening.

'But darling,' shouted a shingle-haired woman who had cornered Haldean, 'surely what you *must* try to achieve is a single integrated abstraction.' She might have been quite pretty, thought Ashley disapprovingly, if she hadn't been dressed entirely in black, including black lipstick and eye-shadow, and wearing a monocle. She waved away a cloud of cigarette smoke and shouted to where a piano was being tortured in the corner by a thin man with bad teeth and a beard which looked as if it had suffered from moths. 'Viktorovich, that's wonderful. So loud. True poetry,' she continued, turning back to Haldean, 'is a single perfect note.'

'Why stick to notes?' shouted Haldean who, Ashley gloomily observed, seemed to be thoroughly enjoying him-self. 'Surely music is a discarded metaphor. The music of the spheres? Nonsense. We need to reach beyond the per-ceptions of human sense, probe into the pure uplands of clarified reality. Real poetry touches the immaterial.'

'Capitalist propaganda,' grunted the piano player, rising after a few final thumps. 'What is the immaterial?'

'What indeed?' agreed Haldean.

'Poetry. Bah! Pretty words fit only for children. The only thing which matters is to create change.'

'Flux,' nodded Haldean.

'Does it support the ideology of power or is it the stinking rags of the bourgeoisie? That is the only criterion I will admit.'

'Boscombe,' muttered Ashley, his mouth close to Hal-dean's ear.

'Boscombe,' said Haldean smoothly. 'Did he support the ideology of power?'

'Boscombe,' repeated Quentin Manderton. He had read four poems to great applause and was now refreshing himself with tea taken from a steaming samovar. 'Jerry Boscombe? Boscombe was a realist.'

'Boscombe was a bourgeois,' grunted Viktorovich.

'Boscombe was a creep,' said the monocled girl, descending to personalities with a bump. 'He really was, darling. You know how he *hounded* poor Richenda and he was terribly mean. And he was always out for what he could get. He'd take anything offered and never give anything back. He lived at Hilda's expense for months, and dropped her like a hot coal when he'd had enough.'

'Good parties, though,' put in Manderton. 'You went, didn't you, Haldean?'

'No,' yelled back Haldean over the noise. 'What were they like?'

'Liquid.'

'He only wanted to impress us,' said the monocled girl, who seemed to have a streak of realism of her own. 'Show off, you know? Darling!' she shouted to a fair-haired man in a seaman's jersey who had just come into the room. 'You've brought your Norwegian violin. How wonderful!' She clutched at Haldean's arm. 'You *must* listen to Ansgar.'

'And I shall play,' added Viktorovich.

Much to Ashley's relief, they didn't stay for the concert.

Seated in the blessedly quiet saloon bar of the Heroes of Waterloo, Ashley took a deep draught of Bass. 'Ah,' he said, and meant it. 'All artists,' he said, with deep profundity, 'are puggled.'

'Puggled?' asked Rackham, putting down his mild-and-bitter.

'Loopy,' translated Haldean. 'Half-baked. Nuts.'

'Too right. God help us, we've seen enough to judge. That Russian bloke and his ruddy piano shouting "Capitalists!" at everyone was bad enough and I tell you, I didn't know where to look when we were at Rupert Lister's.'

'The artist's model?' suggested Haldean with a grin.

Rackham nodded vigorously. 'Say what you like, but I can't concentrate in a room with a completely naked young woman stretched out on a sofa. And did you see his picture? All green blotches and nothing like the right shape. You seemed to get on all right,' he added in reproof. 'All that stuff about mechanical forms and multiple view-points and overlapping planes and so on. I've never heard you carry on like that before. You took the whole thing in your stride.'

Haldean grinned. 'I rather like the opportunity to talk total nonsense from time to time. I enjoyed myself, apart from running into that bloke Ditteridge. You know, the neo-vorticist novelist. He really does hate my guts. I write commercial stuff, you see, and he has a soul way above money. It's not all nonsense, though, Bill. Most of those people are capable of really good work and all the hot air they talk is simply the atmosphere they need to survive.'

'It's not atmosphere but gas, if you ask me,' said Ashley. He looked at the clock on the wall. 'D'you know, it's still early. I feel as if I've been locked up in a lunatic asylum for a year. To get back to business, the general view of Boscombe seemed to be that he was a bit of a phoney, wouldn't you say? He didn't seem to be well liked. Having said that, no one seemed to think he'd stolen anything. Mind you, how they'd know is a question.'

'He had a "bourgeois attitude" towards money,' added Rackham.

Haldean finished his beer. 'Definitely more blessed to receive than to give. Yes, that was the impression I got, too. Look, Ashley, are you keen to get back home right away? I've got a yen to visit the War Office, but I'll be there until at least seven o'clock, I imagine.'

'That suits me,' said Ashley. 'I can always take the train if you'd rather.'

'No, don't do that. We'll run back together, but I do want to go to the War Office. I'll take Boscombe's book with me, if you don't mind.'

'Help yourself. I wouldn't mind an hour or two to

myself. My wife would appreciate something from London and my daughter's got a birthday coming up. What d'you want the War Office for?'

'I want to check Boscombe's book against the official facts.' He pocketed his pipe and tobacco pouch and stood up. 'Nice to see you again, Bill. Ashley, will you meet me outside the War Office at about seven o'clock? That should give me plenty of time.'

Haldean, his spirits sobered by the mahogany-rich fastness of the War Office, smiled with both pleasure and relief as he was ushered in to see Brigadier Romer-Stuart.

He had known the Brigadier, who, despite his rank, was in his early thirties, since the nervous days of the spring of 1918 when Haldean had flown him above the lines. Since then there had been the matter of the mess bill, a scandal which Haldean had quietly defused, and more than a few reminiscent, slanderous and enjoyably long-winded dinners at the Young Services club. Apart from anything else, it was, after the earlier part of the afternoon, a pleasure to talk in coherent sentences without shouting.

His smile of pleasure was returned. 'Jack!' said Romer-Stuart, getting to his feet. 'I had no idea you were in Town. I thought you were down at your aunt's place for the month. How about a bite to eat this evening? Take a pew, won't you?'

Haldean pulled out a chair and put Boscombe's manuscript on the desk. 'I am at Hesperus, Bingo old man, if you see what I mean, so dinner's off, I'm afraid. I'm only up for the day. I've managed to get involved with a bit of nasty business down in Sussex. A bloke called Boscombe got killed at the village fête.'

Romer-Stuart pursed his lips in a whistle. 'I say, is that this fortune teller's tent murder the papers are full of?'

'That's the one. There's been another murder as well, in the same village. A chap called Reggie Morton. I've managed to horn in on it, but I could do with some help.'

Brigadier Romer-Stuart looked a polite, if puzzled, enquiry. 'I want to look up some army records,' continued Haldean. 'I don't know if I'm on the right lines or not, Bingo, but I'd like to see the official account of an incident on the Somme in 1916.'

'I hope you can be more specific than that. There was quite a bit happening about that time on the Somme.'

Haldean smiled. 'It's the Augier Ridge tunnel business. August the 23rd, 1916.'

'Wasn't there a VC awarded for that?'

'Yes, to a Colonel Richard Whitfield.'

'Well, you can have a look at the history and welcome, and anything else you need. The Regimental War Diaries will be helpful, I imagine. Augier Ridge . . . Augier Ridge . . . I seem to remember there was something shady about it.'

'I believe so,' said Haldean. He leaned forward and tapped Boscombe's book. 'This is an eyewitness account written by a bloke who was caught up in it all.'

'Who is he?'

Haldean grinned. 'This is where it gets interesting. He's none other than Jeremy Boscombe.'

'The chap who was murdered?'

'Ker-rect.'

Romer-Stuart whistled once more. 'Bit morbid, don't you think? The voice of the dead and all that. What on earth d'you need to read it for?'

Haldean shrugged. 'Information. Insight. I dunno. I've got the idea that Boscombe was done in because of something that happened in the war. I might be chasing rainbows but on the other hand I might be right. I won't know until I've actually looked at the thing. I've read Boscombe's account before. It's well done and very lively for a memoir. You know, conversation and thumbnail sketches of his fellow officers, that sort of thing. And, as you said, there's something shady going on. As I recall, though, it's rather impressionistic and I'd like to check it against the authorized version.'

81

'Well, impressionistic is one fault the official history doesn't have.' The Brigadier walked to the outer office and looked at the Corporal sitting at the desk. 'Baxter.'

'Sir?'

'Give Major Haldean all the help he needs.' He turned back to Haldean. 'There's a spare office down the hall. You can work there if you like. Corporal Baxter will see to anything you need.'

Haldean followed Corporal Baxter down the hall and into the sparsely furnished office.

'You wanted the official history, sir?' asked Baxter as he showed him into the room.

'Yes, please. I'll probably need some other stuff too, but I'll let you know what later on.'

'Very good, sir.'

Haldean settled himself at the desk and opened Boscombe's book. 'Now then,' he muttered to himself as Baxter's footsteps echoed down the hall. 'Let's see if I've remembered this right, Boscombe, old pal. Because if I have, shady would be a very good description.' He flicked through the manuscript, found the section he wanted and started to read.

Chapter Five

Pro Patria Mori or Saving Civilization
A Memoir by Jeremy Boscombe
Chapter Three
The events of 23rd August 1916. The Somme.

It's surprising what passions can still be stirred by the Augier Ridge affair. I'd like to say that I suspected Martin Tyburn from the first; but I didn't. The only consolation is that nobody else did, either. He was simply the Major, a breed apart from a mere New Army subaltern, who was, as had been frequently pointed out, still wet behind the ears. Of the hero of the affair I can tell you even less. He certainly rescued me (and in the process gave me the worst fright of my life) and, when it was all over, deigned to be treated in the same hospital which had burdened itself with my care, but if anyone wants an insight into the hero's private life they'll have to look elsewhere. I can't write a panegyric about Richard Whitfield VC, because all The Hero did that I can personally testify to was scare me witless. But heroes are like that. I've met a few and they're damned uncomfortable people to be around. They suggest Death or Glory as the only two choices and the third option of keeping your head down never seems to occur to them. Mind you, I wish I'd never suggested the Augier Ridge tunnels to the Major . . .

I've already given my account of the scheme to rid Great Britain of its surplus youth that commonly goes under the title of the Battle of the Somme. With a thoughtfulness that can scarcely be credited, the Top Brass realized that even we couldn't be expected to stand it indefinitely. So it was four days in the front line, four days in support and four days at rest. And as, unlike us, the Top Brass had no days actually at the front, there didn't seem to be any reason why the arrangement shouldn't carry on for ever. If the Germans ran out of young men before we did, our side would declare the battle to be a roaring success.

My particular part in the war to end all wars was the taking of the Augier Ridge. Every day we'd set out across the pock-marked strip of land to the charred and blasted trees that marked the gentle slope of the ridge; and every evening we'd count up those who were left after the Germans had raked us with machine-gun fire. It was a simple game that even a general could understand, but I'd had enough of it.

I mention this to explain my enthusiasm for the tunnels. After trying to go up the ridge, the idea of going under it seemed to have a lot in its favour. So when Sergeant Jesson pointed out the entrance, I was distinctly interested.

We were quartered in a shelled farmhouse and in the course of clearing out the stables the hole came to light.

'It's a hole, sir,' said Jesson, helpfully, standing by the remains of the trap-door.

I looked at him wearily. 'I can see it's a hole, Sergeant. The point is, what's it doing here?'

The face Sergeant Jesson turned to me was a masterpiece of resigned and dumb indifference. Holes *as* holes weren't covered by King's Regulations. And really, if the French wanted to riddle their landscape with mysterious holes in addition to the millions of craters caused by three armies daily bestowing each other with thousands of tons of high explosive, then that, strictly speaking, was none of his business. He didn't actually say that if I knew a better hole I should go to it, but the advice hung unspoken in the air.

I kicked away the remains of the trap-door. It was rotten with age and foul with manure. A flight of steps carved from the chalk of the Somme stretched down into the darkness. It could be a cellar, although why there should be a cellar in a stable was anyone's guess. Jesson stood by, waiting for a command. 'Bring me a torch,' I said. 'And you'd better tell Major Tyburn.'

Half an hour later the Major and I were back on the surface once more. I was excited by what we'd found, and I couldn't understand why the Major seemed so cool. It's obvious now, but at the time I was full of the significance of my discovery. The Major didn't say a word as we re-emerged, but strolled off to the low stone wall which divided the stables from the hummocky fields beyond. He leant his elbows on the wall, looking out over the breeze-quickened downland, quilted with little squares of root and grain. It could have been an English landscape if it wasn't for the shifting line of smoke smudging the air. The Lines. And tomorrow we would be there. Major Tyburn continued to smoke his pipe. Inwardly his mind must have been racing and I wish I could say I guessed then that something was wrong – but I didn't. After all, you can dislike your commanding officer without leaping to the conclusion that he's a Hun spy. And even if I had guessed – well, to accuse the higher ranks of treason isn't the best career move a second lieutenant can make. He, of course, got away with it. He certainly wasn't killed and that put him streets ahead of the poor beggars he led. They do these things, or at least they used to, better in Berlin. Apparently his wife was German. If anyone was serious about finding out what actually happened to the Gallant Major instead of covering up the facts so as not to embarrass their own over-decorated hide, they could do worse than look among her relations. A new cousin, say, who turned up *circa* 1916 . . . it would make you think.

I, fool that I was, couldn't stand the silence any longer. 'Sir,' I said impatiently. 'The tunnel. The compass showed it was running north-east.' I jabbed my finger towards the line of smoke. 'That's pointing directly to the ridge.'

Tyburn tried – and it seemed very natural – to appear

85

sceptical. 'You don't mean to tell me you think it could run all the way to the ridge? Why, it must be over three miles away, man.'

'Why not, sir?' I persisted. 'After all, only part of the tunnel was man-made. It seemed to link into some natural caves.'

Tyburn shook his head. He did this part very well, I'll grant him that. 'Why should anyone want to tunnel to the ridge?'

'To get to the chateau, sir. I heard about it the other day at the hospital.'

'Did you, by Jove,' he said softly. His arrogant stare was enough to make him thoroughly disliked by any man with the usual allocation of feelings. 'Yes, I heard you'd got on very well at the last reception.'

I could feel myself flushing at his raised eyebrow. I had got on well and I knew exactly what he was talking about. One of the brightest spots in this God-forsaken dump was the private hospital run by Mrs . . . Well, I'd better not say the name. Not frightfully pukka to boast. Not that I had boasted, of course. Not really the done thing, and all that, as my frustrated, inarticulate and rabidly jealous comrades in arms pointed out to me afterwards.

It was simply that women, as Major Tyburn might be surprised to learn, actually enjoy talking to men whose conversation doesn't exist entirely of bomb ranges, earth-works and inanely patriotic remarks. I mean, when hold-ing a glass of decent wine and faced with one of the loveliest women in France, I'm damned if I'm going to stutter lame platitudes along the lines of 'Fritz is giving us a tough time, by jingo, but we'll show him yet.' Rank came into it as well, of course. It always does in the army. I'd charmed above my station in life. The lady in question existed on a plane far above that allocated for the use of junior officers who were meant to take their pleasures among her earthier compatriots. A woman who combined the role of Florence Nightingale with the looks of an Italian madonna, she was strictly off-limits to anyone without the requisite number of pips on their shoulder. But even a second lieutenant will occasionally get invited to parties and if a cultured, glamorous woman prefers to talk to him rather than a dull and slightly drunk brigadier, then surely there's no great mystery as to why.

Major Tyburn was still looking at me in a smugly knowing way. I'd have given a lot to wipe that expression off his face but I wasn't going to give him the satisfaction of letting him know he'd irritated me. I decided to play it dead straight.

'Apparently her family used to own the chateau that stood on the ridge, sir,' I said, 'together with a lot of the land around here. She was a d'Augier before she was married. If there *were* an underground passage to the chateau, we could use it to come up behind the enemy.' Good, eh? Real eager, dedicated, medal-winning stuff and if it came off I wouldn't have to go up that hellish slope tomorrow.

The Major was in a quandary. He had to make a show of exploring the tunnels otherwise I and the men would be bound to talk and questions asked, but he made a final attempt to get out of it. 'The thing's impossible.'

'Surely not impossible, sir.' I waved my hand round the old buildings. 'After all, this farm was massively built. I know it's all pretty tumbledown now, but you can see how solid it was. What if it wasn't built as a farm but as a fortification? That would give a reason for linking the chateau to here. And if there's the slightest chance it does lead to the ridge, sir, then we're duty-bound to give it a look.'

Tyburn turned away and leaned his elbows on the wall, smoking. He seemed the picture of calm, but he must have been working out what was an obvious point. If he led a party down the tunnels, then he had a chance of determining what happened to them. If he refused outright then another party was almost bound to be despatched, a party over which he'd have no control. 'All right,' he said eventually. 'I don't suppose it'd do any harm to explore further. God knows, we can't seem to take the ridge by conventional methods. I'd like to give those Johnnies with machine guns a taste of what we've been going through. Get a party together. Make sure they're properly kitted out. I'll inform Staff what we're up to.' He smiled at me and I smiled back, pleased that I had won my point. Stupid of me, perhaps, but then I had no way of knowing that I had played right into his hands.

The tunnel quickly extended into a cave, narrowed back to a tunnel then opened out again. In the light of the torches I could see dark patches against the white of the chalk indicating other passages, but Major Tyburn kept our course directed to the north-east. I was shivering. It was cold down here out of the August sunshine and I didn't have the faintest idea of how deep we were. Adrian Rutledge dropped back beside me.

'I say, Jerry,' he said quietly. 'Where d'you think we are? We must have walked halfway to Berlin by now.'

'We must be nearing the lines, surely. It's hard to tell.'

'Quiet there,' hissed Tyburn from in front. He dropped down on one knee and picked something up from the ground. There were six men in the party and we all craned to see what it was. Lying on the Major's outstretched hand was a cigarette end. I looked at it, feeling the hairs on the back of my neck tingle. It had to be German, which meant . . . Tyburn flashed his torch quickly ahead but no challenge came. I realized I was holding my breath, listening for the faintest sound but there wasn't a whisper of noise.

Tyburn shook his head. 'I don't like this,' he said, keeping his voice low. 'Boscombe, you take the rear. We'll carry on, but it's obvious that someone's been down here. No talking and keep your ears pricked. If you hear anything, turn the torches off and stop moving.'

I slipped to the rear as we set off again. Should I have suspected anything? I don't honestly see how I could. His manner was perfect – but fortunately, on the surface, things were happening.

It was during the next few minutes that I conceived a hatred for underground passages that I haven't overcome to this day. We moved like ghosts along that tunnel and the loudest sound was that of my own breathing. Far louder than my chalk-muffled footsteps. Ahead I could see the shapes of the men outlined in the torchlight. Breathing. That was the only noise. In front of me Rutledge drew up sharply. Tyburn had stopped, hand raised. We snapped off the torches and waited. The darkness was so intense it almost hurt. I strained my ears, becoming abnormally aware of the tiny sounds of six men standing rigidly still. Breathing . . . And the breathing had an echo.

A hand pushed gently on my chest. It must have been Rutledge. 'Go back.' It was the faintest of whispers.

The tunnel exploded in light and noise. A blaze of torches flared, showing Rutledge's face as stark as if it were caught in a bolt of lightning. Shouts, running feet, then a thunderous roaring of guns that left me completely deaf with a head full of ringing bells. Rutledge turned slowly, his arms wide, his mouth opening and shutting, shouting, but I could hear nothing. His forehead splintered into darkness and he jerked back like a dropped puppet. I fell to my knees, trying to unholster my revolver, but my numb fingers fumbled on the stiff leather and the gun skittered out of my grasp. I reached out for it, but someone fell against me, pushing me away. I saw his face, mouth open as if he were singing, and it seemed to take me minutes to work out he was screaming. I thrust him away, trying to get the gun. As I lurched to my feet Tyburn waved me on to be killed, but if I was capable of thinking anything, all I thought of was escape. A bullet bit through my shoulder, hurling me backwards. I rolled on to my stomach and crawled, my left arm dragging uselessly beside me. I scrambled to my feet, doubling over to avoid the shots. I still couldn't hear, but the walls of the tunnel kept on puffing out explosions of dust as the bullets struck home. Then I was beyond the dancing lights, running terror-whipped into darkness.

Perhaps you're wondering, as you read this sitting at home in a comfortable armchair, what had happened to my courage. It had gone, swallowed up in the sick taste of fear. The hero of a boy's comic would have rallied the men and led a charge, indifferent to the bullets whistling round his ears. The hero of a boy's comic wouldn't have a stomach of water, a head full of crashing noise and an arm that jagged with pain. He would have a lovely funeral, with a grand tombstone and a posthumous medal. I'm not a hero. On the other hand I'm still alive.

I crashed into a wall and lay stunned for a few seconds. Back down the tunnel I could see flashlights playing over the walls, but none were moving towards me. I got to my feet very cautiously and felt my way away from the lights. I rounded a bend and stopped. Darkness ahead, light behind. I felt my breathing steady and something approaching rational thought returned. I still had my torch. I'd slipped it into my pocket when we'd stopped. I snapped it on, being careful to shield the light with my body. My shoulder was on fire and my head was spinning and I had to think how to walk. Lift one foot. Forward. Down. Lift one foot. Forward . . . The bitter sourness of panic filled my mouth and I retched miserably. I staggered on, forcing my legs to obey me. The dark mouth of a side passage opened up and I half-fell into the shielding blackness, lying across the mouth of the tunnel. I wanted, more than anything I'd ever wanted before, to lose consciousness, but it wouldn't come. I knew I was whimpering in fear, but I couldn't hear or stop the sound.

I don't know how long I was lying there. Time meant nothing in that intense blackness. I had a bad scare when I heard a faint sound of breathing, then I nearly laughed out loud as I realized it was myself I could hear. Something very like contentment lapped over me as I lay in the tunnel. My ears crackled as sound returned and then, believe it or not, my conscience started to twitch. Should

I go back? No! The sick knot in my stomach returned. Forward? I didn't want to move . . . and then I froze as footsteps sounded in the main tunnel. I scrabbled back further into the side passage. A light shone, illuminating men walking cautiously past the entrance. They were English troops. I tried to shout out, to warn them, but my voice wouldn't work. But I knew what was ahead. Half crawling, half walking, I got into the main tunnel, closed my eyes, swallowed hard and concentrated on producing a shout when a wall of sound hit me with physical force. My small store of courage fled and I shrank back, terrified, curled into a ball of fear. I screwed my eyes shut, trying to lose consciousness, but stayed obstinately, unwillingly, awake.

Then I nearly did faint. A hand jerked my wounded shoulder. I suppose I yelled in pain, but the deafness had returned. A torch blinded into my eyes, making me wince. Then the torch was put down, illuminating the man in front of me. I gave a foolish smile of relief as I saw who it was. An English captain, with, oddly enough, the red tabs of a staff officer on his uniform.

I stretched out my hand, but the Captain didn't take it. He was talking to me – questions, I suppose – which I couldn't hear. His face was horribly grim. I tried to smile again, but he wouldn't smile back. Instead he dropped to one knee and took out his revolver. I shrank back, guessing there must be Germans up the tunnel. I strained into the darkness, but couldn't see . . . and realized the muzzle of the gun was pointed straight at my chest. The hammer raised back, then the Captain whirled and fired a shot up the tunnel. I was weak with relief. God knows what he'd seen. I didn't ask and couldn't have heard the reply if he'd answered. And then familiar faces surrounded me. Dixon, Stafford, Keenan. I was safe.

They got me to my feet and walked some way down the tunnel before halting. They seemed to be arguing with the Staff Captain, and the men were evidently unhappy. The Captain was insisting on something, his body tense with conflict. He smacked his fist down into his hand and the men shrugged. Dixon handed over his rifle and a pouch of ammunition. With a nod of thanks the Captain walked back a few steps and crouched down behind a jutting outcrop of chalk, covering our retreat. I spared him a glance as we walked away. So this was a hero. I've never met a man who frightened me more.

I landed up metaphorically, if not literally, on my feet. The hospital where I'd so recently drunk champagne, toyed with canapés and flirted with the great, if not repressively good, received my fairly battered remains. It was heaven. The care was excellent, the nurses exquisite if unobtainable, and the food a dream. Private hospitals weren't uncommon, but this was one of the best. As far as I was concerned the only drawback was that I was going to have to leave. No one could actually want to return to the fighting but this brief period of civilization gave me a loathing of the trenches which amounted to an obsession. I'd lie awake with thoughts of desertion flitting through my head and I honestly believe if I'd had a gun I'd have tried to arrange an accident. A bullet through the foot, perhaps? But I didn't have a gun and I couldn't think of a convincing reason for getting hold of one. And to be found out . . . That would mean a court martial and a firing squad.

The Second Lieutenant in the next bed – Grant, his name was – had no such worries. His hip and thigh were a mass of bandages. 'Mine's a Blighty one,' he said with horrible cheerfulness. 'What about you?'

'No such luck. I'm damned if I'm going back though.'

Grant laughed, secure in the happiness that comes to those missing half a leg. 'I don't see how you can avoid it, old man. Unless you can pull a few strings and end up on the Staff, you're stuck. Failing that, there's always the RFC.'

The Royal Flying Corps. Now there was a thought. They

didn't sleep in trenches. They didn't go over the top. Their quarters were well behind the lines and those quarters were, if rumour was correct, bloody palaces. The RFC . . . Why the hell hadn't I thought of it? If I transferred that'd mean six months at a home training establishment before joining a squadron. Six months! The war could be over by then. I looked at Grant with real interest for the first time. 'I'll do it!'

'Hey,' he said, alarmed. 'Don't be an idiot. It might sound good but it's not all it's cracked up to be, you know. I had a cousin –'

I wish now I'd listened to the story of Grant's cousin. But I rushed upon my fate. 'Damn your cousin. I've had enough of skulking underground. I'll do it.'

Grant looked at me queerly, then shrugged. 'Suit yourself. What d'you mean, skulking underground? You weren't in a tunnelling company, were you?'

'I might as well have been. I was the fool who discovered the Augier Ridge tunnel. I was in the first party.'

'I say, were you?' That was my first indication of how big an affair this was going to be. The admiration in Grant's eyes was gratifying. If we'd been in an *estaminet* he'd have bought me a drink. He propped himself up on one arm. 'D'you know who's in the private room at the top of the ward? Captain Whitfield himself. That's why *She* keeps going in there.' I didn't need to ask who he meant. There was only one *She* in our constricted world. 'Nothing but the best for The Man Who Saved The Western Front. They say he's up for the VC for what he did. If all staff officers were like him, we'd have shoved Fritz back to Berlin years ago.'

'You think so?' I picked up a four-month-old magazine.

'No, really,' persisted Grant, who seemed to have taken The Hero's cause to heart. 'They say that Fritz was going to flood through those tunnels and if it hadn't been for Captain Whitfield they'd have done it. And he's a staff officer, too.'

'Well?'

'Well, you know the old joke. If bread is the staff of life, then the life of the staff is one long loaf.' He waited for me to laugh but I didn't oblige him. I'd heard that one before. 'But honestly,' said Grant, who could have been the chairman of whatever board it is which awards medals, 'you have to admire him. He held them off single-handed and they had to dig him out of the rubble.' He looked up as a door opened further up the ward. *She*, as Grant would have said, came out of the private room which contained Captain Whitfield. 'Isn't that so, Madame?' he called.

She walked towards us and paused by Grant's bed, straightening out his pillow. 'Isn't what so, Mr Grant?'

'That Captain Whitfield's a hero? Boscombe here was in the tunnels with him.'

'But yes, it is true. I wanted to see you, Monsieur Boscombe. Your kit has arrived.' Her accent gave her voice a delicious tang. 'I saw to it myself. One of the orderlies will bring it up for you.' She reverted to the topic of the moment. 'The brave Captain, he is recovering I am glad to say.' She must have sensed my scepticism, for she became quite delightfully French. 'We all owe him – oh, so much! If the Boche had come down those tunnels then the British would be thrown back to the sea and it would all have been over.'

'They probably wouldn't have made it,' I said. 'After all, we don't know the tunnels went to the chateau.'

'But they do, Monsieur Boscombe,' she said earnestly. 'Remember, it was my home. I had no idea where the tunnels went to, but Papa told me they stretched for miles. We used them to store wine but that is not why they were built. It was the war of Louis the Fourteenth, you understand? When your Marlborough was fighting here and we French and English were on different sides. The great Sébastien Vauban, the most famous engineer of his day, stayed at the chateau and planned the fortifications. My brother, he liked to explore them, but me?' She gave a dazzling smile and a shrug. 'I do not like the dark. They are all blocked off now, with the bombs the Boche threw.

It is better, yes? You were lucky to get out, Lieutenant Boscombe.'

'I was pretty unlucky to be down there in the first place,' I said. 'I could have sworn we didn't make a sound and yet they were waiting for us. I know this Front's lousy with spies. I'm willing to bet we were dropped in it.'

'Dropped in it?' she enquired.

'Betrayed,' I said, translating.

She glanced round the ward quickly, as if to avoid being overheard. 'But yes, there is much in what you say. I heard . . . but no. It was private talk. But I can tell you this, Monsieur Boscombe, that before too long some of your officials will want to talk to you, to find out what you know.' And that was my first hint that things really weren't all they seemed. I asked her for more details, but she refused to say anything. 'Just get better, Monsieur, and before long you will be fighting again. And you will come to another of my parties, yes?'

'Wow,' said Grant as she walked away. 'She even *smells* like a woman. What was all that hush-hush stuff about spies?'

'God knows,' I said, picking up my magazine again. I'd had enough of Grant. I remember there was a cartoon on the inside cover showing an RFC officer with a girl on each arm, lamenting that the war was interfering with Ascot. That was the life for me. Six months at home . . .

'But who's the spy, if there is a spy?' persisted Grant.

'Oh, wait till you read it in the papers,' I snapped, annoyed at having my daydream broken into. I suppose he did read it, later on, and so did the rest of the world. That was one story they couldn't keep quiet.

Chapter Six

Haldean drew his cup towards him and drank his tea, pulling a face as he realized it was cold. On the desk in front of him lay Boscombe's manuscript, various official and leather-bound books and a few sheets of notepaper. He glanced at his watch. He'd have to go. It was nearly seven o'clock and he didn't want to keep Ashley waiting. It had been a long session but he had the information he was looking for.

He ran his finger down his notes. Petrie, Robert Stephen. Royal Sussex from May 1915. Prisoner of war from 23rd August 1916, repatriated and given an Honourable Discharge January 1919. Morton, Reginald John. Second-Fourth Prince Edward's Rifles from May 1917 to the Armistice. Boscombe, Jeremy Andrew. Royal Sussex from January 1916 until September 1916. Transferred to the Royal Flying Corps from September 1916 to June 1918 and subsequently invalided home. He boxed the papers together with his other extracts from service records and glanced at his account of Augier Ridge. Bingo had been right; there was something very shady indeed about it. Boscombe had told the truth after all . . .

The Spyker nosed its way out of London and passed through the last ribbons of houses until the town admitted defeat and became real country once more. Ashley sat contentedly in the passenger seat. On the seat behind him, carefully wrapped in brown paper and sealed with wax, were two records, 'Pick Me Up And Lay Me Down In Dear Old Dixieland' and 'Blowing Bubbles All Day Long', which were, as he had just finished telling Haldean, his daughter's birthday present. Add to that a jazz-patterned silk scarf for Elsie, a fund of stories about the peculiar doings of artists – some not for Elsie's ears – and the feeling of some solid progress in the Boscombe and Morton case, and Ashley felt that the day had been very well spent. 'And what's more, I think your pal, Mr Rackham, had the right idea when he said we had a couple of thieves on our hands. Hotel robberies will be the size of it unless I'm much mistaken.'

'Perhaps.' Haldean was hesitant. He had some ideas of his own, very definite ideas, but what he didn't want to do was present them to Ashley as a completed theory. For one thing Ashley might not agree and for another he was wary of muscling in on what was, strictly speaking, not only none of his business but Ashley's professional life. 'It could be theft, old thing,' he said, easing the car into fourth gear, 'but if theft is at the bottom of it, what were Boscombe and Morton doing in Breedenbrook?'

'I . . .' Ashley frowned. 'Blowed if I know.'

'Let me put it another way,' said Haldean, slowing down as they approached a corner. 'What are some of the various illicit ways of making money? Because we know they had money, quite a bit of it, and they weren't hard-working, sober and honest.'

Ashley scratched his chin. 'Gambling could account for some of it, I suppose. That was Morton's previous form, but like you, I thought that was just a story to keep Miss Sheldon from being too inquisitive. Theft, of course. That's certain, because of Miss Rivers' necklace. Then there's dope-running, although there was nothing to suggest it. Fraud's a possibility with Morton's record, but, again, there's no evidence pointing that way. There's always forgery, but that doesn't seem to fit the bill either.'

Haldean nodded. 'And all those things, with the possible exception of theft, can be done far more profitably in

London.' He gave Ashley a quick glance. Here goes. 'Can I add another one to your list? Blackmail.'

'Blackmail?' repeated Ashley, and paused as the thought took hold. 'Blackmail.'

At least he hadn't dismissed the idea. So far, so good. 'Just think how much it explains,' said Haldean, keeping his eyes on the road. He wanted to make Ashley understand why he was so sure he was on the right lines. 'I told you Boscombe was a beggar for finding a man's weak spot and leaning on it. When I knew him he did it out of sheer devilment, but he wasn't above getting an unfair advantage that way. He'd squirrel away personal details and produce them weeks later when it suited him. He was a moral blackmailer, if you'll let me put it that way. I think there's a fair chance he turned into the full-blown article.'

'Blackmail,' repeated Ashley once more. 'D'you know, Haldean, you might have something there. It's certainly a very powerful motive for murder.'

Haldean gave a silent breath of relief. 'Isn't it, though?' Now the ground of the argument was captured, he had to consolidate it. He had to turn a breakthrough into a breakout, as they used to say in the war, and take Ashley with him. 'I can imagine Boscombe really putting the screws on, demanding more and more. He was living the life of Riley and it wasn't cheap. I think he applied for a pay rise.'

'Who to?' demanded Ashley.

Haldean grinned. 'Now you're asking.' That was the question, wasn't it? 'Let's call him A. N. Other.'

Ashley looked doubtful. 'It doesn't explain the theft of Miss Rivers' pendant though, does it?'

'Well, not as such, no,' said Haldean impatiently, 'but I don't suppose Boscombe limited himself to one sort of crime. I mean, he wouldn't, would he? If he's capable of blackmail he's capable of theft and a good few other things as well, I imagine.'

'Fair enough. But look here, if Boscombe was murdered because he was a blackmailer – and I suppose that goes for

Morton as well – then whoever they were blackmailing must live in Breedenbrook.'

'Perhaps.' That was one way of looking at it, but it wasn't the direction Haldean wanted to go. Not yet. 'At any rate,' he temporized, 'Boscombe knew his victim was going to be at the fête, and, as he was murdered there, we can assume without straining things that A. N. Other, the blackmailee and murderer, turned up. Again, it explains a dickens of a lot.'

'So all we have to do is find out who Boscombe and Morton were blackmailing,' said Ashley thoughtfully.

Haldean laughed. Yes, that was all. 'I like the optimism in that sentence. That's the size of it. Any guesses as to who it could be?' And that was a genuine question. He wanted to hear Ashley's reasoning.

Ashley paused, arranging his ideas. 'It'd have to be someone well off,' he said eventually. 'Anyone with an alibi for Boscombe's murder is out of it, of course. Morton's murder is a lot more open to question, but we can exclude a whole raft of people from Boscombe's.' He looked at Haldean shrewdly. 'You've been thinking about this. Come on. Let's have your ideas.'

Haldean took a deep breath. This was where he'd been heading. He very much wanted to try out his theory on Ashley. He thought it added up, but he knew there was a big difference between a theory which existed in the privacy of his own thoughts and a theory which had been exposed to the cold light of criticism. 'I think it goes back to the war,' he said quietly.

'So that's why you went to the War Office. I see.'

'Ker-rect.' Haldean slowed down so the car was running at a steady thirty-five. Now for it. 'I was concentrating on the Augier Ridge affair. Boscombe had written so lovingly and in such detail about it that I thought, if he'd found out anything, it would be about that. There were notes for subsequent chapters but they were only sketches. Now what actually happened at Augier Ridge was this. The ridge was held by the Germans and attacked by us, us including the Royal Sussex. We got nowhere and suffered some pretty fierce casualties over a period of three or so weeks. Then, during a rest period behind the lines, a tunnel was discovered by our friend Boscombe. It led from an old farm in the direction of the ridge. If, by any chance, it went as far as the old chateau on the ridge it would mean that the ridge could be taken with minimum losses.'

'That sounds like very keen work from Boscombe.'

'Yes, it does, doesn't it?' agreed Haldean. 'He says himself that going under the ridge knocked spots off going over it, and I can't half see his point of view. Anyway, HQ were informed, as they'd have to be, and detailed Major Tyburn, Boscombe's CO, together with Boscombe and five officers and men, to explore it. They must have got a considerable distance before they were attacked by a party of Germans. Boscombe, although wounded, managed to crawl back down the tunnel and there he lay, unable to move. In the meantime, Captain Whitfield, as he then was, turned up from Staff.'

'Is that our Colonel Whitfield?'

'That's the one. Whitfield led a second expedition into the tunnels to try and find out what had happened to Tyburn and his men. According to Boscombe's book, Boscombe heard them go past the side tunnel into which he had crawled. By his own account he tried to warn them of danger ahead, but was too weak to make himself heard. Now at this point the Germans attacked again. Whitfield escaped and came across Boscombe, who by this time had got himself back into the main tunnel. With the Germans down the tunnel they were still in very great danger, when a third party, sent by Captain Hodge from the farm, turned up.'

Ashley winced. 'This sounds as if it's got the makings of a first-rate disaster.'

'It could easily have been very nasty indeed. As it was, it was bad enough but fortunately for us, Whitfield took a firm hand.'

'What did he do?' asked Ashley with interest.

'He reported to Captain Hodge that all the English troops in front of him were dead or captured and that it would only be a matter of time before the Germans advanced. Boscombe was taken to safety but Whitfield insisted on staying behind to cover their retreat. As he was the senior officer present no one could very well argue the toss with him. They retreated in good order until they came to a point that Whitfield thought he could reasonably defend.'

'That was pretty brave of him,' said Ashley thoughtfully. 'I'm blowed if I'd care to wait alone in total darkness, knowing the enemy might strike any moment.'

'He got the VC for it,' said Haldean. 'Boscombe thought Whitfield was a bit *Boy's Own* about it all and there was a touch of the Duke of Wellington – you know, "I don't know if he frightens the enemy but, by God, he frightens me" – but Boscombe was fairly fond of his own skin. He'd always duck a fight if he could. Anyway, as soon as the rescue party with Boscombe reached the surface, another party was commanded to go down to aid Whitfield. They had to dig him out of the rubble. Apparently the Germans had thrown a couple of stick-bombs which brought the roof down and completely blocked the tunnel.'

'Poor devil,' said Ashley. 'I'm not surprised he got a medal.'

'A richly deserved one.'

'But . . .' Ashley stopped and looked at Haldean with a puzzled frown. 'But you said the reason for Boscombe's murder and so on went back to the war. What's there in that story to warrant blackmail?'

'Nothing so far, but hold on. That's only half the story. Now granted we're –' Haldean had nearly said *I'm* – 'looking for someone for Boscombe to blackmail I did briefly wonder about Mrs Verrity. When Boscombe was brought out of the tunnels he landed up as a patient in her hospital. Mrs Verrity appears in his book as the proper, if dispossessed, owner of the Augier Ridge – she's a d'Augier by birth – and an unnamed Angel of Mercy, smoothing pillows and so on. He hints he had an affair with her.'

Ashley gave a derisive snort, but Haldean shook his head. 'She might have done. He wasn't a bad-looking bloke and he could have a world-weary charm when he wasn't plastered. And Mrs Verrity's really something. She's a lovely woman, if a bit much of the *femme fatale* for my taste. However, even if she did have an affair with Boscombe, I can hardly see her stumping up hard cash to keep it quiet.'

Ashley rubbed his chin, frowning. 'She wouldn't want it talked about, though, would she? I mean, a woman's got to be careful of her reputation. She might, granted that there had been something going on, which I doubt, be frightened into paying him to keep quiet.'

Haldean gave him a look. 'Come on, Ashley. Mrs Verrity's not the sort of woman who's looking over the fence wondering what the neighbours think. She's far more sophisticated than that. Say they did have an affair. We're talking about a French widow and a single man in France in the middle of the war. It's a few years ago now and even if Boscombe had some evidence, such as letters and so on, I think her reaction would be, to quote the Duke of Wellington again, to say "Publish and be damned."'

'All the same, she might not like it talked about. No woman would.'

'I don't suppose she would, but even if Boscombe did pop up at the fête to talk about the dear old days with memories of passion spent and so on, she couldn't have killed him if she'd wanted to, because her alibi's vouched for by about a million people.'

'Which rules her out, however lovely you find her,' said Ashley drily. 'That's got much more going for it as an argument to my way of thinking.'

'Yes . . . So she's a non-starter. A pity in a way because I could see her as a bit of a Mata Hari. Of the rest of the

Home Team, so to speak, Colonel Whitfield is also ruled out because of Uncle Philip and so on.'

Ashley gave a wry grin. 'Thank God for that. I can just see the Chief's face if I told him my favourite suspect was a pillar of the community, a VC and a Justice of the Peace. That wouldn't be a good idea.'

'Hardly, but you needn't worry. I've got someone far more interesting for you to think about.'

Ashley looked at him quizzically. 'Who?'

'Major Martin Tyburn.'

'Who? Boscombe's Commanding Officer, you mean?'

'That's the one.' He was approaching the real substance of his theory now. 'When I breezed into the War Office, I met my old pal, Romer-Stuart. His recollection of the Augier Ridge was that there was something shady about it, and Major Tyburn is the shady bit. I checked all this this afternoon and what I found was that we had a good idea that the Germans knew Tyburn's party were in the tunnels. The facts pointed that way and Boscombe, the only man from the first party to get back, said that the enemy were waiting for them. So an investigation was launched and in Major Tyburn's things some highly incriminating evidence was found. Apparently he'd been in touch with the Germans for months. It was known there must be a spy or spies sending first-rate information to the Germans and Tyburn was the man. What d'you think of that?'

Ashley was aghast. 'You mean to tell me that a serving British officer betrayed his men?'

Haldean nodded. 'Not only his men, but the whole army. He was a dangerous man.'

Ashley was quiet for a few moments. 'I hope someone got hold of him. My God, he should have been hanged. To think that while our lads were being blown to bits someone was giving the Germans the information they needed to help them do it. I . . . I . . .' Ashley stopped, unable to find the words. 'It's no use,' he said eventually. 'An enemy soldier is just that; a soldier. You know where you are but this swine . . .' Ashley stopped once more. 'Hold on. If he was ahead of Boscombe in the tunnels he must have been killed. It's a damn shame he was never brought to justice. He deserved it.'

'He wasn't killed,' said Haldean quietly.

'What?'

'He wasn't killed. Not in the attack, at any rate. We had spies too, and got the news back that Tyburn had been lightly wounded and taken prisoner.'

'I wish I'd been in the same camp,' said Ashley grimly. 'Are you sure about that?'

'It was confirmed by the Red Cross. He wasn't a prisoner for long, though. The records do say that but they don't say what happened to him.'

'It doesn't take much to work it out, does it? The Germans must've looked after him.'

'So I thought,' agreed Haldean. 'Presumably it took the enemy a little while to confirm who he was and then I imagine they arranged for him to change his identity. As far as we know he simply vanishes from the records.'

Ashley looked at him thoughtfully. 'So we've got a traitor, a traitor who got off scot-free while his men died in the tunnels, and could be still alive. Where's this going? Are you suggesting Tyburn was the man Boscombe was blackmailing?'

'Not exactly.' Haldean paused. So far he had stuck to provable facts, but now he wanted to see what Ashley would think of his ideas built on those facts. 'It's a possibility, but Tyburn came from Lower Woodbury and that's not too far away from Breedenbrook. Considering that he still faces the death penalty it'd be very risky to come to a place where he could be recognized.'

'Hmm. If he's still with us I think he'd avoid England altogether and anywhere local like the plague.'

'So do I,' agreed Haldean. 'I actually had something else in mind.'

'Then . . . Hold on a minute, Haldean. Where does Morton fit in? So far it fits if Boscombe's the blackmailer, but what about Morton?'

'Spot on. It's interesting, isn't it? I wondered, as I'm sure you have, why, if Boscombe knew something dodgy and lucrative about our A. N. Other, he should wait until last October before putting the screws on.'

Ashley leaned back in his seat. 'And the answer is? Because you've got one, I can tell.'

'Is this.' Haldean took a quick glance at Ashley before looking back to the road. 'I took notes of the service records of all the men who went into the Augier tunnels, and one of them was Robert Petrie, the author of the diary which Morton inherited. Robert Petrie was in the second party. He was captured, spent the rest of the war as a prisoner, contracted TB, and spent the rest of his life in and out of sanatoriums. According to the army pension records, Petrie died last April. Miss Sheldon told us that Boscombe got in touch with Morton at the end of August. Then, as far as our lovely pair are concerned, the party starts in October. Do you see what that implies? Boscombe had some information, Morton had some information, but each one, separately, doesn't add up to much.'

'But put them together . . .' said Ashley slowly.

'Put them together, and you've got, on my reckoning, a recipe for blackmail. The gap between the end of August and October is filled by them tracking down their victim and receiving the first payment. It also explains something of what happened at the weekend. You remember Miss Sheldon said Morton was blazing against Boscombe on Friday night? He said he was trying to double-cross him. I think Boscombe took off on his own to use his personal charm to get some more cash which he wasn't planning to share. Morton spent Friday night going pop, but come Saturday morning decided not to wait and followed Boscombe to Breedenbrook.'

Ashley scratched his chin, jolting as the Spyker ran over a bump in the road. 'Hang on. How did Morton know where Boscombe had gone?'

'Well, if Boscombe knew A.N. was going to be at the fête, there's an odds-on chance that Morton knew it as well and the Talbot Arms is the only place to stay in Breedenbrook. There's something else, too. We know Morton had Petrie's diary on Friday night, because Miss Sheldon told us so. However, it wasn't in the flat so therefore we can presume Morton took it with him.'

'Yes. I'd got as far as that myself.'

'And the diary certainly wasn't in the Talbot Arms.'

'Good Lord.' Ashley drew his breath in and looked at Haldean. 'No, it wasn't. But the room was pulled apart. That has to have been the murderer looking for this diary.'

'And finding it, too.'

Ashley rubbed his hands together. 'You're right. It all hangs together. By crikey, it does. So who do you think they *were* blackmailing? So far you've told me who they weren't, but that's not much help.'

Haldean wriggled his motoring coat further back on his shoulders and increased his speed, savouring the rush of air on his face. This was it. This was the crux of his theory. 'That's where my trip to the War Office comes in again. It was noted in the records that Tyburn had a child. That child must be nearly twenty years old by now. I don't know if it was a son or a daughter. Now if they knew about their father's past, they wouldn't be keen on it getting to be public knowledge who they were. It's a nasty thing to have something like that in your lineage.'

'I'll say,' grunted Ashley.

'And the sins of the fathers, as it were, may cause some serious back-sliding in the sons. To have a traitor as your father could wreck a career, to say nothing of the social consequences.'

'I say it could.' Ashley rested his chin on his hand. 'Yes, it certainly could. They'd want that hushed up and no mistake.' He let his breath out in a whoosh. 'Can you imagine having that hanging over you? It must be a living nightmare.'

106

'A cause for blackmail?' suggested Haldean with a raised eyebrow.

'Too right.' Ashley looked at Haldean with a new regard. 'I think you're on to something. I like the idea of blackmail and it's hard, with that appalling business in the background, to think that Tyburn's treachery isn't connected in some way with what's happened in the here and now. At the moment it's all speculation, but if we can find out who this child of Tyburn's is, then we might find we've got the murderer and the motive all wrapped up. Tyburn's child . . . Whoever it is, they have to be found. I can't let a lead like this go begging.'

'How are you going to go about doing that?' asked Haldean. Oddly enough, he didn't feel too pleased with himself. Yes, Ashley was prepared to consider his theory but in some ways it seemed to ask as many questions as it answered. The sheer slog of digging someone up last heard of twenty years ago as a tiny baby hadn't occurred to him until now and it was a daunting prospect.

Judging by his face, Ashley's thoughts were running on the same lines. 'It's a problem, isn't it? They didn't have the same mania for form-filling twenty years ago that we're afflicted with nowadays. They'll be pretty difficult to trace, especially as they won't want to be found. They're bound to be using a different name.'

'I know.' Haldean hit the steering-wheel in annoyance, increasing his speed in direct index to his frustration. 'I've got a motive but no one to go with it. They could be someone living locally – they'd have to be in a way, if my theory's going to hold water – or they could be miles away, in which case I'm stumped. They could be dead, in which case I'm really stumped. Until we find them we haven't got a clue who killed Boscombe or Morton.'

'We will have, don't you worry. You say Tyburn came from Lower Woodbury? I'll start there. Someone might know something. And if you must drive at fifty miles

107

an hour, would you mind keeping your hands on the wheel?'

Haldean dropped Ashley in Lewes and drove on to Stanmore Parry. It was with a feeling of relief that, as dusk gave way to dark, he turned into the driveway of Hesperus, ran over the bridge and through the trees to the house. It had been a long day and his lame leg, a permanent souvenir of the war, was throbbing from the drive. He parked the car in the old stable block and, as he climbed out, saw an evening-clad figure detach itself from the shadows.

'Ah, Jack m'boy.' It was Uncle Philip, cigar in hand. 'I was just taking a final turn. Have you had a good day? We've finished dinner but I believe your aunt kept something for you in case you didn't get a chance to eat in Town.'

'Oh, thanks, Uncle. That'll be very welcome.' He unbuttoned his motoring coat and stretched his shoulders with a sigh. 'I'm not quite sure how the day went, actually. I know a lot more but whether it's germane or not, I can't tell yet.' Haldean looked at his uncle thoughtfully. 'Did you ever hear of a man called Tyburn? According to his records he came from Lower Woodbury and that's not too far away. He would have been about five years younger than you. Apparently he was married and had a child. I wondered if you knew anything about him.'

Sir Philip stopped. 'Is that the Tyburn who got into trouble during the war?' His face was in shadow but Haldean could hear the strain in his voice.

'Yes, that's the one.' Haldean put his head on one side. 'You do know him, don't you?'

'No . . . At least I met him a couple of times, but that was over twenty years ago. You know his child, though.' He spoke very reluctantly. 'I'm her trustee. It's Marguerite Vayle.'

Chapter Seven

In the deep shadows of the old stables, Haldean stopped dead. He felt sick. All he had said to Ashley twisted inside. He'd been so clever, so ridiculously, smugly clever. 'Marguerite Vayle?' he repeated in a stunned voice. He raised his head and almost shouted. 'Marguerite Vayle is Tyburn's *daughter*?'

Sir Philip stepped forward anxiously. 'Hush, Jack, not so loud.'

One way of escape – the only way of escape – from the logic of his reasoning offered itself. 'Does she know?'

'Of course she doesn't know!'

Haldean shut his eyes in relief. It wasn't her. Thank God, it wasn't her. If she didn't know she was Tyburn's child, all his arguments fell to the ground. He'd been wrong but he didn't care. It wasn't her. His uncle was still talking and he forced himself to listen.

'I . . . We . . . Your aunt . . . We were going to tell her when she was twenty-one. That's when this confounded trust comes to an end but until then . . . Well, it's not the easiest thing in the world to bring up and until now there's been no reason to say anything. Now there's this situation between her and Whitfield we'll have to tell her, I suppose.'

Whitfield! Haldean shook his head. Of all the bitter ironies that it should be Whitfield, one of the few men in England who needed no reminder of what Tyburn had done, who wanted to marry the girl. 'You'll have to tell Colonel Whitfield too, and fairly quickly.'

'I know!' Sir Philip's voice was thin with impatience. 'Don't think I haven't considered it. Hugh Lawrence and I have talked about little else. It's a dreadful worry. Look, Jack, I think you'd better come and have a word with us both inside. You'll need to see Lawrence anyway. He's as much her trustee as I am and I'd like to hear what Alice has to say.'

Haldean paused. 'I don't think I can do that, Uncle. This came up as part of the murder enquiry. I can't discuss it with Mr Lawrence.'

'But in that case . . .' Sir Philip sighed in irritation. 'Now I've let the cat out of the bag I'll have to tell Lawrence. Can't you simply say you got to know without giving too many details?' He saw the hesitation in Haldean's face and pressed his point home. 'Lawrence is all right, Jack. He's been Marguerite's trustee for years, far longer than I have. He's completely trustworthy. His only concern is Marguerite's welfare. Don't think we haven't talked about telling the girl who her father was, but it's a fiendishly difficult situation for all of us. Come into the house.'

Lawrence was in the billiard room with a whisky and soda, practising solitary cannons. Sir Philip rang the bell and gave instructions for Lady Rivers to join them and then tried to pass the time by making conversation of such brittle awkwardness that Haldean greeted his aunt's arrival with honest relief. She came into the room with a puzzled smile.

'What is it, Philip? Egerton said that you wanted to see me. Jack! I didn't know you'd arrived. Did you manage to eat in Town or would you like something now?'

'Later, Alice, later,' said Sir Philip, quickly. 'Something's cropped up.' Lawrence put down his cue and eyed Sir Philip speculatively. 'It's Jack.' He coughed awkwardly. 'He knows who Marguerite really is.'

Lawrence, who had been obviously and understandably perplexed by Sir Philip's manner, became very still. He looked at Haldean. 'How did you find out?'

'I told him,' said Sir Philip. 'Yes, I know we'd agreed not

110

to say anything yet, but Jack had got on to it and I thought it best to tell him the truth.'

'I know half the story,' said Haldean. 'It's to do with Boscombe and Morton's murder.'

Lawrence put his shoulders back slightly and the wariness in his eyes turned to hostility. 'Are you saying that Miss Vayle is implicated in murder?'

Haldean met his gaze squarely. 'No. No, sir, I'm not.' And, thank God, he could say that with a clear conscience. 'But the question of her father's actions came up and it might be relevant.'

Lawrence looked away and picked up his billiard cue once more. 'You're talking about the Augier Ridge tunnels, aren't you?' He tapped the cue lightly on his hand. 'What can that have to do with the murders?'

'That's what we – Superintendent Ashley and myself – are trying to work out. Tyburn's name cropped up and I decided to try and find out a bit more about him.'

'He's dead.'

'Is he?' asked Lady Rivers. 'He disappeared after the truth came out, I know, but are we sure he's dead, Mr Lawrence?'

Lawrence nodded. 'I'm certain of it. There's no proof, I know, but I'm sure of it.'

'He must be dead,' said Sir Philip. 'If he wasn't we'd have heard something after all this time.'

'Would we, Philip?' asked Lady Rivers. 'I wonder. He might have easily changed his name and appearance and he wouldn't want to be found, of course.'

'But there's his daughter, Alice. Surely he'd try and contact her?'

'Martin Tyburn showed precious little interest in her before he was found out,' said Lady Rivers grimly. 'It's not very likely he'll want to get in touch with her now.'

Haldean sat down on the leather sofa and lit a cigarette. 'Will you tell me about him? I only know what I've read in the official records, and that's little enough. For instance, where does Miss Vayle fit into it all? How did you come to be her trustees?'

'Oh, that part's quite simple,' said Lady Rivers. She sat down and put her hands round her knees. 'The Tyburns came from Lower Woodbury and were very well thought of. But Martin Tyburn . . . Well, he always had a reputation, if you see what I mean.'

'He was a rip,' put in Sir Philip. 'He got entangled with a most unsuitable girl whilst up at Cambridge and his father had to buy her off. And then what must the young fool do but run away with a German governess, of all people, whom Cranford, the local doctor, had employed to teach his daughters. I was older than Tyburn, of course, and wasn't here when it happened, but I remember the scandal it caused.'

'They got married though, Philip,' said Lady Rivers.

'Oh yes, I know they got married, Alice, but that only made things worse. There was no getting out of it then, you see. Old Tyburn wouldn't have anything to do with them and they went to live in London.'

'And then Marguerite was born,' continued Lady Rivers. 'It's a pity she wasn't a boy. Old Mr Tyburn might have come round then, but she wasn't.' She sighed. 'He had very rigid views, you know. Very rigid. The real tragedy was that Marguerite's mother died soon afterwards. Martin Tyburn abandoned the baby and left England for Canada.'

'Abandoned's a strong word, Alice.'

'Well, what else would you call it?' she demanded. 'I don't mean he left her on a doorstep somewhere, but he didn't want anything to do with her.' She looked at Haldean. 'He left her in the care of Andrew and Cissie Vayle, who came to be such friends of ours, and they brought her up as their own daughter. They heard nothing from Martin Tyburn for years and then in 1915 had a letter from a solicitor in London. Apparently Tyburn had come back to this country and decided to join the army. Rather late in the day he decided to make some provision for his

112

daughter in case he got killed and set up a trust fund for her. Cissie and Andrew Vayle were one set of trustees and Mr Lawrence here was the other. Martin Tyburn still had no interest in seeing the child, though. He refused to go to their house and although the Vayles met him it was all arranged at the solicitor's office.'

Haldean looked at Lawrence. 'Did you know Martin Tyburn well, Mr Lawrence?'

Lawrence nodded. 'I knew him very well.' He smiled faintly at Lady Rivers. 'I realize you feel bitter about what he did, and I can't blame you, but he was a good friend of mine and a good man. That's why I'm so certain he's dead. I simply can't believe that he'd be in this sort of trouble without letting me know somehow. I guess I shouldn't say this, but he'd have known I would've helped him, no matter what. I never believed he was guilty but even if he was, he'd have had a reason, a good reason, for what he did.'

Sir Philip snorted in disagreement. 'Name me one good reason for being a traitor.'

'Well, perhaps there aren't any. I can't actually argue with you, Rivers, because I agree. But Tyburn knew me and he would have known how I'd react. We owed each other a lot. Personally, I mean. I met him before the war and we started up in business together, but when the war was declared he sold me his share and came back to Britain.'

'Did Tyburn intend to return to Canada after the war?' asked Haldean.

Lawrence shook his head doubtfully. 'I don't think so. He had no reason to any more and he was sure glad to be back in England. I think he wanted to settle down here after the war was over. He was always more English than Canadian and I guess he was homesick. He used to talk about Sussex so much I felt I knew the place. Why, when I came here I'd heard so much about it, it was like coming home. All the high-shaded lanes and the little fields you felt you could pick up and put in your pocket. You know,

113

that sense that people had been living here for thousands of years. All cosy and homey and just about the biggest contrast with the Rockies there could possibly be.'

'And yet he turned out to be a bad 'un,' said Haldean, stubbing out his cigarette.

Lawrence shook his head. 'The only reason I can think of for him going off the rails was his wife. Maybe she influenced him. She was German, you remember, and he might have been inclined to that point of view. But as I say, I never thought he was guilty. I tried to say as much to anyone who would listen and caused a bit of a row.' He picked up his whisky and sipped it thoughtfully. 'With the copper contracts I'd arranged, the government had plenty of reason to be grateful to me, but as far as both the Canadian and British War Offices were concerned, he was guilty and that was that.'

'The evidence was pretty damning.'

'If you say so.' Lawrence finished his whisky and rested his arms on the edge of the billiard table, the cloth reflecting green light on his face. He shrugged. 'All I can say is, he was my friend. Anyway, before he left for France it was all set up that the Vayles and I were his daughter's trustees in case he was killed. Tyburn wrote to the Vayles and the four of us met up in the offices of a London lawyer and arranged the whole thing. He was a rich man by now, Major Haldean, and the money was going to go to her when she was twenty-one or when she got married. The trustees had to approve the marriage, of course.'

'Do you know why he didn't want to see her?'

Lawrence picked up his cue, rolled a white ball into position with the tip and struck it thoughtfully. 'Not really. Maybe he didn't want to disturb her. He knew that these people, the Vayles, were raising her as their own child and he might have thought it was unfair to them. It was probably for the best.'

Lady Rivers unclasped her hands from her knees. 'As far as the Vayles were concerned the trusteeship didn't change anything and I believe they were rather relieved that

Marguerite's father didn't intend to interfere.' She looked at Haldean. 'Do try and understand, Jack. No one concealed anything on purpose from Marguerite but, as I say, the Vayles had always treated her as their own daughter and the question of who she was simply didn't arise. And then when it came out that he was a traitor and had been in the pay of the Germans it seemed impossible to tell her. It was in the newspapers and was a tremendous scandal. The press loved it, because of the contrast between Martin Tyburn and Richard Whitfield. Marguerite was only a child when it happened and it was thought best to keep it from her. Andrew Vayle, who probably would have told her when she was old enough to understand, died in the last year of the war and Cissie only survived him by a few months. Poor Cissie knew she hadn't got long left and asked us to take over as trustees, which, of course, we did. Marguerite was still at school, so all it really involved was having her for the holidays occasionally. Most of the time she went to stay with friends but at Christmas she met Colonel Whitfield and it became obvious that there was an attraction there.' Lady Rivers shook herself. 'We must take some action now, Philip. It's a matter of justice. We can't allow Marguerite to continue seeing Colonel Whitfield without letting her know the truth. I wanted to tell her when you arrived, Mr Lawrence, but you advised waiting.'

'I had a mind to see things for myself,' said Lawrence. 'I'm far from happy about the idea of her marrying the Colonel in any case. It's no secret she's going to be a wealthy woman when she marries and I'm a little suspicious of his motives.'

Lady Rivers stood up. 'This is ridiculous,' she said in a firm voice. 'Here we are discussing Marguerite's future and the one person who's most intimately concerned doesn't know a thing about it. We must tell her. Why not now? It's as good a time as any.'

'Because . . .' began Sir Philip, and shrugged. 'Lawrence? What's your opinion?'

Lawrence put his hands in his pockets, thinking. 'Why not?' he said eventually. 'Let's go and find her. She was in the drawing room the last time I saw her.'

In the drawing room Isabelle was feeling bored. She had been about to suggest a game of bridge when her mother had left the room. She glanced across at her brother, but Gregory was stuck inside a copy of *On the Town*.

Marguerite was sitting by the window, an unread magazine on her knee. She was abnormally still, and Isabelle thought, as she had thought before, just how difficult Marguerite was to get to know. Since Saturday she'd been worse than ever. Not talkative – she was never that – but apprehensive in an odd sort of way. It was as if she was waiting for something to happen. It wouldn't be so bad if she wasn't so quiet, but she never started a conversation and she certainly never gossiped. Maybe she'd suffered from that awful phrase they used to drill into you at school: 'If you haven't anything to say worth saying, don't say it.'

Jack liked her but that, thought Isabelle, had far more to do with Jack's character than with Marguerite's. He was always frantically over-protective to anything or anyone he saw as weak or who'd had a raw deal. He liked her in the same way he'd like the runt of the litter or an unhappy child, which was all very well, but it did mean he was blind to her faults. He wasn't really capable of seeing that Marguerite had any and he certainly wasn't capable – and this *was* annoying – of talking about them.

Dad was much the same. He called her 'a shy, retiring little thing', but Dad could be very dim sometimes. Shy? No. The phrase 'pent-up' came into her mind. Something was bothering Marguerite, bothering her badly, but what on earth could you do with someone who wouldn't talk?

Marguerite glanced up, caught Isabelle's eye and looked away, flushing, her fingers tightening on the magazine.

116

For heaven's sake, this was *ridiculous*. Here they were, two girls of roughly the same age, who knew the same people, living in the same house and they couldn't find a thing to say to each other. Mr Lawrence could always find something to say to her . . .

Isabelle stopped, intrigued by a new line of thought. Mr Lawrence, eh? There was no doubt Marguerite liked him. She was easy and at home with him in a way she wasn't with anyone else, not even her beloved Richard Whitfield. That, in Isabelle's opinion, was nothing more than a crush. She remembered some of the crushes of her own and felt a twinge of sympathy. Maybe Maggie knew what was obvious to anyone looking on, that she was a great deal fonder of Whitfield than he was of her. Maybe it wasn't so much Whitfield she was in love with as the thought of having a home of her own. Maybe that was it. Maggie Vayle didn't have a home. She was cared for, certainly, but she'd spent years inside other people's houses, living by other people's rules.

Marguerite's eyes met hers again. 'For heaven's sake, Isabelle, stop *staring* at me!'

Isabelle concealed her affront with a laugh. 'Sorry. Just a bit bored, I suppose.' She walked across to the gramophone and wound it up. 'Let's have some music.' She put a record on and took the magazine from her brother's indignant hands. 'Come on, Greg, let's dance. '

He made a grab for *On the Town*. 'Stop it, Isabelle. I don't want to dance, I want to read. Besides,' he added, listening to the music for a moment, 'I don't know the steps.'

'I'll show you. Come and dance, Maggie,' she asked with a welcoming smile. 'I'll be the man, if you like, and Greg can watch. It's ever so easy.'

Marguerite unwillingly put down her magazine and came forward.

'That's right,' said Isabelle encouragingly. 'Watch, Greg. Back one, side step, back one . . .' The door opened and she stopped. 'Jack! I didn't know you were here. Maggie and I are trying to show Greg this dance.' She paused. 'Whatever's the matter with everyone? Mother? What's wrong?'

'There's nothing really wrong, Isabelle, but we need to talk to Marguerite.' Lady Rivers smiled at the girl. 'Would you come into my sitting room, dear?'

To everyone's surprise, Marguerite shook her head. 'I think I know what this is about. I've been waiting for you to say something.' She stood rigidly still, her chin pointed forward. 'You'd better say it here and get it over with. After all, it concerns everyone.'

Mr Lawrence coughed. 'This is private, Marguerite. Family matters, you know?'

She looked at him blankly. 'Family matters?'

Lawrence put his hand on her arm. 'Come with us, my dear.' His voice softened and he added, seeing she was reluctant to move, 'We're talking about your father, Marguerite. There's something you need to know. You don't want to discuss it here.'

'My – my father?' She blinked, then gave an irritated shrug, shaking off Lawrence's hand. 'Which one? Daddy – Mr Vayle – or my real father?'

There was a stunned silence. Haldean drew his breath in. Oh no . . . Oddly enough, he didn't have the same sickening feeling as if he'd just kicked a kitten. All right, she knew, but there was another explanation, there just had to be. Somehow his reasoning was at fault. He'd far rather believe that than believe Marguerite Vayle was guilty.

Mr Lawrence spoke first. 'What do you know about your real father?' he asked slowly.

She drew a deep breath and met his gaze. 'I know he was a traitor.' There was a gasp from Sir Philip. The dance music suddenly seemed very loud. 'I know all about him. For heaven's sake, Isabelle, take the record off and stop *looking* at me like that!' Isabelle dumbly complied, her eyes fixed on Marguerite. 'He left me with the Vayles. I'll always think of them as my real parents because he never wanted to have anything to do with me. Then he joined the army and betrayed everyone to the Germans and it was Richard who saved the day. I know. How could I not know?' She was trembling now. 'He thought he could make up for the way he acted by leaving me money. I know all about that, too, but he can't make it better, not ever. And I've been dreading this, absolutely dreading it. Because you're going to tell me I should tell Richard *and I won't!* He must never find out.'

Lady Rivers came forward, took her hands and gently sat her down. 'Why are you so afraid of Colonel Whitfield finding out, Marguerite? If he cares for you then surely it won't matter to him.'

She shook her hand free. 'Of course it'll matter to him. He's got a position – reputation – ambitions. He can't marry a traitor's daughter. The man who betrayed *him*. Even if I am going to have money.' She bit back tears, and her voice cracked. 'Oh leave me alone, all of you! You don't understand! None of you understand!' She got up and left the room at what was nearly a run.

Lady Rivers made to go after her, but was stopped by Lawrence.

'Let me go. I'll talk to her.'

'All right. If you're sure.'

He nodded and followed her out of the room.

'Well,' said Haldean, going over to the sideboard and pouring himself a whisky and soda, 'this is a turn-up for the books. Drink, anyone?' There was a blank part in his mind, the part which had so confidently said *Tyburn's child*. There had to be another explanation . . .

'She knew,' said Sir Philip in stupefaction. 'She knew! When I think of how worried we've been and she knew! My word, Lawrence is a brave man. I'll have a whisky, please, Jack. A good strong one after that. How the dickens did she find out? And why the blazes didn't she tell us?'

'I wish someone would tell me,' said Gregory. 'What's going on?'

'I want to know, too,' added Isabelle, vigorously.

Haldean picked up his drink and draped himself over an armchair. He was deliberately making his actions and words as casual as possible. 'I really think you had better tell them, you know,' he said to his uncle. 'Poor old Belle's going to burst with curiosity in a minute.'

Slowly, and with many interjections from his wife, Sir Philip ran through the story. 'But how she knew,' he finished, 'is more than I can guess.'

'And where's her father now?' asked Isabelle. 'Is he dead?'

'We simply don't know,' said Haldean, sipping his whisky. 'No one's had a sniff of him since 1916. Mr Lawrence thinks he's dead but as the man's got a capital charge against him he wouldn't want to make too much fuss about his continued existence.'

Sir Philip snorted and, getting to his feet, walked around the room in irritation. 'Of course Tyburn's dead. Damn it, Jack, he has to be. Things are complicated enough without you thinking otherwise.' Not nearly as complicated as they could be, Haldean thought, but said nothing. 'Don't you think the poor girl's got enough to worry about without telling her that her father might pop up? She's in an absolute state as it is. What the devil is Lawrence doing? He's being a long time about it, whatever it is.' He picked up a cigar-cutter from the sideboard, turning it over in his fingers. 'I wish he'd take to Whitfield more. If it wasn't for this awful complication I think it'd be a perfect match for Marguerite, but Lawrence seems to be dead set against him.'

'I wonder if he's jealous,' said Isabelle.

Sir Philip put down the cigar-cutter with a click. 'What?'

'Mr Lawrence. I wonder if he's jealous of Colonel Whitfield.'

'Isabelle!' Her father looked at her in shocked disbelief. 'That's an outrageous suggestion. Why, Lawrence is twice her age. The idea's preposterous. He's a good, decent man and a first-rate trustee who, I'm sure, has no ideas about Marguerite beyond trying to secure her best interests. She's nineteen, Isabelle. She's only just out of the schoolroom, for heaven's sake.'

'Well, if it comes to that, Colonel Whitfield's no spring chicken either. How old is he? He must be nearly forty if he's a day. And Mr Lawrence is always fussing around Marguerite. Look at him just now. He was holding her hand and his voice went all squashy. Marguerite looks so helpless she sort of invites it. You do read about guardians marrying their wards.'

'It's a staple of romantic fiction,' put in Haldean. Marguerite and Lawrence? Yes, Isabelle was right about Mr Lawrence's reactions. '*On the Town* must do one with that plot every other month and you do come across it in real life.'

'I don't believe I'm hearing this,' said his uncle, curtly. 'It's an appalling idea. Lawrence is a respectable business-man, not some half-baked hero from a magazine. He's a well-known mine-owner of considerable wealth and has been for years. He's endowed fellowships, set up libraries, and during the war was instrumental in providing this country with enough copper to keep going with no thought of his own gain.'

'But none of that would stop him falling for Marguerite, would it?' said Gregory.

'Yes, it damn well would,' said Sir Philip, exasperated. 'And furthermore,' he added, his voice rising, 'I would ask you all to remember that he's a guest in my house and I expect him to be treated with the consideration he deserves without being subject to this ill-informed specula-tion . . .' He broke off abruptly as the door opened and Marguerite Vayle entered, ushered in by Lawrence.

'In you go, my dear,' said Lawrence, kindly. 'I told you it would be all right.'

She gave him a quick, grateful smile and cast a shy glance round the room. 'I'm awfully sorry. I shouldn't have caused such a scene. Mr Lawrence came and explained everything to me so nicely he made me see that the best thing I could do is come and apologize to you all.'

Everyone tried to think of something ordinary to say to show that things were back to normal, and failed miserably. It was Lady Rivers who, coming forward, took the girl by the hand and led her to the settee. 'Don't worry about it, dear,' she said, sitting down beside her. 'We all realize this must have been a dreadful strain for you. Jack, offer Marguerite a cigarette, will you? And Gregory, I'd like a glass of Madeira and I'm sure Marguerite would like something as well. Now then,' she said when this was all settled, 'if you don't want to talk about it any more this evening, that's perfectly all right.'

Marguerite's voice was shy but determined. 'I . . . I'd think I'd rather, if you don't mind. I mean, I know that's what everyone's thinking about and it seems silly to try and avoid it. I want to get it over with.'

'How did you know who your father really was?' asked Haldean, standing back after lighting her cigarette. The poor kid just couldn't be guilty. 'Tell me to go and boil my head if you'd rather not say.'

'Oh, that's all right. I've always known who he was,' she said, holding her cigarette in fingers that weren't quite steady. Oh, hell. *She'd always known* . . . 'Mummy and Daddy – I mean the Vayles, of course – thought I didn't know I was adopted, but I did. There were various things grown-ups had said when I wasn't meant to be listening which gave it away, so I asked my nurse. I knew it wasn't the sort of question I could ask Mummy. I rather liked the thought I was really someone else. I'd read ever so many stories where the heroine was adopted and turned out to be a princess or something. My nurse was a bit shocked when I asked her who my real parents were, but I went on and on about it and eventually she told me that my real mother was in heaven and that my father was a soldier.' She bit her lip. 'I used to think that my real father would come and carry me off and . . . and I think I liked playing with the idea. I loved Mummy and Daddy but they were ordinary and dull, you know, though in a nice way. I used to dream about my real father who was always wearing a

122

red coat and riding a splendid white horse just like the soldiers in the picture in the dining room. It never occurred to me that he would look like the soldiers we saw in the streets and in the park. Stupid of me.'

She took a sip of the cocktail which Rivers had given her. 'Then one day, a man, who must have been a solicitor, called at the house and I watched him over the banisters. No one knew I was there. Daddy spent ages with him in the morning room and when they came out, the man stood in the hall and said, in a carrying voice, "This will mean that Miss Tyburn's future is secure." Daddy shushed him and said, "She's always referred to as Miss Vayle." They talked for a bit longer and I couldn't hear most of it, but I knew they were talking about me. I asked Nurse that night if my real name was Tyburn and she told me that it had been, long ago, but it was Vayle now and I must never say that I knew, as it would upset Mummy and Daddy as they liked to think of me as their own little girl. And as it didn't make any difference to how things were, I sort of forgot about it but it gave me a nice, secret feeling, if you know what I mean.'

She shook her head. 'Then, what seemed to be years later but was I suppose only really a few months, Daddy made a big fuss about me not seeing the newspapers. Well, I wouldn't have *wanted* to see the papers if he hadn't gone on about it, but naturally I wondered what was there that I wasn't meant to see. There was lots about the casualties on the Somme and I thought for a while they were trying to keep that from me, but there was also a report about a man called Tyburn and what he had done. I had to look "treachery" up in the dictionary. Once I read that, I knew what sort of man he must be.'

There was an uneasy silence, broken eventually by Lawrence. 'Your father was a good friend of mine, Marguerite, and I thought he was a good man. I've always wondered if he was framed, as the Americans say.'

'Oh, don't try and defend him!' Her voice was savage. 'I thought he was a hero too, remember? White horse, red coat. I longed to see him, my father, and all the time he didn't care tuppence. Yes, he arranged trustees for me. It's easy enough to buy off your conscience with money when you have enough, but he never wanted to see me or to know what I was like.' She stopped. 'I'm . . . I'm sorry, Mr Lawrence. I know you're trying to make things better for me but you can't get away from what he did. And . . .' She blinked very rapidly and her voice shook. ' And it's so much worse than you think.'

'How, dear?' asked Lady Rivers, gently. 'Are you worried about Colonel Whitfield? I'm sure it will be all right in the end.'

Marguerite paused. 'Yes.' She seemed to consider the notion. 'I don't want Richard to find out.'

Sir Philip shuffled from foot to foot, exchanged glances with his wife, looked at Lawrence, and, finding no help there, cleared his throat awkwardly. 'I think you're going to have to tell him, though.'

'I know,' the girl agreed miserably. 'Mr Lawrence explained everything to me but . . . I'll do it tomorrow night at the ball,' she added, with a small note of defiance. 'He can't walk away from a ball, can he?'

'No,' said Lady Rivers quickly. 'That would be very wrong, Marguerite. It would be inconsiderate to Mrs Verrity as your host, and very unfair to Colonel Whitfield, to say nothing of the other guests. It would be far better if you told the Colonel privately. After all, you can't possibly want to make such an announcement with other people listening.'

An intake of breath from Sir Philip indicated just how much he didn't want to be one of the other people. 'Dreadful idea, dreadful,' he muttered.

'Don't worry, Aunt Alice,' said Marguerite with a small, twisted smile. 'Whatever happens, I promise I won't spoil the party.'

Lady Rivers looked at her earnestly. 'You mustn't tell him at the ball. What you have to do is see the Colonel tomorrow by yourself and, as I say, tell him privately. He might be shocked at first but you can't honestly think that if he has any feeling at all for you he would let this stand in his way.'

'But that's just what I don't know,' said Marguerite, miserably. 'He seems to like me and yet he . . . he . . .'

'Hasn't popped the question yet?' put in Haldean.

She looked at him gratefully. 'That's just it.' She put her drink down and looked at her intertwined fingers. 'I can't tell you how much I hate all this. I simply want to be happy and it's all gone wrong. I know I could make Richard happy but if this comes out it will affect things, I know it will. And it's so unfair! Why should I be made to suffer for something I had nothing to do with?'

'If he lets it affect him he's not worth having in the first place,' said Hugh Lawrence brusquely. 'You're a fine girl, Marguerite. I can't help wishing your father had made his provisions differently but that can't be helped now. With the money that's in the trust I'd always seen my role as sifting through unsuitable young men, not pleading with some guy to overlook something that happened years ago. You tell him, Marguerite. Damn it, who the hell does he think he is? The Prince of Wales or someone? I'll be honest with you. I think he's too old for you and I suspect he's more than interested in your money.'

Marguerite rose to her feet. 'Not you as well,' she cried passionately. 'I thought you were on my side! And all the time you believe that! He doesn't want my money, you hear, he doesn't! You want me to tell him. All right, I will.' She struck an angry tear from her eye. 'And if he never wants to see me again, because – and only because – of who I am, then perhaps that'll satisfy you.' She moved as if to leave, but Haldean unpropped himself from the mantelpiece and stood in front of her.

'Look, don't go rushing off again. It really won't solve anything. We all want to help. We do, you know.'

He wanted to talk to her alone very badly indeed. He'd been wrong, he knew he'd been wrong, but he wanted to hear some sort of confirmation from Marguerite herself.

'Why don't you come for a walk? It's a corking night – soft summer breezes, any amount of moonlight, flocks of nightingales all tuning up and just waiting for an audience. They get fearfully discouraged if no one pays them any attention. Come and work it all out on me and if you don't want to talk about how absolutely vile things are, I've got no end of stories that will elevate, educate and amuse. Come on. Let's see what Sussex is like in the dim eventide.' He smiled as he spoke and Marguerite reluctantly smiled back.

'All right. If you're sure you want to.'

'Wasn't I making myself clear? Of course I want to. Upsa-daisy. We won't be very long. The garden it is. Yes?'

They went out through the french windows on to the terrace. As Haldean's voice faded away, Lawrence leaned back in his chair and shook his head. 'Oh, hell! Why did I have to say that about Whitfield? Now I've put her back up and she'll never trust me again. I hate her being so upset and yet I'm damned if I know what she sees in the guy.'

'Whitfield's all right,' said Sir Philip gruffly. 'First-rate horseman.'

'Marguerite isn't a horse, Philip,' said Lady Rivers, absently. 'Don't worry, Mr Lawrence. I'm sure Marguerite will come round. After all, she knows you have her best interests at heart and she must be aware of how much you care about her.'

Isabelle looked at her mother sharply. She was probing. Very delicately, very inoffensively, but probing.

Lawrence sighed. 'Care for her! I'll say. Why, her happiness is just about the most important job I've ever taken on, and I've had some tough ones in my time.'

Lady Rivers said nothing. It was not, perhaps, the most reassuring of answers.

Out in the moonlit garden, Haldean was keeping up a gentle flow of chatter which Marguerite was clearly paying

126

little attention too. He came to a stop, but she laid a hand on his arm. 'No, please. Do go on. I was listening but it's so difficult being . . . being . . .'

'Being the centre of attention? It's rotten, isn't it, knowing that everyone's thinking about you and working out what they should say.'

She gave him a quick, sharp glance. 'So you do understand.' She gave a little sigh of relief. 'I hate all this, you know. It was awful having to say those things about Richard, about him not having proposed or anything.' She looked at him with wide eyes. 'I feel so utterly miserable. Everyone talks about Richard as if I'd be doing him such a favour by marrying him but it's all the other way round. If only they knew . . . It makes me feel such a fraud, as if I were making a fuss about nothing. And I could be, you know. Oh, *why* did Mr Lawrence have to come over? Why couldn't he just leave me alone?'

'Because, not unnaturally, he cares about what happens to you,' Haldean said firmly. 'Aunt Alice wrote to him as soon as she thought there was a chance of your being engaged. As your trustee he's got to know what's going on and, you must admit, the circumstances are difficult.'

'Difficult!' She moved impatiently. 'I didn't make them difficult.'

'No. But you've got to live with them. And, I must admit, I think Aunt Alice has a point. If Colonel Whitfield feels the way you want him to, then he wouldn't give two hoots who your father was. Why should he? It wouldn't stop me. It'd make me think a bit, which is only human, but it wouldn't stop me.'

'Oh, you don't understand!' she broke out passionately.

Haldean took her arm and steered her into the summer house. 'Now,' he said, once they had settled themselves on the wooden bench. 'What is it I don't understand?' He tried very hard to keep the anxiety out of his voice and actually managed a smile. 'Don't tell me it's nothing. There's something else, isn't there, Marguerite? Something that's been worrying you.' He put his hand under her chin,

127

turned her face towards him and realized she was on the brink of tears. 'Oh dear. Hang on a mo, I've got a hanky somewhere . . . here we are.' He reached for light-heartedness like a weapon. 'Now you go ahead and sob into that. It's much better than my shoulder. Besides that, this jacket has many virtues but it's ever so woolly and if it gets wet I smell like a dead sheep. Belle refused to have me in the house the last time I got caught in the rain.' A giggle rose up from amongst the sobs. 'That's better.' He put a comforting arm around her shoulder. 'Tell me all, old thing.'

'I . . . I can't. I feel so ashamed,' she said, into his chest. 'When I think how nice everyone's been and Aunt Alice and Isabelle and how they try and how I've treated them . . . I just want to go away and never see anyone decent again. I thought they were going to say something about it in the drawing room and I was half-glad to think it would soon be over and I wouldn't have to face them any more. Then they started talking about my father and trying to guess how I feel and they can't *see* I'm not worth the trouble. They don't know what I'm really like. I'm not worth all that effort.'

He tightened his arm round her bare shoulders. The moonlight though the wicker walls of the summer house laid stripes of silver across them both, making her expression difficult to see, but he could feel her trembling like a captured moth. This wasn't shaping up well but he wasn't going to imagine the worst. Not yet. 'I say, Maggie, old thing, you're not practising to be a nun or a saint are you? I believe they go in for worm-like humility but it's a bit wearing in anyone else.' Now for it. 'What the dickens is it?'

'It's . . . it's that horrible man, Boscombe.'

'Boscombe?' He repeated the name flatly. Boscombe.

'Yes.' She swallowed and then it all came out in a rush. 'Somehow, I don't know how, he knew about Richard and how I felt. I got a letter from him in January saying that he knew who I really was. He wanted me to give him some money.' She wriggled away from him. 'It's no use. I can't tell you.'

Haldean sat for a moment. She was damn well going to tell him if he had to force it out of her. Boscombe . . . Hold on a minute! *Boscombe!* He had wanted money. Maybe it was all right after all. *Boscombe* . . . He reached out his arm to her once more. 'Come here.' He put a hand in his pocket, drew out the collar-stud box and opened it. Marguerite gasped and sat rigidly. He could feel the tension in her muscles as she gazed at the emerald pendant. 'You gave this to Boscombe, didn't you?' Marguerite said nothing. 'You stole Isabelle's necklace and gave it to Boscombe.'

Marguerite covered her face with her hands and burst into renewed sobs. Haldean waited for the storm to die down, relief coursing through him. 'It's true,' she said eventually. 'I'm a thief, a common thief. He wanted fifty pounds. I didn't have the money so I sold some of my jewellery and he wrote back, demanding more. I was desperate, Jack. I've . . . I've taken other things, too. I took Aunt Alice's seed pearl and cameo brooch. She thought she'd lost it because the clasp was loose, but I stole it. I took Uncle Philip's cigarette case, as well.'

'What, his gold one?'

'Yes.' She glanced at his face and drew her breath in sharply. 'Please don't look at me like that. Please, Jack. I know I was wrong, but I was so frightened. Boscombe knew all about me and said if I wanted to keep it a secret from Richard, I'd better pay up. It was dreadful. If you can believe it, I'd never thought before that who my father was could make any difference. Maybe I should have ignored the letter or thrown it on the fire. But I couldn't, you see, Jack, I just couldn't. The idea of him writing to Richard was more than I could bear. I meant to pay everyone back, I really did. As soon as I got my money I was going to make it up to them but I know that wouldn't make it right. When Isabelle said you'd had the necklace made for her, it was dreadful. I didn't know it was so precious, but

129

I love Richard, I do, and now I've ruined everything. I wish I was dead.'

'Oh, glory.' Haldean squeezed her shoulders. So that was it. That was all. 'You idiot. Why, in heaven's name, didn't you tell anyone?'

'I couldn't. I just couldn't.' She tried to break away but he kept his arm firmly round her shoulders. 'I know you hate me for what I've done.'

'Hate?' His voice was very gentle. 'No, I don't hate you. Mind you,' he added with the beginnings of a smile, 'it's not my things which were taken, so it's not up to me to say it's all right, but I doubt if anyone's going to hate you. Count the spoons, perhaps, but not hate you.'

'Don't,' she said with a watery giggle. 'I'll have to tell them,' she added in a small voice. 'I've been wanting to but I couldn't bring myself to do it. And then everyone was so nice to me and I knew how much I owed everyone and that made it worse. It's been horrible.'

'Blackmail is horrible. Look, I'll tell them if you like. And don't worry. You were right about them being decent sorts. They'll understand. But please, Marguerite, if you ever have something bothering you again, something that's simply too much for you to handle, tell someone you can trust. Uncle Philip, Aunt Alice, me, even. But for God's sake tell us. And cheer up, old thing. Boscombe's dead. It's all over.'

'I only wish it was.' She hesitated. 'There's more, you know.'

Haldean felt the hairs on his neck prickle. Like someone revisiting a nightmare, all his fears returned. With a dead weight in his stomach he forced himself to look at her. 'What is it? Tell me.'

She shrank back from his gaze. 'At the fête I met Mr Boscombe. I didn't know who he was until he told me. He thanked me for my letters in a nasty, polite sort of way, then said he was afraid that the contents weren't quite enough. I told him I couldn't manage what he had asked as it was. I gave him my wristwatch. It had been a present from Mummy. I told him so and all he did was laugh. I hated that laugh. Then he said I'd have to do a great deal better than that, otherwise he'd *tell my father*. Don't you see, Jack? I didn't at first but he spelt it out for me. My father isn't dead. Mr Boscombe said so.'

Haldean was stunned.'Your father's *alive*?'

'That's what he said, yes.'

'But . . .' His thoughts were tumbling over each other. 'Did Boscombe say anything more? Had he seen him?'

'I don't know. I didn't want to know. I only wanted to get away from him as soon as I could. I hated being near Mr Boscombe. He was horrible.'

'So didn't you ask him anything? I mean, where does your father live?'

'I don't know, I tell you, and I don't want to know. It's not my fault he's my father. I don't want to know anything about him. Don't you see? He'll ruin everything between me and Richard. Richard couldn't possibly marry me if my father was alive. What if he turned up? What could I do?'

'He's hardly likely to turn up, I'd say. He's got . . .' He'd been about to say *the gallows* but changed it just in time. '. . . er, a serious charge hanging over him.' That hadn't been a very happy phrase either, but she didn't notice it.

'What if someone else sees him? It'll all be dragged up again and there'll be a huge fuss and it'll be in all the papers. Richard would hate it.'

If there were awards given out for single-mindedness, Marguerite would scoop the lot. 'Look.' This had to be sorted out. 'What did Boscombe actually say? Please remember, Maggie, it's important.'

Her lip trembled but she made an effort. 'He said – I think this is what he said – that I'd better pay up or he'd tell my father. And he said something like, "You wouldn't like that, would you? He's hardly the father a nice young lady like you should have." He was so sarcastic and I'm sure he meant it, you know. I didn't know what to do. I couldn't tell anybody, could I?'

131

'So you didn't do anything about it?'

She looked at him in bewilderment. 'No. What could I have done?'

Haldean breathed a huge sigh of relief and pulling her close, kissed the top of her head. 'Thank God. And so that's all you've got to tell me? Is that really all?'

'Why?' she asked with a puzzled expression. 'Isn't that enough? I mean, what else can there be?'

'I'm so glad,' said Haldean, with real feeling, 'that you don't know.'

Chapter Eight

Haldean drew the Spyker into the side of the grass verge under the shelter of the trees, looking doubtfully at the rutted dirt track leading to Colonel Whitfield's stables. Marguerite, urged on by Lady Rivers, had reluctantly decided to tell Whitfield the truth and Haldean had offered to take her in the car.

He was glad he had done. This wasn't going to be easy for her. Tyburn's treachery wasn't an item in the newspapers for Richard Whitfield, a mere footnote to a messy campaign. Whitfield had been wounded and seen the men who had suffered because of that betrayal. Although it would be unfair to blame Tyburn's daughter, it would be very understandable if it told against her. Yes, thought Haldean, despite all his reassurances that the past didn't matter, he knew only too well that it did. He didn't envy Marguerite the interview that lay ahead.

'We'll leave the car on the verge,' he said, cheerfully, trying by tone of voice alone to make everything as normal as he could. 'I don't fancy risking the suspension along that track. Are you sure Whitfield will be here?' It was the first time that morning he had said Whitfield's name to Marguerite. Funny how he'd skirted round it.

'When I spoke to him on the phone earlier he said he'd be at the stables and that we could go riding together.' Her voice was very controlled and she matched it by giving Haldean a consciously bright look. 'We can walk round.'

'Okay.' Haldean switched off the engine and leaned across the car to undo the passenger door. 'Out you hop.

It'll be all right,' he added, trying an encouraging smile. 'I really do think you're doing the right thing, you know, and so does everyone else.'

She got out of the car and, despite the warm sunshine, gave a little shudder. 'I wish I didn't have to tell him, Jack. If it wasn't for Aunt Alice and Uncle Philip saying I must, I couldn't go through with it.' They started up the lane, Marguerite, hampered by her smooth-soled riding boots, picking her way carefully over the stones. 'I know I must, though. It was horrible last night, having to tell everyone about my father and then having to own up to taking their things. That was dreadful but it was just like you'd said it would be. They were all so decent about it and so kind, I wanted to do something, especially for Aunt Alice. I wanted to show her that I do listen to what she says and I'm grateful for everything.' She paused. 'I . . . I didn't really get a chance to thank you properly for paving the way for me last night.'

'Juggins!' said Haldean with a grin. 'You must have said thank you about fifteen times. All part of the service.'

She laid a hand on his arm. 'Well, I was glad you were there. It was awfully difficult to admit what I'd done, but I felt better afterwards. The last few months have been horrible. I know I've let everyone down and Mr Lawrence looked so disappointed in me, even more than Aunt Alice did.'

'Forget about it,' said Haldean encouragingly.

Marguerite gave another little shudder. 'I wish I could. I'm glad you're with me and not Mr Lawrence. He disapproves of Richard so much I can't bear it. He wanted to come with us, you know, but I was afraid he was looking for a row. Do you think he was?'

Haldean hesitated. 'No. No, I can't say that I do. I imagine he wanted to be around in case things went wrong, you know.'

'To pick up the pieces, you mean?' Her lips tightened. 'I suppose Mr Lawrence means well, but he's so silly about Richard. He knows next to nothing about him and yet he's got this ridiculous prejudice. I know Richard's older than me but he's not *old* and it's horrible of Mr Lawrence to even think he's after my money. Richard couldn't care less about that.' She stopped as a groom came down the lane towards them.

The groom, an elderly, whiskery man who clearly knew Marguerite, touched his cap. 'Morning, miss. Morning, sir. You'll be wanting the Colonel, will you? He's in the top paddock. You'll be riding this morning, miss? I'll go and get Saverin saddled up for you.'

'Thank you, Buckman.'

With Buckman beside them, further private conversation was impossible until they stood by themselves once more at the gate to the paddock under the rustling shadow of an ancient oak tree. Across the field a great horse cantered with Whitfield on its back. Marguerite, her eyes fixed on the man, swallowed. Haldean squeezed her hand and she gave him a quick smile. 'I really wish that Mr Lawrence could like him more. Mr Lawrence is such a dear and he's making it so difficult. It's awkward enough as it is.' She waved her arm as Whitfield looked across to them. 'He's seen us now.'

Whitfield brought the horse round the outside of the field, then turned in his heels as he approached a fallen elm trunk which served as a natural jump. In short, sharp thumps the horse's hooves dug into the earth and Haldean heard the quick, snorting breath as the shoulder muscles corded, bunched and rippled, taking beast and rider over the jump in one graceful movement. Whitfield cantered towards them, reined in the horse and dismounted.

'My word,' said Haldean in involuntary admiration. 'Are you going to run him?'

Whitfield shook his head, patting the horse's neck. 'He's too temperamental. He'll go over a jump like that with a steam engine beside him one day, then he'll shy at a piece of paper on the grass. I've come a downright mucker on him more than once.' He looked at Marguerite with a cheerful grin. 'You can bear me out, can't you? I remember you picking me out of the mud.'

'It was the second time we met, Richard. I thought you'd broken your neck. I was terrified.'

'You were wonderful,' said Whitfield, taking the horse's bridle. 'Lots of sympathy and no reproaches.' He put an arm round her affectionately. 'Just what a man needs when he's made a fool of himself. I'd tried him at a jump I knew he didn't like and got thrown for my pains.' He laughed. 'I felt an absolute idiot, I can tell you. My fault, really.'

'It never crossed my mind that you were in the wrong,' said Marguerite with anxious devotion.

Haldean stole a look at Whitfield, wondering if he felt comfortable with such uncritical admiration, but Whitfield was totally at ease. He was either used to it or simply didn't realize the depth of Marguerite's feelings.

Whitfield smiled at her again. 'Have you seen Buckman? I told him you were coming over and to have Saverin ready. Were you thinking of joining us, Major Haldean?' he added, glancing at Haldean's unequestrian brogues.

'Not me.' He tapped his leg. 'I'm not up to riding any more, I'm afraid.'

'Oh, really? Bad luck,' said Whitfield, his face belying his voice. 'Then it's just us, Marguerite. Don't feel you have to wait, Major. I'll take Marguerite back to Hesperus.'

'Thanks.' Haldean glanced at his watch. 'I do have some time to kill, though. I'm meeting Superintendent Ashley at the police station but that's not until one o'clock. Would you mind if I had a look round? I rather like horses.'

Whitfield hesitated. 'Well . . . You can, of course you can. If I hadn't promised to take Marguerite out this morning I'd show you round myself. It's just that the place isn't what it used to be, and that's a fact. What with the war and investments not doing as they should, I haven't been able to make the improvements I should have done.'

Haldean nodded understandingly. 'That's a fairly familiar story.'

'Yes, I don't suppose I'm unique. Here's Buckman with

Saverin. He'll take you round.' The groom approached, leading a fine grey. 'Show the Major the stables, will you, Buckman?' he said. 'Up you get, Marguerite.' He lifted his cap slightly. 'Nice meeting you again, Haldean. You'll be at Mrs Verrity's tonight? I'll see you there.'

They trotted off, leaving Haldean and Buckman together. Haldean had been prepared to radiate encouragement at Marguerite as she left, but it was obvious that Whitfield was absorbing all her attention. Well, he'd thought before that she was single-minded and he was right. Feeling slightly deflated, he turned to the groom. 'What do you think of the Colonel's horse?' he asked, conversationally.

'He'm too nervy,' said Buckman. 'Well called, he is. Satan by name and the devil do look after his own. The Colonel thought he might run the National but a horse has to be willing as well as able.' He spat briefly. 'Near trampled one of my lads but the Colonel wouldn't hear of getting rid of him. We've got better than him in the stables, in temper if not in breeding, I'm glad to say. I don't trust that horse, and that's a fact.' He shrugged dismissively and started to walk slowly back to the stables. 'Was there anything special you wanted to see, sir?'

'Not really,' said Haldean, falling into step. 'It's just I've heard what a fine establishment Colonel Whitfield has.'

'Had, maybe, sir. I don't know so much about has, although there's some as think it's not my place to say so. But I speak as I find.' He shook his head sourly. 'I wish you could have seen it when old Mr Whitfield was alive. There wasn't a better stables in the county. Mind you, those were the days when you had men – and ladies too – that *could* ride, not a crowd of galloping tinkers, all money and no manners. But that was before the war.' Haldean registered the familiar complaint in silence. 'Still,' continued Buckman, 'I mustn't grumble. We were lucky to have the Colonel spared to us. You know he won the VC? There's not many as do that and live to tell the tale. I suppose you was in the war, sir?'

137

'I was in the RFC.'

'Airyplanes,' said Buckman in deep disapproval. 'T'aint natural to my way of thinking. Now here's the old stables,' he said, nodding towards the cobbled yard.

Haldean felt his spirits fall. The yard was set in rolling downland and the rich, homely smell of horses mingled with the tang of the upland air should have been pleasant, but the buildings reeked of neglect. The whitewashed walls were flaking and stained with lichen and a moss-choked water pipe dripped dismally into a leaky water barrel. The stables on the left-hand side stood open and empty and the cobbles in front of them were rimmed with grass.

'I remember when these were all used,' said Buckman. 'A grand sight, it were. But since the war first one horse went, then another, and they'm not been replaced.'

'This right-hand block's been used fairly recently though, hasn't it?' asked Haldean, nodding to where part of a wall had been repointed.

'Not since the autumn, sir. That's when we had to send two blood mares to Tattersall's. Near broke my heart, that did, to part with Nym Queen and Nym Princess. But since the war things have gone from bad to worse. Still, it doesn't do to brood, does it? But it's not a good thing to think on, how we've had to sell our blood stock. There's some right old screws in the yard now. Old Mr Whitfield would have been shamed to see them but they're good enough for men who don't know no better. Tinkers, that's what we have to hire out horses to these days. Tinkers.'

'That grey Miss Vayle was riding was rather nice,' said Haldean in a desperate effort to break out of this slough of despond.

'One of the few left,' said Buckman, refusing to admit a bright side. 'No, I reckon if things carry on as they are there won't be no stables left in a couple of years.' A shout came from across the yard. 'Do you mind if I leave you, sir? That's young Alfred calling for me.'

'Not at all,' said Haldean, easily. 'I'll just carry on poking around by myself. You carry on.' Buckman touched his cap and stumped away. Haldean strolled over to the nearest half-open stable door and made a clicking noise to its occupant. He was rewarded by a velvety nose thrust over the door. He felt in his pocket and offered one of the sugar cubes he had far-sightedly purloined at breakfast. 'Well,' he said, taking in the horse's lines, 'you have seen better days, haven't you, old thing? I wonder what your stable-mates are like?'

He made a leisurely inspection of the rest of the stables then thoughtfully strolled back to the car. A few good horses and a collection of old nags, and this in what had been one of the county's leading stables. No wonder Buckman was so despondent.

At the police station Haldean found Ashley sitting in his office surrounded by neat stacks of paper. He looked rather careworn. 'The Chief called me in this morning,' he announced. 'He thinks the blackmail idea may very well be the right one.'

'Good-oh,' said Haldean, pulling up a chair.

'He's also very keen to get Colonel Whitfield involved.' Haldean pulled a face. 'I know, I know. I wasn't very happy about it either, but the Chief's convinced it's the right way to go. As he says, the Colonel's a JP and he did know Boscombe.'

Haldean picked up a pencil from the desk and tapped it on the edge of the table, thinking. 'I don't suppose you can stop him,' he said eventually.

'Hardly.'

'A pity, all the same. I can't help feeling the fewer people who know, the better. All we can hope for is that Whitfield doesn't blurt it out to half the county. Fine upstanding bloke, and all that, but he doesn't strike me as particularly subtle.'

Ashley sighed. 'Me neither, and the last thing I want to

do is put the wind up any possible suspects. Still, the Chief's the Chief and what he says goes.'

'What else did the Chief say?'

Ashley gave an irritated sigh. 'He wants suspects. To hear him talk you'd think I could pick them off blackberry bushes. It's all very well, he said, having theories – fancy theories is what he actually said – but he'd be a lot happier if we were on the trail of a definite someone. I've been trying to figure out how we can go about tracing this child of Tyburn's. It's difficult to know where to start. '

Haldean took out his pipe and started to fill it. He wasn't particularly looking forward to this and it helped to have something to do. 'As a matter of fact, you don't have to. Start, I mean.' He pushed his tobacco pouch across the desk. 'Help yourself, by the way.'

Ashley ignored the tobacco. 'What do you mean?'

'I know who Tyburn's daughter is.'

'*What?*'

'It's Marguerite Vayle.'

Ashley stared at him. 'Marguerite Vayle? But . . . When did you find out?'

'Last night. Look, I'd better tell you everything that happened after I got back to Hesperus.' He put a match to his pipe. 'Help yourself. This might take some time.'

Ashley listened, unlit pipe in hand, while Haldean briefly recounted Marguerite's story. After it was over, he slowly shook his head. 'Well, I'll be damned. To be honest, I was impressed last night because I thought your theory made a lot of sense, but I wasn't sure – deep down sure, I mean – that it would hold up in the cold light of day. To have it confirmed like this is stunning. Does she know you were going to talk to me about it?'

Haldean nodded. 'Yes. I can't say she was any too happy, but I told her I had no choice. By that time she was so grateful to me for helping her out with what could have been a very nasty situation at home, what with Isabelle's pendant and Uncle Philip's cigarette case and everything, she more or less had to take it. And . . . And . . . ' He took

140

his pipe out of his mouth and inspected the glowing bowl with meticulous care, avoiding Ashley's eyes.

'And what?'

'And I told her that it would be all right.' He looked up, ill at ease. 'She's not guilty, Ashley. Obviously you'll have to talk to her. I told her that you'd have to talk to her, but she's not guilty.'

'Have you told her she's a murder suspect?' said Ashley in a dangerous voice.

'Of course I haven't! Give me some credit. I didn't say a damn thing about it.'

Ashley relaxed. 'Good for you. For a horrible moment I thought you'd warned her exactly what we had in mind.'

'But I haven't got it in mind,' said Haldean plaintively. 'Not now. She's innocent, Ashley. Look, last night was awful. I'd convinced myself that Tyburn's child was the one we were looking for and here was the child in question, popping up at me like the Demon King. She didn't exactly say, "Yoo-hoo, it's me," but she might as well have done. And the more she talked the more obvious it became that she didn't have a clue about the murders. She really didn't, you know. Unless she's a brilliant actress, I'd say she was innocent.'

Ashley looked at him appraisingly. 'Would you? Without any lingering doubts?'

Haldean remained silent. He had been battling this thought since last night. Yes, Marguerite was innocent. That's what he wanted to believe. However, there was a niggle of dissatisfaction that wouldn't go away. She was single-minded. She was obsessive, to put it bluntly. Boscombe and Morton had threatened to come between her and Richard Whitfield, and Boscombe and Morton were dead. She was also, God help him, a traitor's daughter. He was trying very hard not to let that count.

Ashley nodded. 'Yes, I thought that was the size of it.' He drummed his fingers on the desk. 'Marguerite Vayle, eh?'

'She acted exactly as you'd expect an innocent person to act,' said Haldean doggedly, forcing down his doubts.

Ashley shrugged. 'So she's a brilliant actress. Why shouldn't she be? Brilliant actresses do exist and they're not all on stage. By her own admission she was being blackmailed by Boscombe. We were looking for someone who was being blackmailed by Boscombe, remember? She's certainly a thief.'

'She was a terrified girl. And she owned up.'

'She *says* she was terrified. Brilliant actress, remember? And she didn't actually own up until you accused her, did she?'

'No,' said Haldean unhappily.

'What's more, it was you who floated the idea of it being Tyburn's child we were looking for.' He gave Haldean a long look. 'I'll grant you that was before you knew who the child was. Does that really change things so much?'

Haldean pushed his chair back and walked round the room impatiently, eventually pausing with one arm on a filing cabinet. 'No.' His voice was bitter. 'No, as far as the evidence is concerned it doesn't change a thing. And, to be honest, I don't know why I'm so upset about it. I certainly haven't got any tender feelings for her or anything like that.' Marguerite was helpless. Hopeless, Isabelle would say. He felt she'd been trapped and he wanted to help. That was it. But an animal caught in a trap could bite . . . 'Damn it, I don't know.' He clenched his fist, which was better than smacking it down on top of the cabinet. 'It's just that . . . Well, I think she's had a rotten hard time of it, Ashley. Oh, I don't mean she's been ill treated or any-thing, but ever since the Vayles died she's been farmed out from one place to another. She doesn't belong anywhere and now, now that she's looking forward to marriage and so on, with a home of her own, she felt it was all being taken away.'

'Chivalry,' said Ashley. 'You're suffering from chivalry.'

'Nonsense,' said Haldean shortly.

'It's not nonsense,' insisted Ashley. 'I've got it pegged now. That's how you feel. That and a strong dash of pity. It doesn't lead to an objective mind.'

142

And he was right. Honesty compelled him to meet Ashley's eyes. 'I don't suppose it damn well does, no. Why the blazes shouldn't I feel sorry for her?'

'Because it gets in the way.'

Haldean took a deep breath and linked his fingers together, staring at his palms. 'Let's go back to Boscombe and Morton. We know they started putting the squeeze on in October. But Miss Vayle didn't hear from Boscombe until January.'

'So she says.'

'So she says, yes. And I don't know how much our precious pair were getting, but it's more than she could have possibly given them.'

'Is it? She might have been taking things from other places than Hesperus, you know. She was obviously a fairly accomplished thief.'

'But why should she kill Morton? It was Boscombe she felt threatened by.'

Ashley leaned back in his chair with a short laugh. 'Your prejudices are showing. All Boscombe would have needed to say to Miss Vayle was that he wasn't the only person who knew the truth because his pal Morton was in on it as well. So she sees off Boscombe in a fit of desperation and kills Morton as well to make things nice and tidy. The diary's in his room, so she swipes that as well. Look, Haldean, if the evidence fits, then the evidence fits, no matter how sorry you feel for her. And don't you think there's at least the possibility she could have seen off both Boscombe and Morton? I don't know her well, but she seems a secretive type, the sort who bottles everything up. At a guess, that's exactly the sort of person who does strike out.'

Caught in a trap. Ashley had seen it too. Reluctantly, Haldean nodded in acknowledgement.

'She was frightened and she was desperate,' said Ashley, pressing his point home. 'I think she could have been pushed over the edge.'

Haldean looked up. 'Don't forget Greg and I were standing outside the tent.' His voice was tired. 'Neither of us saw her anywhere near the fortune teller's.'

'If she was just about to murder Boscombe she wouldn't advertise the fact she was there, would she? How about Morton's murder on Saturday night? We've pinned that down to quarter past seven. D'you know what she was up to then?'

'I didn't see her,' said Haldean, slowly. 'Gregory, Belle and I had gone for a walk by the river so I wasn't actually in the house, but I don't think she was around.' Where on earth had Marguerite been? 'Hang on. When we got back from the fête Marguerite was looking a bit white around the gills and said she still had a headache. She went up to her room to lie down before dinner. That's it. I remember, now. She looked washed out.'

'So when did you or anyone else actually see her again?'

'At dinner. We didn't bother to dress as it was very informal. It was more of a cold supper, actually. That was about quarter past eight. Her maid would have woken her sooner, at eight o'clock or thereabouts. But she couldn't have walked all the way to Breedenbrook and back in that time and I know she doesn't drive.'

'There are such things in this world as bicycles though, aren't there?'

'Yes, there are, damn it. She's a fairly keen cyclist, too. Oh, hell. That would be possible.' It was beginning to be far too possible for comfort. Haldean made another throw. 'Look, Ashley, I can see you putting it all together and to be honest it sounds horribly convincing.'

'Principally because you pointed the way last night.'

'I know, I know. But there was something else I said last night. Admittedly I didn't make much of it, but there is a chance that Tyburn himself may still be alive. After all, I told you what Boscombe said to Marguerite. What d'you think of that idea?'

'What do you? Honestly.'

'Damn!' Haldean stuck his hands in his pockets and

leaned against the wall. 'You weren't meant to say that, you know,' he said with the beginnings of a smile. All right. Let Ashley argue the case. Let's see where the dangers lie. 'I was going to outline the case for Tyburn's existence with as much dazzling wit and relentless logic as I could summon to my aid and now you've punctured my balloon.'

Ashley grinned. 'I didn't want to play. Go on, though. Say your piece.'

'The trouble is that I can't think of much to say.' Haldean scratched his head. 'Yes, Tyburn could be alive. Yes, Boscombe could have known that.'

'Could he?'

'Oh yes.' And that was true enough. 'He could have come across him and, for all we actually know, Petrie's diary might have a clue to where Tyburn is now.'

'The diary of a man who was taken prisoner in 1916 and spent the rest of his life in and out of sanatoriums for TB? How could he know anything about it?'

Haldean wrinkled his nose. 'I don't suppose he could, unless Tyburn landed up in hospital with him. But if the diary did say that, I don't suppose Morton would have let Edith Sheldon anywhere near it.' That wasn't going anywhere. 'No, scrub that idea. It won't wash. But if Boscombe ran into him that would be different. He would have known Tyburn because he served with him. As a matter of fact, he'd be one of the few people who knew him in the war who would recognize him. The battalion took an awful battering on the Somme and we'd be hard pressed to find anyone else who's alive and could identify him, especially if he's changed his appearance by growing a beard or something. Actually . . .' He stopped. 'Sorry, Ashley. That doesn't make sense. We'd worked out that Boscombe and Morton had to pool their information to make anything of it. If Boscombe had merely seen Tyburn he wouldn't need Morton. He'd go into business on his own account.'

'That's what you said last night,' agreed Ashley. 'I think

you're on the right lines there. But coming back to this identification business. Would Colonel Whitfield, for instance, recognize him?'

Haldean shrugged. 'Blessed if I know. I suppose you could ask him. If nothing else it'd make the Chief Constable think you'd followed his advice and asked for Whitfield's help. Mr Lawrence would recognize him, but he's certain Tyburn's kicked the bucket because otherwise he's sure Tyburn would have asked him to help.'

Ashley thoughtfully tamped down the tobacco in the bowl of his pipe with his thumb. 'So what it boils down to is this. That Boscombe, an acknowledged blackmailer, who was in the process of screwing more money out of Marguerite Vayle on the strength of who she was, frightened her silly by telling her that her father was still alive. Is that it?'

'Yes,' said Haldean reluctantly. 'It is.'

Ashley scratched his chin. 'Convinced?'

'No. Happy?'

Ashley shrugged. 'I'm not happy or unhappy. I'm just making a point, that's all. And the point I would like to make is that whether you like it or not, she does have a motive for wanting Boscombe dead. And Morton.'

Haldean ruffled a hand through his hair, leaving it in a spiky quiff. 'Oh, to hell with it. Yes, she has a motive. I presume she has the means and I suppose she had the opportunity. Yes, she could have done it. Why shouldn't she murder Boscombe? I'd have murdered him myself if I'd spent much longer with the little sweep. I fancy a drink.' He stood up and took his jacket from the peg. 'Do you want to see Colonel Whitfield today? He said he was going to take Miss Vayle back home. We've got a bunfight at Mrs Verrity's tonight so she can't stay out all afternoon. Why don't we have some lunch at the pub and go on to Hesperus afterwards? All shop talk forbidden.'

'Good idea,' said Ashley, rising to his feet. 'Look, Haldean, I know you find it tough to imagine a young girl like Miss Vayle being involved, but I'll have to question her again. In light of what you've told me, I haven't any choice. But I do think your sympathy might be misplaced.'

Haldean shrugged his jacket on. 'I can only hope it isn't. Come on.'

'Hold on a minute. All that stuff about Tyburn was nothing but a smokescreen. Despite how she acted and despite what you said, you think she could be guilty, don't you? Why?'

Haldean didn't say anything for a few moments. He seemed to be concentrating on buttoning his jacket. Then he raised his head, meeting Ashley's gaze reluctantly but squarely. 'All right. Marguerite's character's against her. She's intense. She's crackers about Whitfield and I believe would do nearly anything to marry him. She's passionate about things but keeps it all screwed down inside. You said so, and you're right. It's very hard to know what she's thinking. She fits a possibility I outlined last night. Yes, Ashley, I was flying a kite when I mentioned Tyburn, yes, Ashley, I believe she could have done it and yes, Ashley, I didn't want to say so. Does that make you feel any happier?'

'Not really,' said Ashley, picking up his hat. 'I've got feelings too.'

Lady Rivers looked round the brilliantly lit, noisy ballroom, sipped her champagne and sighed. It was a wonderful ball. *Who cares about money,* sang the vocalist with the dance band, *when love is free. I care about you, baby, it's enough for me.*

From the look of the ballroom *Who cares about money* seemed to be not so much an appropriate sentiment as an unnecessary one. The bright colours of the dresses spun and mingled on the dance floor, punctuated by the black-and-white of the men, with the occasional scarlet exclamation mark of a dress uniform. The light from the chandeliers refracted and shone from the polished wood floor – a properly sprung floor which was a pleasure to dance on – from the glasses of champagne hurried clinking past on silver trays by the waiters and most of all from the decorations of the men and the jewels of the women. It was wonderful, but . . . She was trying to put her finger on what it actually was that made the ballroom at Thackenhurst look so, well, *ravishing*. She sighed again. It was not a contented noise.

Isabelle, who had achieved exactly the effect she wanted in her green georgette, rid herself of Mark Stuckley, shook her head at two other hopefuls and came to stand beside her. 'Are you all right?' she asked.

Her mother turned to her and smiled. 'I'm afraid I was allowing myself a moment of sheer envy about how lavish everything is. Silly of me really.'

Isabelle looked round. 'It's like a stage set,' she said eventually. 'It's beautiful but I'm not sure if I like it. I mean, look at the flowers.'

'But we have flowers at home.'

'Of course we do, but not like this. All those cascades of red and white roses must have cost an absolute fortune. Have you seen the supper room?'

'No.'

'The champagne's in specially carved buckets, all made out of ice. It's red and white ice, to go with the roses and the decorations, and they're all in different shapes such as cars and aeroplanes. It's stunning.'

'Yes,' agreed her mother in a doubtful voice.

Isabelle put her hand on her mother's arm. 'It really is stunning, but I prefer the way we do things, you know. When we have a ball, it's lovely and it looks super, but it isn't intimidating. This is, in a way. Gorgeous but intimidating. Rather like Mrs Verrity herself.'

Lady Rivers exchanged a guilty smile. 'I suppose I should tell you not to criticize your host, but really, Isabelle, I do know what you mean.' She cast another doubtful glance round the room. 'I should simply appreciate all the trouble which has been taken, I suppose. After all, it's all for the Red Cross and it's absolutely splendid. It's just that I remember coming to balls here when Michael Verrity was still alive, before the war. They were grand enough but grand in a different way. In a funny way it was easier to feel at home.'

'Let's go to the supper room and have an ice,' said Isabelle. She was used to the idea that nothing after the war could match up to anything which had gone before. 'Archie Clows-Hunt's bearing down on me and he's got two left feet. I must say,' she added, as they threaded their way round the dance floor, 'that Jack doesn't seem to be intimidated. In fact,' she said, glancing to where the crowd allowed her a glimpse of where her cousin and Mrs Verrity were dancing, 'completely the reverse.'

Haldean wasn't aware of Isabelle's scrutiny. The only thing he was actually conscious of was Anne-Marie Verrity. She had large, very deep blue eyes which were fixed on his from a distance of eight inches away. The body in his arms was slim without being angular and the skin on her bare shoulders sheened with a delicate glow from the Chinese lanterns decorating the ballroom. Her auburn hair was coiled round and held with a ruby clasp and another necklet of rubies decorated her perfect throat. Her steps matched his exactly in the rhythm of the dance and Haldean felt the unmerited if natural satisfaction which came from holding the most outstanding woman in the room. To say she was beautiful was not to say enough; and all other adjectives – grace, elegance, style – seemed like clichés. Which meant, of course, like most clichés, that they were true. He had been prepared for beauty but what had taken him by surprise was her wit and charm. She had the gift of listening intently as if his conversation was the most important event of the evening, then taking a light-hearted remark and capping it.

The dance came to an end and they applauded. The band leader glanced round, tapped his baton, and started on 'The Sheik of Araby'. Mrs Verrity slipped an arm through his and looked up with a brilliant smile. 'A fox-trot. This is a little quick for me. Shall we sit it out?' They walked to the side of the room. Mrs Verrity looked at the dancers and gave a slight shake of her head. 'It's fun but I prefer more elegance. I've been spoiled, of course. I remember Vienna before the war.' She half-laughed. 'I must be careful or you'll think I'm very, very old and I don't feel old at all.'

'I can't imagine you ever being old.'

'Why, thank you, Major. And yet, think of it. Before the war. It seems a lifetime away. I'm sure that child who Colonel Whitfield is dancing with would think I belong in a museum.' She giggled. 'They would have me in a glass case with a label, *Rara Avis: Pre-war Woman*, and everyone would stare and say things such as "Look, my dear, they had women before the war. Fancy that! She looks quite different from how we do nowadays."'

'Which is the loss of nowadays and a perfect example of change unaccompanied by progress.'

She laughed unaffectedly. 'What a lovely thing to say. Do you want to dance again, Major? You dance very well but – excuse me – are you slightly lame?' She spoke with a concerned hesitancy that robbed the question of any possible offence.

'Oh dear, was it as bad as that? I thought I avoided your feet most of the time.'

'All of the time, but with my hospital experience I notice such things. Shall we sit in the conservatory for a while? Perhaps you would be kind enough to bring me a glass of champagne?' He watched her walk across the room, seeing her pause as Colonel Whitfield, who was dancing with Marguerite, detached himself and stood in her way. She shook her head quickly and walked on. Whitfield, annoyance clear on his face, turned back to Marguerite.

Haldean collected two glasses of champagne and went to join her. The conservatory doors were standing open and a welcome whisper of night air mingled with the heavy scent of flowers. He sat down beside her in a cane chair and raised his glass. 'Congratulations, Mrs Verrity. Your ball is a great success.'

She acknowledged the compliment with a quick and wickedly attractive smile. The music was softer out here, quiet enough to talk in an ordinary voice. 'I'm glad you think so. This is only a small affair, of course, but enjoyable, I hope. Parties – balls – I love them, you know. It's fashionable to pretend to be bored, but why bother to pretend something you don't feel?' She stretched out her hand and picked up the glass from the table beside her. 'And you, Major Haldean, I think you dislike being bored, yes? And so you have a hobby.' She pronounced the word with a twist of an accent that made 'a hobby' seem an enchanting occupation. 'You are looking for the killer of that poor man, Mr Boscombe, yes? And that other man who was killed in the pub. You have decided to become a hunter of men.'

'Well, I don't know if I'd put it quite like that myself,' said Haldean, squirming slightly. I mean, she was a lovely woman, but this was a bit much, wasn't it? 'Er . . . How did you know?'

Her eyes opened wide. 'But everyone knows! Marguerite Vayle, she tells Richard and Richard, he tells me, and everybody is talking about what you are doing.'

Haldean said nothing but the mention of Marguerite made him wince. Mrs Verrity mistook his expression.

'You do not like that people should talk about you? Why not? We are interested, you understand? An author who is now a detective. You are famous, yes?'

'Hardly,' said Haldean.

'But you are, Major. Please do not be English and embarrassed and say "Oh, it's nothing. Really, it's nothing to shout about. Anyone could do it. It's just luck, don't you know." You were going to say that, weren't you?'

Haldean grinned. 'Something like that.'

'But why?' She leaned forward, her eyes sparkling. 'The English have many virtues but they're so silly about their accomplishments. And to find you being gruff and modest

151

is ridiculous. You look as if you could be a level-headed Latin. Are you really nothing more than a bluff Anglo-Saxon or am I talking to a member of one of the really sensible races? Please tell me I'm right.'

'My secret is out. My mother was Spanish.'

She sat back and clapped her hands together in delight. 'I knew it! But now you have even less excuse for this pretence. In France we are so much more clear-headed about what we do. You should say with pride that you are a great detective and that no one can escape you for long. For what is detection, after all? Logic and intelligence. You have both those qualities and you must succeed. And privately you know that is the truth, don't you? That no criminal could match himself against you and hope to win.' Haldean made an embarrassed and totally British noise in the back of his throat. 'This murder at my fête and the poor man in the inn – what chance does the murderer have? None. And why? Because you are on their track.'

Haldean, who at first thought he was having his leg well and truly pulled, gave her a steady look and realized she was absolutely serious. 'It's not to say I'll get anywhere though, is it?'

She raised her eyes to heaven. '*Mon Dieu!* What a man is this? Of course you will succeed. One day, not so long from now, you will say to me, "Mrs Verrity, you were right." You will feel compelled to add a great deal of nonsense about luck, none of which you will believe for one second but which is expected of you. By the way,' she added, with a sudden change of tone, 'I don't believe I ever thanked you for understanding me so quickly when Mr Boscombe was found. It was quite dreadful, seeing him there and realizing what that little hole in his temple meant. I looked up and there was the fortune teller, so kindly and so slow, and the other man, puzzled and waiting, and my heart sank at the thought of so many explanations.' She shook her head. 'And then you understood. It was such a relief not to have to spell out what had happened. Thank you. And for taking charge of the fortune teller and that little

152

girl. I couldn't have calmed anyone down at that moment and the idea of facing a crying child and a hysterical woman was more than I could bear.'

'That's all right,' said Haldean quickly, then stopped with an awkward grin. 'You've taken away most of my vocabulary for saying "Don't mention it," but honestly, it really was all right. It was, if you'll excuse the phrase, nothing.'

She rose to her feet. 'It was certainly not nothing, and I am very grateful to you. I must get back to my other guests.' She held out her hand and Haldean, feeling it was expected of him, took it and kissed it lightly. She drew back, smiling. 'And please don't be so English. Remember, I'm a Latin, too.'

He sat down again and picked up his champagne, swirling it round in the glass. So Marguerite had told Whitfield, had she? Well, he might have expected that. Blow Marguerite. He wanted to think about Mrs Verrity. She really was lovely. An extraordinary woman. How much depended on her looks and her voice and how much was character? He tried to imagine her as plain and perhaps slightly plump and failed utterly. He couldn't take away the vibrancy of those eyes and that flawless skin. It had a creamy glow where the light touched her. And that hair!

The music came clearly from the ballroom. *I've had my fun, I've had my fling, but baby, you're the real thing. I'm gonna tell them, you're my favourite doll . . .*

Doll! Haldean half-smiled. ('Hello, everyone. This is Anne-Marie Verrity. She's my favourite doll.') Er . . . no. Apart from anything else, she was surely much, much more than a painted doll. It took real character to set up a hospital, real character to make a successful life in a foreign country, and that character had showed when she had taken command on Saturday. Simple, clear instructions and a plea for help. 'Take Mrs Griffin out of here and get that child away from the entrance.' His mouth curved at the memory of her thanks. A lovely woman. A very desirable woman. And – watch your step, Jack, he warned himself – a woman who must be at least twenty years older than him. He smiled ruefully and, with a gesture of finality, put his glass down on the table.

A footstep sounded, causing him to look up. It was Whitfield. His face was flushed and he held a glass of whisky in his hand. His usual smile was missing and it was with a shock that Haldean realized that the man had been drinking heavily. What the devil had come over him, to get in such a state at a ball? His name would be mud if he were seen. He stood in front of Haldean, rocking almost imperceptibly on the balls of his feet. 'Where's Anne-Marie?' Haldean stared at him as if stung. Whitfield's voice was aggressive. 'I thought she was with you.'

'Anne-Marie?' He couldn't keep the edge out of his voice. 'Mrs Verrity, you mean? She was here until a few moments ago. She's gone back inside now.'

'Damn!' Whitfield sat down carefully in the chair Mrs Verrity had vacated, ran his hands through his hair, then picked up his glass and finished it in a gulp. 'What's the matter with me?' he demanded abruptly.

The obvious, if tactless, answer was 'You're drunk,' so Haldean prevaricated. 'Nothing, as far as I know. Is something wrong?'

'Nothing. Everything. I want another drink.' He looked round and snapped his fingers at a waiter. 'Hey! You! A large scotch and don't take all night about it.' He turned his attention back to Haldean. 'I've got a bone to pick with you.'

'What?'

'A great, big, juicy bone,' said Whitfield, separating each word out carefully. Haldean reminded himself the man had been drinking and decided to be charitable. 'Do you know – because you damn well should – that the Chief Constable's a friend of mine? And I understand that you've got a pal, too. That copper, what's-his-bloody-name.'

'Now –' began Haldean indignantly.

Whitfield carried on without heeding him. 'He's been annoying Marguerite. A whole lot of damned impertinent questions. Grilled her this afternoon. Positively grilled her. Rotten little counter-jumper.'

'Now hold on, Whitfield –'

'And I'm not having it, d'you hear? I'm going to marry Marguerite and I'm not having some nosy copper upsetting her. I've seen Flint – that's the Chief Constable – and told him exactly what I think of his bobbies annoying my fiancée.' He blinked at Haldean. 'That's it. Nothing personal. Don't take offence. No quarrel with you.'

Haldean swallowed hard. Whitfield could be forgiven, he supposed, for being upset on Marguerite's behalf, but he couldn't be allowed to carry on like this. 'Why don't you go home?'

'No. I want Anne-Marie. I know what she's like at these beanos. She'll be tied up with some damn grandee and I won't get a look-in. Women, eh! And I'd like to know where he gets off. I mean,' he continued moodily, 'what the hell have I done to the man? I've never cast eyes on him before and yet he's taken against me and won't say why.' He leaned forward heavily in his chair and fumbled for a cigarette. 'D'you know why?'

'Er . . . who?' asked Haldean, cautiously feeling his way.

'Lawrence, of course. I had it all set up. All set up. Me and Marguerite. Like that.' He twined his fingers together to indicate closeness. 'And what happens? He does. He's breaking that poor girl's heart, you know. Breaking her heart. That's how much he cares. You know him, Haldean. What's he said about me? What reason has he given?'

Haldean shrugged. 'None. It's not really my business, you know.'

'I wish it wasn't his. Let me tell you what happened. You know you dropped off Marguerite this morning at the stables? Do you know what she had to tell me?'

'I had a sort of idea.'

'Well, it hit me like a bombshell. A bloody bombshell.

155

I mean . . .' He lowered his voice to a conspiratorial whisper. 'That she should be Tyburn's daughter! Tyburn of all people! Can you imagine it? And she's all worked up about what that Boscombe feller said about him being alive. Well, I told her. I said, "Come on, old girl, your precious father's dead. Take it from me." That friend of yours – you know, the copper –'

'Mr Ashley.'

'S'right. He wanted to know if I'd known Tyburn. Everybody's talking to me about Tyburn. I never knew the damned man. Why should I? I had nothing to do with him. None of my bloody business. Her father! Can you believe it! I told her it was all right. I couldn't let her go round brooding about it. And then she started crying.'

The waiter arrived with the whisky and Whitfield took an absent-minded gulp. 'Never could bear to see a woman crying. So I said, "Come on, don't you know, I can't deny that it's a bit awkward, but I can't see it makes any difference to us." And then she told me she didn't know if there was an us. Apparently she'd got all upset that I hadn't actually asked her, but damn it, Haldean, I'd sort of taken it for granted. I've never been one for hearts and flowers and all that gush and I didn't think she was either. She always seemed such a sensible girl. It's all very well at the pictures, but this is real life. So I set her straight on that score and thought that, as I had to take her back home, I might as well see the trustees and get everything sewn up properly and stop the silly girl worrying about it. What d'you think of that?'

'Er . . . good idea.' Privately Haldean was appalled. Although he wrote detective stories he usually had a subplot of young love which his editor often warned him to keep in the background, but it had never occurred to him that romance could be quite so ruthlessly subjugated as Whitfield appeared to believe. In their attitude to the Divine Fire, his editor and Whitfield could have been twins. 'How did Miss Vayle take it?'

'Marguerite? Oh, all right. Pleased an' that. Only to be

expected. Damn it, I'd just asked her to marry me. Of course she was pleased.' He slumped back and sucked deeply on his cigarette. 'But you could have knocked me over with a feather. Lawrence refused the match. Sir Philip was all right about it. I'd have no trouble with him, or Lady Rivers either, I could see, but Lawrence? No. And he wouldn't give any reasons, that's what infuriated me. We can't go ahead without his permission. He simply said that Marguerite had to have the say-so of the trustees and he had a perfect right to refuse if he thought it was an unsuitable match. I wouldn't be surprised if he had an eye on her himself, the way he coos over her. Damned old goat. Why should I be unsuitable? What's wrong with me?' he asked, bringing the conversation full circle.

'Look, Whitfield, I don't know what Mr Lawrence's objections are, but I really think you'd better be getting along home.'

'Home? What for?' He looked at his empty glass. 'Never a bloody waiter when you want one. Look,' he said, leaning forward and resting his elbows on his knees, 'You're in with the police. You and that Superintendent feller are as thick as thieves. Do you think there's any truth in this blackmail idea?'

Haldean shrugged. 'You knew Boscombe. Do you?'

Whitfield ran his hand wearily across his forehead. 'Just answer the question, will you? You can tell me. I'm a JP, after all, and Flint told me all about it this afternoon. All I'm asking for is your opinion. Is it blackmail that's behind it?'

'That's the theory, yes. The idea is that Boscombe and Morton were blackmailing someone and their victim shot them both.'

'Oh God.' Whitfield sat very still for a moment. He looked up and the sight of his face shocked Haldean. His skin seemed to have gone flabby, like putty, and the look in his eyes was an odd mixture of fear and defiance, like a dog waiting to be kicked. 'Are there . . .' He swallowed. 'Do you know who it is?'

Haldean shook his head slowly. 'Not yet.'

Whitfield sagged back in the chair, groping for his glass. 'I didn't see how you could. Said as much to Anne-Marie. And Marguerite. She keeps on telling me how brilliant you are. Are you brilliant? You don't *look* brilliant. She says you look clever. But I told her. I said mark my words, all he does is write stories. That's all. Just makes the stuff up. Anyone can do that. Real life's different. It must be easy, making it up. Where's that bloody waiter?'

'It's not that easy,' said Haldean, aware that his sense of humour and his temper were struggling for control.

'Oh, yes it is. I said to Flint, look, if you really want to find out what's what, then you'll get the Yard in, not some damned country copper. Feller ought to be sacked. If he gets on the wrong side of me, he'll be sorry. He'll be in a dole queue before he's much older, I'll see to that.'

Haldean's temper won. 'Superintendent Ashley is a very capable man who won't take kindly to any sort of intimidation. As for me, I *have* done this sort of thing in real life, as you call it.'

Whitfield froze. 'Have you?' He glanced at Haldean, looked away and swallowed uneasily. 'I didn't know that.' He put a hand to his mouth. 'That makes a difference. Yes, that makes a big difference. That's it, then. The case is as good as over. There's nothing more for you to do.'

Haldean's sense of humour started to ebb back. 'Apart from the small matter of finding the actual murderer.'

'What? Oh yes. You've got to do that. I suppose you're going to do that.' Whitfield stopped and rubbed his forehead. 'Wish you luck.' He got to his feet. 'I need another drink.'

'Hold on a minute, Whitfield. What did Boscombe want with you at the fête?'

'Want with me? It was all about his blasted book. Wanted me to write a preface or something. I turned him down. Pestered me all afternoon. You saw him.' He leaned against a pillar. 'Don't you think there could be another reason than blackmail?'

'No,' said Haldean shortly. 'I don't.'

Whitfield half-laughed and straightened up. 'Well, that's it then. Case closed. All the best, Haldean. Good hunting.' He walked off, very self-conscious and very upright.

Haldean looked after him and shook his head. Rattled? You could virtually hear the man. And yet what was he rattled *about*? Marguerite. Of course, it was Marguerite. She'd told him Boscombe had blackmailed her and he'd seen exactly how that could be interpreted, especially with the Chief Constable telling him they were after one of Boscombe's victims. Yes, that would make sense. Poor devil. He drew his breath in. What if Whitfield knew a sight more than he was letting on? What if he actually *knew* Marguerite was guilty? All that bluster and aggression could be rooted in real knowledge. It might not take that, even. All he'd have to do was guess. Oh, hell. He smoked his cigarette down to the stub and threw it away. Feeling thoroughly depressed he got up and drifted back to the ballroom.

'You're looking awfully grim, Jack,' said Isabelle, affectionately slipping her arm through his. He squeezed her arm back, glad of the companionship. She looked to where Marguerite and Whitfield were dancing. 'D'you know, I saw the Colonel earlier and I thought he was a fair way to being bottled. Considering how tanked up he must be, he's making quite a good job of it. Whoops! Missed his step that time.'

He could have hugged her. She was so ordinary and matter-of-fact and a world away from his gloomy imaginings. He looked down at her and grinned. 'Shouldn't you be shocked? A really nice-minded young lady would be.'

She gave a crack of laughter. 'Hardly. I'll tell you what I *was* shocked about though. Marguerite's actually got him to pop the question. She told me all about it and I've never heard of a more ham-fisted proposal in my life. As far as I can make out he sort of grunted at her and told her not to be so damn silly, that of course he wanted to marry her but she didn't expect a lot of sentimental gush, did she?

159

And she was carrying on as if he was Rudolph Valentino. I tell you, Jack, she must be really crazy about him.'

'I sort of gathered that. Hello, what's wrong?' As he watched them move round the dance floor, he saw Marguerite's face change and harden. Then Whitfield bent his head to hers and she smiled again. Haldean followed the direction she had looked in and saw Mr Lawrence standing by the side of the room with Gregory.

'Oh dear,' said Isabelle. 'She's seen Mr Lawrence. I'm being nice to him on purpose because Marguerite's cutting him dead. Shall we dance, Jack? I like this tune.'

'I'll stagger round the floor with you.'

'Charmed, darling. It's horribly uncomfortable. Mr Lawrence and Marguerite, I mean,' she said as they set off. 'She's furious with him because he won't give his consent to her marrying Colonel Whitfield. She can't possibly keep it up at home and it's such a shame, Jack. He really cares about her, you know. I can't help wondering if he has fallen for her.'

'Well, if that is his reason for refusing his consent it's pretty selfish, wouldn't you say?'

'Yes, I suppose I would. It's not that then, because he isn't. Selfish, I mean. I don't think he is, anyway.' They paused while Marguerite, Whitfield in tow, slid past them. 'I don't know what she sees in that stick,' said Isabelle, once they were out of earshot. 'I know he's got the VC, but you can't look at a medal for ever. The only thing he's got going for him are his looks. Mind you, I wouldn't be surprised if he ran to seed in a few years. Those blond, fleshy types often do, and if he carries on putting it away at the rate he has been this evening, he's going to be as fat as a pet pony by Christmas. He's far and away one of the dullest men I've ever met, and I wouldn't be surprised if he and Mrs Verrity had something going.'

'I say, steady on, old thing.' The dance came to an end and under the cover of applause Haldean gave her a warning frown. 'We're in public, you know.'

'No one's listening. Jack, look! Mrs Verrity and the Colonel. They're going outside. What did I tell you?'

'Well, I was outside with her myself earlier in the evening.'

'I know you were. What did you find out? I mean, you were detecting, weren't you?'

'No, socializing. What should I have been detecting?'

'How she did it, of course. You're being very dim about this, Jack,' she said darkly. 'I bet she's a spy working for the Russians or something and Boscombe got on to it. Anyone as good-looking as that at her age has to have something up their sleeve. If she had *femme fatale* stamped on her forehead it couldn't be more obvious.'

He laughed. 'That's absolute rubbish.'

'Just you wait,' she said with a smile. She took his arm again and they strolled back across the room. Sir Philip and Lady Rivers had joined Gregory and Mr Lawrence.

'Time to go, I'm afraid,' said Sir Philip. 'The cars are at the door.' He looked round impatiently. 'Where's Marguerite got to? She was here a moment ago. We'll have to find Mrs Verrity too, of course.'

'I think they're both outside,' put in Gregory. Sir Philip tutted in impatience. 'I'll go and see,' he offered. 'Come with me, Jack?' He led the way out of the ballroom and on to the terrace. 'I want a word with Marguerite,' he said when they were out of hearing.

'What about, Greg?'

'This rotten situation with her not speaking to Mr Lawrence. It'll be utterly wonderful at home with that going on and it's simply not fair. Mind you, I can't help feeling Mr Lawrence is to blame. He won't give any explanation, you know. He just says it's his duty as a trustee to watch over Marguerite's welfare and leaves it at that.' He sighed heavily. 'I wish I didn't have go back to London tomorrow. I hate pushing off and leaving you and Isabelle in the middle of all this. I can't see where it's going to end, and that's a fact. Marguerite's a bit too intense for my liking, but I can't help feeling sorry for the girl and I really feel sorry for all of you, being stuck with it.'

'Yes, Aunt Alice and Uncle Philip especially. They have to be fair to both sides, don't they? It can't be easy for them.'

They looked round the terrace. 'I think Marguerite went this way,' said Gregory. 'Is that her, Jack?'

The light from the ballroom flooded down the steps and across the lawn. In front of them Marguerite Vayle was walking towards a man and a woman who were standing slightly away from the house. The man, Colonel Whitfield, had his back to them, but Mrs Verrity was plain to see, intent on the man in front of her. Colonel Whitfield's voice suddenly cut through the darkness.

'You know why. My God, you know why.'

Mrs Verrity started back and, glancing up, caught sight of Marguerite coming towards them. She caught at Whitfield's arm to silence him, but he carried on, oblivious.

'I'm damn nearly broke. I need the money.' Marguerite stopped, poised and listening. 'It's all right for you. It's not your problem, is it? You've never been short of money in your life but I've *got* to marry her. I'm desperate. I haven't any choice but to marry her. I can't keep on like this.' Mrs Verrity shook her head and covered her mouth with her hand. 'What are you looking at me like that for? I'm not telling you anything you didn't know, am I?'

'Oh, shut up, you fool,' Mrs Verrity said wearily.

They saw Marguerite's slim shoulders go back and she carefully walked the few extra steps to stand beside Whitfield. He spun round and as he saw her his face crumpled. He tried to speak, but couldn't, and stood there pulling at his collar.

'Richard,' said Marguerite, her voice throbbing with anger. 'I think the phrase is "You really have done it now."'

She turned and saw Haldean and Rivers on the steps and stretched out a hand to them. 'Can you take me home, please? I have an apology for Mr Lawrence.'

162

Chapter Nine

Haldean walked across the park to the main gates of Hesperus. It was two days after the Red Cross ball. He had spent yesterday in London and was going to see Ashley later on. He couldn't get his thoughts into proper order and it irritated him.

On the one hand Marguerite was the obvious suspect and on the other he had an uncomfortable feeling that he'd got it hopelessly wrong. How much of that was due to what he sternly felt to be sentimental, woolly-minded and wishful thinking, he wasn't sure. At least there wasn't any chance of Marguerite being summarily arrested. He knew, because she had told him, she had stated in her interview with Ashley that at the time of Boscombe's murder she had gone for a walk in the woods around Thackenhurst to avoid meeting Boscombe again. No one had seen her go. Although it didn't let her out, at least it didn't incriminate her. Ashley, thank goodness, wanted something more solid than suspicion and he had said on the telephone that a further search of the Talbot Arms had turned up nothing.

Marguerite herself was being, he had to admit, a pain in the neck. She had spent most of yesterday out on a long, solitary bicycle ride, much to everyone's relief. When she had arrived home she refused to talk about Whitfield, and as she clearly couldn't think about anything else ordinary conversation was virtually impossible. Broken-hearted maidens were all very well in sad Victorian poems but were horribly taxing to live with.

The only person who could approach her with any cheerfulness was Mr Lawrence. As far as he was concerned, Whitfield was a back number and that was a happy ending. His view – which even he didn't express to Marguerite – was that she would soon 'come round' and realize 'she was well out of it'.

It was concern for Marguerite and the rest of the family that had prompted Haldean to walk into the village. His official aim was to buy some cigarettes and enjoy a stroll in the morning sunshine but his actual intention was to head off Marguerite from a meeting with Mrs Verrity. He didn't know if Marguerite would cause a scene, but he was anxious not to put it to the test.

Marguerite had cycled into Stanmore Parry directly after breakfast. Mrs Verrity had telephoned about half an hour afterwards to ask if she could come round, ostensibly to consult Lady Rivers as a member of the Red Cross committee. He suspected, and Isabelle said, that her real reason for coming was to pick up any crumbs of gossip concerning Marguerite's spectacular bust-up with Whitfield.

A car turned in at the gates and swept up the drive past him, scrunching on the gravel. Mrs Verrity. Haldean smiled. She hadn't seen him. Good. He walked through the gates, then stopped short, retreating fast behind the gate-post. Across the road, a few yards away from the gate, a magnificent black horse was noisily cropping the grass on the daisy-studded verge. Beside the horse, his hand loosely holding the bridle, stood Richard Whitfield. His attention was fixed on the road leading to the village where, in the distance, Marguerite Vayle was toiling up the slope on her bicycle.

Whitfield dropped the bridle and walked into the road in front of her. 'Marguerite!'

Haldean stayed where he was. He could, he supposed, walk back across the park and leave Whitfield and Marguerite in decent solitude, but he wanted to be on hand should Marguerite look as if she needed help. Marguerite hesitated, then held her head high and came defiantly on.

Whitfield stepped in front of her and Marguerite, stuck between running into him or stopping, skidded to a halt. She looked at him for a moment without speaking and, with a toss of her head, put her foot on the pedal once more.

Whitfield reached out and held the handlebars. 'Marguerite! Stop!'

She looked at him stonily. 'If you don't let me pass, Colonel Whitfield, I shall get the lodge-keeper to come and remove you.'

'No. Marguerite, please, no. Wait a moment, will you?' He let go of the bicycle and reached out to her. She ignored the gesture. 'I'm sorry,' he said rapidly. 'I really am sorry. If only I could make you understand what was happening. I keep trying to see you and to speak to you but they won't let me.'

'I gave instructions that I was not at home. And furthermore, Colonel Whitfield, I think it's a mean trick to catch me like this. After what happened at the party I can hardly be blamed for not wanting to see you.'

He shook his head in a bewildered way. 'Stop calling me Colonel Whitfield as if we'd only just been introduced.' Marguerite put her foot on the pedal once more. 'No. No, wait. Please. I shouldn't have said what I did the other night, I know that. I wish you hadn't heard it.'

'I bet you do!'

Haldean relaxed. It seemed as if Marguerite was perfectly capable of handling Whitfield alone but he certainly wasn't leaving her just yet.

Whitfield reached out again. She ignored the gesture. 'I didn't mean it, Marguerite. I was being pestered to death by that blasted woman and I had to tell her something. Look . . .' He paused, then rushed on. 'You've got to understand about Mrs Verrity. She's . . . she's . . . well, she's always had a thing about me. It's been going on for years. When she was married, she used to have these parties – you know what she's like – and I was invited, of course, and it was obvious she liked me. I never took it seriously.

165

Why should I? She was older than me and married and so on but I was flattered, I suppose. I never dreamt there was anything in it. Then, when her husband died, she made it very plain that she wanted me to marry her. She even followed me to France. I was horrified. It's . . . It's hard to cope with, you know? Perhaps she's so used to having men fall at her feet that she simply can't understand I'm not interested in her. Not in that way.'

'Are you certain about that?'

Even to Haldean, Whitfield's voice carried conviction. 'Absolutely certain. My God, yes. It's been awful recently. Ever since she realized that we . . . that I . . . well, cared for you, she's been unbearable. She won't leave me alone. Why did I want to marry you? How could I want to marry you? On and on, every time we met. I can't simply not see her because she comes to the stables, riding. Most of the time she never says anything I can catch hold of. It's all little hints and pointed remarks and if I do take her up on it, it's dismissed with a laugh as a joke. But I'm serious about you, Marguerite. I wasn't going to tell her that. I had to think of a reason she could understand. But surely you don't believe it, do you?'

Marguerite spun the pedal of her bicycle. 'I did . . .'

Whitfield lifted his head at the hesitation in her voice. 'But why? You must know how I feel about you. I know I don't go in for fancy speeches much but that's not my way. It's all been so horribly difficult.' He put a hand to his forehead. 'The last couple of days have been ghastly. I haven't been able to think of anything else. Brooding. I'm going to pieces without you, Marguerite.'

'How?' There was the faint stirring of compassion in her voice.

'How?' He took his cap off and pushed his hands through his hair. 'I can't think . . . Damn it, I've just missed you. Can't sleep properly. Can't concentrate.'

'Richard, you haven't been drinking, have you?'

Haldean felt acutely uncomfortable. There was concern dripping from Marguerite's voice. If she and Whitfield were going to be reconciled, he didn't want to be a witness.

'No. Yes. Of course I've been drinking.'

Haldean began to plan his retreat when a remark from Whitfield brought him up sharp. 'It would be bad enough without that tame dago of yours thinking I know more than I should. All this on top of it is awful.'

Tame dago! Haldean drew his breath in. Talk about listeners never hearing any good of themselves . . .

Marguerite was puzzled. 'Do you mean Jack? What does he think about you, Richard?'

'He made it pretty plain the other night he thought I was being blackmailed by Boscombe. Pestering me about what Boscombe wanted with me at the fête and so on. Damned cheek. I didn't take it lying down, I can tell you. I don't think I'll have any more nonsense like that in a hurry, not after the reception I gave him.'

Haldean bit his lip. So that's why Whitfield had been so rattled the other night. It wasn't Marguerite he'd been worried about but himself. Stupid devil. Didn't he know he was in the clear? Surely the Chief Constable would have told him as much, even if Ashley hadn't. So what was he getting so worked up about? And what reception? Who was he trying to kid? *Tame dago*, indeed!

'Marguerite,' Whitfield continued. 'It's . . . It's taken me all my courage to come here. I tried to see you yesterday but it was no good. I keep trying to understand why any of this should have happened. I don't know why your trustee should have taken against me. I've done nothing to him and it's been damned embarrassing to have to tell you about Anne-Marie.'

Marguerite looked at him thoughtfully and came to a decision. 'Marry me, Richard.'

'*What?*'

Now that, thought Haldean with some satisfaction, had taken the wind out of his sails.'Let's go away together and get married,' said Marguerite firmly. 'What are you waiting for?'

167

Whitfield swallowed. 'But we can't do that. It's got to be approved by your trustees.'

Her mouth compressed into a thin line. 'So much for your feelings. I'm not completely stupid, Richard. I know as well as you do that if I marry without their consent they'll simply withhold my money.'

Good for you, Haldean breathed in silent approval.

'It's not that,' Whitfield bit back angrily. 'It's not that at all. I want to marry you properly, openly, not in some wretched underhand way. If you'd speak up for me, Marguerite, I'm sure Lawrence would change his mind. Why the devil shouldn't he? It's been hell since the other night. What the devil can he have against me? Speak up for me, Marguerite. *Make* him change his mind.'

Keeping her eyes fixed on him she slowly remounted her bicycle. 'I don't really see why I should.'

'Because . . .' He strode forward and took her shoulders in his hands. 'Because of this.'

As Whitfield grabbed hold of Marguerite, Haldean started forward. The bicycle half fell to the ground and there was a confused, struggling moment where she tried to wrestle free. Whitfield tried to kiss her but she wriggled furiously and his lips met empty air. There was a sharp crack and he started back, holding his hand to his cheek. Haldean retreated the few steps back to the gate. Marguerite didn't need his help.

Marguerite, nursing her throbbing hand, for she had smacked him very hard indeed, glared savagely. 'Don't ever – *ever* – try that again.' And with that she picked up the fallen bicycle and set off down the drive, anger showing in every line of her body.

Whitfield stepped back, hand to his reddening face, watching the departing girl. 'Oh, bloody hell,' he said to himself. 'Oh, bloody *hell*.'

Haldean ran across the park back to the house. He wanted to intercept Marguerite before she stormed in. In her present mood and with Mrs Verrity there, there would be fireworks unless he could stop her. By cutting off the

168

angle of the drive, he reached the side door as Marguerite arrived.

Half-blinded by angry tears she didn't see him. She flung her bicycle against the wall of the stables and, furiously wiping the back of her hand across her eyes, marched up the steps and into the hallway of the house.

'Marguerite!' he called, catching hold of her arm.

She whirled on him. 'You!'

'Have a hanky,' he said practically, holding it out to her.

She dashed his hand away. 'How dare you!' she began.

'Marguerite?' asked Lady Rivers, appearing in the doorway of the drawing room. She was flanked by Hugh Lawrence, Isabelle and Mrs Verrity. Haldean felt his heart sink. 'Marguerite, whatever's wrong?'

She shook herself free of Haldean's hand. 'He is!' she shouted, jabbing her finger into Haldean's chest. 'He said Richard was being blackmailed. It's a horrible thing to say. He can't have done anything wrong, I know he can't, and I don't know if he wants me or my money and I hate everyone involved with this and I hate myself because I don't know if he's telling the truth or not and if I really did care for him I *would*.' She raised her eyes and pointed to where Hugh Lawrence stood. 'And I hate what *he's* done to Richard and I wish I were dead!'

'Oh, come on, Marguerite,' said Haldean, rubbing his chest. 'You don't mean that.'

'Yes I do!' she snarled, whirling on him once more. Haldean prudently stepped back a pace. 'Mr Lawrence, why are you so against Richard? He's explained everything to me –' Mrs Verrity gave a lift of her eyebrows – 'but I don't know why you dislike him so. You've always refused to tell me. Tell me now.'

'Now is hardly the time,' he said quietly.

'What's wrong with now?' she demanded. 'If you do know anything bad about Richard, tell me.'

'*Is* there anything, Mr Lawrence?' asked Mrs Verrity. 'After all, it seems an ideal match on the face of it.' Her voice was light but her expression puzzled Haldean. It was as if she were waiting. That was it. Waiting.

Marguerite stared at her. 'An ideal match? After all you said to him? How can you?'

'Marguerite!' Lady Rivers spoke in shocked surprise. 'Please withdraw that remark immediately.'

Mrs Verrity waved her silent, her eyes fixed on the girl. 'No. Don't withdraw it. Explain it.'

'I . . . I . . .' began Marguerite. 'I know you don't want Richard to marry me,' she said desperately.

'I?' Mrs Verrity didn't look disturbed or annoyed; merely curious. 'Why should I have any feelings on the matter? Colonel Whitfield is an old acquaintance but that is all. Who he marries is a matter of complete indifference to me.'

'Oh!' Marguerite stared at her, then dropped her eyes. 'I don't understand,' she said miserably. 'I just don't understand.'

Isabelle came from behind her mother and took Marguerite's arm. 'Come with me, Maggie. We'll go and sit down somewhere and you can tell me all about it. For heaven's sake, get out of the way, Jack, you're blocking the doorway. Come on.' Isabelle glanced round as if to say 'It's all right now,' and Marguerite let herself be led away.

'Well!' said Lady Rivers as they went back into the drawing room. She shut the door behind her and shook her head. 'I must apologize for Marguerite's behaviour. I really don't know what got into her. Jack, do you know what's behind it?'

'She's just seen Colonel Whitfield,' said Haldean. 'I knew she was upset and I tried to stop her from coming in here. I'm sorry I didn't handle it better. She'll feel awful when she realizes how she's behaved.'

Mrs Verrity shrugged. 'She is upset about her young man. When these affairs march badly then it is only natural. Of course it was I to whom Colonel Whitfield was talking when she heard his unfortunate outburst, so it is understandable, perhaps, that she should involve me.

170

Major Haldean, did you really say that Richard was being blackmailed?'

'Of course I didn't. I said nothing of the sort.'

She looked up with a little smile. 'He has, as you say, the wrong end of the stick? But such an accusation would upset him very much.'

'I guess it'd upset any man,' said Hugh Lawrence.

She turned and smiled at him. 'Mr Lawrence, you too came in for some criticism. Do excuse me, but I am a foreigner and therefore have, perhaps, an imperfect grasp of the etiquette in these matters, but I am curious as to why you refused your consent to Miss Vayle's marriage to Richard. I gather you have but there seems to be no obvious reason why you should.'

Mr Lawrence smiled back and shook his head. 'I'm afraid you aren't going to draw me that way, Mrs Verrity. I don't like the guy. Simple as that. I've never believed he could give a snap of his fingers for the girl and I've always said as much. And after the other night who's to say I'm wrong? You heard him, Major Haldean heard him, Marguerite heard him and as far as I'm concerned he's through.'

'So you know nothing?'

'How could I? I'm sure I could find something if I did a bit of digging but the past is the past. As long as he keeps out of Marguerite's way that'll be fine by me. He can do what he likes and good luck to him. I'll go back to Canada and he'll never hear of me again. But there's one thing for sure. He's not going to touch a penny of that girl's money.'

'You are very blunt, Mr Lawrence.'

He grinned at her, the lines round his eyes crinkling. 'I guess I am, aren't I? Why don't you put it down to an imperfect grasp of etiquette?'

Haldean opened the gate out of the top paddock of the

Whitfield estate, standing by to latch it shut after Ashley. 'Did you say that Whitfield was a bit perturbed?'

'Colonel Whitfield,' said Ashley, 'is hopping mad. You seem to have got up his nose good and proper. He saw the Chief again this morning. I suppose he was all worked up after his scene with Miss Vayle, but you came in for some fairly vigorous criticism. '

'My heart is broken and my spirit crushed,' replied Haldean, shutting the gate.

The stables were swathed in a deep blanket of summer afternoon silence, but Young Alfred had informed them that, although the master weren't about, he should be coming along Rickett's Lane soon enough. Screwing his eyes up in the sun, he had professed his astonishment that the gennel'men didn't mind where Rickett's Lane was; waving an explanatory hand in the direction of the top paddock he averred they couldn't miss it. And, oddly enough, they couldn't. The lane ran out of Breedenbrook, up to the fields belonging to the livery stables and stopped at the gate before straggling off humbly as a path across the Downs.

Haldean leaned against the flint-studded gatepost, tipping his hat slightly forward to shield his eyes from the sun. A fresh breeze brought a hint of the distant sea mixed with the scent of grass, thyme and clover. Not far away the roofs of Thackenhurst were visible, but not even a wisp of smoke disturbed the still air. A flock of black-faced sheep on a distant slope were the only other living things in sight. He breathed a deep sigh of contentment and looked at Ashley. 'What did Whitfield tell the Chief I'd done?'

'Hinted that he's been mixed up in blackmail.'

Haldean broke off a piece of grass and chewed it thoughtfully. 'The odd thing is, you know, that I did nothing of the sort. I told you everything that happened at the ball. I'll grant I was a bit short with him, but he'd needled me. I talked about blackmail, certainly, but only because he knew all about it already, thanks to the Chief Constable.

I say, Ashley, you're not in trouble because of anything I've done, are you?'

Ashley sucked his cheeks in. 'I can't say the Chief's happy but that, to be honest, is his business. If he hadn't insisted on telling Whitfield all about it, then none of this would have happened in the first place. But look here, Haldean, you don't think Whitfield really was being blackmailed, do you?'

'I didn't. To be honest it had never occurred to me. When he went up like a rocket I thought he was getting agitated on Marguerite's behalf. I'm not nearly so sure now after what I heard the pompous ass say this morning. D'you know he called me a dago?'

'You said. But he can't possibly have murdered Boscombe. We know that.'

'I'm not saying he did, but he could be another one of Boscombe and Morton's victims. He'd fit the bill, actually, and that would account for him going off pop. He used to be well off, but he isn't any more. Is that a result of bad investments, taxes or blackmail?'

'The last two are more or less the same thing, aren't they?' put in Ashley.

Haldean grinned. 'As you say. Anyway, last autumn he sold two of his brood mares about the same time as Boscombe and Morton cashed in. It might be coincidence, or it might not be. He's got a position and a reputation to keep up and in one thing at least, I know him to have told an outright lie. He said Boscombe had wanted him to write a preface for his book. As far as I can make out that's not actually true. I spent a smoulderingly hot afternoon yesterday trailing round all the likely London publishers to see if any of them had been in touch with Boscombe and requested a preface. The only publishers who had seen the book were the ones I'd originally recommended, Drake and Sanderson, and, as far as they were concerned, Boscombe had withdrawn his manuscript. They certainly hadn't requested a preface from anyone.'

173

'Could Boscombe have wanted a preface by Colonel Whitfield to make his book easier to sell?'

'But why? Drake and Sanderson were perfectly happy with it. To be fair, I can't disprove what Whitfield said, but I don't half suspect it. I think he was lying to cover up what Boscombe had actually said. What that was I don't know.'

Ashley took out his pipe and slowly filled it. 'I'm going to ask the Colonel. It seems the most straightforward way to me. By the way, did you ever get to the bottom of why Mr Lawrence is so against him marrying Miss Vayle?'

Haldean shrugged. 'Belle's convinced it's because he's stuck on her himself. She might be right, or it may be that Lawrence knows something about Whitfield that's none too pleasant. I'd wish you'd heard the exchange between Mrs Verrity and Lawrence this morning. I might be reading too much into it, but it had that significant quality, if you know what I mean. Teemed with hidden meaning and all of that. I've given you the gist of it, but I wish you'd been there.'

'What sort of hidden meaning?'

Haldean hesitated. 'It sounded as if Lawrence was threatening Whitfield through Mrs Verrity if Whitfield didn't stop making a nuisance of himself to Marguerite. Pass your tobacco over, Ashley. I haven't knocked off smoking, you know.'

Ashley handed over his pouch. 'But what the devil was he threatening him *with*? If Mr Lawrence knows something or suspects something about Whitfield, why on earth doesn't he tell us? There's no love lost between them, that's for sure.'

Haldean, having discarded the stalk of grass, was busy filling his pipe. 'Rotten, this, isn't it?' he said, with a sideways glance at Ashley. 'Two solid, hard, unpalatable facts in the form of murder and a mountain of speculation. D'you think we'll get there?'

Ashley shook his head. 'I haven't always, you know, in other cases. I've had my suspicions often enough as

174

to the rights of things, but evidence? That's another matter.' A faint continuous noise sounded in the distance, causing him to look up. 'Hello, is this the Colonel? It's about time.'

They looked down the lane. The black shape of a man on horseback breasted the ridge of the hill at a steady clip, the features blotted out by the sun at his back. Haldean squinted and waved. 'It's him all right.'

The horse cantered towards them before it suddenly stopped, head tossed back and feet splaying in a jinking dance to one side. The head tossed again, ears flat against its skull. Whitfield seemed to be fighting to stay on its back. He leaned over its neck, struggling for control, then, with a braying whinny, the horse thundered towards them.

'Run!' shouted Ashley in shocked disbelief. He instinctively pulled Haldean to one side. 'Run!'

With a jolt of pain Haldean felt his leg go at the knee, sending him sprawling in the dust. There was a brief sight of white, maddened eyes, steel-shod hooves, kicking legs and a monstrous black bulk towering above. He rolled away desperately as the hooves crashed down inches from his ear. The horse reared again. Haldean scrambled to his knees, shying away, then something struck his head in a star-shell of blackness.

Whitfield clung on to the horse's back, one hand matted in the mane. The beast reared and plunged once more, sending him flying. He sprawled in the dust, rolling away from the raging horse. Ashley's world seemed to slow to a crawl. With great deliberation he edged his way between the flailing hooves and the gate. He found the catch and swung the gate back, part of his mind standing back and marvelling at the precision of his movements and the clearness of his thoughts. With the gate open and its way clear, the horse galloped through and raced across the field, where it came to a halt, shivering.

The spell was broken. The world snapped back to its

175

normal speed and with it came noise; a groan from Whitfield, birdsong, the rustle of trees, but absolute silence from Haldean. Ignoring Whitfield, Ashley knelt down by Haldean's side, and carefully touched the blood-caked hair. Resolutely thrusting down the weary sickness that enveloped him, Ashley put a hand on Haldean's chest, closing his eyes with gratitude as he felt the heart quicken beneath the shirt.

There was a scuffle on the road beside him and Whitfield, white-faced and shaking, stood next to them, nursing his upper arm. 'Is he all right? Satan – the horse – I couldn't hold him. He has a filthy temper. Is he all right?' Ashley nodded, not trusting his voice. 'You saw I couldn't hold him? You saw that? Are you sure he's all right?'

'He needs a doctor.'

'A doctor?' Whitfield winced. 'So do I.' He glanced down at Haldean. 'I'll stay here while you go for help.'

'No!' Ashley jerked the word out involuntarily. In Whitfield's glance he had seen something that was there for only a fraction of a second, but which Ashley knew, knew beyond all argument, was hatred. In those few hundredths of a second all his suspicions flared and focused on the man, leaving him utterly certain that he had just witnessed an attempt at cold-blooded murder.

He saw Whitfield's eyes widen in surprise and forced himself to pick his words carefully. There had to be a reason. Think! *I'm not leaving him with you* . . . He couldn't say that. 'You can walk. It's better if you go because you can give instructions to your men.' Steady, commanding voice now, Superintendent. 'Off you go, sir. Every moment may be precious.'

Whitfield paused then nodded, before half-walking, half-stumbling through the gate, across the field, past the now shivering and quiescent horse and into the stable yard.

Ashley loosened Haldean's tie and undid his collar. Taking off his own jacket and bundling it into a pillow he carefully raised the younger man's head and slipped it underneath. As he did so, Haldean stirred and, to Ashley's unspeakable relief, flickered his eyelids open.

'My head hurts,' he whispered.

'You're lucky you've still got one,' said Ashley, his voice oddly shaky. Haldean attempted to sit up. 'For God's sake, man, stay still, will you? Whitfield's gone for a doctor.'

Haldean subsided back on to the jacket and shut his eyes. 'Whitfield? I remember. Whitfield on the horse. He was dancing.'

'Dancing?' Ashley wondered if the injury had affected Haldean's mind. 'Whitfield wasn't dancing.'

Haldean made a slight, impatient motion with his hand and flickered his eyes open again. 'The horse. Danced to one side. They do that – oh, my blasted head! – when they don't know what to do. Conflicting instructions. Charge. Stay still. The horse bolts. He set it up.'

'Quietly does it.' Ashley swallowed and took the plunge. 'I think so too.'

'Good man.' Haldean closed his eyes and breathed deeply. 'Can't prove it. Can't prove anything . . .'

'You'll live,' said Dr Wilcott succinctly. 'You'll probably suffer from concussion to some degree but you've got off very lightly, all things considered.'

Haldean, who had endured being lifted on to a home-made stretcher and carried to the tack room where he had submitted with gritted teeth to the doctor's examination, couldn't quite agree. 'My head's throbbing like the dickens.'

'Lie down. Of course it's hurting.' He looked at Ashley. 'Has he been totally rational? Giddy? Bad-tempered? Shown signs of drowsiness?'

'You sound like an advert for a liver pill,' murmured the patient from the tack-room table. Dr Wilcott allowed himself a smile. 'I feel sick and I want to go to sleep,' he mumbled heavily.

Dr Wilcott cocked an eyebrow at Ashley. 'Well?'

'He's been quite rational, Doctor, but sleepy, as he's said.'

'In that case the best thing is complete rest in a darkened room . . .' He looked up as Buckman, touching his forehead respectfully, creaked the door open. 'What is it?'

Buckman ignored the doctor and spoke to Whitfield who was sitting on a broken-back chair, nursing his arm. 'Here's Mrs Verrity to see you, sir. I told her as how there'd been an accident, and she wanted to come in. Here she is, sir.'

'Can't you –' began Whitfield, breaking off as Mrs Verrity came into the room. She was dressed in tight-fitting jodhpurs and a hacking jacket and looked, if possible, even more striking than she had done in her ballgown. However the sight of her seemed to afford Whitfield very little pleasure. 'I didn't think you were coming this afternoon,' he said with poor grace.

'Nonsense, Richard,' she said, taking in the scene. 'Buckman tells me Satan bolted.'

'I couldn't hold him,' he said, looking her straight in the eyes. 'I've crocked my arm. It's not broken but it jolly well feels like it and he damn nearly killed Haldean here. Trampled him down.'

Mrs Verrity looked at Haldean with a quick, appraising glance. 'A head wound? That could so easily have been fatal.' Haldean made a futile attempt to sit up and she suddenly smiled. 'I am glad to see it was not.' She looked at Wilcott who had unwittingly straightened up to his full height and was adjusting his tie. 'You are the doctor, yes? Is he in any danger?'

'Not now,' said Wilcott. 'He'll have a nasty headache for a day or so and various bruises, but he'll live. No doubt about that.'

She tensed for a moment, then her shoulders relaxed in an almost imperceptible movement. 'And what happens to him now? He is not fit to be driven home, that is obvious.'

'Good Lord, no. He needs something cold on that head. Ice is the best thing, if you have it, and he needs to avoid eating for a day. Fluids but no alcohol. Drink can have very funny effects on concussion cases. That, together with total bed-rest in a darkened room until tomorrow at least, should see him on his feet again.'

'He'd better stay here,' put in Whitfield.

Ashley opened his mouth to speak, but was beaten to it by Mrs Verrity. 'I think not, Richard. After all, you are injured yourself and I doubt if you would be able to give Major Haldean the care he deserves.' She bent over Haldean and stroked the hair away from his forehead. 'You will come to me, to my house? And I will telephone Lady Rivers to send someone to sit with you. It is better that you are not left by yourself, I think.' She glanced at the doctor. 'He will need to be carried there, of course, but it is only a short way over the fields. Can you arrange for that to be done?'

'Certainly,' said Wilcott. 'If he can't be looked after here that sounds like the best solution. If I may use your telephone, Colonel, I can organize things right away. And I must say, Mrs Verrity, that I'm very grateful to you for your help, and yours, Colonel. I don't know about that horse, though. It's not the first time it's caused an accident, I believe. I think you may have to consider having it destroyed.'

Whitfield shifted on his chair. 'It's a damn fine horse, but you might be right. Look, Anne-Marie, I hate to land you with an invalid.' He caught her gaze with his. 'Wouldn't it be better for everyone if Haldean stayed here?'

'No, Richard,' said Mrs Verrity, firmly. 'I think I should take care of Major Haldean. I will call later on and tell you how he is, but first I would like to speak to Lady Rivers.'

Whitfield shrugged, wincing as the movement caught his arm. 'Just as you like. It's only . . . Well, if he stayed here I could have everything arranged for him.'

'I doubt that,' said Mrs Verrity. 'I don't think your

179

arrangements would suit the Major at all. I really think you had better leave the matter to me.'

'I don't like it,' said Ashley, instinctively lowering his voice.

The curtain flapped gently over the half-open window, bringing fluttering fragments of light over the rich bedroom carpet. Haldean stared at it as if mesmerized. The bed was soft and the linen sheets wonderfully cool. He wanted to go to sleep so much it was horribly hard to force himself to speak. 'I'll be all right now.'

'I certainly wasn't going to let you stay with Whitfield, that's for sure, even if I'd ended up carrying you home myself. I haven't got to the bottom of what's going on, but he's up to something.'

'Yes. Good alibi. Can't break it. I might be wrong.' Haldean closed his eyes, feeling sleep mounting like a tidal wave. 'Mrs Verrity doesn't trust him. Do you trust her?'

'At the moment I don't trust anyone but she wanted you away from there nearly as much as I did. I've got to say that Mrs Verrity's been very good. The first thing she did was telephone Hesperus. Your aunt and Miss Rivers are on their way over.'

'Fine. Sorry about the fuss . . . Decent of Belle to come too. I wish I understood things. Better ask Aunt Alice not to leave me alone.'

'Don't worry,' said Ashley grimly. 'I'll make a point of it.'

The next morning, Isabelle and Lady Rivers decided that Haldean, who was sound asleep, was well enough to be left while they went down to breakfast.

Mrs Verrity looked up with a welcoming smile as they entered the room. 'Good morning. How is Major Haldean? Please help yourself to some breakfast from the sideboard, by the way. If there is anything else you would rather have, please say so.'

180

As the sideboard held eggs, sausages, bacon, kidneys, mushrooms, ham, porridge, kedgeree, bread and fruit, it seemed unlikely that there could be anything else that could be wanted for breakfast. Fighting down a mischievous urge to ask for kippers, Isabelle helped herself to bacon and eggs. Mrs Verrity, she noticed, was breakfasting on grapefruit and thinly buttered bread. You didn't get to keep a figure like that by tucking into sausages and ham. 'Can I get you something, Mother?'

'Scrambled eggs, please, dear,' said Lady Rivers, sitting down and taking a sip of the coffee Mrs Verrity had poured for her. 'I'm glad to say Jack had a restful night. When Dr Wilcott arrives I'm sure he will let Jack come home with us. I must thank you again, Mrs Verrity, for your very great kindness. We couldn't have been made more comfortable under the circumstances, could we, Isabelle?'

Thackenhurst was, Isabelle thought, comfortable to the point of luxury. Mrs Verrity obviously had no intention of putting up with the draughts, damp or cold that were almost mandatory in a country house. Although the morning room retained its Regency proportions and a beautiful Adam fireplace, there were also radiators, thick carpets and windows which stayed placidly in their frames without the hint of a rattle. Add to that finely polished walnut, gleaming glass and servants deferential enough to be nearly inaudible, and it was difficult to know whether to envy or admire Mrs Verrity's taste. The only fault Isabelle could find was that the atmosphere created by all this well-being wasn't very English. The French, she thought, had a great deal of sense.

'No, we were very comfortable, thank you,' she said, giving her mother her eggs.

'Think nothing of it,' said Mrs Verrity. 'I am pleased to have been of help. If he had stayed with Colonel Whitfield it could have been difficult. He might have been served with oats and branmash for breakfast!' She smiled at her own joke. 'If your little Marguerite does marry the

Colonel, she will need to make many improvements in the house.'

'I can't see there's much chance of that any more,' said Lady Rivers. 'And really, after hearing what he said at the ball, I should be obliged to advise Marguerite against it.'

Mrs Verrity shook her head. 'Please don't be misled by circumstances. Poor Richard wasn't thinking – correctly? straightly? – that evening. Like a lot of Englishmen he is ashamed at being caught out in an emotion and would rather have some stern, practical reason for his actions. But we are women and can talk without foolishness. He is, in your phrase, not himself, since their quarrel. I went to see him last night, as you know, and he deeply regrets all that has happened.'

'Perhaps . . .' said Lady Rivers, cautiously, but was surprised by pent-up emotion in Mrs Verrity's expression.

'I am worried about him. I have known Richard for many years now and I have never seen him like this. I am fond of him, yes? And I don't like to see what he is doing to himself.'

'What is he doing to himself?' asked Isabelle.

Mrs Verrity looked round quickly as if afraid of being overheard, then leant forward confidentially. 'He drinks. Oh, so much he drinks. Never have I seen him like this before. And his nerves, they are all in shreds. Take the accident yesterday, for example. I doubt that would have happened in normal circumstances. Satan is a brute and ought to be destroyed but Richard has always managed to control him in the past. But please, Lady Rivers, do not doubt the sincerity of his feelings for Miss Vayle. I do not say that he could afford to marry a poor woman –' she gave an expressive shrug of her shoulders – 'but he certainly would not marry a rich one simply for her money.' The oddest expression flickered across her face. 'That I do know. That I really do know . . .' She looked away for a moment, then glanced up with a determined smile. 'But that is by the way. He is talking about writing to Mr Lawrence to arrange a meeting. He feels that if only they could discuss matters properly then Mr Lawrence would be won over. After all, it is hard to see what rational objection anyone could have to Richard. The only reason I can think of is one I couldn't broach with him.'

'What's that?' asked Lady Rivers.

Mrs Verrity looked at her in surprise. 'Why, that Mr Lawrence has a penchant for the girl. Surely you must have considered that idea?'

'I haven't given the matter any thought,' said Lady Rivers, stiffly.

'Oh, but you must. After all, if that were the reason, how easy things would be –' Mrs Verrity broke off suddenly and went to stand beside the window. Isabelle caught her mother's eye, opened her mouth to speak, but was dissuaded by Lady Rivers' slight shake of her head. It was Lady Rivers herself who eventually broke the silence.

'I am sorry, Mrs Verrity. I hadn't realized that you had taken Colonel Whitfield's interests so much to heart.'

She did turn then, meeting Lady Rivers' concerned look with a wry smile. 'His interests? Well, it's inevitable, isn't it? As I said, I have known Richard for many years and it's only natural I should be concerned for him. I am, as you know, older than he is. I feel . . . Let me think how to put it . . . I feel motherly towards him.'

Isabelle finished her breakfast in silence, feeling a genuine stab of sympathy for her. Motherly? She didn't doubt Mrs Verrity's emotions, but motherly? Not in a million years.

'My head,' said Haldean, touching his bandage, 'is bloody but unbowed. 'Scuse the language, Ashley, old thing, but it's poetry and doesn't count.'

'It's good to see you back safely,' said Ashley, leaning over the balustrade. They were standing on the terrace at Hesperus. Haldean had been given permission by Dr Wilcott to return home provided he took things easy. 'I don't mind telling you I was having kittens at the thought of leaving you to Whitfield's tender mercies. I take it Mrs Verrity looked after you all right?'

'She was first-rate,' said Haldean seriously. 'And damn good to Belle and Aunt Alice, too. Look, I know it all seemed perfectly clear yesterday, but was it an accident? Or was I being unnecessarily dramatic about the whole thing?' Ashley gave him a long look in reply. 'I see . . . And Mrs Verrity obviously thought there was something dodgy about things too. I mean, I remember her acting like a cat on hot bricks at Whitfield's suggestion he should look after me. Thinking, I suppose, that there might not be a me in the morning.' He took out his cigarette case and offered it to Ashley. 'Which means, of course, two things. One, I owe her a thundering great debt of gratitude which I happily acknowledge, and two . . .' He tapped his cigarette on the back of his hand. 'That she knows, or at least suspects, that Whitfield's capable of murder. They're very old friends,' he added absently. 'In fact, according to Belle, she's in love with the man.'

'What?' Ashley laughed. 'Come *on*. Not seriously. Whitfield might have said as much to Miss Vayle, but that's nothing more than vanity, surely? I know Miss Vayle's eating out her heart for him but don't try and tell me the glamorous Mrs Verrity's been smitten as well. The other way round, yes, I grant you, but dash it, Haldean, they can't all be in love with him.'

'Why not?' He threw his match away and gave Ashley a quizzical stare. 'He's a remarkably good-looking man, a hero – don't forget the VC – and he's known her for years. She, one would think, could have her pick, but is that really so? She's older than he is and that might have made the difference. It's not fair, is it? No one thinks twice about a woman marrying a man ten years older than herself but the other way round is odd. I know it happens but it's always thought to be odd.'

'Well, it is odd,' said Ashley, dismissing this social conundrum. 'Besides, a woman like that? Come off it. I went to see Whitfield last night, you know, but I couldn't get much sense out of him. He was so half-seas over that I had a job to make him realize who I was. I did wonder if he was suffering from concussion and had ignored Dr Wilcott's advice to lay off the booze, but I think that's a charitable assessment. He certainly sank enough while I was there.'

'Did you get anything out of him?'

'Not a thing, apart from the fact that brute of a horse has a nasty temper and his arm hurts. The mention of Lawrence sent him off pop. He's really got a grudge against him.'

'You don't say. I can't blame him for that, because there's no getting away from the fact that it's Mr Lawrence who's scuppered his plans to do the wedding march. Mr Lawrence says it's simply because he doesn't like the man and for all I know that could be the top and bottom of it, but I can't help . . .'

There was a noise of the french windows opening and they turned to see Mr Lawrence himself come out on to the terrace. He smiled as he walked towards them.

'Just the men I wanted. I did wonder if you'd gone to your room, Major, but Lady Rivers told me you were out here. You look a bit peaky to me.'

'Oh, I'm not too bad, you know. I'll probably have a rest later but I've spent so much time in bed lately that it's nice to be up and about again.'

'Just so long as you don't go overdoing it. Your aunt and uncle were worried about you yesterday when the news came through of your accident. Yes, sir, very worried indeed.' He leaned his elbow against the balustrade and looked at Haldean thoughtfully. 'I've got a question for you that you might think kind of strange.' He paused, drumming his fingers. 'It's just this – and I've got a reason for asking. Was it an accident, Major?'

Haldean and Ashley exchanged looks. 'It certainly appeared so,' said Haldean, feeling his way. 'Why do you want to know?'

Lawrence half-laughed. 'Because I'm as fond of my neck

as most men.' He took a letter out of his pocket and held it out towards them. 'That came by the afternoon post. I'm inclined to go but it did strike me I might be running into trouble.'

Haldean took the letter out of the envelope and held it so Ashley could read it as well.

Dear Mr Lawrence: In an attempt to resolve the differences between us I think it would be mutually beneficial if we could meet to discuss the situation, which I am frankly beginning to find intolerable. I have no quarrel with you, apart from your opposition to my marriage to Miss Vayle, and would be interested to hear the reasons for your stance. It may be that you do not wish to come to my house and, under the circumstances, I do not feel able to come to Hesperus. I would therefore suggest we meet at the old tithe barn on the junction of Rickett's Lane and Gallows Hill at eleven o'clock on Saturday morning. Although technically on my land the barn is unused and we should be free of any interruption. I await your reply, Yours etc., R. T. Whitfield.

Haldean put the letter back in the envelope and returned it to Lawrence.

'Are you going?'

'I don't know,' said Lawrence. 'Was it an accident yesterday? Because it occurred to me that the quickest way out of R. T. Whitfield's problem might be to remove me from the scene altogether. And yet . . . if I saw him face to face I may be able to settle his hash once and for all. He's making Marguerite unhappy. Even after what he said she's still got a hankering for him and I'd like to quash it properly.'

'Do you think you can do that, sir?' asked Haldean.

'Oh yes, I reckon I can. Money, as they say, talks. So, gentlemen, what about it? Was it an accident?'

Ashley took a deep breath. 'It was a very suspicious sort of accident. But that, Mr Lawrence, is strictly between the three of us.'

'I see. Well, forewarned is forearmed. And if the guy's looking for a fight, he can have one.'

Haldean looked uneasy. 'Are you really going alone?'

'I certainly am. Marguerite saw the writing on the envelope and managed to wriggle the truth out of me. She's on fire to come along, but that's out of the question, of course.' He rested his chin in his hand, thinking, then shook his head. 'I'm probably making a mountain out of a molehill. If he intended any funny business I don't suppose he'd write so openly to me. He must've known I'd show it to someone.'

'Yes . . . Well, it's up to you, Mr Lawrence. But if you do want a companion, all you have to do is say so.'

'No. It may be I'll want to express myself in a way I couldn't with someone else listening. If I am going to tell Colonel Whitfield a few home truths about himself, I don't want to have to put a guard on my tongue.' He gave a quick smile. 'In fact, the more I think about it, the more I'm looking forward to it.'

'I wish you'd let me come with you, sir,' said Haldean, seriously. 'I can't help thinking that there might be another – well, shall we say "accident"?'

'He'd be a fool to try anything. No. I guess I'll be safe enough tomorrow.' He looked at Haldean's worried expression and grinned. 'But if he meets me on horseback, I'll be careful.'

Haldean drew the Spyker into the side of the road beside the empty Hillman tourer. Five to eleven. He looked up the winding, deserted lane. It was little more than a track which led to Gallows Hill. It was a road of great contrasts. On one side of the lane ran the high, brick and well-maintained walls of Thackenhurst, glowing a mellow red in the morning sun. On the other side, lying in deep shadow, ran a broken fence enclosing a verge of docks, nettles and scrubby trees. The dark bulk of the barn was just visible through the branches.

He got out of the car and, walking to the Hillman, touched the bonnet. It was still warm. Lawrence had insisted on driving himself, despite the offer of a lift. He ruefully acknowledged a slight sense of relief that he didn't have to explain his presence. Lawrence had been very certain that he wanted to be alone with Whitfield and he wouldn't take kindly to having his footsteps dogged like this. And yet . . .

Haldean leaned against the maroon car and, idly taking a cigarette from his case, gave himself up to a proper examination of his motives for coming. He wished he could have talked things over with Greg, but Greg was in London.

He didn't trust Whitfield. Not now. Not after having seen the way the horse had been forced to act. It was forced, he was sure of it. He struck a match and lit his cigarette, the scrape of the match against the box sounding loud in the silence. It was abnormally quiet and, although the sun was warm, he shivered. Eerie . . . Which was nonsense, he told himself sternly, but there was something creepy about the silent, rutted lane that no amount of brisk common sense could dispel. He wished he could see the barn properly and thought of walking further up the lane, but didn't want to run the risk of being seen by Mr Lawrence. He had a healthy respect for the man's temper. He wouldn't take kindly to being followed and Haldean could hardly blame him.

So why did Whitfield want to see Mr Lawrence? To change his mind? Fat chance. Mr Lawrence was a very stubborn man. Did Whitfield realize that? Probably not. He wasn't the most perceptive of characters and might think all he had to do was talk to Mr Lawrence. He couldn't – could he? – be intending to harm the man.

Haldean sucked deeply on his cigarette. That was, of course, what he was afraid of. It would be incredibly clumsy but Whitfield wasn't a very subtle bloke. What on earth *was* going on? He was certain Whitfield was innocent of Boscombe's death, so why, in God's name, had the talk of blackmail rattled him enough to drive him to that ham-fisted attempt at murder? Come to think of it, was it so ham-fisted? After all, another fraction of an inch and it would have succeeded, and all anyone would have been able to say was that it had been a tragic accident caused by a notoriously bad-tempered horse. Even now he couldn't put his hand on his heart and swear it was anything else. He just thought it was, and his thoughts weren't evidence. If it had come off, it would have been a damn good murder. An impulsive murder, taking advantage of circumstances with Superintendent Ashley standing by as an unimpeachable witness.

He threw away his cigarette in irritation, glancing through the scrubby trees at the barn. For all the use he was, he might as well have stayed at home. Lawrence would be all right, wouldn't he? He certainly hadn't wanted any company while he swapped home truths with Whitfield. But *what* home truths, for heaven's sake? *You're only after Marguerite's money . . .* That wouldn't come as a surprise to anyone. Lawrence had been saying it loud and long ever since he had arrived. Maybe – and Lawrence had hinted as much – he was going to buy off the Colonel and didn't want anyone to know the size of the deal. He certainly expected the meeting to be forthright. Haldean glanced at his watch again. Eleven o'clock. If anything was going to happen, it should be happening now.

Did Lawrence know anything discreditable about Whitfield? Because if he –

A sharp crack rang out. Haldean stiffened. That was a shot. It came from the lane, surely? A second later he was racing up the track, appalled by what he saw.

Chapter Ten

Half-walking, half-staggering, Lawrence came round the bend in the road. He dropped to his knees and, as Haldean reached him, was trying to stand up. There was a gash on his forehead and a livid mark on his cheek. His hair was grimy with dirt, straw and cobwebs, and his jacket and shirt were streaked with dust. He tried to speak, but no words came. Haldean stooped down and put an arm under his shoulders.

'Steady now, steady . . . Just get to the side of the road . . . That's better. What on earth happened?'

'Whitfield . . . Must have been Whitfield. Hit me.'

'Who fired that shot?'

'Shot?' Lawrence looked at him with blurred eyes. 'There wasn't a shot.' He sank down on the grass verge, bowed his head on to crooked knees, then, drawing a ragged breath, fumbled in his pocket for a hip flask. He vainly tried to undo it before Haldean took it from him and twisted the top off. Lawrence took a brief drink, coughing as the whisky hurt his throat. 'That's better.'

'Here.' Haldean knelt down, took the flask, tipped some of the spirit on to his handkerchief and held it to the gash on Lawrence's forehead.

Lawrence's eye's widened. 'Thanks – I guess. Gee, that stings.' He looked at Haldean sharply. 'What the *hell* are you doing here? I thought I told you I didn't want company.'

'I thought you might need it all the same. I wasn't going

to interfere but I decided to come in case . . . Well, in case something like this happened.'

'I suppose I should say thank you,' said Lawrence ruefully. 'Though when I say I want to be alone I'd like to be alone. That guy certainly packed a punch.'

'What happened?'

Lawrence shrugged, then winced. 'You tell me. All I know is that I stood outside the barn like a good boy and blamed fool, waiting for eleven o'clock to show on my watch. I couldn't hear anything and was beginning to think he hadn't come. I walked through the wicket door and – wham! Something hit me like a pile-driver. I went down and must've been out cold for a couple of minutes. When I came to I looked around, but there was no sign of Whitfield anywhere. So I got out and ran straight into you. When I get my hands on that guy . . .'

'Are you sure it was Whitfield?'

'Who the hell else could it've been? He asked me to come here. I guess he meant to kill me. He certainly hit me hard enough. He didn't stay around to find out though.'

Haldean stood up. 'I'd better have a look at the barn. Will you be all right for a few minutes?'

'I guess so, Major. But there's nothing there.'

Haldean left him sitting by the road and walked up the lane. As he approached the barn, he stopped to listen. Nothing. Senses alert, he walked quietly forward.

The barn stood to one side of the road, a solid, oak-built structure bearing the signs of many winters of dereliction. A short, deeply rutted and overgrown track led to huge double doors. Years ago they had swung open to admit farm carts, but now their hinges had long rusted into place. A wicket door cut into the wood stood open. He glanced round for a weapon and, picking up a fallen branch, walked down the grassy track. He saw, with a tightening of his lips, where blood had splashed on a clump of cow parsley. It was deathly quiet.

Using the branch he thrust back the wicket door so it slammed against the inside wall. The creak and bang of the

191

wood reverberated into silence. If anyone had been standing behind the door they certainly weren't there now. Very carefully, and hefting the branch like a club, he stepped over the rotting sill and into the barn. Nothing moved. He stood motionless, letting his eyes become accustomed to the dark, empty space. A rusting plough with a piled heap of sacks protruding beyond it lay at the far end. Scraps of junk – a broken bucket, odd pieces of metal, an old sink, a coil of chain and lengths of earthenware pipe – lay discarded against the wall. He stooped down, gazing at the dusty floor. His face hardened. A heavy old spade handle, its rusted iron rivets still attached, lay on the ground. The rivets were stained and there was a scrape of skin on the heads. There were definite marks of a disturbance by the door and tracks leading across the floor to the old plough. His eyes came to rest on the sacks and he gazed at them thoughtfully, eyebrows lifting.

A sound made him whirl and he turned to find Lawrence framed in the entrance.

'He isn't here, Major. Come on, we're wasting time. When I get my hands on that skunk he'll know about it.' He leaned heavily against the door. 'I suppose I'll have to get someone to look at my head first but afterwards he'd better –'

'Wait a moment.' Haldean walked round the edge of the barn, avoiding the signs of the scuffle in the dust.

'Come *on*, will you,' broke in Lawrence, impatiently.

Haldean looked down at the sacks and nodded. They were heaped up by the old plough and at first glance seemed innocent enough, but he hadn't been mistaken in what he thought he'd seen from the other side of the barn.

'Would you mind coming here, sir? Round the edge of the walls, if you don't mind. That's right . . .'

'I want to get out of here,' grumbled Lawrence, coming towards him. 'This is a waste . . . Good God!' He stopped and gazed down.

Lying on top of the sacks, his feet sticking out beyond

the plough, was Whitfield. A livid gash shadowed his chin and his collar was torn. His blue eyes stared sightlessly at the roof and he was holding a gun in his outstretched hand. The dark stain on his temple showed how he had died.

Lawrence made a choking noise in his throat and bent down to the body. Haldean quickly restrained him. 'Don't disturb it, Mr Lawrence. We've got to leave everything as it is. I'll just see . . .' He quickly touched Whitfield's forehead with his hand. It was still warm. He ran his forefinger over the dark stained temple and delicately rubbed his finger and thumb together. The blood had congealed. He glanced at his watch. Fourteen minutes past eleven.

'I don't understand,' broke in Lawrence. 'He must have committed suicide. You said you heard a shot, didn't you? He must have done it when I was unconscious. Maybe he thought he'd killed me or something. I simply don't understand. We've got to tell someone about this.'

'Yes . . . I don't suppose you recognize the gun, do you?'

'The gun? No, of course I don't. Let's get out of here, shall we? My head's splitting and the sooner the police know about this the better.' He leaned forward again and took hold of a corner of the sack.

Haldean dropped his hand over Lawrence's. 'Don't touch anything.'

'But we can't leave him like this. I was going to cover him up.'

'I'm afraid you mustn't, sir.'

'But it's indecent! Anyone could come in here and find him. I'm going to cover him up.' Haldean shook his head and stood with his arms crossed. Lawrence slowly rose to his feet. 'Are you honestly saying you'd stop me?'

'If I have to.' It struck him with renewed force what he had known before, that Hugh Lawrence was a very power-ful and a very determined man who liked to get his own way. As he met Lawrence's eyes, Haldean sensed menace. Even injured – perhaps even more so now that his physical strength was gone – his personality was compelling. Haldean simply couldn't risk a confrontation. Force was barred to him and he didn't know who would win a trial of will. He smiled to try and break the tension. 'If I didn't stop you from spoiling all the evidence, sir, Ashley'd never talk to me again. Come on, Mr Lawrence. As you said, we need to get out of here.' He put a hand on the older man's elbow. 'And, although I respect your feelings, you need a doctor and I need a telephone.' Haldean breathed a sigh of relief as Lawrence relaxed and allowed himself to be led reluctantly away, to emerge, blinking, into the sunshine.

'Now, Thackenhurst's the nearest place,' mused Haldean, thinking out loud. He remembered being carried through the gardens after Whitfield's horse had downed him. Surely they'd come across this road? He walked a few steps further round the bend of the lane. 'Mr Lawrence! We can get through to Thackenhurst this way. There's a gate.' He jiggled the latch. 'It's open. We'll call on Mrs Verrity, sir. She'll help us, I know.' He opened the gate on to a sweep of parkland. The house lay a few hundred yards away, snuggled down in a fold of land.

They hadn't gone far across the well-manicured lawns when they were stopped by a respectful gardener.

'Excuse me, gentlemen, were you looking for someone?'

'Mrs Verrity,' said Haldean briskly. 'As you can see, this gentleman has met with an accident and we were hoping to find her in. Do you know where she is?'

'She was over at the glasshouses earlier, sir, on the other side of the house. I did see her in the rose garden, but I don't rightly know where she is now. If you call at the house, they'll tell you. Would you like some help, sir? It's a tidy step to the house.'

'I can make it,' said Lawrence. 'That is, if we get a move on. By the way,' he said, addressing the gardener, 'I think you should know that –'

'Come on, sir,' said Haldean firmly, taking his arm again. 'The sooner we get you inside the better,' and, much to Lawrence's annoyance, he bustled him on.

'What's the big idea?' snapped Lawrence, freeing his arm. 'I was going to tell that guy about Whitfield. I think you're taking a lot upon yourself, Major.'

'I know you do, sir, and I apologize, but the last thing we want is a crowd of rustics gaping at the body.'

'I was going to tell him to stand outside and not let anyone in.'

'And you honestly think he wouldn't have a peep himself? The fewer people who know about this until Ashley can get on the scene the better.'

The steps up to Thackenhurst nearly proved too much for Lawrence, but with Haldean's assistance he made it. They rang the bell and the door was opened by a smartly dressed maid whose eyes rounded in astonishment.

Haldean tipped his hat to her. 'Is Mrs Verrity at home? I'm sorry to call so unexpectedly but, as you can see, Mr Lawrence here is rather the worse for wear.'

'Who is it, Norah?' asked Mrs Verrity, stepping into the hall. 'Major Haldean, how nice to . . .' She stopped as she took in Lawrence's battered figure. 'Mr Lawrence! Whatever's happened? Take the gentlemen's hats, Norah, and don't stand there staring. Come into the morning room. Norah, go and get a basin of warm water, a cloth and some iodine for Mr Lawrence. Can you manage to walk in here, Mr Lawrence?'

Lawrence followed her into the morning room and gratefully sank back into an armchair where he sat with his eyes closed. It took Haldean two attempts before he could get Mrs Verrity to realize he was speaking to her.

'The telephone? Yes, of course, Major. There's a cabinet in the hall. I'll stay with Mr Lawrence.'

Haldean stepped into the hall and, with a swift glance to ensure he was alone, rang the station. Ashley's reaction was both colourful and predictable. 'Make sure Lawrence stays at Mrs Verrity's,' he said, after he had taken in the news. 'Can you meet me at the barn? Good. I'll be there as soon as possible. How badly hurt is Lawrence? I see. Well, I'll get hold of Dr Wilcott but he can come to the barn first and see Lawrence afterwards. Mrs Verrity? I'd rather you didn't tell her anything but I can see that might be difficult. The main thing is to keep her or anyone else away from the barn until we've seen it. My God, Haldean, this has upset the apple cart all right. D'you think it really was suicide?'

Haldean paused for a moment to allow the maid carrying a bowl of water to pass by. 'It's certainly meant to *look* like suicide,' he said, keeping his voice low. 'I'll leave you to make the obvious assumption.'

'Right you are. I'll see you there as soon as I can.'

Haldean replaced the ear-piece and went back into the morning room. Lawrence was still sitting in the chair but Mrs Verrity was beside him, replacing the bloodied handkerchief with a professional-looking bandage. She glanced up as Haldean entered, putting her finger on her lips for quiet. She finished the bandage and, getting up, drew him outside the room, motioned for the maid to follow and shut the door gently behind them.

'He is sleepy now. I think it's best to leave him alone at the moment. Take that bowl back to the kitchen, Norah.' She smiled. 'I'm sure that you, of all people, Major, can appreciate how he feels. What happened? It wasn't another accident with a horse, was it?'

He hesitated, mindful of Ashley's request. 'Look, I'm awfully sorry to trespass on your good nature in this way, but I'm afraid I can't tell you at the moment. I've got to leave now but I'll be back as soon as I can. Would you mind looking after Mr Lawrence until then? I'll have the doctor with me when I return and I promise to tell you everything then.'

Her smile faded as she took in his serious face. 'Something dreadful's happened, I know. Is it . . . No, never mind. Off you go, Major. I'll take good care of Mr Lawrence. You needn't worry about that, at least.'

It was half a dozen cigarettes later before Haldean saw

Ashley walking up Gallows Hill in company with Dr Wilcott, a sergeant, a constable and a young man weighed down with a big black box who turned out to be Dutton, the photographer from the village.

'I'm sorry we were so long,' Ashley apologized. 'It took me some time to get everyone together. We've parked at the bottom of the lane. Who does the Hillman belong too?'

'Strictly speaking it belongs to Uncle Philip, but Mr Lawrence was driving it.' He jerked a thumb behind him. 'He's fast asleep at Mrs Verrity's. I was able to get away without telling her anything.'

'Good man. Is this the barn?' Ashley eyed it dubiously. 'Ramshackle old place. Let's go inside and you can tell us what you found.'

'Hold on a minute, there's something I want to show you.' Haldean tossed aside his cigarette and took Ashley to one side. 'Look in the dust here beside the barn. What do you make of that?'

Ashley bent down. 'Bicycle tracks,' he said softly. 'And the grass is crushed against the barn as if someone's stood a bike up there.' He took his hat off and rubbed his hand through his hair. 'How far back do they go?'

'I've tracked them to the bottom of the lane. I couldn't pick them up after that because the road's too hard to take a print.'

'Were they here before Lawrence was attacked?'

'I don't know,' said Haldean with deep irritation. 'I've been racking my brains to try and think if I saw them but I simply can't call them to mind. There was so much else going on that I wasn't looking at the road. I could kick myself, Ashley. I'm really sorry but I just don't know if they were here or not. I've been driving myself crackers trying to remember. When I think how important it could be . . .'

Ashley stood up. 'Never mind. It can't be helped. It sounds as if you had enough to worry about with Mr Lawrence without looking for tracks. I suppose there's a chance the bike could belong to someone other than Miss Vayle but I must admit I don't think it's very likely.'

'She could have been here quite innocently.'

'She could. And if she was, she'll be able to tell me what her reasons were for coming.'

'Ashley,' began Haldean desperately.

Ashley held his hand up. 'Look, Haldean, I'm not jumping to any conclusions but you must admit those tracks are significant. I've got to act on them. Sergeant Sykes! You can drive, can't you? I want you to go to Hesperus right away. You're looking for a Miss Marguerite Vayle. Can he take the Tourer, Haldean?'

'I suppose so.'

'There's a chance you might pass her on the way,' said Ashley, turning back to Sergeant Sykes. 'She's brown-haired, about twenty, and riding a bike. You're not arresting her or anything like that, but at the very least –' this with a look at Haldean – 'she's had a nasty shock. I want you to stay with her at Hesperus. Don't ask her any questions. All I want you to do is see she's all right. I'll need to talk to her, so I want you to see she stays put. Naturally if she volunteers any information, make a note of it, but at the moment that's all I want you to do. Understand?'

'Yes, sir,' said Sergeant Sykes.

'Now then,' said Ashley, turning to Haldean. 'Let's see what's in the barn.'

'All right,' said Haldean, watching the departing policeman. He made a conscious effort to put Marguerite out of his mind. 'There are marks in the dust on the other side of the sill of the door. Follow me and be careful you don't tread on them. It's dark inside and easy to miss your footing.' He stepped into the barn and stooped down beside the spade handle. 'I'd add that to your collection, Ashley. D'you see the blood and skin on it? Someone obviously hit someone else with it damned hard.' *Someone? Could Marguerite hit that hard?* 'Whitfield's body is behind that plough. I didn't see him right away and Lawrence denied knowing he was there at all.'

'Yes . . . It's not immediately obvious, is it?' Ashley walked over to the body and looked at it for a few moments before giving the photographer his instructions. 'Keep clear of this area – there are footprints I want – good. That'll be fine,' he said after a blaze of magnesium from the camera. 'And if you get a picture of these prints here . . . and here. Thanks very much, Mr Dutton,' he said. 'I'm grateful for your assistance. Would you mind waiting outside? There are some more photographs I want you to take. If you come with me I'll show you some tracks we need pictures of and there'll be a couple more after that.' He disappeared out of the barn and they could hear him giving instructions to Dutton. A few minutes later he rejoined them. 'Dr Wilcott? Sorry to keep you waiting, sir. Before you do anything else, just look at the way he's holding the gun. Does that look entirely natural to you?'

Dr Wilcott knelt down beside Whitfield and studied his hand. 'It's difficult to say,' he said, with an irritated click of his tongue. 'He's holding the gun very loosely as you can see. It's very common in suicides for the hand holding the pistol to grip so tightly that you have to crack the fingers to remove it but, like most things in medicine, it's not an absolute law. However, I must say it looks odd to me. More as if – well, as if someone put the gun into his hand after he died.' He pulled a face. 'I won't swear to that though, so don't ask me. The gun was obviously fired at very close range. Look at the powder burns round the wound. They're very noticeable. It's obvious he's been in some sort of scuffle. Now I suppose you want to know when he died.'

'Wait a moment,' interposed Ashley and, taking a pencil from his pocket, carefully inserted it in the muzzle of the gun and picked it up. 'We'll be looking at this outside, Doctor. You carry on.'

They took the gun outside. Constable Hawley spread a white cloth on the grass and Ashley gently placed the gun on the cloth, then went back and, retrieving the spade handle, laid it beside the gun. He took out a bottle of mercury powder and an insufflator and lightly dusted the spade handle and the gun. A series of hoops and whorls sprang into view.

Ashley snorted with satisfaction. 'What d'you make of this, Haldean? There are some nice clear marks on that handle. Look at the muzzle. I bet that's part of a palm. We're on to something, Haldean, we're really on to something.' Ashley raised his head. 'Mr Dutton! Can you take a photograph of the gun and the spade handle, please? Thank you.' Dutton set up the camera on a tripod and disappeared under a black cloth. The camera clicked, then Ashley, using the pencil, flipped the gun over. 'Now this side . . . Good.' Under the mercury powder the gun showed more marks and one clear thumbprint on the muzzle. 'That's it,' breathed Ashley in delight. 'If that wasn't put into Whitfield's hand, I'll eat it.' He pointed to the thumbprint. A smile of grim satisfaction touched his mouth. 'And if the prints on the handle and the gun are the same . . .' They stepped back while the gun was photographed after which Ashley wrapped up the pistol as carefully as if it had been Ming china. 'Now all we need to do is identify that thumbprint and we've –' He broke off as the doctor came out of the barn.

'Finished,' said Dr Wilcott, laconically. 'There's a nasty cut on the left side of his chin that you ought to know about. It looks as if someone thumped him. What? The spade? Yes, that could've been the weapon. The cause of death is definitely a single gunshot to the right temple and the death occurred approximately an hour and thirty or forty minutes ago, give or take fifteen minutes or so on either side. This warm weather makes it a nice matter to judge, but he's been in the shade since he died. What's the time now? Twenty to one? If you call it eleven o'clock you won't be so far out. Yes, Major?'

'I heard what I thought was a shot at eleven o'clock and

when I looked at the body at fourteen minutes past, he was still warm but the blood had congealed.'

'Good man. That ties in with what I thought. I'd say eleven's your time, Superintendent, but don't try and pin me down to the exact minute on the medical evidence because neither I nor anyone else who knows their job would go along with it.' He picked his case up. 'Now, I believe I have a patient to attend to. I hope he's not suffered as a result of my coming here first.'

'I'll join you,' said Ashley. 'I could do with a few words with Mr Lawrence. What about you, Haldean?'

'I'll come too. I'll have to give Mr Lawrence a lift back to Hesperus in any case.'

Ashley nodded. 'Fair enough. Mr Dutton, I'm sorry, sir, but you'll have to walk back to the village, unless you want to wait for my return. If you leave your camera here I'll let you have it back as soon as possible. Constable Hawley, stay here until you're relieved.' He turned back to the doctor. 'Ready when you are, sir.'

They were shown into the morning room by Mrs Verrity herself. Lawrence was still asleep but started to wake up when Dr Wilcott stooped over him.

'You made a good job of this bandage, Mrs Verrity,' said the doctor, approvingly. 'Hold still please, Mr Lawrence . . . The iodine should've helped. This is a nice clean cut. Sore, I should imagine, but not serious. The bruising should fade in a few days. Vision all right? I don't think there's any concussion but if your sight becomes blurred or you start to feel sick or giddy, lie down and have someone send for me right away. That's a nasty bruise on your chin. How did you come by that?'

'I wish I knew,' said Lawrence, feeling his chin tenderly. 'Would it be possible to have a drink? Water, I mean, or tea? And would you mind opening the windows?'

'Of course,' said Mrs Verrity. She threw open the french windows, which, true to her Continental upbringing, had

201

been tightly closed, then rang the bell and gave instructions for a pot of tea to be brought. When the maid had left the room she looked appealingly at Ashley. 'Please, Superintendent, will you tell me what happened?' She swallowed. 'Ever since Major Haldean left I've been dreading what you might say.' She squared her shoulders and pointed her chin outwards. 'I'd rather know.'

'Just a moment, Mrs Verrity,' said Ashley with some gentleness. 'I'd rather hear Mr Lawrence's side of the story first. Now, sir. You'd agreed to meet Colonel Whitfield at eleven o'clock this morning?'

'That's right. You were there when I got his note. I sent back a reply which he should've got in this morning's post.'

'And you wanted to meet him, as I recall, to tell him, as you put it, "some home truths". What home truths were they, Mr Lawrence?'

He shifted in his chair. 'I didn't like the way he was still doing his best to persuade Marguerite to marry him. As you know, I didn't think it was marriage he was after, so much as money. After all, the man admitted it, that night in your garden, Mrs Verrity. As a trustee it was my privilege to turn down any man I thought had unworthy motives, and I thought his motives were as unworthy as they come.' He paused. 'That was it, really. Just the same old stuff.'

Ashley nodded. 'I see. Nothing, in fact, that you hadn't told him before?'

Lawrence met his eyes squarely. 'Nothing new at all.'

Haldean, sitting to one side of Lawrence, was struck by the way his hand tightened on the arm of the chair. He's lying, he thought with absolute conviction. There *is* something else there.

'It seems a great deal of trouble to take when you had nothing new to say to him, sir,' said Ashley politely. 'Surely you could have stated in your letter that you had nothing more to add to your refusal of your consent to his marriage to Miss Vayle?'

202

Lawrence shrugged. 'I guess so.' He felt his chin again. 'I wish now that's what I had done, but at the time I thought if I actually saw the man I could convince him there was no chance I'd change my mind. You see, Superintendent, I felt I was preventing a disastrous marriage. Marguerite had herself pegged as Juliet and me as the old buffer standing in the way of True Love but it wasn't like that. If Whitfield had had any feeling for the girl he'd have either eloped or simply waited until she was twenty-one and free to marry whoever she pleased. But that wouldn't do for him. He wanted the money and wasn't prepared to wait. I wasn't prepared to sit back and let her marry someone like that, even if she hated me for it. I couldn't give a damn what he thought.'

'And so you went to see him. What happened then?'

'It was as I told Major Haldean here. I arrived a few minutes early and stood outside the barn until eleven o'clock. I couldn't hear or see any sign of him but I didn't want to give the man the excuse of saying I hadn't shown up. On the stroke of eleven I went into the barn and something hit me. I went down flat and must've been knocked out because the next thing I recall is coming to and walking out of the barn straight into the arms of the Major. I didn't see anything else. At the time I thought Whitfield had hit me – I still think it was Whitfield – but what happened between me being hit and waking up again I've got no more idea of than the man in the moon.'

The door opened and the maid brought in the tea. 'Put it on the table, Norah,' said Mrs Verrity, absently. 'Mr Lawrence, where is Colonel Whitfield now? I cannot believe he assaulted you in that cowardly manner. Have you been to see him, Superintendent? Why don't you ask him what happened?'

Ashley hesitated and glanced across to Haldean.

Mrs Verrity looked from one to the other quickly. 'What is it?' she asked, a hard edge to her voice. 'Tell me what it is.'

Haldean got to his feet and stood with his back to the mantelpiece. He felt a sudden wave of sympathy for the lovely woman with her tense, white face. 'I'm awfully sorry, Mrs Verrity. There's no easy way to say this. You see, Colonel Whitfield's dead.'

Her eyes grew wider and she gave the tiniest shake of her head. '*Non.*' It was almost inaudible.

'It's quite true, I'm afraid.'

She continued to stare at him then gradually lowered her head. He heard the single whispered word '*Non*' once more and then there was silence. The seconds on the mantelpiece clock ticked away and all the outside noises – the song of a blackbird, the far-off clatter of a lawn-mower – seemed unnaturally loud. 'How?' It was another whisper.

Haldean cleared his throat. 'It looks as if he shot himself,' he began, but she interrupted him fiercely.

'Never! Richard would never do such a thing, never! Someone killed him – murdered him. When did it happen? I might have seen something. One of the men might have seen something. Tell me when it happened.'

'We think it was about eleven o'clock this morning,' said Ashley, his eyes fixed on her.

She put a hand to her forehead. 'Eleven o'clock? Where was I at eleven? I'd been out in the garden most of the morning . . . I can't remember.'

'If you please, mum,' said Norah the maid, with a little bob of a curtsey, 'you were in here at eleven o'clock. You'd rung for your morning coffee and as I was bringing it I heard the clock strike in the hall.'

Mrs Verrity looked at Norah as if she'd forgotten who she was. 'Did it?'

'Oh yes, mum. I remember it as plain as anything. You see, that's my signal, like,' she said, blushing furiously as she realized everyone in the room was looking at her. 'Saturday mornings you have your coffee at eleven o'clock and that gives me time to wash out the cake cupboard before I come back for your coffee things, clear them away, clean the knives, get everything ready for lunch and go and change my dress to set the table. If I miss the clock it puts me out for the morning, you see, and I've got to hurry over the cake cupboard.'

'Thank you . . .' She roused herself with an effort. 'Thank you, Norah. You can leave the tea. That will be all.' She swallowed and turned to Ashley. 'You must ask the gardeners. They might have heard something. Eleven o'clock.' Her face suddenly altered and she spun round on Lawrence. 'Eleven o'clock! You were there, you!'

'Now don't try and put this one on me,' said Lawrence quickly. 'All I know is what I've told you. I'm as much in the dark about this as you are.'

'Oh yes? You hated Richard. Don't try and deny it. All he wanted, God knows why, was to marry that child, Marguerite Vayle, and you stood in his way from the beginning. I didn't want Richard to marry her, I'll admit as much, but you – you stopped him. And to think I felt grateful when you arrived and I found out what your views were. But you! You were at the barn at *eleven o' clock*! And look at you. You've obviously been in a fight. What did Richard do? Hit you? And you shot him.'

'I didn't!' roared Lawrence. 'God damn it, woman, I never laid a finger on the man. I didn't even know he was there until Haldean found him. And as for shooting him – the idea's ridiculous!'

Ashley coughed. It was a polite sound but it seemed like a thunderclap. 'I think it's a little early to start making accusations, Mrs Verrity. There are a number of possibilities we have to follow up before we can do that.'

'Before you announce you've got another unsolved murder, Superintendent?' Her voice was painfully bitter. 'There were no murders before *he* arrived.' Lawrence bristled and Dr Wilcott dropped a warning hand on his shoulder. 'Oh, why did Richard get entangled with her? He did want money, of course he wanted money, but I could've . . .'

'Could've what?' asked Haldean quietly.

She looked at him with dry, bright eyes. 'I could have given him money. I could have given him everything he wanted and instead he fell for that simpering schoolgirl.' She blinked very rapidly. 'I loved him. I've always loved him. Go on, smile. This is a joke, yes? I know what you're thinking. *But she's older than him!* Do you think I cared? I hoped that one day he'd grow to care for me. Other men have found me attractive, so why not him? But although he was willing to be friends he wanted nothing more. I stayed, hoping he would change his mind and grow to be fond of me. I even tried to make him jealous but nothing worked. He liked me, asked my advice, relied on my help . . . but he wouldn't love me. And I loved him . . .'

Haldean shifted awkwardly. 'I'm sorry. Really sorry.'

She looked at him with a trembling lip and tossed her head as if to keep back tears. 'I couldn't believe it when he fell for that girl. What did she have that I couldn't offer him? I couldn't tell anyone how I felt. All I had left was my pride. When the marriage was blocked I felt glad until I realized how unhappy it was making Richard. Because I loved him I wanted him to be happy. Poor Richard. And now he's dead . . .' She sat silently for a few moments, her hands twisted in her lap. 'Please,' she said, very quietly. 'If you don't mind I'd rather you all went now.' She shook herself. 'Talk to the gardeners. Talk to whomever you please but let me be by myself for a while.'

They showed themselves out. Dr Wilcott stayed behind for a few minutes before joining them outside the front door. 'I feel damn sorry for that woman,' he said as they walked down the steps to the Spyker. 'I'm glad she said what she did. It's dangerous to keep emotions as strong as those bottled up. She's got great self-control.'

Lawrence sniffed in disgust. 'I wish she'd had a sight more self-control. I was horrified when she accused me of murdering her precious Colonel. As far as I'm concerned he walloped me, then shot himself and that's the end of that.'

'Unfortunately, sir, it can't be the end of it as far as we're concerned,' said Ashley politely. 'The suicide theory may be correct but we have to look into the possibility of murder.'

'You mean someone was waiting in the barn for both of us? It sounds damned unlikely to me.'

'Nevertheless it's something we have to investigate. I shall need to take your fingerprints, Mr Lawrence –'

'Oh no, you don't!'

'Which you can either let me have before you go home or at the police station. It's perfectly painless and will help us to eliminate you from our enquiries.'

'You'd better take mine as well,' put in Haldean quickly, with an eye on Lawrence's rising colour. 'The idea is, sir, to see from the prints who was in the barn who had a reason to be there. If there's a set of prints belonging to a Johnny we haven't got a record of, then we can look for him. We'll need Dr Wilcott's as well and anyone else who we know was around.'

'Well, if that's all, I guess you can,' said Lawrence, mollified. 'As you wish, Superintendent. And then, I take it, I can make arrangements to go home.'

'Back to Hesperus, sir?'

'Back to Canada. If this is quiet English country life you can keep it. I prefer the Rockies.'

Ashley reached the car and paused, thinking over his words. 'I must ask you to make no such arrangements at present, sir.'

'Are you arresting me, Superintendent? No? Then I believe I can go exactly where I want to.'

'Have a heart, sir,' put in Haldean. 'Think of Miss Vayle. She's going to be really cut up over this. You can't leave Uncle Philip and Aunt Alice to carry the can.'

'As far as Miss Vayle's concerned, young man, now that Colonel Whitfield is out of the picture, I have very few worries. I cannot credit that she will spend very long in mourning for him. I know she'll be upset, but she'll get over it. As for myself, you can't honestly expect me to indulge in any crocodile tears for a man I disliked and distrusted. I came over solely to give or withhold my consent as her trustee, and now the situation has been resolved I intend to sail for Canada as soon as I can book a passage.' He glared at Ashley as if expecting a rejoinder, but Ashley merely shrugged, opened the car door, and stood to one side with a smile.

'In that case, sir, we'd better work quickly. I'm sure you'd like to know the truth of the matter before you go home. After you, Mr Lawrence.'

Chapter Eleven

Haldean tossed aside the newspaper on to the grassy bank and wriggled his back into the knobbly trunk of the weeping willow. This secluded spot by the river was one of his favourite retreats at Hesperus, but it was failing to bring him any comfort. The water gurgling smoothly over the shallow stones showed brown flecked with silver, a black-bird sang as if it was putting the river to music and a blue clump of brooklime flowered like a piece of captured sky, but neither the sight nor the sound had any power to soothe. The newspaper was dire, too. He had intended to put all thought of murder from his mind but Boscombe, Morton and, most insistently of all, Whitfield kept intruding on his thoughts.

Three men, all shot with the same gun. Powder burns on Whitfield, powder burns on Morton. No powder burns on Boscombe but he had been killed from a few yards away. That would be a damn good shot with a small pistol. He was willing to bet it was the same gun that Whitfield had been clutching. But who had put the gun in Whitfield's hand?

He threw a stone moodily into the river. The sound of feet scrambling down the bank made him look round.

It was Isabelle. 'So there you are, Jack. I've been looking everywhere for you. A fat lot of use you've been. Don't you know what's happening?'

'I know exactly what's happening. Maggie Vayle's having a fit. That's why I'm out here. When I got back Sergeant Sykes had taken root in the hall and there were significant and worrying noises coming from the morning room.'

'I'm really sorry Greg's in London,' said Isabelle, sitting down beside him. 'He wouldn't have sloped off.'

'You wouldn't have given him any choice. I couldn't face it, Belle. Maggie was all right. After all, she had you, Aunt Alice and Mr Lawrence all clucking over her. I've already seen one woman in tears today because of Whitfield's untimely demise. I couldn't stick another.' He threw another stone in the water. 'What's she said about it all?'

'She says she killed him.'

'*What?*' Haldean sat bolt upright.

'Oh, don't get so excited. She says he committed suicide because she was beastly enough not to believe him when he explained what he'd said at the ball. According to her, she'd broken Whitfield's heart by being stubborn and mistrustful and it's all her fault.'

'Crikey.'

'Yes. You should have seen that policeman's eyes start bulging when she was carrying on. He couldn't write it down fast enough.'

Haldean sighed. 'I wish to God she hadn't turned up at the barn. What the dickens was she doing there in the first place?'

'She says she cycled over with the idea of listening to hear what Mr Lawrence said to the Colonel. I think that if Whitfield gave a good account of himself she was going to declare everything on again. It wasn't a bad idea, really. At least if he told Mr Lawrence a pack of lies they might be different lies from those he'd told her. Apparently she went out about ten o'clock. She didn't say where she was going, of course.'

'Ten o'clock, eh? That'd give her plenty of time to get to Gallows Hill by eleven.'

'You'd think so, wouldn't you? But she had a puncture and that held her up so it wasn't until twenty past or so that she arrived. She's a bit unclear about the next bit but I gather it involved going into the barn and finding him there.'

'Oh, bloody *hell*! Sorry, Belle. I suppose she left her fingerprints all over the place. D'you happen to know if she touched anything?'

Isabelle shook her head. 'She says not. Sergeant Sykes asked her that.'

'Well, that's something, at any rate. What did she do next?'

'She backed out, got on her bike and was picked up along the way by the Sergeant. They arrived back together and at first she wouldn't say anything at all. Then the policeman told us what had happened and she started saying she'd killed the Colonel and all hell broke loose. Mr Lawrence got back, you dived in and dived out again and the rest you know. She's just staring out of the window now. I don't think she knew we were really there. I preferred it when she was crying.'

'Dear God, did you?'

'I think so,' said Isabelle. 'It'd be easier to cope with in a way. If Mr Lawrence had any sense he'd have given the thumbs-up to their engagement, then let nature take its course. All Colonel Whitfield had going for him was his looks and she'd have got over them soon enough. She'd probably have managed it before the wedding. She'd have certainly managed it afterwards.'

'This is all very cynical, Belle.'

'I feel cynical. I don't believe he ever gave tuppence for her and I could shake her for taking him so seriously. I know he did wonderful things in the war, but he was a perfect stick of a man with no conversation who drank too much. Now he's dead I suppose she'll live in the shadow of his memory and be thoroughly and absolutely dreary about the whole thing for the rest of her life.'

'She could meet someone else,' suggested Haldean. 'After all, she's quite nice-looking when she tries and will be very well off. Money answereth all things, as it says in Ecclesiastes somewhere.'

211

'Now who's being cynical?' countered Isabelle.

Haldean smiled wickedly. 'Ah, but when I do it, it's a mixture of realism and Holy Writ. Have a cigarette, Belle, and entertain me. I'm feeling old and stale.'

'Your only problem,' said Isabelle, accepting a cigarette and puffing blue smoke at a cloud of dancing gnats, 'is that you're grumpy because you haven't solved the murder.'

'Which one?' asked Haldean, settling back against the willow. 'I've got three to choose from. I don't believe for a minute that Whitfield shot himself. That was cold-blooded murder if you like, and Maggie Vayle's trip to the barn hasn't half complicated things.'

Isabelle stared at him. 'You mean she might be accused of killing him? Really killing him, I mean?' Haldean nodded. 'I see.' Isabelle put her arms round her knees and looked at the river. 'That's awkward, Jack. That's very awkward indeed.'

'How come you're not leaping to her defence?'

Isabelle didn't answer right away. 'To be honest, it's not the first time I've thought about her in that way,' she said eventually.

Haldean raised an eyebrow in her direction. 'So she strikes you like that, does she?'

'I certainly wouldn't want to be the one who stopped her from getting what she wanted,' said Isabelle seriously. 'After you told us she'd been blackmailed, I wondered if she would be capable of murdering Boscombe. She bottles everything up so much that it's a bit frightening at times. Maybe she'd be different if she was happy. I've only known her since the Vayles died and she was heartbroken by that. Then this thing with Colonel Whitfield started. I wouldn't be surprised if deep down inside she always knew he never really loved her, so she had to love him twice as much and a bit frantically to make up for it. But she did love him, you know. That proves she's innocent, doesn't it?'

'Unless she finally caught on that he didn't care.'

Isabelle shuddered. 'Don't, Jack.' She shuddered again. 'Please don't,' she begged. 'That's horribly believable.'

There were a few moments' silence. 'I did think,' said Isabelle eventually, 'that the Colonel was the man you were after. When he tried to ride you down I thought he'd tried to kill you. Now he's dead, I suppose he was innocent all along. Was that an accident, Jack?'

'I didn't think so at the time, I must say. He nearly saw me off and came as near as a toucher to getting Ashley as well.'

'So why did he do it?'

Haldean rolled over on his stomach and frowned at the grass. 'Fear. He was frightened, Belle. The Chief Constable told him we were looking for a blackmailer and I put the wind up him that night at Mrs Verrity's. He started laying eggs after that. From what I can gather he hit the bottle pretty badly.'

'From which we infer, Sherlock, that he was being blackmailed, yes?'

'I wish we could infer that. I'm stuck. But I'm certain Whitfield was murdered.'

'What about Mr Lawrence? I don't like the idea but he was there just as much as Marguerite and he loathed Whitfield. Or what about Mrs Verrity?'

Haldean grinned. 'You've got a bee in your bonnet about her.'

'Buzzing frantically,' said Isabelle, stubbing out her cigarette. 'She was nuts about the Colonel and she might have known he intended to patch things with up with Maggie. I bet she couldn't bear to see him go to someone else. She lives next door to the barn. Couldn't she have nipped in and shot Colonel Whitfield?'

'Hardly. The curtain went up at eleven o'clock and at eleven o'clock she was drinking coffee in her morning room. And I was on the spot immediately afterwards, you know. I'm sure I would have seen her or anyone else if they'd tried to get away.'

'Could she have hidden in the barn?'

213

'She *could*, if she'd disguised herself as an old sheaf-binder or a whipple-tree or something. Besides that, I know unrequited love takes people in funny ways, but it'd hardly make her start knocking seven bells out of Mr Lawrence, no matter how stuck on Colonel Whitfield she was. Not only that, she simply couldn't have beaten Lawrence and myself back to the house. We took the most direct route to Thackenhurst just as soon as he was fit to walk.'

'It's Whitfield then,' said Isabelle in a dissatisfied voice. 'It has to be. After all, it might have been suicide. He shot the other two and tried to kill Mr Lawrence before shooting himself.'

'Not only couldn't he have shot Boscombe, it'd be a sight more to the point if he'd shot Lawrence.' He raised his head as a car crunched up the drive and over the bridge. 'I wonder who that is?'

Isabelle ran to the top of the bank, Haldean joining her at a more leisurely pace. 'We're not expecting any visitors . . . I say, Jack, isn't that Superintendent Ashley getting out of the car?'

'He doesn't usually arrive in state like this,' said Haldean in a dried-up voice. 'He knows something.'

Isabelle caught at his arm. 'Come on, Jack. It might not be as bad you think.'

Ashley was standing in the hall with Mr Lawrence when they arrived. He was flanked by Constable Hawley and Sergeant Sykes and he looked, Haldean thought, unusually grim. From the end of the hall appeared Aunt Alice, Uncle Philip and Mr Lawrence, drawn by the instinct that Something was undoubtedly Up. Marguerite was nowhere to be seen.

'Did you want me, Mr Ashley?' asked Sir Philip.

'No, sir. I need to speak to Mr Lawrence here. Mr Lawrence, you stated this morning that you were unaware that Colonel Whitfield's body was in the barn. Is that correct?'

'Why yes, Superintendent,' said Lawrence with a

214

puzzled frown. 'I told you so earlier. Until Major Haldean pointed it out to me I didn't know anything about it.'

'And at no time did you touch either the body or the gun?'

'That's right. I wanted to cover him up but the Major said we had to leave everything as it was. I wish now I'd insisted on it as it might have saved poor Marguerite a dreadful shock.'

'In that case . . .' Ashley took a deep breath. 'Hugh Douglas Lawrence, I arrest you for the murder of Richard Theodore Whitfield. You do not have to say anything but anything you do say may be used in evidence at your trial.'

'Hey,' said Lawrence, seriously alarmed. 'You can't do that.'

'I'm sorry, sir,' said Ashley. 'I just have.'

Haldean looked at the gun on Ashley's desk. 'Can I touch it?' he asked.

'Help yourself,' said Ashley, agreeably. He picked up the gun and passed it over to Haldean. 'We've got all the photographs we need, and I've handled it already. There were six bullets left in the chamber so I unloaded it. The last thing we need is an accident. Neat, isn't it?'

Haldean took the gun thoughtfully in the palm of his hand. A Smith and Wesson seven-shot hand-ejector revolver – a few years old now, by the look of it. It could quite easily be carried in a man's pocket as it only measured six inches or so and didn't weigh much more than half a pound. 'A .22?' he asked.

'That's right. And although there's no way of actually proving that it's the same gun that was used on Boscombe and Morton, the bullets are the same type. We haven't had the post-mortem on Colonel Whitfield yet, but it has to be the gun that killed him.'

'Absolutely,' said Haldean, putting the gun back on the desk. 'And you're convinced, beyond the teeniest, most exiguous shadow of the scintilla of a doubt, that our Mr Lawrence is the man?'

Ashley sighed and leaned back in his chair, then got up and walked to the window, hitching himself comfortably on to the sill. 'How certain do you want me to be?' he said after a pause. 'The evidence is there all right. You can't get round that. The footprints in the barn were too scuffed and confused to make anything of, but Lawrence's fingerprints are on the gun and on the spade too, despite his statement that he hadn't touched them. To be honest, it's the very strength of the evidence which did make me think a bit. If he wanted us to believe Whitfield committed suicide, why on earth didn't he make a better fist of it?'

Haldean drummed a tattoo on the desk. 'It's damned odd, isn't it? However, don't forget I wasn't meant to be there. It might have looked a jolly sight more convincing if I hadn't been on the spot.'

'You mean Lawrence was expecting to have more time to fake the evidence?'

'Yes.' Haldean frowned. 'He can't have expected to be roughed up the way he was. Maybe he was having a breather before going back into the barn.'

Ashley rubbed his chin thoughtfully. 'How about this for an idea? The two men meet, have words and take a swing at each other. Lawrence gets hold of the spade handle and thumps Whitfield with it. Both had obviously been in a fight, so that accounts for that. Lawrence or Whitfield pulls a gun . . . Wait a minute. It'd actually have to be Lawrence's gun, if it's the same one that was used on Boscombe, because we know Whitfield didn't kill Boscombe. Then Lawrence shoots him. Panic-stricken, and in a pretty bad way himself, he quickly makes it look like suicide and lights out to find you waiting for him. He could have been going to clean himself up or stage an accident, maybe a car crash, to account for his injuries. All he'd have to do then is deny ever having been there. But running into you scuppers that option. He wants to stop you finding the body so he invents that thin story about

216

Whitfield making an unprovoked attack and scarpering in the hope you'll take his word for it that Whitfield's not there. Having told you as much, he's got to stick to it, even after you've found the body. He had to risk the finger-prints and it didn't come off. What d'you think of that?'

Haldean shrugged. 'I don't know. If he'd had time to set up a car crash to make it appear that he'd had an accident on the way to the barn instead of on the way back, it might be quite convincing. At the moment his story's got as many holes in it as a Swiss cheese.'

'Agreed. He'd have been better off, once he had seen you, to admit to plugging Whitfield and telling you they'd had a fight.'

'Unless, of course, he was telling me the truth.'

Ashley favoured him with a very long, old-fashioned look. 'Come off it. He's got his fingerprints on the gun and the spade, no one else was in or near the barn, he's very much the worse for wear and Whitfield's dead body is stuck behind the plough. The only alternative to murder, as he sees it, is suicide, so he makes it look as much like suicide as he can in the hope he'll get away with it.'

'What does he say happened? Now you've arrested him, I mean.'

'He says he was telling the unvarnished truth and that's all we're getting. What's eating you?'

'Nothing, apart from the fact I like him. Having said that, he's a formidable type. I wouldn't like to cross him. By the way, it's a bit irrelevant now, but Marguerite Vayle's story adds up as far as I can tell. Her bike has a new patch on the front wheel which conceals a genuine hole. I know because I took it off. However, there's nothing to say when the patch was applied. "Recently" is a bit too vague in this sort of game.'

Ashley sucked in his cheeks. 'So you're still on that tack, are you? To be honest, I think you can stop worrying. I can hardly see her cracking Lawrence over the head, shooting Whitfield, then vanishing into the background while you looked round the barn. That is . . . I take it you could see the barn while you were attending to Lawrence?'

'Oh yes. I'd parked at the bottom of the lane, which, as you know, is out of sight of the barn, but when I heard the shot I ran as fast as I could up to where Lawrence had appeared. No one ran across the road or even out of the door and round the corner of the building. I'm certain of that. Besides, if they had, Lawrence himself would have noticed them. He'd have said if he'd seen anyone. Unless . . .'

'Unless what?'

'Unless, perhaps, that someone was Marguerite Vayle,' said Haldean.

Ashley looked at him. 'What's brought this on? After all, when you thought Miss Vayle was involved you hated the idea. What's the problem?'

Haldean twitched irritably. 'It's times. From the time of hearing the shot to Lawrence appearing was awfully quick. He'd have had to move like the dickens to put the gun in Whitfield's hand. I don't think he was up to moving that fast.'

'That's probably why he made such a mess of it. So you think Lawrence could be protecting Miss Vayle?'

'I don't know.' Haldean shook himself. 'He cares an awful lot about her, that's obvious. This caper's rotten. You start looking at the ordinary, normal people and paw over their actions and their motives until you can't think straight any more. It's perfectly reasonable that Marguerite should want to hear what Lawrence and Whitfield were saying. It's all too believable that she should have a puncture and be late for their meeting. It's only too easy to say "Prove it." She can't, of course. We can't prove most of what we say. We simply take it on trust because most people tell the truth, but who the devil knows what that is in a case like this?'

'I think I've got the truth.' Ashley steepled his fingers, taking in Haldean's strained face. 'This is getting to you, isn't it? When I spoke to Inspector Rackham about you, he

218

said that if you had a fault, you got too involved. You can't afford to be involved, Haldean. You'd prefer it to be like one of your stories, wouldn't you?' Haldean nodded reluctantly. 'But it isn't. The victim, the villain – they were figures on a chessboard. And now the figures have come to life and you want to walk away because you don't want to be responsible for hurting one of them.'

'You're right, damn you.' Haldean got up and moved restlessly about the room. 'It's a rum thing that I've thoroughly liked all the possible suspects and cordially detested all the victims. I went off Whitfield in a big way after he called me a tame dago. Trying to murder me didn't help, either. I suppose I should make an exception of Morton, but that's only because I didn't know him. He doesn't seem to have been an endearing sort of soul.'

'And the little group of suspects that we've assembled contains one who can't be such an endearing sort either. Not if they're prepared to take three lives for their own purposes. But I will say this for Miss Vayle. It seems crazy to drag her in when we've got Lawrence on the spot with fingerprints to prove it.'

'Maybe. Not that, as far as my lacerated feelings are concerned, I'm any happier pinning it on Lawrence. And what about the motive, Ashley? Admittedly he loathed Whitfield, but if he killed him then he must have killed Boscombe and Morton as well. It was the same gun, after all, or the same sort of bullets at least.'

'Well, surely the motive's obvious. If he cares about Miss Vayle as much as you say he does, then he murdered them because they were blackmailing her.'

'But he didn't know.'

'He says he didn't know. He might have guessed what was going on.'

Haldean shook himself in frustration. 'He might. Oh, to hell with it. Why the blazes didn't I pay more attention to Boscombe that day at the fête? He was full of himself, the little creep, bubbling over with "I know something you don't know" and horribly smug. I suppose that's why

I got rid of him as fast as I could, that and him being offensively drunk. Back in the war, you know, he used to adore getting one up on someone. He'd nurse little snippets of scandal to himself and drip them out bit by bit and quite frankly, my heart used to sink when I saw him in that venomous mood. When I saw him at the fête, so damn pleased with himself as if he had something up his sleeve and so –' Haldean broke off and stared blankly at the opposite wall.

'So what?' prompted Ashley, but Haldean didn't hear him.

'So horribly smug,' Haldean repeated in a whisper. 'Smug. That's it.' He looked at Ashley, his eyes bright and his face alert. 'That's it!' he said in ringing tones. 'He was so disgustingly smug. He was on to something *new*! D'you know what he said to me? He said *Give a man enough rope*. That's what he said. *That's* the motive. It makes sense. Everything makes sense.' He snatched up his hat. 'I've got to go to London.'

'London?' said Ashley, completely bewildered. 'Whatever for?'

'I've had an idea but it might take me some time to root it out. Don't bother about me. Just carry on as if nothing had happened.'

'Oi!' shouted Ashley as Haldean opened the door and raced out of the room. 'You'll have to tell me a bit more . . .' But Haldean had gone. Minutes later Ashley heard the roar of the Spyker's engine. *Give a man enough rope?* What the devil did that mean? He retreated disconsolately back to his desk.

'Haldean?' Brigadier Romer-Stuart walked across the lobby of the Belvedere Club. 'What the dickens are you doing here?'

Haldean smiled apologetically. 'Sorry to barge in on you like this, Bingo, but it's urgent. It might be, anyway.

I called at your rooms and your man told me where you'd be. Are you in the middle of anything?'

'A fairly tedious dinner. Why?'

'Good. That it's tedious, I mean. If it's that much of a frost perhaps you won't mind leaving. I need to check some records at the War Office.'

'At this time of night!' The Brigadier's eyebrows shot up. 'It's Saturday. You know, the weekend. That's the bit where you don't work, remember? The place is closed until Monday morning. Can't it wait until then?'

'I'd rather it didn't, Bingo, old man. You see . . .' Haldean hesitated. 'You see, there's a man in prison.'

Romer-Stuart sighed. 'Well, I'm very sorry for him, but I don't see why I should skip dinner and watch you leafing through files on the strength of it.'

Haldean grinned. 'Come on, Bingo. I mean, I know you're here in gilded splendour, quaffing and supping and what-have-youing, but just think how much fun it'll be watching me put in some really hard work.'

'About as much fun as a wet weekend in Skegness.' The Brigadier looked at Haldean's dark, eager face and wavered. 'Damned if I know why I'm doing this,' he grumbled. 'I suppose, although you haven't mentioned it, I do owe you a favour for sorting out that mess bill business. All right. Give me a few minutes.' He disappeared back into the club to re-emerge shortly afterwards with a broad smile. 'They've just got on to the speeches. I don't mind cutting those. I said that something urgent had come up and I had to get back to the War Office. I could see everyone itching to ask me what it was. The rumours were starting as I left the room. If you hear we've declared another war, ignore it. I hope this is worthwhile.'

'Now that,' said Haldean, as Romer-Stuart got his coat and hat, 'I can't honestly say.'

Sir Philip wandered in through the dressing room and sat

down on his wife's bed. 'Have you seen my reading glasses, Alice?'

'They're round your neck, dear.'

'What? Oh yes, so they are.' He looked at them absently but made no move to go.

She put down the book she was reading and, sitting up against the pillow, reached out for his hand. 'Are you worried?'

'Worried?' Sir Philip gave a snort. 'I should think I am. I asked Jack outright before he went skittering up to London. "Is Lawrence guilty?" And all he said was, "Wait and see." I tell you, I don't like it, Alice. How he can even think Hugh Lawrence might have killed Whitfield is more than I can imagine. Why the devil should he? The man's our guest. It's a ridiculous idea. Why . . . I like him, dash it. Why on earth we all just can't accept Whitfield shot himself – although that's bad enough for heaven's sake – I don't know.'

'I rather think Jack was hoping to get at the truth.'

'Truth? I know the truth and so should he. As for these other two characters who died, I'd be glad if someone could tell me what they're supposed to do with Lawrence. You mark my words, it'll turn out that they shot themselves as well. Arresting an innocent man! I don't know what the country's coming to.'

Lady Rivers sighed. 'Doesn't it seem a little odd to you, Philip, that three men should shoot themselves in the space of a week?'

'It happens,' said Sir Philip, belligerently. 'There could be any number of reasons. I can't tell what's going on in someone's mind.'

'I wish I knew what was going on in Marguerite's mind,' said Lady Rivers, reflectively. 'She was shocked, of course. I wish she hadn't seen the body, but it's a strange thing, though. I believe she was as upset about Mr Lawrence being arrested as she was about the Colonel dying.'

'That shows very proper feeling,' grunted Sir Philip in approval.

'But unexpected, wouldn't you say? I did feel sorry for her. She said that everyone she'd ever cared for had been taken away. The Vayles, Colonel Whitfield, Mr Lawrence – there was no one left. After we'd been to see Mr Lawrence this evening she was so quiet and thoughtful. I expected her to be up in arms against him but she wasn't.'

'She didn't say anything at all as I recall.'

'Not when we were there, no. But do you know she called to see Mr Lawrence again? Afterwards, I mean. Isabelle met her and she was so white and shivery that Isabelle made her go to bed. Marguerite said she couldn't bear to think of what was happening and it was all her fault.'

'How on earth does she work that out? I can't get the hang of her at all, Alice. She seems to take things so much to heart.'

'Well, you'd expect her to, wouldn't you, Philip? After all, it's a horrible thing to have happened. I was surprised that she came down when Mrs Verrity arrived.'

'Now that was an odd thing. What the devil did the woman want? I didn't know what to say to her, especially if she really was fond of Whitfield as you suggested. I mean, I couldn't offer my sympathies because I'm not meant to know that they're required. It must have been the most awkward game of bridge I've ever played. Fancy being expected to concentrate on cards with all this hanging over us! Still, it was better to have something to do rather than sit round gazing at each other. I wish I knew why she'd come here.'

'That's fairly obvious, I would have thought,' said Lady Rivers, yawning. 'Don't you see, dear? She was lonely.'

'Eh, what?' Alan Romer-Stuart blinked and stirred in his chair.

'I said I'd finished,' repeated Haldean patiently.

'I'm very happy for you. What time is it?' Romer-Stuart sat up and, blinking sleep from his eyes, looked at his watch. 'Good God, it's nearly quarter to three.' He got to his feet, stretching out his cramped limbs. 'That must be the most uncomfortable chair in London. D'you say you've finished? Get anywhere?'

'I think so. I might have. There are two possible names. One lives in Cromer, which is a bit off the beaten track, but the other lives in Battersea. I'll try the London one first.'

Romer-Stuart stopped mid-stretch. 'Not tonight, I hope.'

'No.' Haldean grinned. 'I think it's a bit late for social calls. Come on, Bingo, you look all in. I'll run you home. And thanks, old man.'

'I suppose I should say, "Don't mention it," but I'm jolly well not going to. I can put you up on my sofa for the rest of the night if you like. It's a bit basic, but it'd be better than that blasted chair you wished on me.'

'I'll take you up on that. Thanks. Cheer up. You've slept in worse places. And it's better than prison.'

'I don't know so much about that,' said Romer-Stuart, grumpily. 'You get a bed in prison.'

Hugh Lawrence stirred and looked at the lighter barred patch of grey against the dark wall of his cell. He was conscious of a quiet despair. He'd been a fool to announce he was going back to Canada; that had put the police on their mettle. Better, perhaps, though, than being arrested on the ship. If only it wasn't for Marguerite; at the thought of her his insides twisted. She was safe, anyhow, and that was worth everything. Would she ever know how much he loved her? Perhaps . . . What had she said this evening? 'I don't love you yet. You can't expect me too. But I might, in time.' That was nearly a promise. And Whitfield was dead. God help him, he was glad Whitfield was dead. For a moment his mind leapt ahead, clearing all obstacles and seeing only himself and Marguerite, together at last, and he smiled, conscious of being on the edge of a deep well of happiness. He turned over in bed and his smile faded. His clothes were on a peg on the wall, jacket and hat together. In the dim light they looked like a hanged man.

'I got your telegram,' said Ashley, walking down the path of his neat, semi-detached house. 'Thanks for saying you'd call for me. It saves a lot of waiting about at the station. But I don't know about this, Haldean.'

'It's worth trying, all the same. If I'm right it'll explain an awful lot.'

'Well, I'll agree with you there, and no mistake,' said Ashley, opening the gate and walking on to the pavement. 'Is he in the car?'

'He is. We're parked a few yards down the road. Here we are.' Haldean led the way to where the Spyker stood. A small, black-button-eyed man sat in the front passenger seat. 'Mr Stafford? This is the Superintendent, Mr Ashley, I was telling you about, so you can see it really is all above board.'

'Pleased to meet you,' said Mr Stafford with a broad Cockney grin. 'Don't mind me not getting out. I'm not as handy on my pins as I used to be. Got one less leg than I started off with. Oh yes, my running days are over. The wife says it suits her as she always knows where I am. She don't know so much at the moment though, does she? It's nice to have a bit of a trip out. I've never been in a car before, not all to ourselves, as you might say. I'm still not sure what you want me to do though, Major.'

'Just say whatever comes into your head,' said Haldean getting into the car and pressing the self-starter. 'Are you ready, Ashley? That'll do fine, Mr Stafford.'

'I always do say what I think. Got me into trouble a few times, that has. I don't usually get paid a fiver for doing it, though. Is it a long way to this police station?'

'Not very far.'

'Especially driving as you do, Haldean,' muttered Ashley. 'I was at the station this morning. Miss Vayle came to see me.'

225

'Oh yes? What did she want?'

'Well, she actually came to see Mr Lawrence, but she took the opportunity to tell me he was innocent. She had various suggestions, such as a tramp being to blame, which I told her was highly unlikely, and then she came up with something that really baffled me. She suggested that the Colonel might have shot the other two and killed himself so that Lawrence would be hanged for murder. She said she'd read a story where a jealous woman had committed suicide so as to lay the blame on her husband.'

'Oh, I know that one,' said Haldean, increasing his speed as the road straightened out. '"The Problem of Thor Bridge". It's a Sherlock Holmes story.'

'It sounds crazy to me. I mean, why go to all that trouble? It's not natural. It'd be much more straightforward *and* believable, granted you were going to top yourself anyway, to shoot the person you wanted to, then do yourself in.'

'You wouldn't have a story then. However, I agree, and I certainly don't think that's what happened here. What the devil's got into Marguerite though? I'd have thought she was the last person to suggest her beloved Whitfield could be anything other than squeaky-clean. I wonder . . .'

'What?'

'Nothing,' said Haldean with a sidelong glance at Stafford. 'Just rambling.' And the rest of the way to Breedenbrook he talked exclusively of the Great War.

They arrived at the station where, having been helped from the car, Ernest Stafford looked around with disapproval at the deserted village street. 'Quiet sort of place, isn't it? Not much happening here on a Saturday night, or any other time I should say. I like a bit of life, myself. People talk about Battersea and I'll grant you it's no beauty spot, but there's always something going on.'

'There's been a bit too much going on for our tastes, Mr Stafford,' said Haldean with a smile at Ashley. 'Can you manage the steps? Oh, you're used to it, I can see.'

226

'No trouble at all, Major. I still don't know what you want me to do, though.'

'Just speak your mind, Mr Stafford.'

'Well, that won't come hard. In here, is it?'

Hugh Lawrence was lying on his bed, reading, when they walked in. He looked more fine-drawn than Haldean remembered and the brightness in his eyes had gone.

Haldean hesitated at the door with Ashley and Stafford behind him. 'I'm . . . I'm awfully sorry, Mr Lawrence.'

'What for?' Lawrence managed a smile. 'I won't be here long. Your uncle assures me it's all a ghastly misunderstanding which he's sure will be cleared up soon. He seemed to think you might do something to help and I'm open to offers.' He stood up as Ashley and Stafford came into the cell. 'Anything you can do . . .' His eyes widened and his voice trailed off into a whisper.

Stafford stumped forward and took a long look at Lawrence. 'Here! I know you! You're that bleeder Tyburn who did for us all. It's him! It's him from the Augier Ridge I was telling you about.' He turned to Haldean and Ashley. 'It's him, I tell you. No moustache and his hair's gone grey, but it's him. Don't try and deny it, because I know.' His fists clenched. 'Cor! I'd like to get my hands on you. When I think what you did . . .'

Ashley dropped a heavy hand on Stafford's arm. 'We can't allow that, Mr Stafford. You're certain this is Major Martin Tyburn?'

'Course I'm sure. That's what I'm telling you, ain't I? Look at him. It's written all over him. He's that bugger Tyburn.'

'Oh hell,' said Haldean. He looked absolutely wretched. 'I told you I was sorry, Mr Lawrence.'

Chapter Twelve

'Well?' demanded Ashley bluntly. 'Is it true?'

Hugh Lawrence looked from Stafford to Ashley and Haldean, then back to Stafford once more. He put his shoulders back and sighed. 'There doesn't seem to be much point in denying it, does there?' The Canadian twang faded from his voice and he seemed a much older man than seconds before. He faced them with an air of wary, sick-hearted defiance. Like a man who's been told of a fatal illness, thought Haldean, or someone before a firing squad . . .

Stafford shrugged off Ashley's restraining hand. 'Don't worry, mister, I'm not going to slug him. Bleeding clever, weren't you, *Major* Tyburn? Leading me and my mates up the garden path like you did. We trusted you. We'd have followed you anywhere. Precious few of us left to trust you now, ain't there? How much did they pay you then?'

'I believe the going rate is thirty pieces of silver.'

Stafford flushed with anger and he aimed a swing at Tyburn before Ashley could stop him. Tyburn caught the flailing fist easily and held it firm. 'Don't be such a bloody fool, Private Stafford.' He flicked a glance at Ashley. 'Get him out of here – stop it, man! – and I'll answer your questions. God knows, I've got little enough to lose.' He let go of Stafford's fist. 'Go on.' He sank down on the bed. 'You've done your part.'

Haldean drew Stafford away. 'Come on, Mr Stafford, I'll show you to your hotel.'

'And what about him?'

'You can leave him to us. Come on.'

Tyburn glanced up as Stafford got to the cell door. 'By the way, where did you lose your leg?'

'Fricourt. Out of all the boys there was me, the Sergeant and Harry Brinton left alive after that. You'd seen to a good few and your Jerry pals finished the rest. Happy about that, were you?'

Tyburn flinched. 'No,' he said bleakly. 'No, I can't say I was ever happy about that.'

Haldean delivered Stafford into the care of Constable Hawley with instructions to see him safely established at the Talbot Arms. When he got back to Tyburn's cell, Ashley had been joined by Sergeant Sykes who was sitting at the table, his notebook in front of him. Tyburn was sitting on the bed, his back against the angle of the wall, cigarette in hand.

Ashley looked up as Haldean entered. 'I'm glad you're back. Mr Lawrence – Tyburn, I should say – refused to say anything before you arrived.'

'It's odd to be called that once more,' interjected the prisoner. 'He – Tyburn – belongs to another age.' He flicked his ash on to the floor and looked up with a twisted smile. 'And as for you, Major . . . Well, you seem to have worked everything out. The only thing you're lacking is the truth.' He waved a hand at Sergeant Sykes. 'Tell him to write this down. I don't want to go through it twice. I'm Tyburn. Martin James Tyburn. I'll give you the story from the beginning. You might as well hear it all. I've got nothing to be ashamed of, but little cause for pride.'

He put his shoulders against the wall and sighed. 'It's hard to know where to start. I got into trouble at Cambridge with a woman a good few years older than myself. She knew what she was about all right and I . . . well, even at that age I should have known better. She threatened an action for breach of promise and my father bought her off. There'd been a couple of other girls, too. It was nothing serious, but I was a good-looking young devil and my head was easily turned. There was a hell of a scandal and

229

not only did I get sent down but the guv'nor hauled me back home to reflect upon my sins. I can sympathize with him now. He was heavy-handed but right and had got me out of an awful mess. He wanted me to go to Australia and make something of myself out there. I, unfortunately from his point of view, met Beatrice Ziege. She was teaching the local doctor's girls. I've never known anyone like Beatrice, before or since. She was . . .'

He shook his head. 'Well, I can't describe her, so I'm not going to try. If she could have called herself *Von* Ziege I don't suppose my father would have objected. There was a stinking row which ended with us going off to London together and getting married. We were both of age, so there was nothing he could do about it. He washed his hands of us and for the next year and a half we were completely happy. I tried to make it up with the guv'nor, but he'd have none of it. I think what made it worse, from his point of view, was that instead of starving, as he'd foretold, I actually did rather well. Motor cars were getting popular, and I got a job as a demonstrator with a garage on Warren Street. And then Bea had Marguerite.'

He threw his cigarette on the floor and slowly took another from his case. 'She died. Beatrice died. There were all sorts of explanations I was given but the solid truth was that this baby, who Beatrice had been longing for, had cost her mother her life. I remember the doctor saying to me, "You've got your daughter," but I didn't *want* my daughter. I wanted Beatrice. I could hardly bear to look at the child . . . Cissie and Andrew Vayle were my salvation.' He glanced up. 'The Vayles were good people, Haldean. They were from Lower Woodbury but always came up to Town for the season. I'd run across Andrew whilst show-ing him a car and he'd invited us to dinner. There was a lot of local feeling about me and Beatrice and how the guv'nor had acted. Some supported him, some didn't, and the Vayles, who were only a few years older than us, rather took our part. After Marguerite was born, Andrew and Cissie came to see me. He was both tactful and honest. He guessed how I felt – I'd made no secret of it – and said that the one big regret in their lives was that they had no children. Placed as I was, could they look after the baby? They'd never pretend to be anything more than foster parents and I would always be her father. I feel sick when I think of how I answered him. I told him he could have the damn child and call it Vayle. I wanted nothing more to do with her, ever. If they'd take her off my hands, I was getting out of this bloody country and never coming back. At this point the baby wailed in the next room and Cissie got up without a word. I heard her talking to the nurse, then she came back into the room holding the child. She said, "Oh, Andrew . . ." and looked. Gets you when a woman looks like that.'

He smoked his cigarette down to the butt, then abruptly shook himself. 'From then on Marguerite belonged to the Vayles. And I? I'd got what I wanted. I didn't feel pleased or regretful, just numb. They went off with Marguerite and I was free to go. Cissie stood at the door and asked me if I wanted to say goodbye to my daughter but I couldn't. She wasn't mine any longer and I didn't want to interfere.

'Well, the next couple of years I spent drifting until I found myself going further and further into the Canadian west. Eventually the news caught up with me that my father had died but I had no desire to return home. I gave instructions for the estate to be sold and a few months later had a sizeable chunk in the bank. Then I met the man whose name I borrowed, Hugh Lawrence. I ran into him by taking his part in a fight with some toughs in a bar at Black Springs. By the time we'd put them to rights we found we were friends, and we've remained friends ever since. Lawrence is the goods. He's one of the best men I've ever known. He had a nose for copper and was itching to develop a site he'd found on the Peace River. With my money and his knowledge we prospered until a small town had built up around the workings. But Lawrence didn't really care about money. It was the excitement of the

231

find he was after and he'd often go off on lone trips, prospecting. He had the wonderful gift of being able to be friends without wanting to turn you inside out but eventually got to know all about Beatrice and the baby. Andrew wrote to me occasionally and a couple of times enclosed a photograph of the child. Lawrence tried, without pushing it, to make me see it wasn't the child's fault and, eventually, something of what he was saying took root. Then war was declared and I started thinking about home and the more I thought, the more I realized that's where I wanted to be. I sold my share to Lawrence and we travelled to London together. He fancied seeing England and wanted to put some deals through in London. When I got to London I put most of my money into a trust for Marguerite. If I got killed it wouldn't be any good to me and if I survived I could rely on Lawrence to give me a start back in Canada. I had a hankering to see her but – well, what was the point? She was happy with the Vayles. Following my wishes, they'd let her believe she was their daughter and I didn't want to disturb her for purely selfish reasons. There was one thing I did which I came to regret, though. I wanted Marguerite to be free to marry without the unhappiness I'd endured, so made the proviso that she should be able to have her money on marriage. Lawrence and the Vayles were the trustees and they had the sense to put in the clause that any marriage before her majority must be approved by them. Thank God they did. I was later to be very grateful for their foresight.

'I went to France, was commissioned, and avoided dying long enough to be promoted. I'd mixed in with all sorts of men in the previous years and learnt enough to be popular. Then we came up against the Augier Ridge. Major Haldean, you know that country, don't you? A rise of fifty feet is mountainous and the Germans were sitting on the top of the ridge with machine guns. There had been a chateau but by August 1916 it was in ruins. We tried four times to take it and every time were thrown back. Then Boscombe – the guy who was killed the other day – found a tunnel. I couldn't believe the tunnel would lead any-where useful but it was worth a try. I contacted Staff and received permission to take a party to explore. We got a fair way when the Germans jumped us. I can't tell you much about what happened. I stopped a bullet and woke up on the other side of the lines. It was a few weeks later before I found out what I was meant to have done. Some fresh prisoners came into the camp and were full of the story of my supposed treachery. That got pretty nasty, I can tell you . . .'

He shook his head and lit another cigarette. Glancing up, he shrugged. 'What can I say? I knew I was innocent, but the evidence was damning. One black mark against me was that I spoke German fluently and, as a result, got on better with the guards in the camp than most of the other prisoners. And it was clear enough I didn't hate the Germans. How could I, knowing that Beatrice was a German herself? There had been some ill feeling about my supposed pro-German tendencies and the idea I was a traitor was only too readily accepted. No one believed me and, partly for my own protection, the Germans decided to remove me to another camp. I escaped by jumping the train and, because I spoke the language, was able to get up to Rostock with little trouble. I stowed away on a Danish boat, got to Harwich and made my way to London. What I learned there convinced me that any attempt to clear my name would be futile.'

'Hold on a minute, sir,' asked Haldean. 'What did you do for money?'

Tyburn shrugged. 'It won't do him any harm to tell you now, I suppose. Andrew Vayle helped me. It was Andrew who pointed out that feeling was running so high, I'd better wait until the end of the war at least, before trying to restore my reputation. He took my word, but no one else in England would've done. I called myself Stockland – my mother's name – sailed for Canada and made my way back to the Peace River. Lawrence had heard the story and done what he could to protest my innocence. Useless, of course. It was Lawrence who suggested I stay put. He'd opened another mine fifty miles or so upriver and insisted on making me a present of it. He gave out that I was an old American friend of his who had come into partnership, and the firm of Lawrence and Stockland flourished. Most of the men who had worked for me as Tyburn had gone and the handful that were left failed to recognize me. There wasn't a lot of contact between the two mines anyway, and I'd shaved off my moustache, which altered my appearance a good deal. If I'd come across someone who'd known me well as Tyburn, the game would've been up, but as it was, I was safe enough. Then we got the news that Andrew Vayle had died and, at Christmas 1919, Cissie Vayle died too. Lawrence, as trustee, was invited to England, but . . . but Marguerite was my daughter, after all. The solicitor who had dealt with Lawrence when the trust was established had retired and I decided to risk a deception. I came over in Lawrence's place and he spent the time I was in England to go on one of his solitary trips using the name of Stockland.'

'You changed identities?' asked Ashley.

Tyburn smiled for the first time since he had started his story. 'Yes. It appealed to Lawrence's sense of humour, apart from anything else. He'd become quite a big noise and he relished the chance to leave it all behind and travel without any fuss. I thought there was little danger of anyone remembering Martin Tyburn and I could forge Lawrence's signature well enough to pass muster on any documents. I went to Marguerite's school.' He sighed. 'I fell for her, hook, line and sinker. Although she didn't look like her mother, odd things she did – the way she held her head, the way she walked – all reminded me of Beatrice. I'd ignored her for years; now I was crazy about her. I had another reason for visiting England, too. As Lawrence it was reasonable that I should want to find out the truth about my "old friend" Tyburn. I employed a lawyer – Bell of Moreland and Bell, Lincoln's Inn – and quickly got the gist of it. There had been a flood of first-

234

class information to the Germans and it was obvious there was a fairly senior spy at work. After I failed to return from the Augier tunnels there were documents found in my kit that pointed directly to me. Whoever the spy was had found a convenient scapegoat in me. There was no doubt in anyone's mind; I was the traitor.'

'Did the spying continue after your capture?' asked Haldean.

'Yes. That much was obvious. However, there was always some leakage of information, so it didn't raise anyone's suspicions, and things had quietened down for a few months after I'd gone. But I *knew* I was innocent and therefore the real spy had escaped scot-free. It had to be someone with access to my things because I certainly hadn't put the papers there, which narrowed it down to the men who were at the farm with me. I did wonder about Boscombe, who I always disliked, but he transferred to the RFC, and was posted to a training school in England. He couldn't have done any spying from there. I simply couldn't bring myself to suspect the rest of my officers. Most of those who survived the tunnels were killed at Fricourt, as Stafford reminded me just now. I realize that spies can be killed as other men are, but my suspicions centred on the one man who had been in the tunnels, who survived the war, and who might have had access to my kit.'

Haldean nodded. 'Colonel Whitfield?'

'Colonel Whitfield,' agreed Tyburn. 'I knew nothing about the man but I made it my business to find out. He'd gone from the cavalry to the staff, and who better than a staff officer to have information that the Germans would want? He'd been awarded the VC – what a cover that made! I was very leery of the good Colonel.'

'So what did you do?' demanded Ashley.

Tyburn shrugged. 'What could I do? He was secure. Major Tyburn had disappeared and was popularly supposed to be dead. If I started making a fuss then the spotlight would fall on me and for the sake of Lawrence, who had shielded me, and for Marguerite, who would be bound to be caught up in the mess, I decided to let matters stand. As Stockland I was respected in Canada. As Lawrence I could come to England and see my daughter. And so it went on. Then I got a letter from Alice Rivers . . .'

Tyburn drew deeply on his cigarette, shaking his head in disbelief. 'Of all the men in England my daughter had fallen in love with Whitfield. In a way I could have expected it. Since the Vayles died, Hesperus has been Marguerite's home and a good home, too. With Breeden-brook being so close it was inevitable that they should meet, but it struck me like a thunderbolt. I hurried across and threw an almighty spanner in that gentleman's works. I suspected he had been a spy and a traitor; I was certain his interest in Marguerite began and ended with her money. No one could understand why I refused the match but I didn't have to explain. The more I saw of him, the less I liked him. I would have done anything – *anything* – to prevent Marguerite becoming his wife.'

'And what did you do?' asked Ashley.

'I refused my consent. I know what you believe but you're wrong. Whoever killed Whitfield it wasn't me. I can't see why he shouldn't have killed himself. I suspect he was nearly broke and he was sodden with drink. When I refused to budge on the marriage, he may well have thought that was the best way out. But I didn't kill him. I could get what I wanted without resorting to murder. I agreed to meet him because I intended to buy him off. He was disturbing Marguerite's peace of mind and I meant to stop him. I knew he had no idea who I was, as we'd never met each other until a fortnight ago, so I intended to say enough about the Augier Ridge to let him see that one person, at least, was wise to him. If he'd been guilty he couldn't have mistaken my hints. As it was, I never got to say anything to him.'

He paused, putting his hands round his crooked knee. 'It all happened exactly as I said. I arrived at the barn, walked

236

into a punch like a pile-driver, went out like a light and, when I came to, got out as quickly as I could. I had no idea Whitfield was there until Major Haldean showed me his body. I don't know how my fingerprints got on the gun. I've been racking my brains to remember if anyone could have shown me a gun or a gun-barrel I might have touched without knowing, but I've drawn a blank. I don't remember hearing a shot. I think I must have been unconscious when it was fired. Not being a complete fool I realize how thin it must sound, but it's the truth.'

'Are you sure you don't wish to revise your statement?' said Ashley.

Tyburn met his gaze. 'No. It would be easy enough for me to say I'd seen Whitfield before I came out of the barn but I'm not going to. If I could think of some believable explanation I might try it, but I can't. All I can tell you is that I'm innocent. Damn it all, man, why *should* I kill him? Can't you see how awkward this is going to be for Hugh Lawrence? I wouldn't drag him into it if I could think of a way round it. Hugh's been good to me. I'd never repay him like this.'

'Does Miss Vayle know who you are?' asked Haldean.

'She does now. I told her last night.' He smiled. 'The odd thing was I think she was beginning to suspect. She certainly wasn't as surprised as I thought she might be. She believes in me, thank God. That's been a great comfort to me over the last few hours. But . . .' His face lengthened. 'I didn't want her to find out like this and when I think of the people who've trusted me – Philip and Alice Rivers but most of all Hugh Lawrence – and all the trouble it's going to bring them . . . Well, it's a hard furrow to plough but it's not of my making.'

Ashley coughed. 'I'd like to ask you about Jeremy Boscombe.'

'Boscombe? What about him?'

'Apparently he knew who your daughter was and had been blackmailing her from January onwards. He also told her that you were alive.'

Tyburn's lips tightened. 'Little swine. I'd had no idea he knew who Marguerite was. When she told us what she'd been through, it was damned hard to restrain myself. When I think of her being forced to sell her jewellery and actually take Isabelle Rivers' necklace . . . I wish I could've got my hands on him, I can tell you.'

Ashley looked at him thoughtfully. 'The question is, Mr Tyburn, did you get your hands on him?'

'What? Murder him, you mean? No, I didn't. I can't pretend I'm sorry he's dead but I didn't kill him. I wasn't aware he was at the fête. Obviously enough, I wouldn't have gone if I'd known he was going to be there. I didn't know he'd seen me. The first I heard about it was last Monday night when poor Marguerite told us what had been happening. I'm not sure how he knew who she was, but I think I might be indirectly to blame. I used to keep a photograph of her and the Vayles propped up against my things in France. We used to talk about our homes and families of course, and it turned out that Captain Hodge knew the Vayles slightly and had actually met Marguerite. She was only a child then, of course, so he couldn't tell me much about her, but the fact I had a daughter I'd never seen aroused quite a bit of comment. There wasn't any secret about it, you see, not then. Boscombe was interested in it, as I recall. He might have recognized her name if he came across her later on. Andrew Vayle was fairly well known and there were various pieces in the newspapers about him when he died. That's the only thing I can think of. Hodge, poor devil, was killed at Fricourt.'

'I can guess what you're going to answer to this question, Mr Tyburn, but I have to ask it anyway,' said Ashley. 'Were Boscombe and Morton blackmailing you?'

Tyburn's eyes opened wide. 'Blackmailing *me*? Of course not. Boscombe had his knife into Marguerite but I don't suppose he had any idea I was alive until he saw me last Saturday. Why, I've been in Canada since the end of 1916.

I'd never heard of Morton and I hadn't seen Boscombe since the Augier Ridge.'

'You hadn't come across Boscombe on one of your trips to this country?'

'Absolutely not. Let me explain. I knew my position was delicate, to say the least. I felt safe enough coming to Sussex because it was years since I'd lived here. As a youngster I'd been away at school and then up at Cambridge. I don't resemble my father particularly and I couldn't see why anyone would connect the young Martin Tyburn with the middle-aged Hugh Lawrence. And, of course, no one did. But I was wary of anyone who'd known me in the army. I had a list of four people I had to avoid. All the rest had either only known me in passing or were dead. But these four I knew I mustn't see. They were Stafford, who you managed to dig up, Jesson from Norfolk, Petrie from London and Boscombe. They had known me well and although it *might* be all right, I wasn't going to take any risks. I reckoned that if I stayed out of London I'd be safe enough. I never thought Boscombe, a city creature if ever there was one, would come anywhere near Breedenbrook. No, Boscombe never approached me.'

'And yet his death must have been convenient for you, sir.'

Tyburn chewed his lip. 'Convenient? Yes, it was convenient but do you really think that a man in my position could afford to risk a murder? Quite honestly, if Boscombe had tried to blackmail me, I'd have probably paid up to keep him quiet. I know you're not meant to admit that sort of thing but what choice would I have had? One word from him in this country would not only have ruined me but made things horribly difficult for Marguerite and downright impossible for Lawrence. Once I'd got back to Canada, it would have been a different matter. There I was known as Stockland and Hugh would've been able to prove he'd been in Canada throughout most of the war. They could've investigated Lawrence until the cows came

239

home without finding anything to his discredit. And, while we're on the subject, I may as well tell you I had nothing to do with that other chap's death. Morton, I mean, the man who was killed at the Talbot Arms. I've told you the truth, Mr Ashley. Someone used me as a scapegoat in France and someone's using me as a scapegoat again.'

Tyburn looked at Haldean. 'Your uncle told me you've got a flair for working out the truth. Work out the truth of this business and it'll be one of the best things you've ever done.'

Haldean avoided his eyes. Work out the truth? He'd done that and the reward was bitter indeed.

Sitting in the garden of the Lamb and Flag, Isabelle picked up her glass and swirled it round, seeing how the liquid danced a reflection on the underneath of the sycamore leaves spreading above her head. She sipped her gin-and-ginger thoughtfully, looking at her cousin. He seemed drawn and unhappy. Tired, as well, which wasn't surprising after driving to London and back twice in two days.

It was Monday morning. Ernest Stafford, the richer by five pounds, had been taken back to Battersea the previous day. Her father, after refusing to believe Lawrence was Tyburn until he heard it from his own lips, had first sulked, then badgered Jack to prove that Tyburn was an innocent man. Marguerite wouldn't consider any other possibility and was only stopped from having a blazing row with Haldean by the presence of Lady Rivers. Isabelle found herself allied with her mother as the keeper of an uneasy peace. She felt distinctly sorry for Jack.

She had gladly fallen in with his plea for company in the car that morning. 'I need some time off,' he explained. 'I've always loved Hesperus but the atmosphere is pretty poisonous at the moment . . .' He let the sentence trail off expressively. 'I wish Greg was here. I'd like to chew things over with him.' He'd not wanted to go back to Hesperus but instead had taken her for lunch in the pub. Sitting by the noisy stream which gave Breedenbrook its name, she noticed the lines around his mouth and the shadows under his eyes. 'It's been rough, hasn't it?' she asked gently.

He didn't pretend not to understand but gave her a quick, grateful glance. 'It's been putrid. Ashley's full of praise for my having completed the case, and can't understand why I've got any reservations at all. To him, my producing Stafford was like a magician pulling a rabbit from a hat, but there wasn't anything magic about it. I was thinking about Boscombe and it suddenly struck me what he'd said at the fête. *Give a man enough rope.*'

Isabelle looked puzzled. '*And he'll hang himself,*' she completed. 'I don't get it, Jack. How did that lead you to Mr Lawrence? Tyburn, I mean.'

He half-smiled. 'Don't you see? Where did they use to hang people, Belle? Think about London. Oxford Street, you know, where Marble Arch is now.'

'Tyburn,' said Isabelle slowly. 'Jack! *Tyburn.*'

Haldean nodded. 'That's what Boscombe was going on about. He must have seen Mr Tyburn at the fête and been over the moon. Blackmail with a capital B. No wonder he was so full of himself. He was so up in the air about it he couldn't help boasting and it made it all the more fun for him that neither Greg nor I had a clue what he was talking about. When the penny finally did drop, it made so much sense. If Mr Lawrence really was Tyburn it explained why he had been so protective of Marguerite. We all sensed his feelings ran deeper than those of a trustee to his ward. We guessed the wrong motive, that's all.' He ran a hand through his hair. 'Once I had the idea I had to prove it. It didn't take me long to work out that if there was a war pensioner who'd served with Tyburn before the Augier Ridge tunnels, the War Office would have a note of his current name and address. I hadn't got the mechanics of it, but guessed there was some sort of substitution going on. Hence Ernest Stafford's visit to Breedenbrook and Mr Tyburn's number was well and truly up.'

'Wasn't it a bit chancy? I mean, Stafford might not have recognized Mr Lawrence – Tyburn, I mean – anyway.'

'I'd talked to Stafford so much about the war that he must have thought I had an *idée fixe* on the subject. I didn't put the notion into his head, just made sure he was thinking along the right lines. And that's magic. The quickness of the 'and deceives the h'eye. Brilliant, wasn't it?' he added bitterly.

Isabelle shook her head. 'Don't be like that, Jack. It was really clever of you to work out what Boscombe was going on about.'

He half-smiled once more. 'You think so? That puts you in a minority consisting of you and Ashley. He thinks I'm wonderful. He should talk to Marguerite and Uncle Philip. Aunt Alice has been a bit frozen, too. My God!'

'Jack,' said Isabelle cautiously, aware she was treading on delicate ground. 'You said something about reservations. Have you really got any?'

'Oh Lord, yes. Him, mainly. Tyburn, I mean. He was so utterly convincing about his innocence that it was damned hard not to believe him. I stood in that cell, watching him being so sincere and so ruddy brave that I could feel myself really wanting him to be innocent. It worked, you know? I did wonder afterwards if he'd been too convincing. I could feel myself being swayed and I didn't like it, Belle. Do you know what I mean? Someone, someone powerful, tells you what to feel and you *do* feel it. Later on, when you've come out from under the ether and the effect's worn off you begin to think that you might have been led up the garden path. He finished off with a direct appeal to me, Belle, to the man who'd just landed him in it. He knew I'd brought Stafford along. So why ask me?'

'Because he wanted you to help?'

'By doing *what*?' Haldean stopped just short of banging the table. 'Look, I like him. It'd be hard not to like him but he has a real ruthless streak. That's there, too. By his own showing he's a tough and successful copper miner. Anyone, I suppose, can have a lucky strike in somewhere as

God-forsaken as the Rockies, but you don't develop it and turn it into a wealthy business without making some hard choices. I sensed how powerful a personality he has that day I helped him out of the barn, the day Whitfield was killed. You know you said you wouldn't like to stand between Marguerite and her getting what she wanted? Well, she inherited that trait from her father and no mistake. The evidence is there too, Belle. Wonderful, scientific, fingerprint evidence. Get round that. Just because his wife died under tragic circumstances doesn't mean he's an innocent man.'

'I can see that, but . . .'

'But what? He's dippy about Marguerite. Admittedly, not for the reasons we thought, but he's crackers about the girl. Boscombe, Morton and most of all Whitfield all threatened her well-being and he's not the sort of man to take that lying down. Not only that, but Boscombe recognized him at the fête. What's to say the recognition wasn't mutual? Just think what that'd mean to Tyburn. I know he said he'd be all right once he was back in Canada, but he wouldn't, not really. The best he could look forward to was a lifetime of blackmail, the worst, and this would have seemed much more likely, was exposure, arrest and the rope. Not only that, but the whole scandal would have been dug up again and Marguerite's future would have been utterly blighted. My God, no. Tyburn fits, Belle, he fits. It's a bit like doing a jigsaw, you know. You put in all the pieces round the edge, then pick up the final piece – the murderer – and carefully lay that down. I've put Tyburn into the gap marked "Murderer" and there aren't any chinks showing.'

Isabelle pushed her plate away and, taking a cigarette from her case, leaned forward for him to light it. 'I can see a chink,' she said. 'It's you.'

Haldean struck a match. 'What d'you mean?'

'If you believed he really fitted into your jigsaw then you'd be . . . happy's the wrong word. Satisfied. You're not. And I don't understand why Colonel Whitfield tried to murder you on that horrible horse. I know you said Mr Law . . . Tyburn might have recognized Boscombe and that's fair enough, but you also said he would have killed him if he'd known what he was doing to Marguerite and I don't believe he did know. She was so secretive about it that she wouldn't tell *anyone*. I think you were right to begin with and Boscombe and Morton were killed because they were blackmailers, but who they were blackmailing, except for Marguerite, I don't know.'

He started to laugh. 'I think I followed all that.'

'I should hope you did,' she said, returning the smile. 'So was Boscombe blackmailing anyone apart from Maggie?'

'Oh yes. He was blackmailing Whitfield.'

Isabelle breathed deeply. 'Jack, will you *please* explain?'

'Okay.' He took a long drink of beer. 'Think about Whitfield, Belle, think how he acted. The man was scared stiff by the mention of blackmail. That's what made him attempt to murder me. That and my telling him I wasn't a complete dud, that I'd done this sort of thing before. He'd got me on the raw and I said more than I should. Something you don't know – this is in confidence, of course – is that his bank account shows that, whereas before October he was making fairly hefty payments to cash, after October it sky-rocketed. Another seventy-five pounds a month started going out regularly. If he'd carried on at that rate he'd have been ruined by the end of the year.'

'But what were they blackmailing him *for*, Jack?'

A wry smile lifted the corners of his mouth. 'That's obvious, isn't it? He was the Augier Ridge traitor.'

Isabelle stared at him. 'But he can't be. He just can't. If he's the traitor then Mr Lawrence – oh, bother it, you know who I mean – Tyburn – is telling the truth and he's innocent.'

'Innocent of what?'

'Well, everything. The spying, the murders – everything.'

'It doesn't prove anything of the sort.' Haldean pulled deeply at his cigarette. 'Ashley doesn't believe a word of this, by the way. He thinks I'm clutching at straws. He argues that if Whitfield's the traitor then presumably he put the incriminating documents in Tyburn's kit. Now when could Whitfield have got at Tyburn's things? As Ashley says, Whitfield might have gone into the mess-room of the farmhouse but he'd have been lucky to get into Tyburn's quarters undisturbed. It was their rest day, you see, when you'd expect the farmhouse to be full.'

He frowned. 'Ashley – and I have the deepest respect for Ashley – thinks I'm making complications for the fun of it. He rightly points out that the simplest explanation is that Tyburn put the papers in his own kit because Tyburn was the traitor. Oddly enough, in a way it doesn't matter.'

'How on earth do you work that out?'

'Easy. Say Boscombe was blackmailing Whitfield. He comes down to the fête to screw some more money out of him, runs into Marguerite Vayle, and just to make his cup of happiness complete, spots Tyburn. So far so good?'

'I suppose so, yes.'

'Now Whitfield, who, by my reckoning, had every reason to murder him, didn't. Unfortunately that's a sheer physical impossibility, worse luck. But Tyburn, the resolute, determined Mr Tyburn, is waiting in the wings. He might not have been a traitor; I don't believe he was. That's not the point. Everyone believes him to have been a traitor and one word from Boscombe spelt ruin.'

She moved impatiently. 'Don't tell me you believe all that, Jack. This is Mr Lawrence we're talking about. I haven't known him very long, I agree, but I like him and trust him.'

'His name isn't Lawrence. Trust him in what way?'

'The usual way, I suppose. You know, truthful, reliable, all that sort of thing.'

'But can't you see, Belle, that's exactly what he isn't? He didn't tell us the truth. He came here pretending to be another man.'

'He had a pretty good reason.'

'I know that, old thing, but he was terribly convincing as

Lawrence. He made us all believe him. He's a brilliant liar. Now I think Whitfield is much more likely to have been the traitor, because it fits in with everything that happened afterwards. But don't you see that *because* Whitfield was the traitor Tyburn had a compelling motive to murder him? When you think of what Whitfield had done to both him and his men, sheer revenge would make Whitfield's death seem more like a justifiable execution than a murder. And as for saying he didn't do it – well, I repeat, he's a brilliant liar.'

Isabelle finished her drink in silence. 'I still trust him,' she said in a small voice.

'I'm afraid that doesn't amount to a hill of beans.' Haldean picked his glass up and stared at his beer. 'Why beans, I wonder? Jolly useful things in their way, legumes. Broad beans, butter beans, runner beans, french beans, kidney beans, haricot beans . . . Don't pay any attention, Belle, I'm rambling.'

'You always do talk nonsense when you're worried.'

'Do I? Windsor beans . . .'

'They're the same as broad beans,' put in Isabelle, starting to smile.

'Are they? Yes, I suppose they are.' He finished his drink and put the glass down firmly on the table. 'But whether they're undisguised or operating under an alias, they amount to the same thing; nothing. And that, old scream, is what trust is in a case like this; nothing. Have you finished your Mother's Ruin, by the way? Fancy another? No? Let's go, then. I don't mind telling you,' he added, picking up his hat and giving her his arm, 'that I wish I'd never started all this. I was so damned keen to get involved. I'll know better next time. Shall we walk along by the brook to the car? I think the path should bring us out in more or less the right place.'

'I still like him,' said Isabelle obstinately.

'So do I. Why d'you think I feel such a complete heel?'

Isabelle looked at him and squeezed his arm. 'Jack,' she said slowly, stepping on to the narrow path and skirting round a clump of nettles, 'couldn't you try and believe him? You know, take that as your starting point. Imagine everything he said was the truth. How would that affect things?'

'It makes them just about impossible, I would have said . . . *Morton!*'

'What?'

'Morton!' He grasped her arms eagerly. 'Don't you see? I've assumed Boscombe and Morton came here to dig more money out of their victim. Now Morton was really ticked off with Boscombe and followed him down afterwards. If I'm right, then Morton wouldn't have known anything about Tyburn. It was Whitfield he was after. Once Boscombe recognized Tyburn, he wouldn't have told Morton anything about it, even if he could have done. He must have thought it was like finding money in the street. So why did Tyburn murder Morton? How could he have known the man existed at all? Unless, damn it, Boscombe told Tyburn as a sort of insurance. "Don't try anything on me, I've got a pal who knows all about it." Hell! I thought I had something there.'

'But you have, Jack, haven't you?' asked Isabelle, looking up at his crestfallen expression. 'Boscombe didn't know Morton had come here. He might have talked about his friend in London, but he didn't know his friend was on the spot.'

Haldean stopped and looked at her open-mouthed. 'By God,' he whispered. 'By God, you're right! Belle, I could kiss you. Damn it, I will kiss you.' He put his arm around her and suited actions to words. 'From now on I sit humbly at your feet. Of course! Tyburn *couldn't* know Morton was at the Talbot Arms. What did you say, O Mentor? That I should start from believing everything he says is the truth? I'll try it. I don't know what the dickens I'm going to do about those fingerprints, but I'll try it.'

'I'm glad to hear it,' said Isabelle, detaching herself with a giggle. 'Stop, Jack.' She pushed him away. 'For heaven's sake, don't grab me again. There's a row of cottages along the path and people will be looking.'

'Let 'em. Mind you,' he added, sobering slightly and resuming their walk, 'I still don't see what happened. I can't quite manage the mental gymnastics of the Red Queen and believe six impossible things before breakfast. It'll take until dinner-time, at least. But it's a start, Belle, a start. Believe he's telling the truth, eh?'

'That's right. Just take what he says in good faith.'

Haldean clicked his tongue. 'It's not faith so much as a brainwave I need. Faith without works is dead, as St James says . . . Faith? We need evidence. Proof. I haven't got the whole story yet and, by crikey, I want it.'

She squeezed his arm once more. 'You'll get there.'

They had drawn level with the backs of the cottages and on the narrow strip of scrubby grass that separated the back walls of the houses from the path, a little girl sat playing with an old kettle and three mismatched cups. A doll was propped up beside her on a hummock of earth. She looked up as they approached then, with a squeak of joy, flung herself at Haldean.

'It's you! It's you what gived me my dolly!'

'It's Sally, isn't it?' said Haldean, bending down with a smile. 'You remember Sally from the fête, don't you, Belle? Say hello to Miss Rivers, Sally.'

'Hello, Miss Rivers,' said Sally politely. Haldean felt a hot little hand tug at his. 'Come and see my dolly's tea party. I had to call her Mabel 'cos my other dolly was called Daisy but she's being a good girl and eating up all her tea. Come and see.'

With utmost gravity, Haldean allowed himself to be conducted to where Sally had arranged a meal of elderberry flowers, daisies, buttercups and laburnum pods on plates of leaves.

'You won't eat these, will you, sweetheart?' said Isabelle, stooping down and picking up the laburnum seeds. 'They're poisonous, you know.'

'I know that,' replied Sally witheringly. 'I'm only 'tending. Do you like my plates? I've got to have leaf plates 'cos I haven't got a proper dollies' tea-set.'

'I'd rather have leaves,' said Haldean, sitting on the grass, and solemnly receiving a cup of muddy water from the old kettle. 'Jolly good tea, this. Is Mabel having some?'

Sally put a cup to the doll's lips. 'There,' she said with great satisfaction. 'She's drunk it all up and now it's time for her nap.' She picked up the doll and put it carefully into the waiting cot, covering it up with the blanket. 'I wish I still had Daisy,' she said wistfully. 'Daisy's cot had roses on the blanket and the pillow. I liked the roses. Poor Daisy got all trodden on. I found her cot but it had got broken but I never did find Daisy's pillow. Still,' she said, brightening, 'Mabel's a good dolly. She's fast asleep now.'

There was an inarticulate exclamation from Haldean and Isabelle laughed out loud.

'You're not meant to *really* drink it,' said Sally, watching Haldean wipe the water from his lips. 'It's not *really* tea. I told you. I'm just 'tending.'

He froze for a few brief seconds, then relaxed. 'Of course you are. I should have known better, shouldn't I? I say, Sally, about Daisy's pillow. Are you sure you looked everywhere for it?'

'Everywhere,' she said with round eyes. 'Mummy helped me too, because it had roses on it.'

There was a shout from the yard behind them and a young, apron-clad woman came to the gate. 'Who're you talking to, Sally?' She stopped as she saw Isabelle and Haldean, looking at them enquiringly.

Haldean scrambled to his feet and raised his hat. 'Mrs Mills? I'm Jack Haldean and this is my cousin, Miss Rivers. We met your little girl at the fête the other week.'

Mrs Mill's face cleared. 'Oh, you're the gentleman who gave Sally her doll. That was very kind of you, sir. Wasn't it a shocking business what happened?'

'Terrible,' agreed Haldean. 'Look, Sally, Miss Rivers and I have to go now, but if Mummy says it's all right, here's something for your money box.' He took out his pocket-book and gave the awe-struck child a ten-shilling note. 'It is all right, Mrs Mills, is it?'

'Why, yes sir. And it's very kind of you, I'm sure. Say thank you, Sally. But you shouldn't have done that, sir. It's far too much.'

'No, it's fine, really it is.' Isabelle caught the note of suppressed excitement in his voice. 'She's just helped me to think of something that's been bothering me. I'm very grateful to her. And perhaps, Sally, if Mummy agrees, you could buy a dollies' tea-set with some of the money.' He tipped his hat once more. 'It's nice to have met you, Mrs Mills.' He ruffled Sally's hair. 'Enjoy your tea-set, won't you?'

'What is it, Jack?' asked Isabelle urgently, as soon as they were out of earshot. 'I know there's something biting you.'

He looked at her with a jubilant gleam in his black eyes. 'I can't tell you.'

'Jack!'

'No, I really can't – don't hit me, woman! – because I don't know what it is yet. I might if you let me work it out. There's a ghost of an idea but it needs to be left in peace for a while. There's one thing I can tell you for certain though, Belle.'

'What's that?'

'You said I needed faith. I've never needed anything less. I've been a damn sight too trusting altogether. Cynicism is what I need, *real* cynicism. Trust? Forget it.' His lips set in a hard, straight line. 'It's about time I started disbelieving everything I've been told.'

Chapter Thirteen

Anne-Marie Verrity sat up on the sofa of the morning room at Thackenhurst and looked at Haldean in undisguised astonishment. 'Monsieur Haldean, are you serious? It is true, yes, that I own the Augier Ridge and what remains of the chateau.' She shrugged. 'I have never thought about it, but I suppose that as the entrance to the tunnels is on my property, the tunnels are also mine. But why do you want to go down them? They have not been entered for years and I cannot see why you should want to do so now. They cannot have anything to do with Richard's death. If I thought you could help poor Richard by doing such a thing, then of course I would give you my permission. But how will such an action benefit anyone?' She got up and walked to the window, pointing across the grounds in the direction of the tithe barn. 'That is where Richard was killed. That is where you should be looking for evidence to convict the horrible man who murdered him.' She turned and shook her head. 'The tunnels and the war – they are yesterday. They cannot affect what happened to Richard.'

Haldean shifted forward in his chair and looked at her seriously. 'It's precisely because of Richard Whitfield that I'm asking you to let me go. You see, everything that's happened here has its roots in the past. Martin Tyburn . . .' Mrs Verrity snorted at the name. 'Martin Tyburn swears he's not the traitor.'

'Who then does he accuse?' asked Mrs Verrity savagely. 'Richard?'

He looked at her with great sympathy. 'I'm afraid he does.'

She froze, then very slowly walked across the room and rested her hand on the table. Her tension was nearly tangible. 'He says that? He says these things about *Richard*? No one will believe him, I tell you, no one. As soon as he says it, it will be dismissed like that.' She snapped her fingers together. 'Richard was a hero. He had the VC for his bravery. He and he alone stopped the Boche in the tunnels. Tyburn – who cares what he says? He will be laughed at, you hear me, laughed at.'

'He'll still have said it.' She tossed her head dismissively, then turned, compelled by Haldean's measured voice. 'When Tyburn comes to trial he'll be allowed to make a statement. It's his right under the law and he proposes to base his defence on Colonel Whitfield's guilt. Of necessity it will be discussed, debated, argued over. And, even if it's ultimately rejected, you will always have a rump of people – influential people – who will think there's more to Colonel Whitfield's heroism than met the eye. Mr Tyburn's a likeable man, Mrs Verrity. He has the gift of persuading people that he's right.'

Her hand clenched. 'This is nonsense.' Her voice shook. 'An outrage.' She jerked her head up and glared at him. '*Et vous, vous le croyez?*'

'No,' said Haldean quietly. 'I don't believe it. I am merely pointing out what will happen if Tyburn is allowed to make his statement. Colonel Whitfield cannot defend himself, but if I am allowed to find out the truth – *and prove it* – then his good name might be preserved. I'll be honest with you, Mrs Verrity. I hardly knew Colonel Whitfield but he meant an awful lot to Marguerite Vayle and I know, if you'll excuse me mentioning it, he meant a lot to you.'

Mrs Verrity raised her hands high. 'But how will going into the tunnels prove anything, Major Haldean? Still, I do not understand.'

Haldean hunched forward, resting his elbows on his knees. 'Let me try and explain. The Allied end of the

252

tunnels was blocked off by German grenades but beyond the landfall things should be as they were left that day in 1916, unless the Germans interfered, of course. But really, once the link to the British lines was closed they would have no reason to enter the tunnels again. The soil, as you know, is chalk. With only a little bit of good luck everything should be bone-dry and therefore perfectly preserved. Mr Tyburn has said enough to make me curious as to what really is down there. I might as well tell you that I wonder if there's another element in the case we haven't looked at.'

'Such as?'

'Well, such as someone else, another man altogether, being the real traitor. Boscombe, as you know, wrote a book about his experiences in the tunnels. But that wasn't the only record of what happened that day. Robert Petrie, who also went into the tunnels, left a diary. Now we haven't been able to find the diary, more's the pity, but we know enough to have a pretty shrewd idea of what was in it. And it's those ideas, Mrs Verrity, that I want to have a shot at either proving or disproving. I *think* I know who Petrie implicated, but I can't know I'm right and certainly can't prove I'm right until I can get into the tunnels.' He half-smiled. 'I might be completely up the creek of course, but I don't think I am. After all, look how much it would explain. Tyburn's story might be true, as far as it concerns the Augier Ridge.'

'Nonsense! He is lying. How can there be another man? Even if there was, you will not find him in the tunnels. I will hear none of it. This Tyburn is the traitor and is blaming Richard to save his own skin.'

'And that also is possible. But –' he smiled apologetically – 'I really want to know. Obviously I'm not expecting to find the bloke in there waiting for me, but he'll have left evidence of his activities that should put me on his track. But with no proof, I'm helpless. I can theorize until I'm blue in the face but once I'm in the tunnels *I'll know*.'

She lifted her eyebrow. 'You have great confidence, Major Haldean. What if I refuse my permission?'

'Well, there's more than one way of skinning a cat.' She looked at him curiously. 'I've learnt enough to have a good chance, a very good chance, of obtaining the information elsewhere. But that would take time. I'd probably get there in the end, but this is the simplest way. And, of course, there's nothing to stop me taking a short holiday in northern France . . .'

'No!' She shook her head vigorously. 'Please, do not even think of it. You will be on my property without my consent but, believe me, that is not the reason I say no. Have you any idea how dangerous that land is? Why, I have tenants – farmers – on the ridge who thought that after the war all their troubles were over. But the land is full of unexploded bombs and rotting mines. One of my tenants, Raoul Rimet, has a barn full of old rifles, ammunition and shells that he has dug up from his fields. I would be surprised if the Boche did not use the old cellars to store their fearful weapons. There might be many tons of explosive under the soil. I tell you, Major, I do not care to live near the Chateau d'Augier any longer. To go into the tunnels? You would be in great danger.'

Haldean gave her a brilliant smile. 'I survived the war. I think I'll be able to survive the tunnels.'

She bit her lip, then, shaking her head, came to a rapid decision. 'I will come with you.'

'*What?*'

'It is better so. I know the old entrance from the cellars of the chateau. The building is destroyed but the cellars are still there.'

'No.' Haldean shook his head. 'You can't do that, Mrs Verrity. Why, you've just told me how dangerous the place is. I can't possibly let you risk it.'

Her eyebrows rose. 'It is not for you to say what I can and cannot risk.'

'No, but . . .'

'But rather than have you climb over the ruins I would

254

prefer to take you a way that I know is safe.' She smiled briefly. 'You are young and courageous, Monsieur Haldean.' She crossed the room to him and held out her hand for him to take. Her smile increased. 'You are also inquisitive and – I am old enough to say this – very handsome.' She looked down at him thoughtfully. 'I would not like you to come to any harm.'

'Well, if you're sure,' said Ashley unenthusiastically.

'Of course I'm not sure!' exploded Haldean. 'If I was *able* to be sure I wouldn't have to go down the damn tunnels at all. But you must admit that what I've said makes sense. Lots of sense. It adds up, which is something that no other theory does. No loose ends. You said yourself I was on to something.'

Ashley grudgingly nodded. 'And I wouldn't be surprised if you were right. In fact the more I think about it, the more convinced I am. But it's hellishly risky, Haldean.'

'Knowing I've got your support takes as much risk out of it as it's possible to do. And Greg's in on it as well. I can't tell you how much his backing means to me. I really think we should do this, Ashley. After all, what have we got to lose?'

'Your neck, you young idiot,' said Ashley wearily.

'Only if I'm right.'

'Which will be a great consolation to anyone who's allowed themselves to care tuppence about you.' Ashley drummed his fingers on his desk and sighed. 'Leave it with me. Yes, of course we'll do it. God knows what you'd get up to if I said no. You'd probably go ahead without me, as there's absolutely nothing I could do to stop you. I'll have to get permission, of course, but with any luck that shouldn't be a problem. I can't say I'm happy, though. I wish . . .' His mouth tightened, then he shook his head. 'Oh, forget it.'

'Cheer up,' said Haldean. 'I might be wrong, you know.'

'Fat chance,' grunted Ashley. 'You know damn well you're not.'

'Now there you're mistaken, old son,' said Haldean seriously. 'I think I'm right; you think I'm right. But until we can prove it we can't *know* we're right. And as I said to Mrs Verrity, I really want to know.'

It was the British Fifth Army that had eventually taken the Augier Ridge in a grim struggle which included Beaumont-Hamel. Picking over the charred timbers that rose like dead men's fingers from the smoke-blackened stones of the chateau, Haldean had a sudden recollection of flying over this insignificant hump of ground. One eye on the sky around him – his stomach churned at the memory – and the briefest of glances at the ant-like figures crawling up the hill. Take out the machine guns; those had been the orders. God, he'd loathed strafing ground troops. Every man armed with a spark of light that turned into bullets. Three flights a day, four when the light was good. Height; dive; fire; zoom; height. No use twisting in aerobatics here. Skill was redundant when death was a many-headed monster. And the only response to the men who plunged to the earth below was another scrawled letter to some English town. They'd taken a beating here. The Germans had fought savagely. Or gallantly. It all depended on your point of view. The ruins of the chateau faded from sight and superimposed themselves on a creased map and a board of aerial photographs. And the ants? There must be a name carved on some memorial for every square foot of ground. He shuddered, then turned as he felt a hand touch his arm.

'Major Haldean? You are all right, yes?'

He shook himself and forced a smile. The aerial photographs faded and he was standing in a ruined house on top of a blustery ridge overlooking lush valleys filled with pale living gold and green. If it wasn't for the chateau you'd never know there'd ever been a war . . . 'I'm sorry,

Mrs Verrity. Just thinking back. It must be hard for you, seeing your old home like this.'

She shrugged. 'The first time, yes. But I have made my home in England and I am happy with my choice. It is not the first time I have been back, you understand, and, of course, I was here during the war. Every so often I like to visit my tenants. It keeps them "up to the mark", as you put it. And, I think, they are pleased to see me.'

'They certainly made us very welcome,' said Haldean, diplomatically. They had gone by hired car from the hotel to the farmhouse of Raoul Rimet and his wife. Here Madame Rimet had insisted on Haldean trying her home-made cheese washed down with wine of startling rough-ness, while Monsieur Rimet took Mrs Verrity on a tour of the farm. From what he could follow of the torrent of rapid and idiomatic French, Haldean guessed he was attempting to negotiate a decrease in rent. His slightly surly farewells indicated how well he'd got on. 'Have we got very far to go?'

'By no means, Major.' She pointed to where part of a wall still stood. 'If we go through what remains of that doorway it will bring us to what were the servants' quarters and the entrance to the cellars.'

It was a depressing walk through the ruins. What struck Haldean as odd were the remnants of occupation that remained. A wall which still showed fragments of eighteenth-century wallpaper, rich with flower-entwined urns. Scraps of what had been inlaid woodwork. Countless crystal beads from a chandelier scattered over the stones and, still hanging drunkenly on part of a wall, most of a heavily gilded picture frame, its gilt faded by the rain and sun that now came freely through the few remaining rafters. They came into an area which had obviously been the kitchens. A doorway yawned open, leading into blackness.

'These are the cellars,' said Mrs Verrity. 'The entrance to the tunnels is down there.'

Haldean snapped on his torch and prepared to lead the

way when Mrs Verrity stopped, frowning at the ground. 'What is it?'

'Someone has been here.' She pointed. 'Look, in the dust the other side of the door. That is a footprint, yes?'

'It could be someone helping themselves to stone,' suggested Haldean. 'With all this free building material lying around, it's only to be expected.'

'This is my property, Major Haldean. Anyone who wants to come here should seek my permission first. Even ruined, it is still mine. No matter. I shall see to that later. Shall we go down?'

'Right-oh.' Haldean picked his way round a fallen timber then turned to give Mrs Verrity his hand. 'Carefully does it – that's right. Shall I hold your bag for you? It looks a bit heavy. You might find it easier if I take it.'

'I am fine, thank you. You have the torch to manage.'

Following the beam of white light they descended the steps and Mrs Verrity confidently led the way through cobwebby cellars which still contained rack upon rack of empty wine-shelves. There was smashed glass but no wine; the Germans would have seen to that and the British cleared up any which remained. Room led on to room. In the fifth cellar she paused before an ancient trap-door set with an iron ring.

'This is the entrance. I will hold the light for you.'

Haldean grasped the iron ring and heaved. The door rose up and Mrs Verrity peered down the flight of rough-cut steps that sloped away into the earth. Suddenly she swung round, sending the light flickering round the cellar walls.

'What is it?'

'I felt . . .' She shuddered. 'I felt as if I were being watched. Excuse me, it can be nothing but nerves. The dark – I do not like it. There is an English expression . . . Ah yes . . . *Someone is walking over my grave.*'

'Look,' said Haldean, laying the trap-door back flat against the cellar floor. 'There's no need to come with me, you know. I'm no end grateful to you for showing me the way here. I can find out everything I need to know by myself.'

For a moment she hesitated, then shook her head. 'No, Major. I think I would rather come with you. After all –' she tried a smile – 'my brother and I sometimes used to explore the tunnels. It is not a new thing that I do.'

'Well, just as you like. You take the torch and go first, though. Those steps look a bit dodgy to me. You'll be able to see your way better if you're in front.'

'If you prefer.'

There was the slightest of sounds in the absolute blackness of the cellar as Haldean followed Mrs Verrity down the steps. It was, perhaps, the scuttle of a rat.

The steps ended in a small room cut out of the raw chalk. Haldean took back the torch and shone the beam round the walls. This had obviously been the German HQ. A backless chair, a desk, some filing cabinets and a bank of telephones, their wires long gone, remained. Paper scattered the room. Everything was covered in a thick layer of dust. The black mouths of two tunnels opened out in front of them, bringing a faint, stale breeze.

Haldean took out his pocket compass and checked the direction in the light of the torch. One tunnel ran west, the other south-west. He cocked an eyebrow at Mrs Verrity. 'Which way should we go?'

'The western tunnel leads to store rooms, as I remember.' She handed him back the torch. 'I never explored the other properly.'

'Now's your chance,' said Haldean with a smile. He flashed the light down the south-western tunnel. The roof was about eight feet high and five men could have walked down it abreast. 'I'll lead the way, shall I? Have you noticed it's always "Ladies first", unless it's something exciting?'

'You find this exciting?' asked Mrs Verrity in surprise. '*Mon Dieu*, you are younger than I thought. Please, Major Haldean, be my guest.'

They set off down the tunnel, Haldean keeping up a

constant flow of comment as he followed the circle of light. 'It's widening out here a bit, isn't it? Obviously all this is man-made. It must have taken them ages to do. I'm amazed the tunnellers could breathe down here in all this chalk. They must have worn masks or something. We'll look as if we've been let loose in a flour mill by the time we get out of here. The air's not bad though, is it? I say, what's this?' He stooped and picked up a small brass tube. 'A stray bullet. German, by the look of it. I think we're getting warmer, don't you?'

'I am rather cold,' said Mrs Verrity distantly.

Haldean grinned. 'That's not exactly what I meant. I mean we're –'

'Stop!' Mrs Verrity turned, her head on one side. 'Shine the light back up the tunnel, Major.'

Haldean obediently did so. 'What's the matter?'

She impatiently waved him quiet. The only sound was that of their breathing. After a little while Mrs Verrity shook her head. 'I thought I heard something. Listen!'

'I wouldn't have thought there was anything to hear. Perhaps it's just being down here that's giving you the heebie-jeebies. I say, these tunnels aren't meant to be haunted, are they?' She ignored him, her head tilted slightly to one side. 'Shall we get on? I'd like to know where this tunnel ends up. Strictly speaking it should be –'

'Major!'

'Sorry.' Haldean fell silent.

She heaved a sigh. 'I could have sworn I heard . . . No matter.'

'I didn't hear anything. Mind you, I wouldn't be surprised if you did start imagining things. We must be the first people to have been down here for years. D'you think there'll be rats?'

'I sincerely hope not.'

'Well, we'll soon find out. Come on. Best foot forward and all that, unless you want to go back?'

'And find my way through the cellars in the dark? No,

thank you, Major. I am staying with you.' They walked on, Haldean doing his best to keep up the flow of conversation, but she was at best a distracted listener and at worse an impatient one.

'Well, there's one thing,' said Haldean, trying hard. 'We can hardly get lost down here. Boscombe's book gave the impression there were any number of tunnels running off the main one, but we haven't passed any, yet.'

'They must be further along.'

'D'you think so? It must be awkward to find your way round when all the tunnels start interlinking. Be rotten to be lost down here in the dark without water. It sort of catches your throat, doesn't it? This is one of the driest places I've ever been in. I suppose you'd die of thirst in the end. You wouldn't last long, although, if someone was looking for you, a shout should carry a long way . . .' Moved by a sudden impulse, he threw back his head in a resounding bellow. 'Hello!'

The sound rolled down the tunnel, echoing off the walls, reverberating into the far distance until it rumbled to a grumbling halt.

'Major Haldean,' said Mrs Verrity, tightly. 'If you do that again, I shall take the torch and leave.'

'Sorry.' He grinned apologetically. 'I had no idea it was going to be so spectacular, although that's not really the right word to describe a noise. My word, it was loud, wasn't it? Enough, as you might say, to wake the dead. But perhaps that's not the happiest of images, either.'

She contented herself with a look.

A few minutes later he stopped. 'There seems to be something in the way up the tunnel. Either that or the ground's very uneven.' He took a few paces forward, then paused quietly, running the light over the humps on the floor. He took a deep breath. 'Bodies.'

Mrs Verrity gave a whispering gasp.

Haldean went down on one knee and reached out his hand, then stopped. 'No. I'll leave the poor devils. Their war ended quickly, at any rate.' He stood up, brushing the chalk from his knees. 'All British. This must have been one of the parties Boscombe talks about.' He shone the torch further down the tunnel. 'Look, there's another group down there.' He walked swiftly away before halting for Mrs Verrity to catch up with him. 'More men,' he said sombrely. 'Again, all British.' He focused the torch on a khaki-clad figure on the floor. 'He was ambushed from behind. You can see where the bullet went through his back.' He flicked the light over the dead men and shook his head. 'Some of these poor blighters were jumped as well . . . They didn't stand a chance. I say, Mrs Verrity, are you all right?'

She swallowed, and closed her eyes for a moment. 'Walk on, please. I had no idea these – these things – were down here. Please, Major, let's go on.'

'Right you are.' He stood for a moment, then shook his head. 'There's damn all we can do for them now. I wonder why the Germans didn't remove the bodies? There's precious little point, I suppose. After all, they're further underground than any burial party could dig. And they were mourned long ago. It's funny, isn't it, to think that up there, over the Channel in England, there are women who remember these men as they were. And now there's nothing but bones.'

'Is there any reason at all for us to be here?'

Haldean glanced at her. 'Can these bones live, you mean?' She gave him an irritated, puzzled look. 'That bit in the Bible – Ezekiel, I think it is – where the dead bones rise up and clothe themselves in sinews and flesh. It always struck me as creepy. But it's just possible these bones may speak . . . I say, you're not looking any too bright. Shall we go on?'

After what seemed a long time but was, in fact, just under ten minutes by Haldean's watch, they came to the entrance to another tunnel running off to the west. 'I wonder,' murmured Haldean and, crouching down, he shone the light along the dust-clogged ground. 'I bet this is the tunnel Boscombe hid in, you know. There's a very gentle depression to one side as if someone's lain there.'

'That would have vanished after all these years.'

'Would it? Perhaps. I may be mistaken. There's obviously been a good deal of traffic down the main part of this tunnel. Look at all the foot-marks.' He straightened up. 'Any idea where it goes to? It was pretty well used.'

'None. I never came this far.'

'Shall we go down it?'

'No. Please, Major Haldean, either find what you are looking for or admit this has been a mistake. There can be nothing down here that can tell you what happened to Richard.'

Haldean seemed rather crestfallen. 'Perhaps I have been barking up the wrong tree,' he said reluctantly. 'Still, as we are here, we might as well see it through to the end.'

A few hundred yards more brought them to an absolute halt. The tunnel had narrowed and now stopped altogether in a landslip. The only way was back.

'I suppose,' said Haldean thoughtfully, 'this is where Whitfield made his last stand. They dug him out of the rubble on the other side of this wall.'

'And now you have seen the place where poor Richard was attacked, perhaps we can go? I have not enjoyed walking down here and I am anxious to get back to the surface. I am sorry you have not had a successful voyage, but never could I understand what you hoped to find.' She looked back at the yawning blackness of the tunnel and gave an impatient shudder. 'And now we have to go back and it has all been for nothing.'

Haldean put the torch down on a large lump of chalk, leaned against the wall, and shook his head. 'Not quite for nothing, Mrs Verrity. You see, I've found the evidence I came for.' He studied his nails for a moment. 'And the case, if you would like to put it like that, is closed.'

She stared at him, then laughed. 'What? What can you have seen that I have not? It is ridiculous what you say there.'

'Not really.' He looked up and smiled. 'You see, I now know who the traitor was, why and how Boscombe was murdered, why Morton was murdered, why Colonel Whitfield had such an overpowering desire to marry Marguerite Vayle, and why and how the Colonel himself came to be murdered in turn. It's an interesting tale. Slightly sordid in parts, hinging as it does on some very basic human weaknesses, but interesting all the same. Would you like to hear it?'

'Of course. But can you not tell me on the way back, Major?'

'Oh, this is as good a place as any. You can see what actually happened if we stay here. This landslip, for example. Such a good, solid, convincing fall of rock with Whitfield on the other side, brought down while he hero-ically held off the Germans. Odd that there aren't any Germans, isn't it?'

'I – I don't understand.'

'Don't you?' He picked a piece of chalk from the rubble and made idle patterns on it with his thumbnail. 'Whitfield was supposed to have been in a fight. Where's the enemy? We – the British – took his word for it that beyond the wall were Germans but, as you can see, here we are on the other side of the wall and not a single Fritz in sight.'

She licked her lips nervously. 'The bodies must have been moved.'

'Perhaps. Strange, though, that they left all the Tommies. Unusual, that. Let's say that is what happened. They must have been a jolly thorough working party. They obviously cleared away every single spent bullet and cartridge case as well.'

She shrugged. 'Perhaps they did.'

He raised an eyebrow. 'Perhaps,' he repeated, drily. 'After all, a great many things may be possible to troops who are invisible.'

'What do you mean?'

'Don't you see, Mrs Verrity? The British were attacked from the rear. *But the only tunnel down which the Germans*

264

could have come had Boscombe lying across the entrance. If they had passed him he would have known – and so would they. He would have been taken prisoner and spent the rest of the war behind wire, instead of coming to enliven my life in the RFC.' He tossed the chalk from hand to hand. 'And so, on the evidence, I'm afraid that our Colonel Whitfield stands convicted not only of being the Augier Ridge traitor, but of shooting his own men. Can you imagine that? They, faces to the front, watching for the enemy, while the man who offered to lead them quietly drew his gun . . . Some of them must have known and turned but he got them nevertheless and left them here dead and dying. We're in a tomb, Mrs Verrity. They have long since ceased to live and their bodies have crumbled to dust, but their bones tell the story. Their bones spoke after all.'

She tried to laugh but it was an unconvincing sound. 'You have the good imagination, yes? Tell me, Major, if poor Richard had done what you say, why were stolen documents and German messages found in Tyburn's things? I cannot believe Richard put them there. He would not have had the chance.'

'Of course he wouldn't,' agreed Haldean. 'You did that.'

There was a moment of frozen silence. Then Mrs Verrity gave a real smile. 'So. You know. I was beginning to wonder if you did, Major Haldean. I suppose you know how I murdered Boscombe, Morton and poor, dear Richard himself?' Haldean nodded and Mrs Verrity's smile grew. 'I was right about you, Monsieur Haldean. I thought you were dangerously clever when I met you and, *mon chéri*, I was not wrong. I should have taken care of you the night you stayed at my house. Richard wanted me to, but after his clumsy attempt to kill you, you were under the eye of the doctor and your friend, the policeman. It would not have been safe for me to take the action I wanted. Perhaps I should have risked it after all.' Her hand moved to her bag.

'Don't do that,' said Haldean, pleasantly. 'I'd hate you to pull a gun on me now.'

Her hand stopped and she shrugged. 'Ah, well. It is permitted, then, that I smoke a cigarette?' With his wary eyes on her, she slipped a hand into her pocket, brought out a flat silver case and, opening it, took out a cigarette. 'Have you a match?'

Without taking his gaze from her Haldean leaned forward with his lighter and, as the sweet smell hit his nostrils, he knew he'd been tricked. He gave a little gasp and crumpled forward.

Anne-Marie Verrity pulled deeply on her cigarette, looking at the sprawled body at her feet. Then she casually threw the cigarette down and ground it into the dust with her heel. Opening her bag, she took out a heavy, stick-shaped object with a bulge at the top, looking at it critically. It was a German hand grenade. She placed it on the ground beside her, reached in her bag once more and took out a small, blue-sheened revolver. She pointed it at Haldean, then shook her head regretfully before turning it round in her hands and holding it by the muzzle. Going on one knee beside him she carefully brushed back his hair from the temple. She raised the gun, butt end high, to strike . . . And a hand caught hers.

She whirled and screamed. A British soldier stood in front of her, tall, relentless and ghost-white with chalk.

'We can't let you do that.' He took the gun from her numb fingers and covered her with it, but it was unnecessary. She crammed her hand into her mouth to stop the screams but the noise came out as whimpering sobs.

There were running footsteps in the tunnel and lights bouncing off the walls. Ashley, flanked by three other men, came panting up beside them. He dropped a hand on the soldier's arm. 'Well done, Captain Rivers.' He bent down beside Haldean as he opened bleary eyes. 'Are you all right?'

Haldean looked at Rivers and a half-smile touched his mouth. He took the proffered hand and stood up. 'My God, Greg, she must have thought you were the living dead.' His grip tightened. 'Thanks, old son. It might have been nasty without you.'

Chapter Fourteen

'It might have been very nasty,' said Haldean thoughtfully, picking up a glass of brandy and cupping it in his hands. They were in the Wedgwood blue drawing room at Hesperus. The curtains were drawn back and through the open windows a tranquil dusk was gliding into night. Haldean sipped his brandy with widening eyes. 'My God, Uncle, what are you giving us?

'It's the '75,' said his uncle, with a touch of pride. 'There are still a few bottles downstairs and I wanted to drink it before it "went back", as they say. However, it needs a special occasion.'

'This would make anything into a special occasion,' said Haldean, reverently swirling the pale liquid in his glass. 'Here's to you, Greg. I couldn't have done it without you. As a matter of fact, I wouldn't even have tried.'

Gregory Rivers looked suitably abashed. 'Well, it wasn't that difficult. But come on, Jack. Here we all are. We've given you a corking dinner, and I want to be told the whole story, not just bits and pieces. You've got to sing for your supper.'

'Tell us properly,' said Isabelle. 'I want to know what was behind it all. How it all started and why. And none of your "with one bound Jack was free" stuff. I knew it was Mrs Verrity,' she added happily. 'I suspected her like mad. I said so, didn't I, Jack.'

He grinned at her. 'I know you did, old prune, but it's a fat lot of good suspecting someone without any proof.'

He took a cigar from the box on the table beside him and

looked round the room. Aunt Alice by the coffee tray, Uncle Philip standing by the sideboard, Greg and Isabelle on the sofa, Martin Tyburn with one hand casually covering Marguerite's, and Ashley, looking very much at ease with a glass of brandy in one hand and a cigar in the other, all waiting to hear the story.

He picked up the cutters and carefully clipped the end of his cigar. 'Well, you asked for it. Here goes.' He lit his cigar, snuggled back in his chair and blew out a contented mouthful of smoke. 'Mrs Verrity's a good person to start with, though, Belle, because it all began when Anne-Marie Verrity, who was at a loose end after her husband died, set up her hospital outside Auchonvillers in 1915. It quickly gained a reputation as a thriving social centre as well as one of the best hospitals on the front and that, as far as anyone knew, was all fine and dandy, because it ensured a steady flow of donations to keep up the good work. What *wasn't* known was that Anne-Marie Verrity had had a scorching affair with a German Royal in Vienna, which resulted in her being recruited to the Kaiser's Secret Service. There were some rather illuminating letters found in her house which helped to dot the i's and cross the t's. With a constant flow of top brass to and from the hospital, Mrs Verrity was in the position of being able to keep the Germans up to date with authentic snippets of information which she had painlessly extracted from her visitors. The Germans had set up their HQ in the Chateau d'Augier and Mrs Verrity could stroll in any time she liked by using the western tunnel whose exit was on d'Augier property near the hospital but whose entrance was in the cellars of the chateau. She was pretty keen I didn't go down that tunnel and I'm not surprised. It was obvious it had been heavily used.'

He frowned at the ashtray beside him. 'I'm not sure how she got her claws into Whitfield. Probably the most obvious explanation is the correct one, for he was fairly ornamental and sure to attract her attention. She'd known him in England and the affair might have started here, but once in France I imagine that Whitfield, the staff officer, was simply too useful to give mere crumbs of information. She wanted hard facts and once he'd supplied them, she had him nailed. Then came a real crisis; Boscombe discovered the tunnels. Now this spelt Trouble with a capital T. Not only did it give us an unparalleled chance to break through the line and take the Augier Ridge, it would also mean the discovery of Mrs Verrity's activities. That western tunnel was far too convenient to be overlooked, and she wasn't the sort of woman who would keep mum about her confederates. It's a good guess, as well, that the Germans had records in their HQ of where their information had come from and, lo! Whitfield's name would lead to all the rest. He *had* to stop us from reaching the chateau. When the news came through his first action would be to inform Mrs Verrity and then it was up to him. He went to the farm and took control of the second party.'

Haldean glanced at Tyburn. 'You had already gone into the tunnels, sir, and met with a warm reception. The Germans, alerted by Mrs Verrity, were waiting for you. Boscombe managed to crawl away and hide in the nearest tunnel, where he lay while Whitfield's party went past. From his perspective the second party were also attacked by the Germans who had killed his comrades, and the next thing he knew was that Whitfield was running back down the main tunnel. Whitfield saw him and Boscombe relates in his book how he thought Whitfield was going to shoot him. He was right, of course. Then the third British party turned up and Boscombe was saved. Whitfield, as we know, went on to perform some entirely imaginary heroics, artistically stretching as far as a few minor wounds and placing himself in the rubble. It was, as far as he was concerned, a happy ending. He was awarded the VC, acclaimed as The Man Who'd Saved The Western Front, and only he and Mrs Verrity knew that his gallantry consisted of blocking the tunnel and making sure none of his men survived the frontal attack by shooting them in the back as they faced the enemy. Not nice, is it?'

Tyburn's hand tightened on Marguerite's. 'I thought he was a traitor, but I had no idea he was a murderer as well.' His face was grim. 'Those people were my friends.' He took a deep breath. 'Why did he pick on me to carry the can?'

Haldean took another sip of brandy. 'It wasn't so much why as how you came to be dropped in it that puzzled Ashley and myself for a while. It was Boscombe's book which gave us the clue. There's a bit where he's in hospital and Mrs Verrity tells him she's had his things brought over. The implication is that she had access to the officers' and men's belongings. They'd all have been piled up together and she could have slipped the papers into your kitbag then. She had to choose an officer to make it credible that he would have access to enough information to be a spy, so she chose the highest-ranking man who had been in the tunnels. It wasn't, if you like, personal.'

'It *felt* personal,' growled Tyburn.

'I daresay it did,' agreed Haldean. 'Of the men who survived, two decided to write down their experiences. Boscombe in the form of a highly polished memoir and Petrie as a war diary. We haven't been able to find the diary, so what follows is pure speculation, but I think we're on the right lines. Petrie was in the second party, the one Whitfield attacked. Now, although in the confusion of the attack Petrie wouldn't have known who was shooting at them, he would have realized there was an enemy behind. And that, much, much later, gave Boscombe, who was a bright boy, cause for thought. Because, you see, Boscombe *knew* there were no Germans behind the British. If they had entered the tunnels he would have seen them. When Boscombe read Petrie's diary, which had been left to his friend, Reginald Morton, his mind was full of the war because of writing his book. But if the Germans hadn't attacked Petrie and the rest, who had? The man who had given him such a fright in the tunnels, of course, our hero, Richard Theodore Whitfield. And Boscombe, as he put it to me afterwards, saw an opportunity for private publication . . .'

'I don't get it,' said Isabelle, her nose wrinkling. 'Why are you so sure Petrie's diary didn't just name Whitfield?'

'Because Morton, who owned the diary, and Boscombe were in it together. If it had been as simple as that, they wouldn't have needed each other to put the squeeze on. And Morton let his girlfriend read it. By itself, you see, it was harmless.'

Lady Rivers put down her coffee cup. 'I can't get over Mrs Verrity being so ruthless, Jack, to say nothing of her keeping up a pretence for so long.'

'She was a ruthless woman,' said Haldean, 'and a very credible one, too. I think, you know, that she'd been playing a part for so long it came as second nature to her. It might reflect something of her love of power. People would only know exactly what she wanted them to know. She was in control of their reactions, you see, or thought she was.'

Lady Rivers put her head on one side. 'I think you're right. It's odd how often I sensed something artificial around her, but it was her surroundings, not her, that seemed slightly out of key. I must admit I felt very sorry for her at one point. I thought she really cared about Colonel Whitfield.'

'The funny thing is, Aunt Alice, that you may be right. Yes, I'd love some more brandy, please, Uncle. Thank you very much. I must admit I'm guessing here,' Haldean continued, picking up his refilled glass, 'but it's a guess which fits the facts. Anne-Marie Verrity was used to having her own way with men. As well as being a real corker in the looks department, she had . . . well, It. Pure S.A. Any man, me included, simply couldn't help looking at her. Now although Whitfield had presumably started off by falling for her, I think the gilt wore off the gingerbread pretty quickly, and our Anne-Marie wasn't used to having her boyfriends turn sour on her. Those letters from Vienna make fascinating reading. I think he grew to hate her and she resented it. So, not being able to obtain his uncritical adoration, she decided to have the next best thing, which was his attention.'

He paused. 'She – well, she wasn't a *kind* woman. She'd have loved getting under his skin and it was very much to her advantage to keep an eye on him, because although she knew some pretty damaging facts about him, by the same token he also knew some ruinous things about her. She ensured his silence by blackmail.'

Gregory Rivers raised his eyebrows and whistled. 'Blackmail, Jack? Are you sure?'

'Quite sure. You tell them, Ashley.'

'We were able to get at both Whitfield's and Mrs Verrity's bank accounts,' explained Ashley. 'Whitfield had been paying about fifty pounds a month out to cash ever since the war over and above his legitimate expenses and Mrs Verrity had been raking in the same sum. Apart from the money, it must have made her feel very secure. It gave her the upper hand, you see.'

'And that arrangement looked set to continue indefinitely,' said Haldean, 'when along came Boscombe and Morton. They really put the cat amongst the pigeons. They demanded seventy-five pounds a month and Whitfield had to pay up. Although the stables had never really flourished after the war – and no wonder – from October onwards they started going downhill fast. Salvation, as far as Whitfield was concerned, arrived in the shape of you, Marguerite, at Christmas. If Whitfield could get his hands on your money he'd be safe.'

She swallowed. 'Was that really all there was to it?'

Haldean shrugged. 'It's never easy to say, is it?' His voice was gentle. 'I don't believe he had any real feelings for you, no. I'm glad to say there are far better men around than Whitfield, and you've got to remember he was desperate. He saw his stables going to rack and ruin while Mrs Verrity spent money like water. But that's a question I can't really answer. Marrying you must have seemed a very agreeable way of obtaining some money and he must have been flattered by your feelings for him. Anyway, Boscombe upped the ante by getting greedy. Like many another, he found his expenditure kept pace with his income, and so he applied, as you might say, for a pay rise, without mentioning it to Morton. Whitfield, stretched to the absolute limit, couldn't brass up. Now at this point I rather think we can see Mrs Verrity coming into the picture. She was in as much danger as Whitfield. If Whitfield cracked and the truth became known, he would make pretty damn sure that she shared in his downfall. Boscombe came down to see Whitfield to apply a bit of personal pressure and, by doing so, signed his death warrant. For, although he didn't know it, he had come up against Anne-Marie Verrity.

'It was a shock for everyone when Boscombe arrived at the Red Cross fête at Thackenhurst. Boscombe, to his delight, saw not only Whitfield, but you, Mr Tyburn. He couldn't get to you directly but used the opportunity to screw some more money out of Marguerite. If he had lived, you would probably have received a billet-doux from him in fairly short order. Mrs Verrity, who had a very French grasp of practicalities, realized that the quickest way out of the dilemma was to kill Boscombe. Now here's where, if I had been paying attention, I could have got to the bottom of things. It worried me that Boscombe was shot, because who on earth takes a revolver to a fête? The answer is no one, of course – after all, this is Sussex, not the Wild West – but Mrs Verrity had by far the best opportunity to get a gun. After all, all she had to do was walk into her own house. I should have realized that, you know.'

'And so did Mrs Verrity shoot Boscombe?' demanded Isabelle. 'I don't see how she could have done.'

Haldean grinned at her. 'Perpend, old thing. I think the original plan was for Whitfield to do the deed as and when the opportunity arose. But his best chance, which was when Boscombe, who by this time was bottled and sleeping it off in the fortune teller's tent, was ruined by the vicar

274

arriving wanting to talk about ponies. D'you remember Whitfield's reaction, Greg? He was pretty shirty about it and went off with very bad grace. Then you met up with him, Uncle Philip, and escorted him back to the cake competition stall where he finally managed to see Mrs Verrity. You saw them, Belle, if you recall, round the side of the tent. You said they seemed to be having an argument. I bet they were! It ended with Mrs Verrity taking back her gun and deciding to tackle Boscombe's demise herself. She knew from Whitfield that Boscombe was laid out in Mrs Griffin's tent, so decided to get Mrs Griffin out of the way by awarding her first prize in the cake competition. That meant no one would go in the tent until Mrs Griffin returned so, unless Boscombe decided to move, which was unlikely in view of his condition, he was safe for the time being. Then she walked back with Mrs Griffin, in order to congratulate her the better. Credible, isn't it? For otherwise we just might have wondered what the sophisticated Mrs Verrity was doing in the fortune teller's tent at the village fête. And then came the master stroke which I didn't spot and deserve kicking for. I helped her, you see. She laid a trap and I fell right in.'

He smoked his cigar down to the butt and crushed it out in the ashtray. 'Mrs Griffin went into the tent and came out giggling about "the gentleman" being drunk. Now Mrs Verrity didn't have to ask who "the gentleman" was. She realized straight away it was Boscombe, which should have rung some alarm bells. I'm ashamed to say it did nothing of the kind. She took command and marched into the tent to ask him to leave. All of us, Mrs Griffin, Belle, Greg and myself, crowded in after her. D'you remember what she did? She looked down at Boscombe, started, fixed us with a glance and asked us to get out and fetch help.' He paused. 'Belle, you were there. What did you think had happened?'

'I thought he was dead, of course. I didn't know until afterwards that he'd been shot.'

'Bang on. And Greg thought he was dead and so did I. He wasn't.'

'*What?*'

Haldean leaned forward. 'It was so simple. She contrived to have herself left alone with Boscombe, who was too drunk to know anything about it, and when we left, she shot him.'

'Good God.' Rivers looked at him with wide eyes. 'She shot him *after* we'd seen him? Are you sure, Jack? I mean, I could see we wouldn't hear a shot beforehand, because of all the noise and not listening out for one, but surely, *surely*, she was taking a terrible risk afterwards.'

'She was taking a calculated risk,' agreed Haldean. 'And that's where my little friend, Sally Mills, came into it with her doll. Sally had put the doll, cot and pillow down and when she came back the pillow had been taken. She told me afterwards she and her mother had looked everywhere for it. I don't know how she struck you, Belle, but she seemed a most determined child to me. I couldn't help thinking that if the pillow was there to be found, she'd have found it. When we met her the other day it occurred to me that although the doll, cot and blanket were found, the pillow had gone for good. But why should anyone take part of a child's toy? What could it be used for? And then a glimmer of light dawned. It's a nice, handy shape, a doll's pillow, and stuffed thick with flocking, or whatever it is they use. Just the right size to be hidden in a handbag or a pocket, for example, and just the right thickness to be used as a silencer on a gun. I put the idea to Ashley, and he did some experiments with the .22 in his possession.'

'It wasn't a bad silencer,' agreed Ashley. 'Despite what people think, you can't silence a gun completely, but you can cut down the noise dramatically. And although we could still hear the shot, it would be faint enough to pass unnoticed at the fête, especially with all the other racket there was going on. If you'd heard anything, you would have probably thought it was a crack from the air rifles or the trap-shooting. The fact that she'd used the pillow as a

276

silencer explained why there were no powder burns on the body. Naturally there weren't. All the burning was on the cloth. It would have taken a real crack shot from the tent walls to plug Boscombe in the temple like that. If he was shot by someone holding a gun to his head it was easy. I liked the idea and the more I thought about it the more I liked it. It took all the mystery out of the affair, you see. We didn't have to wonder how some unseen man had parted the tent walls and shot Boscombe so accurately. Instead you'd had a murderer who walked up to their victim as bold as brass and pulled the trigger.'

Haldean nodded. 'It *felt* right, didn't it, Ashley? And, of course, once we'd got that far with Boscombe's murder, it led us on to Morton's. That was tough, because no one knew he was in the Talbot Arms. So why did Mrs Verrity go there?'

'She wanted to search Boscombe's room,' said Isabelle, slowly.

'And the Talbot Arms is the only place you can stay in the village,' put in Greg.

'Absolutely. And Boscombe's key was in Boscombe's pocket, with his room number on it. So that gave Mrs Verrity his room number on a plate, so to speak. After Whitfield's poor showing at the fête I can't see her trusting him to break in and search the room without making a complete pig's ear of it. I think she simply slipped into the office and took the spare room key without anyone knowing. I managed to do it, so it was perfectly possible. Then, of course, she went up to Boscombe's room and found Morton, waiting for Boscombe's return. As we know, Mrs Verrity had a fairly short way with anyone who crossed her path. She shot him and disappeared with the diary. You believe she burnt it, don't you, Ashley?'

'Almost certainly,' he agreed. 'I can't see her keeping it. It'd be far too dangerous.'

'Horribly dangerous.' Haldean took another cigar from the box. 'But an even bigger danger to her was Whitfield. When he found out the police were looking for someone who had been blackmailed, he went up like a flushed pheasant.' Haldean carefully examined his cigar. 'I can't blame him, either. As someone who had been blackmailed for years, he must have thought his position delicate, to say the least. And, of course, he'd recently been presented with what he referred to as "a bombshell".'

He looked at Marguerite. 'When you told him who your father was and said there was a chance he was still alive, it must have been like a nightmare. That meant that not only was there one man who *knew* that Tyburn wasn't a traitor but that same man probably had a jolly good idea of who the traitor was. But he still desperately wanted to marry you because of your money. He needed that as much as before to keep Mrs Verrity satisfied. He tried to kill me, you know,' said Haldean, reaching for the cigar clippers. 'Compared to the other murders it was a clumsy affair, but it nearly came off. If he'd been lucky, he'd have got us both with that great brute of a horse. As it was . . . well, our luck held, didn't it, Ashley?'

'Thank God. It was a close-run thing though, Haldean. I didn't realize the risk I was taking by leaving you at Mrs Verrity's.'

'No, although I was probably safer there than almost anywhere else. Mrs Verrity knew I mustn't suffer a fatal relapse or you and the doctor would ask some very searching questions. Perhaps, if she'd been in it by herself, she might have seen me off and brazened it out, but she couldn't trust Whitfield. Even though it meant the loss of his blackmail money, he had to go.'

'Didn't she have any affection for him, Jack?' asked Isabelle. 'After all, they had been close, if I can put it like that.'

'I think what she liked was power, and you must remember how dangerous he was to her. He was drinking like a hydroptic fish, and might at any moment spill the beans about the whole business. And she didn't like –' he nodded towards Marguerite – 'saving your presence – the company he was keeping. The very day Whitfield tried to

278

ride us down, she'd been round digging away about you, Mr Lawrence. Boscombe had said that Tyburn was alive and I think she left convinced in her own mind that you either were Tyburn or knew far more about things than you should. You'd threatened to look into his past life if Whitfield persisted in attempting to marry Marguerite and she certainly didn't want that to happen. All in all, it would be a healthier world for her if both you and Richard Whitfield ceased to exist.'

Sir Philip frowned. 'Why did she go about it in such a complicated way, Jack? Surely if she suspected Lawrence was Tyburn, she could have killed him without involving Whitfield? After all, even though it makes me cold to think about it, once Tyburn was dead she'd have nothing to fear from Whitfield any more. Whitfield could have married Marguerite –' he glanced apologetically at the girl – 'because although I deplored his behaviour at the party, I know I would have eventually let you have your own way, my dear.'

'You'd think that'd be the size of it, wouldn't you?' Haldean lit his cigar and blew out a cloud of blue smoke. 'But she looked at it from our point of view. If Lawrence, as we then knew you, sir, was murdered, who would the police look to first? Why, Whitfield, of course. And we'd have had a good circumstantial case against him. After all, Lawrence was the one who was preventing his marriage to Marguerite and Whitfield was in such a state I doubt if he'd have been able to stand up to any prolonged or serious questioning. But if she murdered Whitfield in such a way that Lawrence appeared to be guilty, that was a different kettle of fish. Mr Lawrence's dislike of Whitfield was well known and she had arranged for them both to be at the same spot at the same time without witnesses. She got Whitfield to write a letter asking to meet Lawrence. It would be, she probably told Whitfield, a good opportunity for him to find out what Lawrence really did know.'

'I fell for it,' said Tyburn grimly. 'I must admit I welcomed a meeting with Colonel Whitfield with nobody else

279

around. I intended to offer him money to leave Marguerite alone and I would've been very surprised if that hadn't done the trick. If it didn't, I thought an odd hint about his VC would have worked. I had a whole story planned, about how I had bumped into a German way up the Peace River who had dished the dirt, but I never got a chance to say a thing. Even now I can't see how she did it. If you're telling me a woman like Mrs Verrity can land a punch like a prize-fighter, then I'm going to have to dissent, Major Haldean.'

Haldean grinned broadly. 'She didn't. And do, please, stop calling me Major. I feel as if I'm on parade.' He held his hands wide. 'She knew you'd be at the barn by eleven o'clock and probably a bit sooner. She must have arranged to meet Whitfield there earlier. By that time he was in such a state of nerves he'd probably want her moral support fairly badly and he'd also want her to hear what Mr Lawrence had to say. So, at about twenty-five to eleven at a guess, she put her plan into operation. I think she drugged him first. She used ethylchloride on me in the tunnels, and I bet she used it on Whitfield as well. You might have had it at the dentist's. It produces instant unconsciousness for about two minutes or so. She made it look as if he'd been in a fight by walloping him with the spade handle. Then she shot him, arranged his body as if he'd committed suicide, and waited by the door for you, Mr Tyburn. Do you remember how dark the barn was after the sunshine outside? When you came in, blinking, she slugged you with the spade. We saw the blood on it. You went down and she completed the good work by applying the ethylchloride. That gave her up to two minutes and she must have gone like the clappers. She'd previously wiped the gun, of course, and it wouldn't take her long to put your fingerprints on it. Then she placed the gun in Whitfield's hand, roughed you up a bit, made sure your prints were on the spade as well, and scooted off across the road to the garden gate of Thackenhurst, where, once safely behind the wall, she fired the shot with her other revolver which brought me hurtling up the road. I was an added bonus, of course, but she did want there to have been a shot. It would have looked grim enough anyway, but she must have been delighted to find that I'd heard a gun go off at eleven o'clock. Well, you know what happened next. We went across to Thackenhurst to be met with a fine display of grief and the statement by Norah the maid that at eleven o'clock her mistress had just rung for her morning coffee.'

'And how did she manage that?' demanded Gregory Rivers. 'Magic?'

'Not a bit of it. She put the clock back. As simple as that. It'd chime the half-hour again, of course, but that would be mistaken for the quarter if anyone was listening. In through the french windows, which she'd prudently left open, adjust the clock, ring the bell, and there's Norah ready to swear that at eleven o'clock her mistress was deep in coffee without a care in the world. Not actually being there I can't prove that's what she did, but it's by far the easiest way. Good, eh? It was risky, like Boscombe's murder, but she brought it off brilliantly. She must have been highly amused in the days which followed to see my industrious efforts to land poor Mr Tyburn still deeper in the soup. Once Stafford had identified him as Tyburn she could breathe again. But fortunately we ran into little Sally Mills. I hope she got her tea-set, Belle. If ever a little girl deserved one, she did. Anyway, this excellent and meritorious child pointed me in the right direction. I badgered myself to death for the best part of the afternoon, went to see Ashley and by the end of the evening we had a plan.'

'A dangerous plan,' grunted Ashley.

'A successful one,' countered Haldean. 'And once you'd secured the co-operation of the French police and Greg had weighed in on my side, I stopped worrying. You see, it was one thing being certain in our own minds what she'd done, but proving it was quite another matter. We had to draw her out somehow and so I paid Mrs Verrity a visit. Having so publicly appointed herself as Whitfield's champion she more or less had to go along with me. She certainly didn't want to take me down the tunnels, but I dropped so many hints about what I hoped to find that she must have thought I was crackers. Because, on the face of it, what on earth could there be? She'd never read Boscombe's book. She'd only read Petrie's diary and, as I remember saying before, you had to read both of them to spot the flaw. I made references to a mysterious Mr X – she must have thought I was chasing moonbeams – and told her my intention of going with or without her. I was almost certain she'd buy it. After all, she *thought* she was safe but I managed to raise enough of a question mark in her mind for her to ensure she was. And if I did, by some weird chance, find anything, she wanted to be on the spot.

'And so we went to the Chateau d'Augier. It's a dismal place. Not nice at all. Not any more. What she didn't know was that in the tunnel, arrayed in his old battledress, was my long-suffering cousin, Gregory Rivers.' Haldean raised his glass. 'Here's to you, old pal. It must have been a grim vigil.'

'It was,' said Rivers with feeling.

'And, in the cellars, were, of course, Ashley and three officers of the French police. Now what *I* didn't know was that she'd helped herself to a grenade from the stack of weapons that French farmer, Rimet, had. However, I did notice her bag seemed jolly heavy.

'It nearly went wrong at the outset. She noticed a footprint at the cellar entrance, but I fobbed her off with a tale of peasants looking for free bricks. She was as jumpy as a cat all the way down. She sensed someone was watching. And honestly, Ashley –' here Haldean broke off to gaze severely at his friend – 'I could have done without all the scuffling in the cellars as we were going down the steps into the tunnel.'

'We were getting ready,' said Ashley. 'I half-expected her to whack you over the head and shut the trap-door on you.'

'Yes . . . it occurred to me as well. However, I insisted she went first because the thought of her behind me was not pleasant. Once in the tunnel I wanted to get the layout. Once I'd seen that, put together with what I already knew and suspected, it was clear what had happened to you, Mr Tyburn. It gave her a real shock when I made the accusation. She'd gone from being wary of me to thinking I must be loopy. I kept up a flow of inane chatter, which she could be forgiven for wanting to murder me for, to tell everyone where we were. At one point I let rip with a shout to tell you we were coming, Greg.'

'I heard it,' he said with a grin. 'That was the signal to get my head down.'

'And, as you know, she confessed all. She was perfectly safe, you see. As far as she knew, there weren't any witnesses for miles and it must have given her some considerable pleasure to boast about how clever she'd been. She'd already decided I was going to have an accident. The ethylchloride took me by surprise. I hadn't realized at that stage she must have drugged you in the barn, Mr Tyburn. I thought she'd simply thumped you with the spade. I should have known she'd want to be a lot more certain than that. She couldn't shoot me, of course. My body was almost bound to be recovered, even though she intended to chuck a bomb at me to bring the house down. However, I believe she was caught in the act of clubbing me with the butt-end of her gun.'

'I've never moved so fast,' said Rivers. 'I'd come as close as I dared to hear what she was saying, but you went out like a light and she raised that damn gun . . . It was a nasty moment, Jack.'

'It was,' agreed Haldean warmly. 'But you gave her a nastier one. When you rose up in front of her, I thought she was never going to stop screaming. She must have really thought the dead had walked. And, although I don't want to be vindictive, I can't help thinking it served her right. After all, she'd helped to kill them.'

'They were my men,' said Tyburn sombrely. 'I shall have

their bodies brought out and decently buried. It seems the least I can do. I'd like to think they had a proper memorial and a grave. They were good men. Decent men.'

'That's the most any of us can hope to be,' said Haldean quietly. He raised his glass. 'To the dead.'

They drank the toast in silence, then Tyburn raised his glass once more with a broad smile. 'You can't drink this, Haldean, or you, Superintendent Ashley, or you, Captain Rivers. Because this is for you. I've got two priceless things returned to me which I thought were gone for ever; my reputation and my daughter. What was the toast of the RFC?'

'My favourite one was "Happy landings",' said Haldean.

'Happy landings,' repeated Tyburn. 'It's been a tough flight. But here's to the pilot.'